RAVEN'S RISE

ALSO BY ELIZABETH COLE

Honor & Roses

Choose the Sky

A Heartless Design

A Reckless Soul

A Shameless Angel

The Lady Dauntless

Beneath Sleepless Stars

A Mad and Mindless Night

Regency Rhapsody:

The Complete Collection

Raven's Rise

Elizabeth Cole

SkySpark Books

PHILADELPHIA, PENNSYLVANIA

SkySpark Books
Philadelphia, Pennsylvania
skysparkbooks.com
inquiry@skysparkbooks.com

Ordering Information:
Quantity sales. Special discounts are available on quantity purchases by corporations, associations, and others. For details, contact the "Special Sales Department" at the address above.

RAVEN'S RISE / Cole, Elizabeth. – 1st ed.
ISBN-10: 1-942316-22-4
ISBN-13: 978-1-942316-22-0

Chapter 1

England, 1144

THE SOUND OF CLASHING SWORDS rang out, followed by hundreds of ecstatic cheers. A man dressed in full chain mail armor with a yellow surcoat fell to the ground, his knees sinking in mud. He swung his sword upward to parry yet another blow, but it was too late. His opponent's stroke masterfully knocked aside the blade, sending it flying into the mud beside the yellow knight.

"I yield," the yellow knight gasped out. "You win, Sir Rafe. Again."

The triumphant knight wore blackened chain mail armor and a white surcoat with a black raven blazoned across the chest. His round shield was striped red and black, and the horse he rode earlier was black as well. Such a remarkable vision would have caught everyone's attention if he'd been doing nothing more than traveling the path through the normally sleepy village of Ashthorpe, which lay in the very heart of England. But seeing him in the midst of an attack was spectacular. It didn't matter at all that this attack was—ostensibly—for show. The crowd cheered wildly throughout the whole joust.

The battle was part of a festival with a special tournament hosted by the local lord to celebrate the tenth year of his reign. More than a dozen professional fighters came to compete, and it seemed the whole population for miles around came to watch.

The black-clad knight glanced at the crowd, then raised one hand in an acknowledgment of their adoration. The cheers increased and he smiled, as if pleased. In truth, he felt nothing. Absolutely nothing inside.

He'd defeated his opponent, true. But Rafe always defeated his opponents. In every tournament and joust and show battle he'd participated in over the past two years, he'd come away triumphant. And after each one, he searched for any sort of pride within himself, and found none.

As for the crowds, he was beginning to hate them as well. They were always so eager to see blood at these spectacles. These same folk who claimed to despise battle and war, largely because of the taxes and the disruption to their daily lives, were nonetheless happy to watch men risk wounds and death in a field for their entertainment.

And what does that make me? he thought. After all, no one was forcing him to fight in these tournaments. He'd once served a lord, but had forsaken him, along with his old life. Now all he had was his sword. He had to make a living somehow.

His current way of living meant that he had to put on a show, to impress the spectators. He strode over to his fallen opponent, who was still lying on the muddy ground. Rafe pointed his sword toward the man's neck, emphasizing how easy it would be to kill him. The other man went still.

A voice boomed out, "The Knight of the Raven is the victor!"

More cheers.

Rafe looked toward a small, raised platform. The baron of Ashthorpe, who organized the event, sat in comfort, surrounded by several other people of enough importance to rate an invitation.

"My lord, what is your wish?" Rafe called out. It was a formality—but one that gave the lord immense satisfaction, since it let him play God.

"Mercy, Sir Rafe," the baron called back. "Let him live!"

"As you command, my lord!" Rafe bowed, then sheathed his sword. He turned back to his opponent and offered a hand.

"Need a bit of assistance to get on your feet, eh, Louis?"

The other knight grimaced. "Go to hell, Rafe." Nevertheless, he took the proffered arm and scrambled to his feet. "I had you until I slipped in that damn patch of mud."

"Of course you did," Rafe said with an easygoing grin. "It had nothing at all to do with the fact that you're not as good at fighting as I am."

"You're lucky."

Rafe snorted. "Lucky or not, I'll be taking the spoils today. Don't worry, I'll see that your contributions go to a worthy cause."

Louis's expression soured further. "I'd call you greedy, but you take even that small satisfaction from your victims, don't you?"

"You can complain to the church, if you wish."

It was customary at tournaments and jousts for the winner to claim what the loser owned—which meant that Rafe would walk away with Louis's horse and equipment he'd used today, as well as the prize purse offered by the baron. Such stakes ensured that only knights who were confident in their skills would enter a tourney. It also meant successful fighters were rewarded with the means to keep fighting. Horses, weapons, and armor were very expensive.

Since Rafe won so often, he quickly found himself overburdened with a particular kind of wealth. His solution was political as well as practical—he offered much of his winnings to the local church for the purposes of charity, and he gave away many small coins directly to the spectators. His growing reputation as a generous, open-handed man meant he had a following. Local clergy who otherwise objected to tourneys—viewing them as frivolous or dangerous or both—were more than happy to receive the benefits of Rafe's donation. Local commoners crowded around him in hopes of receiving a handout, and women were impressed by the stories of Rafe's supposedly unselfish nature—which was something he very selfishly took advantage of when opportunity knocked.

He saw an opportunity now, as he walked from the field to the platform. One of the watching noblewomen stood up as Rafe approached her. She was absolutely gorgeous, with rich dark hair and a knowing smile.

"Sir Rafe," she said, clapping her hands together as he got closer. "Well done! You surpassed all expectation."

"All thanks to you, my lady Sybilla," he replied, touching the pale green ribbon tied around his upper arm. "Your favor gave me strength to endure."

"Is that so, sir knight?" She took a deep breath, causing her chest to strain against the tight bodice of her gown. "I had heard tales of your skill, but tales are nothing compared to seeing such a magnificent fighter with my own eyes."

Rafe bowed, then said, "To please a lady is all the payment I need."

She leaned over the railing, under the guise of reclaiming the favor she'd offered at the start of the tournament. In a low voice, she said, "If a lady's pleasure is the payment you seek, find me tonight after the feast."

He kissed her hand and gave her a smile, though not a promise. Rafe didn't give promises to anyone.

He left Lady Sybilla, collected his winnings from the baron's seneschal, and headed out of the tourney grounds and toward the village. All he really wanted was sleep.

However, he was soon surrounded by local people congratulating him, praising him, and wishing him good health. They all had their hands out, some more desperately than others. Rafe thanked them for their kind words, and pressed many small coins into many palms. Most were copper, but a few silver coins were mixed in, glinting in the sunlight.

Rafe reached his hand in the pouch once more and dropped a few coins in a young man's outstretched hand.

"Bless you, sir!" the recipient cried out, his pale blue eyes bright as the sky.

Rafe saw the reason for the lad's astonishment. Rafe had by chance pulled out four silver coins.

"It's nothing," he said to the lad, before he was swept along. The crowd barely slackened when he reached the first buildings of the village. Only when he got to the inn where he was staying did he get a chance to breathe.

Rafe always took care of his armor and weapons himself, which was a bit unusual. He could afford to hire a boy to act as page and all-around servant. But Rafe had his reasons for traveling alone. Thus, he had to attend to all the details of maintaining his tools of the trade. He cleaned and sharpened his sword and daggers. He laboriously scraped the debris from the tiny rings of his chain mail, cursing the previous foul weather that turned the tournament grounds to mud that day. This winter lingered. It was after Candlemas, when the weather should be growing warmer. Or perhaps he'd traveled far enough north that he could no longer rely on his old reckoning. In truth, Rafe wasn't always sure what shire he was in.

He finished cleaning his tools. Only his clothing, including the surcoat decorated with the sign of the raven, did he entrust to others. One of the maids who worked at the inn came by to take all the dirty clothing.

Rafe handed her an extra coin. "Joan, see that these things are returned to me by this evening."

"Tomorrow is not soon enough?" she asked, a little pout on her lips. "When are you leaving? Surely you will stay the night." From the way she looked him over, it was evident that the maid hoped to provide more services in the dark hours, in order to increase her income.

Had Rafe given her the impression he was interested in such services? Probably. Though he was trying to be a better man than he used to be, he continually failed to rise above his sinful tendencies in one department—women.

He loved women. He'd never been *in love* with a woman, but he loved them as the glorious creatures they were. He loved how they were shaped, how they kissed, how they felt under his hands. He flirted incorrigibly with nearly every pretty one he met, whether or not he had any actual intention of taking her to bed. A beautiful woman was his weakness.

The maid was still looking at him, expecting an answer.

"I'll probably stay for a while," Rafe told her, "but make sure the clothes are cleaned by tonight, all the same. I like to be ready for anything."

"Ready for anything," Joan echoed with a saucy grin. "Indeed, sir."

She left, but her lingering glance suggested Rafe would see her again before the night was out.

Rafe washed himself, dried off, dressed, and went downstairs to the tavern room to eat a hearty meal. Then he drank. His mood was dark for a man who'd won glory and gold that day. Joan's question had stuck in his brain. *When are you leaving?*

Soon. He was always leaving soon.

That wasn't how it used to be. He once lived at a manor called Cleobury, the closest thing he had to a home. But he made a mistake, and now Cleobury wouldn't ever be home again. Since he'd left two years ago, Rafe hadn't lingered in any one place for more than a few weeks. The feeling of being hunted kept him moving.

All that travel, all those months on the road, tourney after tourney, had now brought him here, to a lowly tavern in a town whose name he couldn't even remember.

He took a long drink of ale.

Despite his unsocial stance, arms crossed and his body hunched over the bar, people persisted in speaking to him. Most were congratulations, which he accepted. Some were offers of drinks, which he accepted more warmly.

Then someone had to bring up politics.

A thick-set man leaned next to him and started talking.

Rafe didn't mind that much till the man said, "What do you think of the news from the south? The tide seems to be turning in Stephen's direction."

Rafe put his mug down. "Where are we right now, friend?"

"This is the village of Ashthorpe."

"So we're not on a ship?"

The stranger looked very confused. "Um, no."

"If I'm not on a ship, then it's no matter to me how the tide turns." Rafe glared at the stranger. "Let a man drink in peace."

"You're for the Empress, then?" the man pressed, evidently not getting the message.

"I'm for finishing this ale without interruption," Rafe said. He put his hand to the hilt of his dagger.

That cleared the matter up. The stranger turned away, muttering something under his breath. Rafe ignored him and applied himself to getting drunk.

He was doing quite well, on his fourth or fifth ale, when another interruption came.

"Beg pardon, sir knight," a voice said.

"God's wounds, not another one." Rafe turned in his seat, ready to chastise whoever dared intrude on his solitude. He confronted a man about his own age...well, actually somewhat younger. Twenty at most. He stood strong and broad-shouldered, but with a certain hesitation in his bearing. Rafe looked him over, trying to guess his occupation. Farmer turned soldier, probably, like so many others in this anarchic kingdom. "What is it?"

The man gave a little bow, causing straw-colored hair to flop over one eye. "My name is Simon Faber. Apologies for disturbing your evening, but I have a proposition for you."

"I don't gamble," Rafe said, already half-turned back to his drink.

"It's a job for hire."

"I don't need money."

"But I do," Simon said.

Rafe looked back, feeling a spark of curiosity in spite of himself. "You take it then. Why even tell me? What is the job?"

"A lord in this shire needs to hire an armed escort for a journey. A family member must travel some distance and must be protected along the way, with the state of the country being so uncertain. I have two friends I trust—"

Rafe took a long sip of ale. Two friends was two more than he had himself. Yet another mistake for which he had only himself to blame. The reminder didn't help his mood.

"—but the lord will be more inclined to give the job to an established name," Simon continued. "I fear he'll not consider me. But if *you* were at the head of the group, Sir Rafe, he'd hire us without question."

"So," Rafe said slowly. "You want me to help you get a job escorting some pimply-faced noble for miles through the forest, all by using my reputation as a fighter to secure the job, and in return, I expect, you think I'll give you and your friends all the pay, because I'm such a charitable soul. Correct?"

Simon's faced reddened slightly, and Rafe knew he'd guessed correctly on that last part.

"Your generosity is spoken of. You give most of your winnings to local churches, and Lord Otto would surely trust a good Christian such as yourself."

Rafe smirked into his mug. He wasn't a good any-thing. And escorting nobles around the country was hardly in his field of expertise—in fact, the one time he'd done it in the past led to his downfall. Then again, what else was he going to do? He could find yet another tournament. Humiliate yet another opponent. But what was to be gained from that?

"Where's this lord live?" Rafe asked.

Simon's eyes brightened. "North of here, half a day's ride."

"Then tomorrow we'll go and see him. Meet me here, about an hour after dawn."

"I shall, Sir Rafe." Simon paused, then added, "Um, will you be sober by then?"

Rafe lifted his mug in a mock toast. "If God wills it."

Chapter 2

IVORY AND GOLD TOWERS STRETCHED upward into a pure blue sky, until they were lost amid clouds of brilliant white. No hint of grey marred the sky—there could never be a storm here.

The great structure seemed to be built entirely of priceless marble, in hues of creamy white and rose. The roofs glinted gold and silver in the light.

In front of the structure lay fields of emerald dotted with wildflowers in all imaginable hues. A golden road cut through the fields, inviting the viewer to step forward and see what marvels lay in store.

The woman gazing at the scene wished with all her heart that she could do exactly that…but she was not free to do as she wished. She was confined in the dreary halls of Dryton Manor. She could be free only in her mind.

She reached for the pouch tied around her waist. Inside it was a tiny silver box, wider than it was tall. She undid the silver catch, and opened it to expose the contents—a lock of hair. The light brown curl made her smile softly, and she pictured the owner of the hair. Her son Henry, only ten years old and now far away from her. He'd always loved the scenes she created, and she wished more than anything that he could be with her to see it.

"Truly remarkable," a voice said from over her shoulder. It was the priest who lived at the manor, Father Mark. "Is this what you saw in your vision of heaven, my lady Angelet?"

"Yes, Father." Angelet closed the box and looked over the scene she'd embroidered, elaborately stitched in many colors of silk thread, the stitches laid so close that the underlying fabric was hidden entirely.

She had worked hard on the altar cloth, and she had been permitted to purchase expensive materials all the way from London: not only gold and silver thread, but even purple, which was more costly than the gold, due to the great rarity of the dye.

Angelet labored over the design for a long time, and the result was a vivid scene of unusual detail. It depicted a soul entering heaven, surrounded by all the splendor Angelet had seen in her visions: blue and purple clouds parting to reveal an otherworldly palace. In the middle of it was a set of doors worked in gold and silver. The doors were open, and in the space between them stood an angel, a six-winged seraph ready to welcome the righteous into Paradise. Emerald green vines covered the borders of the cloth, and white lilies bloomed in the corners.

"In my vision," she said to the priest, "the scene was far more beautiful. I tried to recreate it as best I could, but it is only a poor imitation."

"It is a gift from God," Father Mark said. "You must never doubt that, child."

"Lord Otto does not share your opinion." Otto Yarborough ruled over Dryton Manor, and thus over Angelet as well. Otto was her father-in-law, but he never treated her much like family. Angelet's marriage to his first son had been brief—Hubert died less than a year after their wedding, shortly before Henry was born. However, Angelet remained with the Yarborough family, hoping to be reunited with her son. Her own home in Anjou seemed worlds away, and it was unlikely she'd ever be sent there again.

First, there was the war. With Stephen and Maud fighting over the English throne, everyone living in England was touched by the conflict. Since Angelet's family supported Maud's claim and Otto supported Stephen… well, it was a point of contention, and it transformed Angelet into a hostage of sorts. Then there was her dowry. As long as Otto had Angelet, he had control of her dowry too, until Angelet should marry again. But Otto didn't seem to want her to. The result was that Angelet found herself in the position of so many women of her time. She was weak and without practical power, at the mercy of stronger men.

And finally, there were the visions.

Angelet didn't want the visions, however beautiful they were. The visions were as much a curse as a blessing. They terrified the household when they occurred, though her descriptions of what she saw in her visions drew many listeners afterward. Father Mark encouraged her to write down what she'd seen—Angelet was literate and had a passable hand. She dutifully recorded many of her early visions, which were filled with descriptions of the beauty she saw—a world of bright light and palpable joy. She knew Father Mark passed on some of her writing to other priests he knew. Even Otto took a passing interest in the visions, largely because they made Angelet marginally useful due to the scenes she created from them.

Otherwise, Angelet was a useless ornament. She had few skills—only those that a lady was expected to know. She did have an exceptional hand for embroidery, and she could play the harp, and she possessed a naturally sweet voice that people told her was a pleasure to hear singing. But there her skills stopped. The manor functioned without her participation, and no one seemed to care very much if she was present or not.

The only person in the world who did care about her was Henry, and he had been sent away to be fostered with another family. It was common practice among the wealthy lords of England, but Angelet hated that Henry had been sent so far away, all the way to Dorset in the south.

She looked out the open window. The morning had dawned cold and bright, the late frost sparking on young shoots of irrepressible green grass. Winter was nearly over, and soon the spring would calm the bitter winds and warm the whole world.

But Angelet's soul felt as cold as ever. "I dreamed again," she told Father Mark.

The priest's eyebrows rose, and he leaned forward eagerly. "Another one of your visions?"

She shook her head. "No, Father. Just a dream, an ordinary dream. I dreamt of Hubert. He was alive, and as old as I am now. We were still together, him and me, and with Henry too. We were happy." She'd actually felt warm in the dream, feeling safe in the arms of her husband. It had been so long since she'd felt such affection.

"My child, of course you think on your late husband with longing, and it is natural that you would have such a dream. It is a comfort sent from God."

It did not feel like a comfort to Angelet. It only served to remind her of how alone she now was. "But does it indicate…that I am…"—she paused, hunting for the right word—"discontent?"

"Yearning is the lot of all mortals," Father Mark said. "You are not unique in this, Angelet. Indeed, we all know you yearn most ardently for greater things—the special visions you see are proof. God has graced you, Angelet."

Angelet sighed. The visions that occasionally came upon her *were* glorious, and more. They uplifted her, transported her from a dull life into pure light and sound, filling her with utter peace and joy.

Unfortunately, the price she paid for such visions was high. Her body shook violently, then seized up, sometimes for hours. She'd collapse, too weak to even crawl. A great pain blossomed in her head, so strong she could barely eat or sleep. Any light was too much for her—even a candle made her wince. Sometimes it took a full day for her to recover enough to be able to stand up.

Worse, Angelet rarely had much warning that a fit was coming. Once, she was seized while walking outside of the manor grounds, and she lay helpless for hours, until a passing fieldworker happened to find her and summoned help. Since then, she kept to the manor, afraid of what might happen if she ventured forth again.

"My child," the priest was saying. "To think of what you have lost is no sin in itself. But I worry that you are dwelling too much in the past, and not looking to the future."

"What future is there for me?" she asked dully. "What purpose can I serve, other than as a vessel for these visions? Am I to marry again? I doubt it." The truth was that she held very little appeal as a potential wife now.

Father Mark sat down beside her, letting out a thin sigh as his knees creaked. He was over sixty, with white, wispy hair cut into a tonsure. His heavily wrinkled face wrinkled even more when he smiled, which was often. Mark aspired to be a shepherd, and always tried to lead his flock very gently. Rather too gently, one could say, for Otto and those under his rule often disregarded Mark's teachings and counsel. There was only one world that interested Otto, and it wasn't the heavenly realm.

"Ah, these bones feel the damp!" Mark said. "Every spring seems damper, too…unless I'm getting older!"

"We are all getting older. For instance, I am too old to be a bride now," she said, choosing the most obvious objection first.

"I have performed weddings for couples older than you, dear, and seen them thrive together. You'd find that many men would court you, pretty as you are." He chucked her affectionately under the chin as he spoke.

Angelet smiled. True, she was very pretty. She'd been a pretty girl when the betrothal was struck, she'd been a pretty young woman on the day of her wedding. She was a pretty young widow on the day her husband died. And now she was a pretty, useless ornament that no one thought twice about.

"I would not object in theory," she said. "But Otto is the one to ask about a marriage. He seems to think I should remain as I am."

Father Mark wrinkled his nose in distaste. "Women are not meant to be alone. Eve was created as companion to Adam. So you should be a companion to another. I will speak to Lord Otto on the matter."

"As you think best, Father," Angelet said, though she

knew Otto's mind was unlikely to be swayed by any new argument.

In fact, she would be interested in another marriage, *if* the man was worthy. And that was the issue. Angelet would have no say in any marriage Otto might arrange for her. The man could be old, or cruel, or sick, or violent. *Be careful what you wish for*, she reminded herself. It would be foolish to throw herself at the first man who offered for her. What were the chances that she would actually be matched to a man whom she could love, or even respect? A handsome or strong man who would actually care for and protect her? An intelligent man who could succeed in the world? No, she shouldn't press too hard for a change in her circumstances. Let Father Mark argue if he liked, but she would say nothing.

Then Otto himself walked into the chamber. Though he was over fifty, his hair was still mostly brown, with only a few silver strands at the temples. His eyes were clear and missed nothing, a fact that all the manor servants knew all too well. He was a subtle, clever man, always eager for news of the world, mostly so he could use it to his advantage.

"Good day," he said. His voice was the warmest thing about him, always well-modulated and deceptively friendly.

Father Mark stood immediately. "Good day to you, my lord. God's blessing upon you."

Otto nodded graciously, as if accepting a gift from the priest. "What goes on here? Counseling our Angelet away from sin?"

"The lady needs little counsel of that nature, my lord. She is virtuous and good, and a fine example to others. In fact, since we are speaking of her…"

"Not now," Otto said, with a slashing motion of his hand. "I have other matters on my mind, and you may go." He then surveyed Angelet. "This altar cloth you're working on. How close are you to finishing it?"

She gestured to the table, proud of what she'd accomplished. "See, it is nearly done, my lord."

"How astonishing," another voice said. A thin woman stepped from Otto's shadow.

"Good day, Lady Katherine!" Father Mark said as he reached the door. "I didn't see you there!"

Katherine was Otto's wife, and it was common for people to not see her. Otto eclipsed her in every way. She was as quiet as he was talkative, as meek as he was bold. She seemed content to always walk behind him and never speak her own mind. A perfect wife.

After Father Mark left, she leaned over the table to look at the cloth with sincere admiration. "So very beautiful. I've never seen such colors."

"I hope not, considering what the materials cost," Otto said, chuckling. "But all the better, for it will be a most impressive gift."

"A gift for whom?" Angelet asked. "Should I embroider a name onto it?"

Katherine shot an almost guilty look toward Otto, but he only said, "No need. You just work to finish the design. A few days will suffice?"

Barely. But Angelet gave a little nod. "I will try, my lord."

"Do not overtax yourself," Katherine warned in her wispy voice. "If you have another fit, you will lose a day of work."

Now Otto's expression soured. "God's wounds, it's been three months since her last fit. I thought we might not see another."

"I do not choose it, my lord," Angelet whispered, hoping to calm the coming storm. "I do not mean to trouble the household."

"Yet trouble it you do, either with your tales of heavenly glory or your fits and seizures. It is intrusive to daily life, Angelet. You are a selfish creature to expect us all to stop what we do simply because you cannot keep control of your body or mind. It is a moral failing on your part."

"I am sorry, my lord. You could send me home to my family in Anjou."

"Unlikely. The d'Hivers are for the Empress, and would the king like me any better if I sent one of their own back to them, even one as pathetic as you? No, I will do my duty and keep you in Britain. If it stays the hand of one soldier in a battle, it is enough. Never speak of that again, Angelet."

"Then what will you do with me?"

"God knows, but I'll think of something. Thank God I was quick to move young Henry to a foster home. If you'd mothered him any longer than you did, he might have fallen prey to the same curse."

"It's not a curse," she protested, though it certainly felt like one.

"My lord," Katherine said. "What harsh words to tell a mother! And the mother of our grandson, at that. When Hubert left for fostering all those years ago, I could feel my heart break."

"But you endured, my lady, and Hubert returned home in time for his wedding." He broke off then, probably recalling that Hubert hadn't lived very long after his return home. The look on Lady Katherine's face suggested she remembered all too well.

"I do miss my Henry," Angelet said, with a grateful nod to Katherine. "More than I can say."

"Finish the cloth, Angelet," Otto grunted, and left the room. Lady Katherine patted Angelet's hand before following in his wake.

Angelet closed her eyes and hot tears slid down her face. She hated it here, and everyone here hated her.

"God save me," she whispered.

An image came to her—a familiar one, one she'd seen many times since the visions first began. It was strangely comforting, though in truth it wouldn't sound so if she described it out loud. She saw a great light, bright but not harsh, and somehow both pure white and a deep, royal purple—an inexplicable phenomenon that she explained to herself by deciding that in heaven colors were seen with the soul, not the eyes. It was a warm, gentle light, and in front of whatever the source of the light was, she saw an outlined figure, nothing more than a black shadow in the shape of a person. She did not know if it was male or female, and it did not matter. The figure never moved or spoke, yet she felt calmer every time it appeared to her. An angel, she thought. A personal guardian to watch over her during the worst times, when she was rendered helpless from the crippling after-effects of her visions. She never named it. She never dared.

But she was overjoyed when it appeared again. "Oh, thank God you've come," she whispered, her voice no louder than breath. "I've no one else."

The figure did not respond—it never did—but Angelet felt surrounded by love, and within moments she could breathe normally again.

Chapter 3

AS INSTRUCTED, ANGELET WORKED DILIGENTLY on the altar cloth, remaining in her little solar each day from dawn until the midday meal. The light was best there, due to the southern exposure, and it was warmer too. She spent most of her time embroidering, though mending and some other work could also require her attention.

She wondered idly who the altar cloth was for, but not too hard, for Angelet never worried overmuch about Otto's dealings. Probably for some other baron with whom Otto wanted to make an alliance. Otto, an adherent of King Stephen, was deeply concerned with the progress of the war between the royal cousins, and worked constantly to better his position. Angelet had no strong feelings either way. Let the great powers struggle among themselves for earthly glory, so faint and fleeting. Neither faction had use for her, so she had no use for either of them.

A few days after Candlemas, the morning dawned bright and sunny. She worked through the midday meal, but in the afternoon she heard a commotion below. Visitors? Curious, she went to the window to see what was happening. In the courtyard, a small group of men had just ridden in. Their horses steamed in the cold air as they dismounted and offered cheery greetings to the stableboy who had rushed forward.

Travelers, she guessed. They may only be staying the night, or perhaps they were on some official business that involved Otto in some way. Angelet surveyed the men, leaning further out the window to do so. They looked much like mercenaries, with mismatched armor and a smattering of weapons among their gear. One stood out, though.

That man wore a black surcoat over his chainmail, and everything about him looked more professional than the others. He must be the leader. His shoulder-length hair was just as black as his surcoat. He tipped his head up to look around the courtyard, and Angelet actually gasped when she saw his face. His deep blue eyes were bright and full of intelligence. He wore no beard, so his mouth was clear to see—a beautiful, sensual mouth. All in all, an uncommonly handsome man.

His gaze crossed hers, and Angelet quickly drew back into the safety of the solar. She ought to behave more modestly, instead of hanging out of a window staring at strangers. What would Father Mark say? She remembered his talk of marriage, and briefly pictured a husband who looked like the man in the courtyard. That might convince her to marry, if she also knew him to be good.

The man in black did not seem precisely *good.* Something about him made her nervous—a premonition that he was going to intrude upon her life for better or for worse, and there was nothing she could do about it. Her hands began to shake, a telltale sign that a fit could occur. She took several long breaths, putting one hand over her belly to measure her breath and keep herself calm.

"Mother Mary, Queen of Heaven, help me," she prayed. "As your son healed the sick, I beg you to intercede for me. I am weak and a sinner, but I swear I love thee and thy blessed son. Please, have mercy on me. Don't let me fall into darkness again."

The prayer helped, and she repeated it several times until the worst of the feeling passed. She would survive this. No matter what happened, she would endure it with grace.

Angelet sat down at her work table again, willing herself to put the image of the stranger out of her head. He meant nothing to her, and she had work to do while the light remained good.

A half-hour later, the door swung open, and a servant girl stepped through. She eyed Angelet suspiciously and said, "Lord Otto says you are to join the family in the hall for supper this evening. Dress well, for there are guests. You have one hour," she added, as if Angelet were the servant to be ordered.

"Send Bethany to my room to help me dress then. I'll be there in a moment." Angelet didn't bother to correct the servant's rude behavior. After years at Dryton, she was used to it.

Angelet's chamber was tiny, because she was the only person who slept in it. The other women of the house objected to sleeping near her, due to her affliction. So despite being born a lady, she slept in a place more like an anchorite's call. She didn't mind much, in fact. She valued privacy.

Her privacy came to an end when Bethany stormed in.

Bethany's head came only to Angelet's chest, but a lack of stature in no way humbled the maid. She tore though the room in search of everything needed to dress

Angelet for supper.

"No word ahead, and then I'm supposed to leave off my own work to get a lady ready for show," she muttered, the rest of the complaint lost amid the fabrics spilling out of the chest the maid was hunting through.

"The white gown will do," Angelet said. "I'll wear the rose surcoat to make it look more stately." And to hide the stains on the front of the underskirt. Angelet's wardrobe was not well-attended to on wash days.

Bethany performed the bare minimum of assistance to get Angelet dressed. Then she left the room. Angelet tied the laces down the sides of the surcoat herself. She deliberately made the ties loose, allowing the surcoat to billow out a bit, and to make the armholes extra large. Angelet didn't like it when clothing hugged her curves too tightly. When she was finished, she looked down at her outfit with a satisfied nod. The rose over the white was pretty but not ostentatious, and the loose fit ensured that she'd be comfortable throughout the evening.

She brushed her hair to a glossy sheen, and left it mostly loose, braiding only a thin crown around the back of her head to hold the rest in place. The fine, light blonde strands tended to fly when let loose. As a lady, however, Angelet couldn't remember the last time she'd let her hair be completely free.

She wore two silver rings—one was a gift from her mother on the day she left home and the other was a wedding band. Normally, that would be the only jewelry she'd wear. But something made her open the little box on the table.

She pulled out a necklace of five large, oval moonstones set in silver. She put the necklace on, peering in her small hand mirror. The necklace was the one valuable thing she owned, and it was meant for truly important occasions. Not an ordinary supper. But she kept it on, liking the weight of the stones around her neck. Otto would be annoyed she wore them, and Angelet looked forward to seeing his expression.

She went downstairs, wondering what she was supposed to do that evening. Otto rarely called for her attendance for any events when visitors came to Dryton. He preferred her out of sight and out of mind. Yet he called for her specifically tonight. Why?

In the great hall, she saw the group of men who'd ridden into the courtyard earlier. There were four in total. So they weren't simply travelers asking accommodations for the night. They were important enough for Otto to invite to table. Interesting.

The black-haired man was just as handsome as he'd seemed at first glance, perhaps even more so. He looked around the hall, and when his eyes met hers, he smiled warmly, as if he knew her already. Angelet quickly looked away. She didn't want to encourage anything, especially from a knight likely to be as arrogant as he was good-looking.

Unfortunately, there was another arrogant man in the room, and he was walking directly toward her. Her brother-in-law Ernald Yarborough was a thorn in her side. He had a knack for finding her at the worst possible times, and she hated the way he looked at her.

She greeted some people as she made her way to her usual seat. The men in the hall looked at her, and most didn't bother to hide their appraisal. The villagers and servants about the manor were circumspect—the difference in class was ingrained from birth, and very few of them would ever dare to insult a lady by a too-blatant appreciation. But the men-at-arms were different. Rough in personality and manners, they thought nothing of staring at her, and even muttering a few choice words that only she could hear.

Angelet didn't even respond to them. Instead, she moved past as quickly as she could, finding the nearest group of people to protect her by their presence. She'd learned to keep an eye out while pretending to notice nothing. She always knew where it was safe to walk and what hours she should remain in her chambers or with other women of the manor. No one taught her this—no one cared enough to do so.

But Ernald was different. He was unavoidable.

"Look who's come from her tower. Angelet the visionary. And with such jewels!" her brother-in-law said. "You're asking for attention."

"Lord Otto wanted me to attend," she murmured coolly. She wasn't asking for attention, and she certainly wasn't asking for Ernald's.

"Then you'll sit by me."

"I will not."

"No point seating you by a guest," he said, glancing about jealously. "What will you discuss with those men? Embroidery? Or do you think yourself so pretty you don't need to say anything?"

Angelet was used to such remarks and paid them no mind. "Enjoy your supper. I will find my place at the table."

"Your place isn't for you to decide." Ernald stepped closer, his expression turning ugly. "If you won't act as part of this family, you should take your meal in the kitchen. Or better yet, the courtyard, with the beggars and freaks."

Then, with no warning, the black-clad knight appeared between Angelet and her tormentor.

"Such comments are not polite," he said flatly. "Apologize to her."

"Or what?" Ernald asked, amazed that anyone would speak to him like that in his own home.

"I'll decide it's a matter of honor," the stranger said. He didn't seem the least bit taken aback. Did he not understand Ernald's rank? "You definitely look old enough to have been taught the concept of honor by now."

"What does *that* mean?" Ernald snapped.

"It means we'll fight. And lately, every man I've fought has either surrendered or died. I care not which it will be for you."

Ernald inhaled, puffing out his chest in offense. "I am the only living son of Lord Otto, to be a lord in my time. You're nothing more than a soldier. Who are you to teach me lessons in manners?"

"Sir Rafe. I'm also called the Knight of the Raven."

That name had some effect on Ernald and the others standing within earshot. Angelet didn't know what special meaning it held. All she knew was that no one had come to her defense in nearly ten years.

Now that defender turned to her. "My lady? What is your wish? Should I press this matter for your sake?"

She looked at the sweating Ernald, picturing him bleeding on a field, and finding a perverse and primal joy in the image. Then she sighed. "No, sir knight. He is my brother by marriage, and I would not wish to be the cause of his death."

"His own stupidity and rudeness would be the cause," the knight argued.

"Nonetheless, I humbly beg you to overlook his rudeness and stupidity," Angelet said. "Trust me, no amount of education will repair those flaws."

The knight smiled slightly at her words, and Angelet felt a stirring of satisfaction in saying them. For once, there was someone who *heard* her, if only for a moment.

"I am Sir Rafe," he said, bowing. "Whom do I have the pleasure of defending?"

"My name is Angelet," she replied, warmth spreading through her. Up close, the man had truly beautiful eyes, and she found herself blushing at his attention.

"May I defend you through supper, my lady?" he asked.

"Why…yes." She couldn't believe he would want to dance attendance on her. She was nobody. "That is, if you wish to spend your evening with a woman of no renown."

Escorted by him, she walked to her usual seat and sank down on the little cushion placed there.

"I've renown enough of my own," he said, taking the seat beside her. He spoke in such a way that it was impossible to tell if he was joking or not. "In truth, I wish the company of a civilized person for a few hours. The road is not civilized, and I've had enough of it."

"Where have you come from?"

"Most recently, from the south, by way of Ashthorpe. I follow the tourney circuit," he added.

"The Knight of the Raven. I know that name now," she said, finally connecting it. "It is said you always win."

"It is said correctly," he acknowledged. "Do I offend with my lack of modesty? I've never been a modest man."

"So long as you speak truth, I cannot see how anyone could object."

"Truth is rarely much appreciated," Rafe said. "In fact, it usually gets me into trouble."

Otto and the rest of the family sat, as did the others in the room. Suppers were often large affairs, with many people partaking of Otto's largesse. Tonight was one of those nights. The mood seemed almost celebratory.

"What brings you to Dryton?" she asked. "Are you just passing though? You mentioned travel."

"So I did, but the fact is that my companions and I are hoping to be hired for the job Lord Otto needs done."

"What is that?" she asked.

Rafe looked puzzled, but said, "Someone from Dryton is to be escorted somewhere. That's all I know. You have not heard of this?"

"No, but Otto does not consult me on such matters. Why does he want to hire outside men? We've plenty of men-at-arms here."

Rafe said, "He may not wish to reduce the ranks of defenders. Though the fighting has quieted down this past winter, it could flare up again, anywhere. These are nervous times."

"That must be it," Angelet said, seeing the sense in the soldier's words. "I know little of the details of the struggle between Stephen and Maud. To be honest, I know nothing."

"Excellent. Just don't ask me about it either. I despise politics," Rafe said.

"Don't you need to know what's happening?"

He took a bite of his meal and looked unimpressed. He said, "I used to think so. Now I need only know if the road ahead of me will be affected. It's all that matters."

She pondered that. His mode of living was so entirely different from hers.

After a long moment, he said, "The stones around your neck. What are they?"

"Moonstone." She touched one of the cool jewels. "Have you not seen such before?"

"I don't think so," he said thoughtfully, as if trying to recall something long past. "Unusual," he added, "and beautiful."

She smiled, pleased he liked them.

Rafe laughed once then, at himself. "To think I missed that opportunity! I'm more tired from travel than I thought. You must pretend I said that they are as beautiful as the woman who wears them."

Angelet was delighted at the compliment, transparently flattering as it was. "I thank you, sir."

"It's a lie, of course," he added, the charming tone gone from his voice.

Angelet looked down. "Oh."

"They are not nearly as beautiful as you," he said, his voice low and urgent. "Even though they are among the more remarkable stones I've seen, they are nothing next to you."

Warily, Angelet raised her eyes to look at him. Which of his statements was she to believe? Or any? Was he teasing her, just like all the others?

"It's truth," he said, not looking away.

She swallowed. "You say so?"

"From what I've seen just in this room? Yes, I say so."

Angelet wasn't sure how to reply, and in any case, it didn't matter, because Otto stood up and called for attention.

"Everyone, everyone! Still your tongues for one moment, for I have something to tell you all. The dinner you are enjoying is a celebration. I wish to acknowledge someone here: none other than our Angelet." He swept a hand toward her, and after a moment of surprised silence, the crowd began to clap.

"Yes," Otto said after a moment. "She is such a part of the manor, and so modest that many might not think of her. But tonight is her night."

Angelet had no idea what he was leading up to, and leaned forward so as not to miss anything.

"How desolate the manor of Dryton will be, upon losing such a singular person," Otto went on. "Yet it is time for Angelet to follow her destined path. I am pleased to share with you all some excellent news. The abbot of Basingwerke has agreed to accept Angelet as a postulant. She will be escorted there by these fine soldiers, who will keep her safe until she reaches Basingwerke Abbey. Then she will pass through those gates, to begin her life as a holy nun."

Chapter 4

ANGELET COULD NOT HAVE HEARD properly. The words Otto just spoke made no sense to her. "Postulant," she murmured, in an uncomprehending echo. "Basingwerke."

"You intend to take the veil?" the knight at her side inquired. "You didn't say *you're* the person we are to escort."

She shook her head slightly, as if that could open her ears. "I don't…"

"Angelet!" Now Otto stood by her side, looming between her and Sir Rafe. "You are extremely fortunate, my girl. I know the news comes as a surprise, but a welcome one, I hope."

"It is indeed a surprise, my lord," she said, her mind swirling. "I have many questions!"

"Then I'll answer them," Otto said heartily. "This moment in fact, to put your mind at ease. Come with me." He emphasized his command by putting a meaty hand upon her shoulder.

"Please excuse me, Sir Rafe," she murmured.

"My lady." He rose to his feet when she did, a courtesy her own family often ignored. His expression was polite, but when she caught his gaze for a moment, she saw some speculation there, a recognition that the upcoming trip might be in doubt.

But then Angelet was being driven along by Otto, like a lamb before a shepherd's dog. He directed her to a little alcove in one corner of the great hall. It was shadowed by a curtain that fell halfway across the opening. There was a comfortable padded bench, but Angelet remained standing.

"My lord, we have never spoken of this!" she began. "I've no wish for a religious life, and no calling for it."

"You have visions of heaven, Angelet," Otto countered.

"I do not want them," she insisted. "If I could be free of the occurrences, I would do it in a heartbeat…"

"That is what the abbot of Basingwerke offers."

She blinked several times, as Otto's words sunk in. "He knows of my visions?"

"He does. Father Mark has reported news of your visions to his superiors, along with some details of what you recorded. Other visitors have their own tales too. Some are quite moved by what you claim to have seen, and by the scenes you've created out of mere thread and cloth."

"I do not seek fame for what I experience. Only an end."

"An end is precisely what you will find at Basingwerke. The abbot there has seen similar instances before. If you are merely sick, you will be treated. If you truly experience divine visions…well, what better place for you to be than in a house of God?"

"But at the cost of remaining there? For the rest of my

life?"

"Everything comes with a cost, Angelet."

"But…" If she were confined, who would be there for Henry? Her own life didn't matter so much, but her son still needed an advocate. "What of Henry? He needs a mother…"

"Young Henry can certainly visit you there. That is a fair deal, is it not? You may be healed, and you'll be safe and well occupied, and you'll be able to write to your son and accept visits when his time allows. Perhaps he'll inherit one of my manors close to Basingwerke. Or, even sooner, I could have him fostered by another family in the shire. Wouldn't that be a happy solution? "

She stilled. So that was the true bargain. Otto knew her vulnerability all too well. The implied promise was that if she behaved and went along with Otto's plans, she'd be reunited with Henry in some limited way. Unlike now, when he was kept from her entirely. "I see."

He added in an annoyed tone, "Have I not done well, to seek out assistance for your singular plight? No one else has done as much for you. Where is your thanks?"

"I thank you most sincerely for your consideration, my lord," she said in a more obedient tone. "I only wished for more warning."

"You have it now. By the way, do not speak of any of this to the hirelings."

"Why not?"

"They are soldiers, and strangers," Otto said. "They would not understand the complexities of the situation. If any of them asks, tell them merely that it is your ardent desire to take the veil. Do not mention your visions, or the physical afflictions that follow."

Ah. He was afraid that Sir Rafe and his men would

refuse the job if they knew about Angelet's infirmity beforehand. Of course they would. Who would want to worry about escorting a sick and raving woman through the woods? "Am I to be alone then? Will no one who knows my state be there in case of an emergency?"

"Don't be simple. You'll have a female companion for the journey. One of the maids will go."

Then Otto walked her back to the main table, after warning her to show joy about the decision made for her.

Sir Rafe stood once again as she returned, and waited for her to sit before he also sat.

"Where were you raised, Sir Rafe?" she asked, hoping to steer talk away from herself. "You have the air of a man used to the court."

"Not at all," he said. "I was raised at a manor in Shropshire. My environment was no more refined than here."

"Have you been to court?"

"A few times. But I've seen the king more often on campaign…a setting where courtly manners mean little."

"You've seen the king?" she asked, surprised. "King Stephen? In person?"

"Aye, and spoken with him once—on the day I was knighted. He wouldn't remember me. My liege at the time owed allegiance to Stephen."

"And now?"

"Now I have no lord," Sir Rafe said, his eyes distant.

She nodded, though his answer puzzled her. Masterless men were not particularly welcome in the world. It was too chancy to have free lances wandering the land. That was how bandits gained strength, she was told. It was easier to steal and kill than to serve honorably. Yet Rafe seemed an honorable man. What had caused him to leave his lord's service?

"Is it lonely?" she asked. "To be your own master?"

"Sometimes. But not always. For instance, there are times when I get to dine with a lovely woman." His smile made her heart flutter, but she pushed the feeling away.

"You are a flirt," she said, attempting to sound annoyed by it.

"True," he admitted. "What harm is there in a little flirting?"

"You might break a lady's heart."

"I never have before."

"I doubt that very much. You likely have cut a swath through the country, now full of women lovesick at knowing that you've smiled at them once and will never pass by again."

"Now who's the flirt?" Rafe asked, his eyes warming. "You look like an innocent, but I suspect you're more than you seem."

"I'm a widow," she said suddenly. She touched the moonstones. "My husband gave me this necklace as a wedding gift."

Rafe looked chastened. "I did not mean to be impertinent." His smile returned. "Well, I did a little. It's been said that I'm incorrigible."

"Have no fear, Sir Rafe," she said. "You will not break my heart."

"I would not dare," he returned. "And anyway, what chance would I have with a woman about to take the veil? You must be ready to leave all such worldly things behind." His tone was light, but there was skepticism in his eyes.

"I hope to find peace at Basingwerke," she said. She couldn't outright lie about her situation, but she could dissemble. *Think of Henry. Think of seeing him again.*

"Do you not have peace now?" he asked.

Angelet saw Ernald staring at her hungrily from where he sat. She turned back to Rafe. "No. It is difficult to explain. Please do not ask me anything further."

He relented immediately. "Then I will ask you if you'd like a little more wine."

"Very kind. Thank you."

Following the course of sweets and nuts, during which even more wine was poured, the hall grew noisier, filled with the contented babbling of dozens of people, full and drunk and happy.

Just as Angelet was about to excuse herself, Otto stood up once again. "Attention!" he called. "Attention!"

"Saints help me, now what?" she muttered, fearing a worse announcement than before.

The room fell quiet. Otto gestured for two servants to bring something toward the center of the hall, just in front of the high table. They rolled in a small cart on which was set a heavy wooden chest, the lid on but not secured. Next to it on the cart was a coil of heavy chain and a great iron lock. The contents must have been heavy, to judge by the grunts of one servant.

Everyone strained for a better look. Those in front leaned in over the tables. Those in back rose to their feet to see.

Otto chuckled as he walked around to where the chest sat. He made another impatient gesture. "Candles! Bring some here to better show the spectacle!"

Rafe leaned over to Angelet, whispering, "What manner of magic trick is this? Will some bird fly out of the box?"

"I know not," Angelet replied, equally perplexed.

"Otto is not above a little showmanship, but I have no idea what he has planned tonight."

The candles were brought, and soon a pool of bright light shone on the chest and on Otto's face. His expression was almost smug.

"I announced earlier that the lady Angelet was traveling forth on a journey to take the veil. Well, a nun's place at Basingwerke Abbey does not come without cost. A bride of Christ must still bring a dowry with her."

He seized the lid and swung it upward. The squeak of the hinges was a little comic, but that meant nothing in light of the revelation of the contents.

Gold. Gold and silver coins glittered and gleamed in the candlelight, drawing shouts and excited gasps from the viewers. Angelet herself was stunned. She didn't think she'd ever seen so much wealth in one place before. That was her dowry?

She glanced over at Rafe, expecting to see him also agog over the display. Instead, he leaned back a little, his eyes narrowed as he studied not the gold, but Lord Otto.

Otto himself was still basking in the attention of the whole crowd. His long fingers curled around the lid, and then snapped it shut. "There, there. You've all seen the dower gift, and you'll be the last people to see it, until the abbot himself receives the chest." Otto picked up the coiled chain and began to wind it around the chest, looping it several times, tightly enough to make the chest impossible to open without removing the chain first.

And that would also be hard to do, because Otto's final touch was to loop the end links of the chain into the heavy wrought-iron lock. He snapped the lock shut. "Safe and secure," he declared, holding aloft an iron key. "May this gift bring favor from heaven, and may Angelet's holy service bring equal favor." He turned to her. "You will say prayers for the Yarboroughs, Angelet. Every day."

Angelet nodded wordlessly. So Otto found a use for her after all.

Chapter 5

FROM THE MOMENT HE SAW the lady Angelet earlier that day, Rafe knew he was in trouble. She'd been high above him, watching from her room, and the wind had picked up that pale blonde hair and waved it like a banner in the sun.

How was he supposed to ignore that?

He had no reason to think that he'd see her again, but then she appeared in the great hall, looking even more beautiful at close range. Nothing like his usual fare, but striking. Slim and pale, with long hair so light blonde it was nearly silver, and she possessed wide-set, light green eyes that he wanted to swim in.

Before dinner, when Rafe still didn't even know the name of the woman, he already wanted to throttle the stupid lordling who was mocking her. That the man should turn into such a sniveling coward the second Rafe confronted him only added to his fury. The lady had been so dignified, even when she was being assailed with harsh words. She was obviously hurt, but she didn't snap back or let the man's behavior drag her own down. Maybe that was why Rafe jumped in. Someone had to defend her, and it looked like no one in this whole hall of people was willing to take the task on.

Granted, Rafe hadn't realized he was challenging the lord's *heir* until he'd committed. But it wasn't as if Ernald had many supporters leaping to back him up either. Only a few sycophants lingered behind the young lord. None of them looked like a threat.

Still, Rafe used the pretext of protecting her to sit next to the lady at supper. He enjoyed every moment of her company, and the subtle way she deployed her wit, unafraid to exchange a barb or two. Her unusual beauty also helped keep his attention—not that she was anything like his type. She was too willowy, and too fey. He got the sense that those pale green eyes saw more than most mortal eyes. Lady Angelet was in danger of being carried away by fairies. Perhaps he could negotiate to be her protector. He certainly carried enough iron and steel to keep the otherworld at bay.

Rafe had caught himself and steered away from further ideas about getting closer to the lady. She was a dinner companion, nothing more.

Then Lord Otto spoke.

Whatever she said afterwards, Angelet had been stunned by Otto's announcement. Rafe saw it in her face, and that gave him grave misgivings about the job. He had no issue with escorting a woman to a nunnery—he didn't want to escort a woman against her will, however. And from Angelet's horrified expression when the news was announced, this decision was not of her choosing. But when he tried to ask her about it, she insisted she really did want to go. What could he do?

He could drink, and he did so, slowly, his mind working the whole time. For some time after the lady Angelet had excused herself for the evening, Rafe remained at the table, drinking the wine provided. He'd been a soldier for far too long to pass up the opportunity to drink on someone else's bill. The wine was quite good, the ale barely drinkable. The wine must have been imported from a good vineyard, while the local brewmaster had some lessons still to learn.

Eventually, Simon beckoned, and Rafe stood up, walking over to him.

"Come, let's go outside," Simon said. "We ought to talk."

Rafe agreed wholeheartedly. Once they got to the courtyard, Simon took a huge breath of cold night air.

"Did you *see* that chest of gold?" Simon demanded, as if there was the slightest chance that anyone could have missed it.

"I did. So that's what it costs to have a holy sister pray for you every day," Rafe said. "The price seems steep, but then, glory is often more expensive than you first expect."

"That is cynical, Sir Rafe," Simon said. "Surely Lord Otto's motives are pure. The lady wishes to join the nunnery and that is the cost."

"I'm not sure she does wish it. She was as surprised as anyone at the news."

Simon looked uncomfortable. "Well, that may be, but if so, it's not for us to decide. It's between the lady and her family."

"And the soon-to-be paid abbot! Otto's buying much more than a place in the cloister for his daughter-in-law. He's buying bragging rights and influence in the church. Mark my words, the lady is the least important part of this transaction."

"You should not say that. Reducing a holy vow to a

mere exchange in the marketplace is…"

"Blasphemous? It's true all the same. That man was putting on a show in the great hall, burnishing his name by creating a scene. And worse, he made our task harder."

"How so?"

"Do I have to act it out for you?" Rafe asked. "After that spectacle, rumors will be flying on the road before us…rumors of a small cortège weighted down by a chest of gold! We'd attract attention no matter what with a noblewoman like the lady Angelet in tow. But now we've got to worry about thieves and bandits who know exactly what sort of prize we carry."

"But the chest is chained up. Locked," Simon protested.

"So? All they have to do is *take* it…after killing us, of course. The chain and lock are impressive, but an axe will open that chest soon enough. Otto was a fool to advertise the gold."

"Is it advisable to call our client a fool?" Simon asked, looking around to see if any of the locals had overheard.

"He's not paying us to flatter him." The more he thought about the whole scene, the angrier Rafe got. "Why couldn't he have interviewed us about the job first, instead of making us wait until tomorrow to discuss it?"

"Will you refuse it?" Simon asked worriedly. He and his friends were the ones who needed the job, not Rafe. But Rafe was the logical person to take the lead and speak to Otto on behalf of all the others.

"It's too late tonight to say anything," Rafe replied. "I'll speak to him on the morrow." Then he smiled. "Perhaps this can be turned to our advantage. The extra risk requires extra reward, after all."

"Be careful."

"Not to worry, Simon. I know what I'm doing." Rafe didn't actually, but he knew there was something to be gained from a negotiation. However, to truly gain an advantage over their potential employer, Rafe would need more information.

And the person who had that information was Lady Angelet.

Rafe left Simon behind and returned to the main house. He had a fair amount of experience when it came to finding women in a discreet manner, so even though he'd never been inside of Dryton before, he was able to navigate the narrow hallways and rooms without attracting attention. He hoped to find Angelet in an out-of-the-way place so he could get some more honest answers out of her than he had so far.

However, when he caught sight of her again, she wasn't alone.

Ernald had her by one arm, and despite Angelet's efforts to extract herself from his grip, he kept her close, until she was backed against a wall and couldn't go any further.

"…never do this," she was saying as Rafe got closer to the pair. "Just let me go!"

"You'll be gone soon enough," Ernald returned. "You sure you didn't tell him to do that? To get you out of Dryton? I know you've been trying for years to get out of here. Marry me, and you'll be able to travel if you want. If you'd only listened to me—"

"No! I'm not interested in that," Angelet said. "I've told you that over and over."

"Shame." Ernald leaned over, eclipsing Angelet's form, hiding her expression from Rafe. "Then give me a goodbye kiss, Sister."

Angelet's next words were cut off as Ernald tried to claim a kiss.

Rafe covered the last fifteen paces at a speed he usually didn't try for. He clamped his hand down on Ernald's shoulder.

A second later, Ernald was flying backwards until he stumbled against the far wall. Rafe stepped between Angelet and the now-prone Ernald, keeping his back to the lady.

"Are you out of your mind?" Ernald hissed, rubbing at his jaw. "You hit me, fool!"

"I did," said Rafe. "I suppose I could have waited for the lady to slap you, but I'm impatient. And it would hurt more if I hit you."

The other man stood up, leaning against the opposite wall for support. The candle burning in the sconce a few feet away cast stark, deep shadows over Ernald's face. He sneered. "Aren't you the high-minded protector. Do you always lurk in corridors, waiting for women to save?"

"Not always, but I'll step into the role when needed."

Ernald rolled his eyes and attempted to skirt around Rafe to get to Angelet. Rafe shifted and half-drew his dagger.

"Stop."

"Do you dare get in my way?" Ernald asked with honest amazement.

"I dare a lot of things," Rafe drawled. "Which is why I've got plenty of notches in my sword while you're too cowardly to attack anything tougher than that over-cooked roast from supper. If you take another step toward the lady, I'll open up your stomach with this blade and pull out what's left of your meal."

Ernald paled, but said, "That's disgusting."

"So is raping your sister-in-law."

"I don't have to listen to this slander," Ernald snarled. "I'll report your actions to my father. Once he's heard what you've done, he'll never give you the job of escorting Angelet anywhere!"

Rafe kept his gaze steady on the lordling and made sure to keep himself between him and Angelet. "Guess you'd better hurry off, then."

Ernald's eyes slipped past Rafe, but he must have realized that even if he ordered Angelet to leave with him, Rafe wouldn't permit her to go. He turned and stalked away down the hallway.

Behind Rafe, Angelet let out a sigh of relief.

He spun in time to see the disgust on her face as she watched Ernald's retreat.

"That happen often?"

"He wouldn't have…." she started to say.

"Are you that innocent despite having been married? I was watching him all night. He looks at you like a wolf looks at a sheep. You're better off leaving this place."

"I'm glad to be going."

"Even to a nunnery?" he asked shrewdly. The few words he'd overheard suggested not.

"Um, yes." She looked at him with those wide, green eyes. "But now the journey will be delayed. I am so sorry to cost you the position!"

He smiled at her. "I haven't lost it yet. Not till Otto himself says so. How much weight will Ernald's words have?"

She frowned, thinking it over. "He'll lie, change the story to one that suits him better. He'll say he found *you* attempting to ravish me, and that he's the hero. Ernald will claim to have stopped you from attacking me."

"In that case, surely he'd have grabbed you and taken you away to safety. You'd be in Otto's presence when Ernald gives his account."

"True!" Her eyes lit up. "And Otto will certainly ask me what happened. Ernald and he have crossed words often enough that he won't trust Ernald's account alone. If I can't be found, the whole charge might fall apart."

"Where can you hide?" Rafe asked. "Especially if Ernald raises a fuss and asks for a search?"

"I know a few spots where I'll be quite safe," she said, smiling. "Listen. Should there be a search, *someone* ought to find me. If it happens, come to the chapel with one of your companions. You both can meet me there—I'll keep an eye out for you from my hiding spot—and I'll say I was in prayer the whole time. Then it will seem that Ernald made the whole thing up."

"Good enough." He touched her hand. "By the way, I wasn't in the hallway by chance. I do have questions for you about this journey."

"Then we'll talk more. Later. I don't want to be found by Ernald or his lackeys just now." She paused. "Why did you intervene? You could have walked away."

Rafe said, "Let's just say that I like you better than Ernald. And he needed a reprimand."

Her fleeting smile felt like a spring breeze. "Find me in the chapel. Good luck!"

* * * *

Angelet knew of many hiding places around the manor of Dryton, because over the years she learned it was better to be forgotten than noticed. Thus, she had favorite spots to dash to no matter where she was, whether on the grounds or in the manor house itself.

When Sir Rafe left her, she slipped down another hallway and hid in a shadowed alcove when she heard two other people walking toward her. She held still, scarcely breathing. From the tone of their conversation, it was only two servants. But she knew Ernald would be out to find her very soon.

So Angelet kept moving whenever she was alone and unwatched, making her way toward the chapel. Ernald probably would send men to the chapel looking for her, but she had a hiding place there too, a nook behind a curtain where Father Mark kept extra candles and oil. From there, she'd be able to see anyone who entered the space. When she saw Sir Rafe, she'd reveal herself again.

The chapel was empty when she got there. Father Mark went to sleep quite early, since he rose during the night to observe Matins and Lauds, the holy offices that took place during the hours before dawn.

Angelet entered the quiet chapel and moved to the hiding place. She took a few deep breaths, thinking of what an odd day she'd had. First Sir Rafe arrived, disturbing her placidity like a stone thrown into a pond. Then there was Otto's surprise announcement, and Ernald's display of dominance. Thank goodness Rafe appeared to thwart him. Angelet didn't think Ernald would have gone beyond a kiss, but that was bad enough. She never liked Ernald, even when she first came to Dryton. Hubert had been sincere and sweet. Ernald was the opposite, selfish and calculating.

In fact, Ernald first ignored her completely, until she was widowed. After her affliction began to plague her, he teased her for her visions and her strangeness. But then Ernald also began to press Otto to let him marry her. Otto always turned down the idea, but Ernald revived it often.

Despite her words to Rafe earlier, she was well aware that Ernald watched her. How had Rafe put it? Like a wolf watches a sheep. Yes, it was time to get away from Dryton, even if a nunnery was her only other option.

If that's the price I pay to see my son again, then I'll pay it, she thought. And she'd pray for the saints to intercede with a better ending, if they chose to. Either way, she'd get free of Dryton and the Yarboroughs.

She felt lighter as she thought of leaving Dryton at last. She'd been stuck here for far too long, within the dreary walls and the dour lands around. The journey, at least, would be new. She would see new vistas and new towns. Perhaps she'd get to meet a few interesting people along the way.

If she was lucky, maybe they'd travel along a route that would let her see a spectacular sunset, like the ones she remembered as a child. Dryton, confined in a wooded valley, never had sunsets like the ones she dreamed of, all gold and red beams in the sky, opening up as if it was heaven itself.

Closing her eyes, she imagined the scene, hoping to make it real. The colors seemed to burst in her mind, and she felt lighter and lighter, more joyous every moment. She could almost touch the sky…

Angelet drew in a shuddering breath. Too late, she realized what was happening. This was no idle dream, but the start of another fit. She scrambled out of her little hiding place. She had to run to find some sort of help before the seizure worsened, leaving her unable to move.

As she reached the altar and turned to the door of the chapel, she saw the same bright colors of her sunset, but now the color streamed in through the doorway, dazzling her. And in the midst of the vibrant, violent burst of light was the black outline of the figure she had seen so often before. Her angel.

"Help me," she said, reaching out to it. Pain stopped her from going any further. Her arm struck something at her side, and then she was falling, falling, falling, and everything went dark.

Chapter 6

AFTER WARNING ANGELET TO REMAIN hidden until the corridor was silent, Rafe had left her. He went to the dormitory, a long, low roofed room where male guests could stay. There were several mattresses laid directly upon the floor. No walls divided the space—it was little more than a barracks. Rafe was quite familiar with the set-up, after serving as a soldier and a knight.

His new companions were settling in. Simon, Laurence, and Marcus all took beds in a row. They were sitting on the middle one, about to start a friendly game of dice, so Rafe joined them.

The group was just starting the betting when a local guard walked in with the news: Otto wanted to speak to Angelet, but she could not be found. Ernald must have given his own account of the incident, just as expected.

Rafe told Laurence and Marcus to start searching near the outer walls of the manor, while he and Simon would begin with the buildings.

"Won't the residents know where to look?" Laurence asked. "We're strangers here."

"Then perhaps we'll see something that they've overlooked," Rafe countered.

About half an hour later, though, no one—local or stranger—had located the elusive, lovely Angelet.

Simon eventually gave a sigh and kicked a wall with his foot. "I swear we've been through every hallway and room three times by now. Still no sign of the lady. How can she simply vanish?"

Rafe said calmly, "There's no magic or mystery at work here. I'm sure she'll be found, and all will be explained."

"God willing," said Simon. "To be out of a job before it begins! My father will laugh at me. He's a carpenter, and my older brother's a carpenter, and Lord, I don't want to be a carpenter too. I was sure the soldiering life couldn't be so difficult, yet I'm failing from the first. How can we escort the lady through half the kingdom when she can't be located inside one manor house?"

"She'll be found." Rafe smiled, then looked around. "Come, let's try another tack. We've scoured the manor house, so let's go outside. Perhaps she's somewhere else on the grounds. Someplace where she might not have heard any commotion of those looking for her. Someplace quiet and peaceful…"

Simon's eyes lit up. "My God…the chapel!"

"Good thinking," Rafe said, happy Simon had picked up the idea Rafe so carefully suggested. "Let's go there."

Rafe entered the chapel with Simon on his heels. Next to an upright, carved wooden crucifix, a candle set in a heavy wrought iron candlestick burned on the altar, the only light in the space. Rafe was a little surprised, since he expected that Angelet would have lit at least a few other candles while she was waiting there, as they had agreed.

"The other candlestick is missing," Simon said then.

"What?" Rafe turned to the other man, who was staring at the altar in puzzlement.

"The other candlestick." Simon pointed to the altar. "I stepped in here earlier, and there were two candlesticks, each flanking the crucifix. They should always be lit. Yet now there's just one. That's strange."

"Someone may have needed light," Rafe hazarded. It was a ridiculous suggestion, and he knew it. No one would have taken a heavy candlestick from the altar itself. There were other candles in more humble holders to be used. Something was not right. "Lady Angelet?" he called out. "Are you here?"

There was no answer.

Rafe made his way up the center aisle. "Lady Angelet, people are looking for you. If you're at prayer, we can at least tell everyone where—"

He broke off, because when he reached the altar, he saw a pool of white of the ground. A woman's skirts. Angelet lay at the far side, the heavy candlestick nearby, its light now doused. "Jesu," he muttered.

Behind him, Simon asked, "What is it?"

Rafe knelt beside Angelet, reaching for her hand. It was ice cold, and she didn't react at all to his touch.

"Oh, dear God," Simon said, now seeing what Rafe saw. "Is she dead?"

Rafe bent to her face, and felt the slightest puff of breath from her open lips. "No. She's alive. Go get help!"

Simon dashed off immediately, and Rafe turned to the unconscious woman at his feet.

"Angelet," he said, quietly. "Wake up. We're alone. You need not act now."

She did nothing, said nothing. Rafe realized that whatever was happening now, it was no act to explain away her absence. Something serious happened to Angelet, leaving her alone and helpless on the cold stone floor.

Moments later, several people entered the chapel.

"Thank God," Rafe muttered. He raised his voice. "Over here!"

"I sent out a cry, sir," Simon said. "This is Bethany, one of Lady Angelet's maids."

After Bethany, Ernald came in, along with a few of the manor's guards.

The petite maid looked down at Angelet's prone body with narrowed eyes, then spoke. "So that's why we couldn't find her. She had another seizure and couldn't hear us calling."

The utter lack of concern in her tone made Rafe tense up. "This happens often?"

"Often enough," Ernald said. "Sometimes months go by between her fits, but it's no surprise to see another."

"How do you care for her now?"

"Naught to be done," Ernald said with a shrug.

Bethany added, "When she rouses, she can go to her bed and rest till the headache fades. She always has a headache afterwards." The maid gave the last bit of information as if it were a grave personal failing on Angelet's part.

"You would just leave her here till she wakes on her own?"

"There's no waking her now, sir. Trust me, we've tried all manner of tricks. Screaming in her ear, banging pots, striking her…she sleeps on."

Rafe was appalled at the maid's list of abuses. He couldn't rely on the manor's inhabitants to care for her, so he'd have to do what he could. He gathered Angelet in his arms. She did not weigh that much.

"I'll carry her to her bed," he announced.

Ernald blocked his path. "I should do it."

"Then why didn't *you* pick her up?" Rafe asked. "I've got her, so let me by. Jesu."

The lordling sneered but stepped aside. "Bethany, show him the way," Ernald ordered.

Bethany led them out of the chapel and across the courtyard to the manor house. Rafe followed, trying to keep his stride steady so as not to disturb Angelet more than necessary.

Not that she seemed the slightest bit aware of her surroundings. Her head lolled against his shoulder and one arm slipped down, dangling toward the ground.

"Simon," Rafe ordered. "Her arm."

Simon, who'd been like a faithful shadow, now circled and gently laid Angelet's arm across her stomach. His expression was still stunned, and Rafe knew the young man was highly disturbed by Angelet's condition.

The little party made its way through the manor house. A few other residents stood by as they passed. Some muttered, a few crossed themselves hastily. None offered to help.

On the upper floor, Bethany opened the door to a corner chamber. "This one, sir."

Rafe passed through the doorway to find a small space enclosed in darkness. He saw the narrow bed as a faint patch of lighter color and laid Angelet down on it. "Light a candle," he ordered the maid.

Bethany did so, grumbling about Rafe's officiousness.

Ernald came in then. He looked at Angelet, lying on her bed, then at Rafe. "You can go now, sir knight."

"She can't be alone."

"I'll stay with her," Ernald said.

Rafe almost laughed out loud. As if he'd let Ernald near Angelet after what he'd seen earlier that night. "No."

"I'm her family. You're nothing."

Simon, who'd been silent thus far, now stepped forward. "That's an insult!"

"Simon, stand down," Rafe said quietly. He thought for a moment. "Please find someone who can tell us more of what's going on. Lord Otto, if that's what it takes."

"Yes, sir."

Ernald snapped, "Bethany, come with me. I would speak with you."

After they left, Rafe sat on the stool next to the bed, leaning against the wall. He waited, listening to the shallow breathing of Angelet.

He wasn't sure why it felt so important to remain beside her, other than the pure shock of seeing her so lively, and then a short time later so still. He also didn't trust the household to look after the lady, not after Bethany's callous response to seeing Angelet helpless on the floor.

About a half an hour passed, during which time Angelet didn't stir even the slightest bit. Rafe stayed at the bedside, watching her to make sure she didn't worsen. Not that he'd know what that would look like.

Then there was a stir in the hall. The lady of the manor walked in, flanked by two new maids. One bore wine and the other some cloth and a bowl of warm water.

Rafe stood up.

"I am Katherine," the lady said. "Your man Simon found me and told me what occurred."

"Will she recover?" Rafe asked.

"She has before." The lady directed the maids to put

down their things, and began to give them a series of detailed instructions. Then the older woman said to Rafe, "I will stay with her through the night. You may retire, sir knight."

"I'll stay outside in the hall," he told her. "In case there's need."

Katherine blinked, and then seemed to focus on him for the first time. "You're the knight my husband will charge with escorting Angelet to the nunnery, are you not?"

"I'm one of the soldiers."

"You take your duty seriously."

He could have given simple yes, but something in him made him retreat. He did not want the lady to see just how profoundly Angelet had affected him. "Expediency, my lady. I can't get paid for a job if the client dies first." Rafe smiled as he spoke, the same smile he always used to charm.

Lady Katherine gave him a long, searching look. Then she said, "You may wait outside the room. Though with Angelet, all we can truly do is wait for her to come back to herself."

Rafe nodded and took up a position just outside the door. The maids exited a little while after. But Lady Katherine remained inside. The slight sounds of movement, the rustle of fabric and the clink of the dishes suggested she was doing something. Then things quieted down.

An hour passed. Another. Rafe must have dozed, because he jerked awake on hearing some small sound.

"What is it?" he asked out loud, reaching for the dagger at his side. His brain was muddled, and his instinct was to expect a battle.

No one was there, but he heard the sound again, a soft moaning. It came from Angelet's room.

He took a breath, then eased the door open. The candle had burned low, but still illuminated the room. Lady Katherine sat in the only chair, her head nodding over her chest.

Angelet, however, appeared to be waking. Or at least her sleep was no long the deep catatonia that gripped her before. A thin sound escaped her lips.

Rafe sat on the edge of her bed, there being nowhere else to sit. He leaned over, putting a hand to her head.

"Angelet?" he asked quietly. If Lady Katherine woke, she would not look on the scene with much sympathy. "Angelet."

Her brow wrinkled up, a sign of some internal pain.

Rafe immediately bent and laid a kiss on her forehead, hoping to soothe her. He pulled back to find her eyes now open, staring at him in wonder.

"What has happened?" she asked. "I was waiting for you in the chapel, and…" she trailed off. "Oh."

"You remember?" he asked.

"It's coming back. You found me?"

"I did. You were near the altar, unconscious."

"It happened again," she said in a small, hopeless voice. "I hoped I would be free of it for some time, but luck was not with me. Well, perhaps it was, if you found me."

"Simon and I both found you, and brought you back here when your own servants showed no inclination to do so."

Then she blinked, seeming to realize something for the first time. "You stayed with me."

"Just outside. Lady Katherine remained here. See?"

She looked over, but immediately returned to him.

"But you hardly know me, and you stayed."

"Well, you needed me to," he said.

"It was most kind."

"Self-interest, nothing more," Rafe said. "If you die, I'll have no one to escort to the nunnery, and then no one gets paid." He leaned over as he spoke, his fingers sweeping strands of that unusual silvery blonde hair from her face.

Angelet smiled. "Your words are harsh, but your gesture too tender. Part of you is lying to me, Sir Rafe."

"No knight leaves a lady in distress. What else can I do for you? Do you need food or drink? There's wine here."

"I need only rest. I hate this part most of all, when I can barely rise from my bed. My head hurts so."

He put his hand to her head, very cautiously. "Where?"

"Behind my eyes, but also at the back by my neck, and, well, everywhere."

Rafe began to stroke her head with his fingers, moving lightly from her temple to the base of her neck. "Does that feel better or worse?"

She closed her eyes. "It's…not worse."

Good enough. He continued to do it, to soothe at least a little of the pain. Angelet shifted to lie on her side, her hands tucked up under her chin, her eyes closed. Rafe glanced over her. The dip of her waist and the rise of her hip showed plainly under the blanket, the sort of curve he liked to see in bed.

He couldn't recall the last time he'd been alone with a woman that hadn't led to pure carnality. Yet here he was, alone with a beautiful woman and thinking of nothing more than how to heal her.

Well, not *nothing*. She'd certainly caught his interest, even though she was not his usual type. But he had no intention of acting on his impulses in this situation. The idea of taking advantage of a helpless woman was repellent.

After a moment she whispered, "You said there was wine? I am thirsty."

He reached to the table, where a glass of wine stood. Then he slipped his free arm behind her shoulders. "Just rise a little, so you can drink this down."

Angelet dutifully sipped several times. "Enough," she said at last.

Rafe eased her down, then replaced the goblet on the little table. "How do you feel?"

"Less thirsty," she said, with a tiny smile. "I'll take what victories I can."

"Sleep, Angelet," he said. "I'll stay here."

"That's good," she whispered, her eyes closed. He remained by her side until she drifted off again. Then he moved back out to the hallway. He used the old tricks he learned on campaign to stay awake during sentry duty, and only when dawn colored the sky did he allow himself to relax.

* * * *

Later in the morning, Otto himself came to Angelet's room. Rafe stood just inside the door as the lord looked her over. "How are you, girl?"

"Better," Angelet replied. "I am most grateful someone found me and brought me to my room." She didn't say Rafe's name, probably to maintain a bit of discretion.

"Well, I shall remain with you this morning," Lady Katherine said. "You will need some bread and a little broth, I think, to revive you."

"That would be most welcome," Angelet said.

"Quite a commotion you caused last night," Otto told Angelet.

"The fit came on without warning," she said. "As they always do."

"You knocked the candlestick off the altar," Otto said. "It's damaged."

"I'm sorry," Angelet said meekly. "I have no memory of that."

"The candlestick is your concern?" Rafe asked. "Not your daughter?"

"She's not my—" Otto snapped, then checked himself. "She has an affliction that no one here can deal with. Of course we're all concerned for her health."

"Of course," Rafe echoed, not believing it.

"I had wanted to speak to you last night," Otto said, again turning to Angelet. "Ernald insisted something important occurred, and you would know what he was speaking of."

Angelet's eyes grew wide. "Did he? I'm not sure what he could have meant."

"Do you not?" Otto grunted, and looked sidelong at Rafe.

Rafe jumped in. "In fact, my lord, I have some questions of my own. Shall we let the lady rest? We can speak elsewhere."

"Very well."

Otto led Rafe to another part of the manor house, and then to what must be his private room. There were documents, sealed and unsealed, filling cubicles along the wall. In one corner stood the chest of money that Otto presented last night, the whole thing still bound with the chain and lock.

Otto sat in a large, high-backed chair. Rafe continued to stand, since there was no other place to sit.

"About last evening…" Otto began to say.

Before Otto could bring up Ernald's trumped-up accusations, Rafe launched his own offensive. Always keep an opponent on his toes. "Did you hope to hide the lady's condition? What if she'd had an attack on the road? None of us would know what to do!"

"The matter will be addressed. The maid Bethany has seen the attacks before," Otto said. "She told me early this morning that she will be pleased to accompany Angelet on the journey."

"Will Bethany's knowledge be sufficient?" Rafe remembered Bethany's cold reaction to Angelet's collapse and her total lack of any assistance. He narrowed his eyes, waiting for Otto to come to his senses.

The lord finally shifted in his seat, looking a bit uncomfortable. "I suppose I should have mentioned it."

"Yes, you should have."

Otto grumbled, "What do you want? An apology?"

"More money."

"*What*?" Otto's eyebrows nearly rose off his forehead.

"This job is not what was first described. Your reticence about the lady's health and your choice to flaunt the gold in that chest both mean the journey is much riskier than you implied. If you want me and my men to guard the cortège from here to Basingwerke, it will cost more. Double, in fact. And you'll pay *before* we move out."

"Ludicrous."

Rafe shrugged. "Very well, my lord. If you don't like

my terms, then hire another group. Farewell." He headed for the door.

"Hold, sir knight!" Otto said quickly. "Angelet needs to travel now. There's no time to wait for another group."

Rafe smiled to himself. He'd gambled on Otto's impatience, and it paid off. But when he turned back to Otto, his face was serious. "And how much is your time worth?"

"Double the original price is too high. I could offer you…half again as much."

Rafe made a show of considering it. "Agreed."

Otto clearly hated being outmaneuvered, but he said, "Done, then. And I'll lend your group four of my guards as well, to ensure the safety of the venture. But you must leave tomorrow."

"Certainly, my lord. We'll leave as soon as the wagons in the cortège are loaded…and the payment is in my hands."

Rafe nearly skipped out to the courtyard. Negotiating with Otto had gone better than expected. It was almost too easy, in fact.

He gave Simon and the boys the good news.

"This is amazing," Laurence said. "We'll eat beef for a year!"

"He must value the lady's safety highly," Simon murmured.

Rafe disagreed. "He wouldn't weep if the lady didn't make it to the end of her journey. But the money is another matter. That's what we're really guarding."

Simon chewed his lip. "Did Lord Otto say that to you?"

"No," said Rafe. "He didn't have to. You've got to learn to listen to what these lords *don't* say. It's just as important as what they speak in words."

"God's wounds, I'm even greener than I thought," Simon groused.

"That's why you enlisted me, is it not?" Rafe clapped him on one shoulder, a gesture of camaraderie that he didn't really feel. Yet it seemed to mean a lot to the other man.

"I suppose so. Well, I'll learn a lot on this trip, that's for certain. And we'll see both the lady and her dowry safe to her destination."

Rafe was going to have to teach Simon the trick of expecting the worst.

Chapter 7

FREEDOM. GLORIOUS FREEDOM.

Angelet's spirit lightened the moment her carriage left the grounds of Dryton. Even though she had grave doubts regarding her ultimate destination, she was away from the place that oppressed her for so long, and the air was cool and clear, and she could pretend that all was well.

That morning, the small cortège had been ready to go, making it clear that Otto had planned this for some time, waiting until the very last moment to tell Angelet her fate. His trickery irked her, but what could she do? Facing the inevitable with grace was her only option. So she cooperated with Otto. She allowed the meek Lady Katherine to assist her in final preparations for the journey, suffering her mother-in-law's platitudes about how fortunate she was to be going to Basingwerke.

Katherine had carefully folded and packed the completed altar cloth, putting it into Angelet's possession rather than alongside the chest of gold. "Keep this safe, dear. You put so much of your heart into it. You can hand it to the abbot personally. No matter what may happen, you'll have a lovely gift to give. And soon enough, perhaps, you'll get a visit from Henry. I'll ask my lord Otto about it…" The older lady trailed off. She'd never spoken very much, and this speech seemed to use up all her words.

Father Mark bid her goodbye as well, commending her to God and telling her he would pray for her happiness always. "Your soul is a candle in the dark, little Angelet," he said. "You hardly know your influence. Faith and charity and love are your most powerful gifts."

"Not embroidery?" she asked wryly.

He chuckled. "When you sew with faith and charity and love, my daughter, then yes."

"I'll miss you." Father Mark was the only person she would miss from Dryton.

"God willing, we'll meet again." He kissed her forehead and spoke a blessing.

Otto himself was less sentimental. Right before they left, the chest had been ceremoniously loaded onto the carriage that Angelet would travel in. She didn't like that decision at all, but she had little say in the matter.

Upon being told, Sir Rafe nodded crisply. "Of course, my lord. A sensible decision to put all the valuables in one place. It will be easier to guard."

"All the valuables?"

"The gold and the lady," Rafe said. "What could be more valuable than the life of one we're meant to escort?"

"Ah," Otto said, clearly having forgotten that Angelet was worth anything at all. "Yes. How true." He turned to her. "Angelet, come with me."

"In a moment, my lord." She handed Rafe her own bag. "Please put this in my carriage, where I can get to it easily."

Rafe took it. "What is it?"

"Just a few personal effects."

"I thought you were giving up all worldly goods at the end of this journey."

"But not until the *end* of the journey, Sir Rafe," she countered impishly. She was feeling remarkably good, and excited to be leaving Dryton.

She followed in Otto's wake, curious as to what he could want. A final warning, probably. She was to keep her mouth shut and not interfere with anything. She was not to have more fits—as if she chose to! She was not to smile or laugh, or enjoy her brief time of relative freedom before the gates of the nunnery would slam shut and lock her away for life.

"Yes, my lord?" she asked politely. "What is it?"

He looked around, saw no one, then produced the iron key. "Keep this with you until you give it to the abbot himself. Tell no one you have it. These soldiers may well turn upon you if they think they'd have a chance to steal the money for themselves."

Angelet's mouth dropped open. If Otto thought that was possible, why was he hiring them in the first place?

"My lord," she said at last. "If you don't trust them…"

"Oh, they seem solid enough. But one never knows, and gold makes men do strange things. So be wary, daughter. Keep your own counsel, don't fall into easy confidences, and remain aloof until you arrive safely at Basingwerke. Understand?"

"Yes, my lord." Angelet tucked the key into the small bag slung about her waist. Otto never called her *daughter*. What a strange parting this was turning out to be. "I suppose I should rejoin the group. They can hardly start off without me."

"Very true," Otto said, putting a hand awkwardly on her shoulder. "We have not got on, Angelet. But all else aside, you're the mother of my only grandson, and I'll never forget that. You did your duty as a wife to Hubert. And I think you also made him happy, to the end of his short life."

She nodded and turned away, unable to think of anything to say. Otto made her life hell for years, and now he wanted…what? Gratitude? Reconciliation? She had nothing for him. "I must go."

Armed with the key, conscious of the weight of it in her bag, she returned to the cortège.

Rafe stood by the door of her personal carriage, his hand out. "Ready to go, my lady?"

She put her hand in his as she stepped up into the cushioned interior. His grip was strong and steady, and she would have enjoyed it more if the maid Bethany hadn't been glaring at her pointedly from her own seat.

She still had difficulty believing that Bethany volunteered to accompany her. It would be better to do without a maid at all, yet she could not be devoid of female companionship on the journey. Even as a widow, she must appear chaste.

Angelet let go of Rafe's hand as though it were on fire. "I am ready to go, sir knight."

"Expect a few moments wait, my lady, and then we'll be moving." Rafe shut the door, smiled at Angelet through the open window, and walked off.

"What caused you to dally?" Bethany asked.

"My reasons are not your concern," Angelet replied, feeling a surge of confidence at the thought of leaving Dryton Manor at last. "Conduct yourself according to your station, Bethany, and we'll have no trouble."

"And if I don't?" the maid asked.

"You can walk."

"You're not in charge."

"If not me, then who? Ernald? Otto? Or is there another one of noble birth tucked away in the supply wagon?" Angelet looked hard at Bethany. "If answering to me chafes you so, hop out now before we leave Dryton."

"What will you do without a maid?"

"I'll hire another one in the next village." Angelet had never done such a thing before, but judging by Bethany's shocked expression, the maid believed it possible.

The next few hours passed in silence. Angelet stared out the windows, eager to see anything outside her own small world. The view was not inspiring, mostly mud and still-bare branches. But the air was crisp and smelled cleaner than the manor's did. That was enough.

Her carriage was well-supplied with cushions to make the journey more comfortable, and curtains to block dust and rain, as well as any too-curious stares.

In addition to her own carriage, there were two supply wagons stocked with food and equipment they'd need along the way. It was expected that they'd find shelter at other homes or in towns for most of the nights. But to travel in this day and age meant to always be prepared for the unexpected: a storm, bad roads, a washed-out bridge, or worse. Rafe told her they'd likely be sleeping at least a few nights on the road. For most of the party, that was no hardship—they were commoners and soldiers, used to rougher living. She was apprehensive about the notion of sleeping outdoors, but after all, she wouldn't be alone.

If only she felt less alone.

Chapter 8

THE FIRST EVENING, THEY HALTED in a village Angelet had heard of but had never been to. The inn there was quite acceptable, and the innkeeper was familiar with Otto and Dryton, so Angelet was given the best room. She would have been even more pleased, except that the sour-faced Bethany would share it with her, to preserve her honor.

Rafe came up to them and pointed to a small pyramid of sacks and boxes. "Bethany, those items all go up to the lady's chamber. You should be able to take care of it in three or four trips."

Surprisingly, Bethany nodded and went to work.

Angelet was happy…then she noticed the chest of gold. "What are you doing with that, Sir Rafe?"

"It's also going in your room, my lady."

"Must it?" she asked, as Simon and one of the Dryton guards wrestled it upstairs.

"Tactical decision. Both you and the maid will be near, and I'll see that guards are within earshot of the room. Someone will always be awake."

"Would a thief actually try to come into my room?"

"It's a risk," Rafe said. "But better that the gold is inside, instead of left in the carts."

"If you think it best." She looked up the stairs, then felt Rafe touch her arm.

"I promise you'll be safe."

She nodded, feeling a little better. He was the Knight of the Raven after all, undefeated in all the contests he entered. Otto would have hired the best.

They ate well that night, since the inn was a prosperous one and Angelet was a better class of guest than most. She had thinly sliced beef in a sauce rich with the taste of red wine, which soaked into her trencher, turning the hard bread into a very satisfying course. However, despite the meal, or perhaps because of it, she felt rather restless.

She stood up, only to find that Rafe stood too. "My lady?"

"I was cooped up all day in that rolling box. I need to move. I'll take a walk through the town. Bethany can come."

"Yes, my lady," the maid said quickly enough. Her earlier pique was gone. In truth, Bethany was perfectly good at all the skills a maid should be good at. Her changeable moods created all the problems.

Rafe shook his head. "You may take a walk, my lady, but the maid can stay here. I'll escort you." He put a hand meaningfully on the hilt of his sword.

Angelet said, "Surely I'm not in danger in a village a day's ride from Dryton?"

"You won't be in danger if you've got a soldier as escort."

The daylight was waning when Angelet stepped out of the inn, followed by Rafe. The feeling of being guarded was novel. She had never been considered important enough to guard before, beyond the usual restrictions imposed on all women of her birth. She would have expected it to annoy her—being constantly under someone's view. But in fact it felt comforting to have Rafe near her, perhaps because she was certain that no one would dare harm her while he had that sword strapped to his side. Or just perhaps because he was a pleasure to look at. Any woman would be pleased to have such a man walking by her, wouldn't she?

The town was compactly built, with the slightly taller buildings all huddled up together along the main road, so that the sky above was just a narrow strip of clear purple, like a silk ribbon.

Warm, gold light from candles and cooking fires shone out of windows and doors, thanks to the mild weather. Angelet hummed to herself as she peeked into the lives of these strangers. She saw families of all types. There were young couples chasing after little wild things pretending to be children—the shouts of the boys made her smile. There were fat, content older couples who lived more quiet lives. There were merchants and laborers, apprentices and traders. But no ladies like her.

A sudden feeling of intense loneliness assailed her, and when she saw an open field with a pond on the other side, she took the narrow path cutting through it. All the while, Rafe had said nothing, content to be her shadow.

But Angelet grew curious. She asked, "Is this a common task for you, Sir Rafe? To act as a bodyguard, or an escort?"

"No. I'm only here as a favor to Simon Faber."

"So you know him well?"

"Barely at all, to tell the truth. We met in Ashthorpe.

He proposed I join his group to seek the job offered by the lord of Dryton. If he hadn't spoken with me in the tavern, I would probably be miles away right now, looking for the next tourney to compete in. That's what I usually do."

"I'm happy you're here instead," she said, feeling very shy. "You take well to this work—the men all respect you. I saw today how they jump at the slightest command. You're a natural leader."

Rafe laughed at that. "I'm nothing of the sort. Simon and his boys are just green. Any authority would seem wise to them."

"You are too modest."

"That, my lady, is not something I've ever been accused of." Rafe gave her a wicked grin.

"What is a more common accusation?" she returned playfully.

"Oh, too handsome, too charming, too clever…that sort of thing."

"Not modest at all, then."

"As I warned you when we first met," he said.

Seeing a large fallen log near the edge of the pond, she stopped. "I'd like to sit here a while."

"We have time."

"You could sit with me…unless you need to keep watch, lest a deer or a rabbit comes to attack me?"

"I'll risk it," he said, sitting down just close enough that if she reached out she could touch him. "The local rabbits are probably not a threat."

She laughed. "You don't act like any other knight I've met. Not that I've met many. I enjoy talking to you."

Rafe gave her wink. "Don't get used to it, my lady. At your nunnery, you'll endure days of silence. Or endless prayer."

She wrinkled her nose in distaste.

"Why is it to be a nunnery?" he asked, more intently. "Why not marry again? You were widowed so young. How have you not gained more suitors?"

"I have nothing to offer. Who would wish to marry the broken widow of a minor nobleman's son? Even aside from my affliction, I bring no great lands, nor distinguished name. And…" she broke off.

"And what?"

"Nothing."

"Were I a lord, I'd offer for you."

"Were you a lord, you would need to make alliances, or gain land, or get an heir, like any other man. You'd choose a young bride with a great dowry to bring to the marriage bed."

"Just as well I'm not a lord then. None of those things do I want. Not lands, or alliances, or an heir."

She was skeptical. "What man doesn't want a legacy? What would your father say if you told him such?"

"I don't know, because I don't know who my father is," Rafe said. His tone was careless, but she saw a flash of pain in those deep blue eyes. "Maybe he's one of the great lords of England. Or maybe he was a common soldier, dead a day after siring me. I have no idea, and no loyalty to a man I have no name or face for. Let that be my legacy—that I won't do the same to a child that my father did to me."

"Oh," Angelet said, reaching out to cover his hand with hers. "Don't say that. You don't know where you come from, but I am sure you were loved. Your mother, what of her? Did she tell you nothing of your birth?"

"My mother's identity is a mystery to me too. I don't remember her at all. I think she must have got rid of me the first moment she could after I was born."

"You can't say that about your mother!" Angelet said, thinking of what she'd do to see her own son again.

"I can and I will," Rafe said bitterly. "The cold fact of the matter is that I was born a bastard and then instantly abandoned. So don't speak to me of family name or legacy. They're empty dreams, stories nobles tell each other to convince themselves they're better than the peasants plowing their fields. I'll make my own way."

"Is that why you're a soldier?"

"It's a profession where skill is all that matters. Doesn't matter how noble a man's blood is…he can still lose it all on the battlefield."

Angelet winced at the thought of him dead.

"Forgive me," he said. "None of these things are subjects to discuss with a lady. I shouldn't have said anything. In fact, why am I telling you any of this?"

"Do you not normally confide in a woman?" she asked.

His expression became more closed off than before. "I don't confide in anyone."

"You must have someone," she said. "I refuse to believe you're alone, without friends or companions or someone you love."

"Why does it matter to you?" he asked. He turned toward her, his expression dark. "I don't want pity—"

Without knowing that she was going to do it, Angelet leaned over and kissed him.

It had been a terribly, terribly long time since she'd kissed a man, and the initial touch of his mouth to hers sent a shock through her whole being, as if she'd been brushed with fire. She leaned closer, deepening the kiss as she laid her hands on his shoulders.

She didn't know what she thought he would do in reaction to her wanton advance, but she expected something faster and fiercer than what he did.

Rafe slipped one work-roughened, calloused hand behind her neck, teasing the soft skin there. He took his time tasting her, running the tip of his tongue along her lower lip. Angelet moaned a little as she pressed herself closer to him. The dusk surrounding them weakened her inhibitions, allowing her to indulge in this unwise but most tantalizing folly.

He drew out the kiss slowly, as if they were the only people in the world. Angelet desperately tried to remember how she was supposed to kiss, but with every passing second, her mind spun further and further from reason, lost in the maelstrom of sensation caused by Rafe's mouth on hers. No need for her to remember how to kiss…he knew what to do. When she felt his tongue flick against hers, she gasped and pulled back for a second, but Rafe didn't let her go far—by now he'd somehow wrapped both arms around her, and she was molded against him, kissing him over and over.

Only when the cry of a night bird pierced the air did she recall exactly where she was, and why. She pushed herself away from Rafe, breathing hard. "A moment," she gasped. "I need to…I don't know what I need…" She shook her head, too embarrassed to look him in the eye. "Forgive my behavior."

"Nothing to forgive, Angelet. I liked it." His voice was warm, easy. "If that's how you show pity, maybe I do want to be pitied after all."

"It wasn't pity," Angelet confessed. "I don't know what I was thinking. I'm not like this normally."

"Or you are, and you just needed to get free of your

prison to know it."

"I'm not in any prison," she objected, remembering all the details of what brought them both here. "Remember, I'm going to join a nunnery."

"That's another word for prison, if the going isn't your choice."

"I *do* want to go there," she insisted. And indeed she did, if that was where she could be cured of her affliction and if it meant she would see her son again.

"You're hell-bent on a heavenly reward, even after a kiss like that. So you're not going to invite me into your bed along this journey? You don't need a lover, one last wild indulgence before you lock yourself away for the rest of your life?"

She gasped at the suggestion. "I can't take a *lover!*"

"Why not?" he asked, sounding far too reasonable. "Consider, my lady, that you have what—a week? two?—before you lock yourself away behind walls for the rest of your life. You might never see a man again. You certainly won't see one as handsome as me."

Despite everything, she bit her lip to stop a giggle.

He continued, "For a little while, you're on your own. You can do anything you like, experience anything you like. Including some pleasures which are denied you by the circumstances of your widowhood."

"You offer to be my lover," she said, to ensure she heard correctly. She couldn't have. His words were too bold and too scandalous to be real.

Rafe nodded, his eyes locked with hers. "If you like, Angelet. If you don't like, I'll never press you. You have my word. And if you do take me as a lover, you can rely on my discretion. I'll never betray a confidence, not during, and not after. And while we're together, it's on your terms."

"My terms?"

He gave her a little smile. "I'll obey your every command, indulge your every whim, satisfy your every curiosity."

"Oh." Angelet had never heard an offer quite like that before.

Rafe took her hand in his. "I'm not modest—I admit that. But I also don't boast about something unless I can back it up. If you take me as your lover, you won't be disappointed."

"Oh." Eventually she'd have to start breathing again. Rafe's proximity was making her feel distinctly lightheaded.

"And what have you to lose?" he added. "We're together a fortnight, at most. Then it's over and we go our separate ways. You to your nunnery, and me to…wherever. Either way, soon we'll never see each other again."

"What if we spend a night together and I wish to end it there?" she asked, hardly believing this conversation was happening.

"Then it's ended. I mean what I say about obeying your every wish."

"Oh." Sweet Mercy, stop saying oh, you fool, she thought.

He waited, his eyes intent on hers. She waited for some hint that he was teasing her, or that it was a joke. But everything in his demeanor suggested he was serious.

At last, she whispered, "I must think on this."

"Of course. It's an unusual proposal, to be sure."

"I may never speak of it again," she warned.

"That's an answer in itself." He took her hand, laid a soft kiss on the back of it, and then released her, showing her that he didn't just take what he wanted. He was content to wait for it to come to him. And his words made it seem quite natural for her to want to come to him.

"You're a most perplexing man," she said.

He smiled and it nearly took her breath away. "Yes, I know," he said. "It's part of my charm."

She realized she was already leaning in for another kiss. Lord, he was dangerously attractive. Too bad he knew it.

Trying to recover a modicum of dignity, she rose to her feet. "It's well past time to return."

"You're undoubtedly right."

But she just stood there, overwhelmed by emotions.

Rafe stood too, never taking his attention from her. He raised one eyebrow. "What's the matter? One foot in front of the other, beautiful. That's how I manage it." Now he was teasing her, but his teasing felt gentle rather than cruel.

"I'm *moving*." She took a step. There. She did remember how to walk. Then she stumbled in the darkness.

Rafe's hand was at her elbow. "Careful," he said in a low voice. "If you get a scratch, it will look very bad on me. Not to mention on you."

Rafe walked Angelet back to the inn. It was as if the kiss and his outrageous proposal never happened. But Angelet could still feel his mouth on hers, and his arms around her, a sort of protective circle that urged her to forget the whole world and focus only on him. She had no doubt that if she allowed him into her bed, it would be… memorable. He made no secret of his flirtatious nature and his experience with women.

However, actually accepting his proposal was out of the question. She was a modest lady, a widow, a soon-to-be postulant in a nunnery. She was not some woman ruled only by her lust.

In fact, she'd been good and modest her whole life… and what had it got her except being sent away to a place where there was no other choice but to be good and modest? She curled a lip in irritation. Why should she never be allowed to enjoy anything in life on her own terms? She was always being ordered by someone else. A man with more power and authority than she'd ever have.

I'll obey your every command.

The more she thought about it, the more Rafe's offer made her blood catch fire. What would a night with him be like, if he truly obeyed her every command and indulged her every wish? Wouldn't that be worth it, considering the years of solitary, holy loneliness that awaited her?

Chapter 9

BACK AT THE INN, RAFE took Angelet directly to her door, and he was actually grateful the maid Bethany was there, attending to some task by candlelight. Two guards stood outside, just as Rafe ordered, which also kept him from making any remark that was too familiar.

On the left stood Dobson, one of the four men-at-arms that Otto had included as part of the revised agreement after the value of the chest had been revealed.

Dobson nodded a greeting to Rafe. "We're to switch watches halfway through the night, sir?"

"Yes. Two others will take your place."

"Are two guards at a time necessary, sir?" Dobson's tone was diffident, but he obviously thought that it was overkill to guard a door inside the inn at all, let alone with multiple men with multiple watches.

"I hope it's not necessary, Dobson," Rafe said, keeping his manner easy. "But those are my instructions. Understand?"

"Yes, sir." Dobson looked to be about forty—in other words, old enough to have learned that questioning an order wasn't worth the hassle. "You're in charge."

Rafe relaxed. The last thing he needed was an insubordinate soldier on his first outing as a leader.

"Get some rest, my lady," he told Angelet. "We leave early tomorrow."

She nodded graciously, her manner not giving a hint that they'd exchanged a wildly inappropriate kiss. "I thank you for your advice, Sir Rafe. After such a long day of travel, and knowing my door is guarded so thoroughly, I shall sleep well indeed. Good night."

He turned away and then got the hell out of range. Her words, designed to be neutral, immediately caused Rafe to picture Angelet laying on a soft, white featherbed. Her hair would spill out on the fabric, and her body would be just as soft as the feathers themselves. God, what he'd give to see that with his own eyes, to have her smile and invite him to join her, to spend a whole night with her.

However, she hadn't accepted his offer, and who knew if she ever would? Rafe guessed she wasn't quite as demure as she seemed as first—after all, she had been married, and *she* had kissed him. But she didn't exactly jump at his offer, either.

Until she did, he wouldn't do anything about it. Well, he would try not to. Old habits died hard, though. Rafe spent most of his life indulging his vices, which happened to center around women. Over the past year or so, he'd been trying to be a better man. Truly. And in many ways, he had improved his behavior. But he'd never run into a temptation like Angelet before. Beautiful and intriguing and somehow still very innocent. He'd never been attracted to the fair, wide-eyed type. But he *was* attracted to Angelet. Far too much.

Even before her unexpected kiss, she had affected him

in some strange way. He told her about his parentage—or lack thereof—which was something he hated to think about. He certainly never chatted about it, not to anybody. And there he was, offering up his history without the slightest reservation. He was worried by how much he'd already revealed, not thinking of the consequences. Something in Angelet's fey eyes made him forget all his defenses. He couldn't risk anyone in this party learning of his past transgressions.

The bitter truth was that Rafe hadn't merely left his lord's service to pursue fame and glory on the tourney circuit. He'd violated an oath, nearly killed one of his only true friends, and betrayed the blood of the one man who'd offered him a home.

As a very young boy, Rafe knew that he owed everything he had to Rainald de Vere. Rafe was a bastard, a child of no importance or distinction. He didn't even know how he'd come to Rainald's attention, in fact, but once it became clear that he had an aptitude for fighting, Rainald allowed him to join the small group of boys who were at his manor for training.

They were sons of the gentry, and in one case the nobility. Allies often sent their children to be fostered elsewhere as a way of strengthening bonds and taking advantage of each others' resources. De Vere employed an excellent master of arms and several very skilled veteran knights. Now retired from active service on campaign, they still served their liege lords by training up new men to be squires and knights.

For some boys, the training was rather perfunctory. A young lord needed to know the basics of battle, but not much more than that. One of Rafe's cohort, Luc of Braecon, had been a proud and annoying little snot, assured of his place and certain of a comfortable future due to his family's wealth and connections. Luc participated in practices for swordplay, riding, and hand-to-hand fighting. But he had aspired only to competence—his true interest lay in politics.

Rafe was the opposite. He knew little of politics and cared less. However, he could make a name for himself on a battlefield. In a world perpetually at war, skilled fighters were always in demand. Rafe was blessed with natural athleticism and innate skill for combat. He could see weaknesses in any opponent, and he trained himself to know how to exploit those weaknesses. From the age of fourteen, Rafe could beat Luc every time they met on a practice field.

In fact, Rafe's only true competition was Alric of Hawksmere. He was the son of a knight, so his dedication to training equaled Rafe's. Alric was big and broad, even as a boy, and he was nothing to laugh at when it came to a duel. Still, by the time they finished training, Rafe usually triumphed against Alric too. He was just a little quicker, a little more adept, a little more driven.

"No question. You're the best of us," Alric had often said after practices. The other boy never knew how much those words meant to Rafe. To hear someone praise him—to confirm that Rafe had worth at least in one setting—was music to him. Without a mother or a father, or any family at all, Rafe never heard such things.

When they all grew from boys into men, they fought together on the battlefield, relying on each other to stay alive. Those experiences forged a bond among them, one eventually solemnized with an oath they each gave to the others. Rafe promised, on his life, to be a brother to Alric and Luc.

Well, Cain was a brother to Abel, he reminded himself. And it is written how that ended.

He still remembered the day he broke his vow. The day that started his descent from a respectable knight to what he was now…a mercenary and a vagabond.

Since fleeing from his old life, Rafe hadn't stayed in one place for more than a week or two. The longest he'd stayed anywhere was London. He thought he'd be able to fade away, lost amid the thousands of other bodies. And for a while he had been happy there—well, not happy, but at least not miserable.

Then, one day, he saw a familiar face across a market square. The face and figure of Octavian de Levant was unmistakable. There was more than one African-born, black-skinned man in England. But only one who was friend to Alric and Luc, and who saw Rafe's misdeeds up close. So when Rafe noticed the young knight in the market, he ducked behind a linen seller's stall.

He felt like an idiot. Octavian couldn't have seen him, and in any case, he was probably in London on his own lord's business—he wasn't searching for Rafe. But that didn't mean that Tav wouldn't send a message to Lord Rainald if he learned Rafe's whereabouts. So Rafe left the city the next day, and had kept moving ever since, usually to the next tournament he could find. Winning at tournaments was a profitable living, but it wasn't a vocation. When he got Angelet delivered to her destination, he'd be able to take a few days to decide his next step. And he might need those few days to forget Angelet, who already occupied more of his brain than he wanted to admit.

In the morning, the wagons and carts were packed up again, the chest once more secured, and the cortège made its way out of the village. By midmorning, they were once again on the road, which ran through patches of woodland and then farms and then woodland again. Rafe should have been irritated by the slow progress. No one in the group besides himself—not even Otto's four men-at-arms—ever served in a real army, and none of them were seasoned travelers. They had little notion of how to pack efficiently or move quickly. The journey to Basingwerke might take longer than he first guessed, especially if they didn't pick up a little more speed.

On the other hand, a slower pace meant more time with Angelet. Rafe glanced toward her well-appointed carriage and caught her leaning on the sill of the window, gazing out at the passing scenery. When her gaze crossed his, she averted her eyes, ducked her head, and pulled back within the darker confines of the carriage.

He chuckled to himself. A shy, embarrassed woman was a woman thinking of things she shouldn't. And Rafe liked that quite a lot. Then he sighed.

"Nun," he muttered to himself. Angelet and he should never have crossed paths. Even though they were now traveling together, he had to remember that in a very short time they'd never see each other again. He never should have mentioned a liaison. He'd revoke the offer the next time he could speak to Angelet privately. He'd apologize. He'd be the better man he told himself he wanted to be.

"Behave for a week," he told himself. "Two weeks. You can do that. Anyone can do that."

"Sir Rafe?" Simon asked, startling the hell out of him.

"Gah! What?"

"Did you need something, sir? You were talking."

"Taking to myself," he said. "It's nothing."

He just had to *keep* it to nothing. Nothing between him and Angelet. Ever.

They rode on. The day was sunny and bright, perfect for traveling. Yet Rafe didn't share the cheerful mood of nearly everyone else around him.

Rafe turned in his saddle, casting a look backwards at the road they'd traveled so far. There was nothing amiss. Nothing out of the ordinary, just fields of freshly turned soil, with little green seedlings beginning to wake up. Beyond, there were a few copses of trees and a distant farm, the low buildings now just specks in his vision.

But he couldn't shake the feeling that something was wrong. Rafe trusted his gut when it came to such things. He'd be dead a dozen times over if he ignored that familiar creeping sensation along his spine. *Something* was wrong. Someone was after them.

He said nothing to the others of his suspicions, largely because he couldn't prove anything, and also because even if someone was following the group, it could be as much for Rafe as for the chest of gold. He didn't particularly want to explain to the others why someone had sent men to track him down.

He looked again, scanning more slowly, taking in the whole landscape. It was a part of the world that was unspectacular, though very pleasant. Rolling hills and scattered woods lay between the farms and villages—the very heart of the country.

Plenty of places to hide, he thought. In the few years since he'd fled his old home of Cleobury, this had happened more than once. A figure, sometimes two, would edge into his vision and Rafe could tell they were there for a reason.

Someone wanted to know where he was, and was willing to pay people to find him. *Alric*. It had to be. Rafe betrayed Alric, nearly killed him, and despite an awkward confrontation and apology on Rafe's part, it was very likely that Alric wanted a more thorough accounting for Rafe's actions. Hence the paid henchmen sent to dog Rafe's trail.

Sometimes, Rafe got a message from an innkeeper that a man stopped by looking for him, and wanted to talk. Rafe left quickly whenever that happened, not believing that "talk" was all they wanted. Every so often, Rafe had actually seen one of those pursuers at a distance, allowing him plenty of time and space to slip away. He followed the tourney circuit because a wanderer had no home, and no place where he was vulnerable. Rafe could pick up and move on at any moment. He needed nothing other than his sword and his horse, Philon. He could run forever.

Or could he? Someday, he'd miss the signs. He'd be caught unaware, and whoever was following him would catch him.

"Not today," he muttered aloud. He'd keep his eyes and ears open, deal with the pursuer, slip away…

"Damn." That was the difference. This time he couldn't slip away, because he had to see Angelet all the way to her destination.

He'd have to deal with this particular shadow in another way.

They halted for a midday meal, drawing off from the line of carriages and carts to a little clearing just off the track. Everyone seemed content to linger, since adjusting to the constant jarring motion of riding a horse or in a wagon was unpleasant.

Angelet had barely spoken to him all morning, undoubtedly regretting whatever impulse had led her to kiss him. Understandable. Angelet was a lady, and a lady had no business dallying with a mere soldier like Rafe. It had been loneliness and pity that had driven her, and it was Rafe who turned her kiss into something more. No wonder the lady kept Bethany by her side all day.

At the moment, the two women sat on a green grassy slope, eating the last of their meal, which was largely bread and cheese. Rafe approached, offering a friendly greeting. "Happy to get out of the carriage for a while?"

"By the saints, a carriage is a weapon," Bethany moaned.

"It must be borne," Angelet said, with more equanimity. "At least we got to rest for a bit."

"Are you still hungry?" he asked. "Do you need anything else?"

"Before we leave, I should refill my flask from the stream," Angelet said, patting the newly sprouted, long grasses around her. "Where is it? Did I leave it in the carriage?"

"I'll fetch it, my lady," Bethany said, sounding much less cranky than usual. The meal must have soothed her temper.

"No need," Rafe said, gesturing for the maid to stay seated. "I'll make myself useful."

He left the women to relax, and walked to Angelet's carriage. Laurence, who was leaning against the back of it, nodded when Rafe approached. Rafe had insisted that the carriage holding the chest never be unattended.

Rafe opened the door and saw the flask Angelet used for water. It was made of horn, with a cork stopper and a leather strap, a much finer product than the waterskins most people carried. He was just about to snag it by the strap when he saw something else lying there, half hidden on the cushioned bench. It was a velvet pouch, barely the size of his palm.

He'd seen it before. Last night, when Angelet had gone into her room, she'd moved directly to her bed and picked up the same tiny pouch, clutching it as though fearing it would be stolen. And now it was still close by, though Angelet tried to hide it from view while she was gone from the carriage.

Rafe picked it up, curious what Angelet would conceal like this. He opened the drawstring and shook out a tiny silver box. It was etched with a pattern of a curling vine, looping over and over around the box. He thumbed the catch, lifting the lid to reveal the contents.

Inside was a lock of hair, a curl of light brown about two inches long. One end was carefully stitched together to prevent the hair from scattering. Rafe was puzzled, until he saw the inside of the lid, where an H was inscribed.

Angelet had mentioned her husband's name once when they had been talking at Dryton Manor. Hubert.

Rafe snapped the lid shut and jammed the little box back into the pouch. He yanked the drawstring shut and replaced the pouch where it had been before, then walked away with the flask.

Lord, he was a churl. Here he'd been flirting with Angelet, even offering to seduce her, while she clung to a memento of her long-deceased husband. She must still be in love with him. And she was going to a nunnery. Whatever her physical response to Rafe, which had been real enough, she still harbored strong feelings for another, keeping a secret token of her love with her every day. He wanted to curse himself. Even after he'd vowed to try to live better, to be better, he still fell into the trap of his own self-indulgence. He saw Angelet and wanted her, and he didn't even stop to think how she felt or if she wanted anything from him.

He filled the flask and gave it to Angelet, keeping his usual flirtatious remarks to himself. She looked at him with curiosity in those big, pale green eyes, but said nothing.

Chapter 10

OVER THE NEXT FEW DAYS, they continued along the road, the whole cortège inching northward to Angelet's inevitable fate. So far, they'd been fortunate to reach an inn, or in one case the home of a local lord, before dark. The weather had been dry and mild, too, which meant that travel was safer, faster, and much less muddy than it might be.

She ought to be praying for thanks, thinking holy, sanctified thoughts, or pleading with the saints to intercede for her when it came to keeping her from sin.

Instead, she felt more and more drawn to earthly distractions. From the safety of her carriage, she often tracked Rafe's movements, noting how perfect his body was, how well formed from years of fighting and training. What that body would look like stripped bare…

Angelet quickly looked down at the ground. Lord, what was *wrong* with her? She could hardly glance at Rafe without thinking distinctly carnal thoughts. It didn't help at all that the man was gorgeous. Those blue eyes were so deceptively soulful, so sad and sweet. Then he'd smile and she knew there wasn't anything sweet about him. Sir Rafe lived for the moment, and he sought only pleasure. Such a man could not be trusted.

However, though Rafe was still attentive to Angelet, he hadn't crossed any line since the night she kissed him. Indeed, his flirtatious behavior vanished almost completely. He didn't seem like the man she'd kissed that first evening. Had she dreamed the whole thing? Was it some devilish departure from her usual visions, where instead of heavenly sights, she experienced a powerful illusion of a more worldly nature?

One bright morning while the men-at-arms were loading all the supplies and readying the animals, Rafe helped her into her carriage. All he did was offer a hand to steady her as she climbed in, but that contact was enough to make her think of the kiss once again. In fact, every time she looked at Rafe, she thought of the kiss.

But his expression was neutral. "If you don't mind my saying, Lady Angelet, you look a little drawn. How did you sleep?"

The truth was that Bethany tended to snore, and Angelet had a lot on her mind. But neither of those facts was appropriate for casual conversation. "No need to be concerned, Sir Rafe."

"I am concerned. You're my responsibility while we're traveling."

"I will tell you if something serious happens," she said. "But truly, I slept well enough."

"You'd sleep better with me," he said, his voice low and close to her ear.

Her heart hammered and she was having trouble breathing. And why did she like how he smelled? She shouldn't—it was a smell of the road, and oil and leather and iron, and something else. Yet, she wanted to lean right into him and breathe deep.

But then Rafe said, “Lord. Forget I said that. I meant to apologize for what I said that first night. The…offer. It was inappropriate.” He looked truly taken aback.

“I thought the inappropriateness of it was the charm,” she said, not quite hiding her disappointment.

His eyes flicked over her face. She realized that he hadn’t lost interest in her since his offer—she guessed he’d just been worried he offended her.

“I can’t read you, my lady,” he said, still watching her closely.

“I’m not a book. How do you read a woman?”

“Accept my offer and I’ll show you.”

She took a breath. “So the offer is back on the table? Didn’t you just rescind it?”

“Oh, it’s back. On the table or wherever else you’d like.” Then he was gone, off about his tasks as if he hadn’t just tried to scandalize her in broad daylight.

Oddly, she didn’t feel nearly as scandalized as she ought to. She actually felt better, since Rafe shared her memory of the kiss and his subsequent offer. And he still wanted her.

Warmth spread through her limbs. Being wanted by a man like Rafe was novel for her. It made her feel excited rather than scared, eager rather than wary. Foolishness, she told herself. The man was dangerous, and he didn’t even pretend his intentions toward her were honorable. Not once had he breathed the word *marriage,* yet even that worked in his favor. At least he didn’t think her stupid enough to fall for an empty promise. She’d spent the last several years with people who considered her either mad or vacant or a holy idiot. Now she’d finally met someone who treated her as a grown woman. Unfortunately, she met him a fortnight before she had to foreswear contact with virtually *all* men.

Angelet often wondered if Satan meddled in people's happiness directly, or if he sent subordinates to carry out the work. Why else would Angelet be tempted into sin at exactly this moment, after so many years of dull, unchallenged widowhood?

"My lady, are you going to have a fit?"

Bethany peered at her from the other seat in the carriage. The cortège was rolling along the track by now, and the maid had taken her place in the carriage without Angelet even noticing.

"What?" she asked. "No. No, I'm quite well. Why?"

"You were staring at the sky with a look like you were seeing an angel," Bethany explained. "I half think you'll collapse in a minute…though in your fits, you never speak."

"I'm not about to have a fit," Angelet said, more crossly. "Anyway, I suffered one less than a week ago."

"So?" Bethany retorted. "Good thing that abbot is willing to take you."

"The abbot might know of a cure," Angelet said.

Bethany's expression was not one of great confidence for any mortal to cure Angelet, but she just sighed meaningfully and went to work at mending something. There was always mending to be done. This item looked like a shirt from one of the men-at-arms. Angelet took out her own needle and thread from the bag she packed. It would be a long, long day.

That night, the group once again reached an inn. This one was more run down, and the sleeping rooms were little more than partitioned spaces, with thin walls and doors that closed only most of the way. Angelet and Bethany got the one at the end, with a little window for light. As usual, the chained and locked chest was carried to Angelet's room, this time by Rafe and Dobson. They placed it near her bed.

"I'll take first watch at the door tonight," Dobson told Rafe. "I'm not sleepy. Tad can take first watch as well."

Rafe nodded. "That will do. Wake Laurence and Simon when it's time."

"Aye, sir."

The whole party ate the evening meal in the tavern room below. The food was better than the accommodations, and Angelet was soon yawning. She rose to her feet and gestured to Bethany. The maid dutifully followed her, after draining her glass of ale.

There were no bed frames, just narrow straw mattresses. Luckily, Angelet was so tired she doubted even a pokey straw mattress or Bethany's snores would keep her awake tonight.

Indeed, she dropped right into sleep, though it was a dream-filled sleep in which a tiny part of her remained alert, listening to the sounds of the inn and the outdoors, weaving every noise into fractured, fantastic dreams. Angelet heard the stomping of footsteps on the stairs, and dreamed she was in a high tower like those of her visions. She heard an owl cry, and saw a gigantic, dusky owl alight on the foot of her bed. Bethany's snores became the heavy breath of a sleeping dragon, which the owl would hoot at impatiently.

Lost in her dream, Angelet was certain that the owl knew something of vital importance regarding her family, and she kept asking it over and over to give her news of her parents, or her brother, or her son. But the owl merely asked, "Who?" and the cycle began anew.

Then Angelet woke up. There had been a sound—a real one.

"Who's there?" she asked as she sat up. "Bethany?"

But Bethany was still sleeping on her pallet. A different, larger shape loomed near her bed.

"Who—" was all Angelet managed to get out before a massive hand clamped down on her mouth. She gasped for breath. Whoever was trying to silence her was doing too well. She couldn't get any air.

Panic blossomed, and she jerked away from the figure, desperate to free herself. She bit at the hand.

"Bitch!" Her assailant pulled his hand back.

Angelet dragged in a huge breath and screamed.

Another scream echoed hers and she heard the stomp of footsteps.

But then the hand was back, pushing her head down against the pillow. Angelet struggled, this time with no success. She bit again, and nothing happened. She tried to breathe, and couldn't. Sparks and flashes of light began to pop at the edges of her vision. Air. She needed air.

Just as she began to black out, the pressure vanished. The man attacking her wheeled backwards. She could just see another man grab him from behind.

At that point, light flared. Bethany stood in the doorway with a lit candle.

Gasping for air, Angelet sat up and slipped off the pallet to get away from the two men locked in a savage fight in the middle of the room. One was fully dressed and armed with a long dagger.

"Dobson?" Angelet gasped out loud. He'd been guarding her room, and he was one of the Dryton men-at-arms who'd served Otto for years. Angelet never would have suspected he'd go against his lord like this. Trying to kill her, and then to kill…

"No!" she choked out when she saw him raise his arm to stab his opponent, who was none other than Rafe.

Rafe must have run in immediately after hearing her scream, for he was only partially dressed, and unarmed. Dobson was going to kill him.

But just as Dobson's arm began to arc down, the blade flashing silver, Rafe moved with stunning speed. He somehow stepped to the side, ducked out of the weapon's path, and then struck Dobson with a sharp blow.

The guard grunted, but didn't lose his grip on the dagger.

Rafe didn't look as if he was worried in the slightest about Dobson's bigger size and heft. "Drop it," he advised. "I don't want to kill you. I've got questions."

"You? Kill me?" Dobson growled. Then he attacked, wielding the dagger like a madman.

Angelet was sure Dobson would soon win the fight. But Rafe was trained to a degree Dobson was not, and nearly every blow Rafe struck landed, while Dobson's often went wide, as Rafe's superior reflexes allowed him to dance out of the way.

The two continued to struggle, until Rafe knocked the dagger out of Dobson's grasp. It seemed like time had stopped, though less than a minute had passed.

Dobson gave a roar and lunged for the dagger. Rafe got there first. At the last second, Rafe snatched up the dagger and plunged it directly into Dobson's chest.

Dobson's eyes widened, but he made no sound. Rafe's aim had been true, and the dagger blade pierced the heart. The off-white fabric of the man's shirt turned into a vivid red, and a second later, Dobson's body sank to the floor, his now sightless eyes staring upward.

Angelet had seen death in her life, but never this violently, or this close. And yet, her first feeling was relief. *It's over*, she thought.

Rafe swiped the blood from the dagger with the edge of Dobson's shirt. Then he stood up and glanced at the various shocked people in the room.

"Tad was on watch with Dobson," he said, very calmly. "Someone find him and get him in here. Now."

Laurence hurried out. Rafe turned to Angelet. Bethany had reached her and flung a blanket around Angelet's shaking shoulders. It wasn't just for warmth, but for modesty as well, since Angelet wore only her thin shift.

"Should someone fetch your shirt, sir?" the maid asked as she shot a look directly at Rafe's bare upper body.

Angelet looked too. She couldn't have avoided it, not when he was right there in front of her, still breathing fast from the short but vicious fight. Angelet knew she shouldn't be staring at his perfectly conditioned torso, or his arms, or shoulders…every muscle starkly contoured by the light of the few candles in the room.

"Bethany," she whispered. "Please do that. Fetch his clothes. Immediately."

The maid left and returned with Rafe's shirt, which he pulled on. Not that it mattered now. The image of him was seared into Angelet's mind.

"What happened?" Rafe scarcely raised his voice, as if this was an ordinary conversation and there wasn't a dead body at his feet. "Angelet? I need to know."

"I…I'm not sure. I wasn't sleeping well, and I heard a noise, and I woke up to find someone here in the room. I asked who was there, and he rushed toward me. I didn't even see who it was, but he capped his hand over my mouth. To keep me quiet, I thought. But his hand was over my nose, too, and I could barely breathe."

"Then what?"

"I bit the hand. Then I screamed. That woke Bethany. She screamed and ran from the room."

"To get help," Bethany added. "I pounded on the door next to ours."

"That's true," Simon confirmed. "The screams woke us, but the pounding on the door got us all up. But by the time we reached this room, you had already got here, sir."

Rafe nodded, then turned back to Angelet.

"So, from when Bethany left to get help, what happened?"

She shuddered, thinking of it. "Dobson had his hand on my mouth again, and I knew it wasn't to keep me quiet. He meant to suffocate me. I just kept trying to get free of him, and trying to breathe. Then you were there, and you pulled him away. You know the rest."

Rafe looked down at the body in disdain. At a word, Simon and Marcus hauled the body out of the room. Immediately after that Laurence came back with a rather disheveled-looking Tad at his heels.

"Found him sleeping, Sir Rafe," Laurence reported. "Seems even the commotion didn't wake him."

"Sleeping. When you were supposed to be on watch." Rafe's gaze was cold. "Tad, explain what the hell happened. Where were you?"

Tad shuffled his feet and said, "I had rather more ale than usual, Sir Rafe. About an hour into the watch, Dobson told me I was nodding off…he said I should just go early to bed, and he'd rouse the second watch himself."

"Leaving him alone and unobserved to sneak into the

room and try to steal the gold from the chest. God damn."

"I swear I didn't know what he was up to! I'd never have gone along with it!" Tad looked utterly ashamed, and every time his gaze fell on Angelet, he dropped his eyes to the floor. "What's to be done with me, Sir Rafe?"

Rafe glared at him. "I'll think on it. Meanwhile, get back to bed and stay out of trouble."

"Yes, sir!" Tad was out of the room faster than Angelet had ever seen him move.

Rafe pointed toward the empty basin. "Bethany, please go draw some fresh water from outside. Now."

The maid hurried out of the room once more. Rafe ordered the men still there to take the body out, then turned to Angelet. His expression was far more concerned than before. "Are you all right?" he asked in a low voice. "Truly?"

"Yes. He didn't manage to harm me."

"What about your condition? Did what just happened...will it trigger anything?"

"I don't think so. But it's possible. I'll tell Bethany to watch me carefully."

Rafe sighed. "Jesu. You seem to be in danger both from within *and* without."

"The seizures are rare."

"But could happen anytime," he said. "And even if you do not suffer from that, we cannot forget that one person has tried to kill you to get at the gold. There could be another."

She shivered. "You're probably correct."

"I need to think of some way to lessen the risk."

"How?"

"I've no idea," he admitted. "Give me the night, and with luck some saint will slip the answer in my brain by morning."

"I'll pray for your success."

He gave her a tiny smile. "However you wish to use your lips on my behalf, I won't complain."

"Rafe!" she scolded. The blood still surging through her veins after the terror she'd been through now heated up at his innuendo. Terror and excitement felt very, very similar, she realized.

His eyes widened in mock innocence. "What? Did you think I meant something besides prayer?"

Her cheeks burned. "I know what you meant. You're —"

"Incorrigible. Yes, I know. It's part of my charm."

"How can you joke after…"

"Killing a man?" Rafe shrugged. "He was a killer himself. Should I weep over him?"

"I don't know," she whispered.

Rafe's expression cooled. "It was his life or mine. The whole point of being my own master is that I decide my fate."

She tried to reach out, to tell him she didn't blame him for what happened. "I didn't mean—"

But he shook her hand off his arm. "Get some rest, my lady. We still have a long way to travel." Then he left.

* * * *

Angelet didn't think she'd sleep again after what happened. Even Bethany, in a hushed voice, asked to shove her pallet next to Angelet's so the women might sleep next to each other. Angelet agreed instantly, feeling there was some sort of safety in that. She woke in the morning to find that she had slept after all, and this time, blessedly, she remembered no dreams.

In the tavern room below, the mood among the men-at-arms was grim. From the fragments of conversations Angelet overheard, everyone was perturbed by Dobson's attack on her life. Even the few who muttered that a man might break his oath and steal so much gold were still aghast that one man went beyond theft to attempted murder.

"But not Dobson," one of the men muttered to his companion. "He served Otto since they were boys!"

Rafe finished his breakfast quickly and stood up. He gestured to Simon and Angelet. "Come along, please," he said.

Curious, Angelet followed as Rafe walked to her personal carriage, where the chest had just been loaded. Laurence was there, guarding it.

"Simon," Rafe said curtly. "We're going to move the chest from Lady Angelet's carriage to the supply wagon. Laurence, keep an eye on the inn. I don't want everyone to see what we're doing. My lady, keep an eye on us the whole time to reassure yourself we're not tampering with anything."

She nodded, relieved that the chest would be further away from her on the journey.

It didn't take long for the two men to wrestle the chest out of her carriage and onto the ground. They grunted as they hefted it up and walked it back to the supply wagon. Angelet went ahead to clear a space for it.

"Move the hay aside," Rafe grunted.

She clambered up and pushed at the loose hay meant for emergency animal feed. The men lifted the heavy chest up and slid it over, nearly pinning Angelet to the wall of the wagon in the process. She yelped in surprise when the corner of the chest hit her right ankle. "Ouch!"

"Apologies, my lady!" Simon said.

"No matter." Without being told, Angelet started to replace the hay over the chest, helping to conceal it from casual view. When she was done, she was on her knees, with straw all over her skirts, but she felt much better.

"Well done, my lady," Rafe said, from behind her. "Come, I'll help you out of there."

She edged backwards and then felt his hands on her waist as he helped lift her out and set her on the ground. She sensed the strength in his arms, and momentarily forgot what she was going to say when her gaze caught his eyes.

He looked her over from top to toe, then said, "You're missing a shoe, my lady."

"What?" That wasn't what she expected to hear. She looked down. Her right slipper was gone. "Oh. I must have lost it when the chest hit my foot."

"Do you want me to retrieve it for you?" he asked.

It was probably buried under hay. "No, thank you. I have another pair that will serve."

"Very well. Then let me walk you back to your carriage. You can set it to rights before the others get called from inside."

He helped her into her carriage, once again distracting her with his nearness and the simple touch of his hand in hers. She didn't ever remember being so aware of a man, and definitely never in a way that created such a buzzing in her body.

She worked to restore the carriage to its proper order, covering the place where the chest had been with a few more boxes and cushions. "There. No one should see any change. Except Bethany. She'll notice soon enough, since she's traveling with me."

Rafe said, his expression intent, "Shall I tell her she's to go elsewhere?"

"That negates her purpose," Angelet replied.

"No one will be able to threaten your honor while the carriage is in motion, guarded by soldiers," Rafe pointed out. "I'll instruct the girl to find a spot elsewhere while we are actually traveling. Then you can enjoy some solitude."

He returned to the inn, presumably to do exactly that.

When Bethany came out a moment later she frowned, looking Angelet over with a critical eye. Angelet was painfully aware that her gown was scattered with bits of straw snared in the wool, and she was still missing a shoe. She looked very much as if she'd been, well, rolling in the hay.

"Sir Rafe informed me that you would not need companionship today."

Angelet felt embarrassment and rage flare up inside, but she kept her face blank. "Correct."

"You can't just tell me where I'm to sit or walk!"

Suddenly Rafe stood near them. He said, "Lady Angelet made her wishes clear. Now, Bethany, you may walk, or ride on the back of one of the carts, or ride if there's a spare beast for it. Don't bother the lady until she calls for your service."

Bethany gaped at Sir Rafe, who towered over her, his expression cool. His hand rested lightly on the pommel of his sword.

It dawned on her that there was no hope for negotiation with the black-clad knight, and she had no standing to argue. She whirled around and stalked off.

Rafe gave Angelet a little wink. "Satisfactory?"

"Quite. Thank you."

"Just following orders, my lady. I'll do anything you ask of me." His tone was light and teasing, but heat shot through Angelet.

There was no way he'd chosen those words by chance. He was reminding her of his scandalous offer. If only the idea of him following her every order didn't sound so interesting.

Rafe still stood there, apparently waiting for something. Oh, yes. He'd asked a question while she was daydreaming.

"Repeat that?" she asked.

"Did you need anything else before we depart? We'll ride until dark, or until we find a suitable place to stay the night."

"Oh. No, thank you. I don't want…anything…" she trailed off. She wanted so many things, and she'd get none of them. "Wait! There is one thing."

"Yes?"

"I forgot to tell you last night."

He raised his eyebrows. "You remembered something?"

"No. I just meant I should have told you…thank you. For saving my life."

He looked surprised for a moment, then gave her a half-smile. "Live to serve."

She retreated into the carriage, sinking into the cushioned seat. She reached out only to pull the curtains closed. She needed to be alone and unobserved for a little while, so she could recover her normal calm demeanor.

Lord, someone tried to *kill* her last night, and here she was dreaming of Rafe as though nothing had changed. Yet, despite everything she knew about his personality,

Rafe was the one person she felt she could trust.

Chapter 11

ANGELET ENJOYED THE RELATIVE PEACE that riding alone in the carriage offered her, though nothing dulled the monotony of travel, especially as the surroundings grew wilder, with almost no villages or farms along the way.

That evening was the first time they were forced to make a camp. The road had become lonely, with no hint of any village or manor in the vicinity. Laurence had ridden on ahead of the group just to be sure, and brought back the news that the group would have to make its own shelter.

The men all worked to set up the camp, relying on Sir Rafe's instructions for nearly every element. The single large tent was set up for Angelet and Bethany. There were several more smaller, simple ones for the men, although the sky was clear and fine, and the air quite warm, even with the sun sinking low.

Angelet was contemplating the effect of the setting sun through the young leaves, thinking it looked just like the stained glass windows in a church, when Bethany interrupted her.

"Where is the chest?" Bethany demanded. "I looked in the carriage and it wasn't there!"

Angelet said, "After what Dobson tried to do, Sir Rafe thought it best to move the chest."

"Moved to where?"

"That is hardly your concern." She looked the maid over. "It is quite safe, and there the matter ends."

"I'll tell Lord Otto you disobeyed him!"

"You mean after I've gone to a nunnery, where I'll be subject only to the rules of the Church? Carry your tales to whomever you wish. It matters not to me." Angelet laughed. For years, the greatest threat anyone at Dryton could offer was to alert Otto that something might displease him. Such a threat was meaningless now.

Bethany realized the same thing. She pursed her lips, then said, "How do you know Sir Rafe isn't going to steal it himself?"

"At this point, I'd give the chest over to anyone who came to take it," Angelet said wearily. "It's brought us nothing but trouble."

The maid nodded. "Who knew Dobson would be so vicious? He's Otto's man, after all, here on the lord's orders. Otto asked him special. Excuse me, my lady. I have to take care of something before it gets dark."

Bethany hurried off. Angelet watched her go with idle interest, since she had nothing better to do. But when she saw Bethany actually leave the camp and walk purposefully off into the woods in the direction of a large hill to the north, she wondered just what the maid was up to. Surely she didn't want to climb a steep slope simply for a call of nature.

Without telling anyone else, Angelet began to follow the maid. The underbrush was more or less completely leafed out now, obscuring much of the ground, and Angelet had to move quickly to keep on Bethany's trail.

She clambered over a few rocks and tried to keep pace, although the path was fast turning from dirt to rock and making her progress more difficult as she slowly got closer to the hill's summit.

She paused from time to time, listening for the crash of Bethany's steps up ahead. She was fairly certain she was still on the right path—she hadn't seen any other trails diverge from this one.

The trail flattened out for a short stretch, along a natural clearing, and she got an unimpeded view of the rapidly darkening eastern sky. The valley below was already in shadow. In a few minutes, the woods she just passed through would be much harder to navigate. Perhaps she ought to return…

"But where did Bethany go?" she muttered, looking ahead once more.

All of a sudden, she felt someone grab her hand from behind. She whirled, about to scream, when she saw it was Rafe. A very annoyed Rafe.

"Where the hell do you think you're going?" Rafe demanded. "After what happened, you should know better than to be alone. Ever."

"There's no one around but us!"

"You don't know that," Rafe said tersely. "Until you're safely to Basingwerke, my lady, we have to assume that you're in danger."

"You think like a soldier," she said.

"I *am* a soldier."

"Well, I'm not and I won't live looking over my

shoulder."

"You don't have to, Angelet. I'm going to watch over your shoulder whether you like it or not. Now tell me what possessed you to wander away from camp just now."

She pointed toward the summit. "I think Bethany is up ahead. I saw her leave the camp and I was suspicious. I followed her, or what sounded like her. And now you've slowed me down…"

"I saw Laurence leave the camp," Rafe said, relaxing. "Heading this way too. Then I saw you go on the same trail and I followed."

"So Laurence may go where he likes, but I can't."

"Precisely." Then his eyes sparkled. "So what you're saying is that you saw Bethany walk away from camp shortly after I saw Laurence…you may want to be less adamant about locating your maid just at the moment."

"You mean they're together….oh." She broke off abruptly. "Well. If that's what they're up to, then I wouldn't really want to interrupt… that is…"

"Why don't we head back to camp, my lady?" Rafe suggested.

"Yes." She looked around, then noticed something. "Wait!"

Rafe instantly had his hand on his sword. "What?"

"Nothing to slay, sir knight. Look!" She pointed toward the eastern horizon, where the first sliver of the moon was emerging over the horizon. "I want to watch the moon rise. Please. We can linger that long, can't we?"

* * * *

Rafe knew he should say no, but the idea of telling her that she wasn't allowed to watch a moonrise just seemed cruel. Who knew how many more moonrises would be available to her?

"All right, then. Only a little while. Wouldn't want anyone to get the wrong idea," he added under his breath.

Angelet didn't even register his comment. Her gaze was locked on the moon, a sort of rapture in her expression that was almost pagan.

And completely beautiful.

Her beauty had nothing to do with her outward appearance, either. The hem of her gown was stained with dirt. Dirt was an inevitable part of travel, but he was a little surprised that Angelet was so tolerant of it, until he remembered that she had never been expected to show herself off at Dryton. For many women of her class, appearance was the only consideration. A woman could spend hours a day making herself ready to be shown off for her lord or some other event. Angelet had been ignored for so long that she didn't follow those practices, despite her arresting natural beauty.

Angelet could have been a very useful tool in Otto's political arsenal. How strange for the man to overlook her…there must be a reason. Angelet's affliction wasn't explanation enough, since it was only occasional and didn't reduce her prettiness by one bit.

He must have been staring at her like an oaf, for she gave him a quizzical look. "What?"

"The moon suits you. That's all." It was true. She was a creature of the moon, with her silver blond hair and fey eyes.

"You're teasing me, but there's no court to impress."

"Angelet, you're the only one I'm interested in impressing at the moment."

She looked a little uncertain. "I am?"

"Don't tell me you forgot about my offer."

By the way she bit her lip, she definitely remembered.

He walked up to her, standing right in front of her. "What have you been thinking about, then?"

She put one hand on his chest, keeping him a few inches away from where he wanted to be. "I'm thinking about the moonrise. You're blocking my view."

He shifted fractionally to the right, still in front of her but letting her look beyond him. "Pardon. I'll try not to do that again. You enjoy your view… and I'll enjoy mine."

"Rafe, is this quite—"

He bent to lay a kiss on her neck, just under her jaw-line, and was rewarded with a little intake of breath.

Rafe pulled away and looked her over with approval. "So you *have* been thinking about my offer."

"That is not true," she breathed out. Yet he could tell by her breathing that something stirred her interest. And he'd bet it wasn't the moon.

"If it's not true, then why are you holding me as if I might get away?"

Angelet glanced down, seemed to realize that she had reached for him, and gasped in dismay. Her hands flew up, fingers splayed wide.

He caught her hands in his, then put them back exactly where they'd been. She took a breath, then said, shyly, "If you wanted to…you could kiss me again."

He wanted to. Rafe wanted to do a lot of things with her, but he only kissed her, because that was what she asked for. He concentrated on her neck, laying little, teasing kisses on her skin. How the hell was it possible for a woman to be so soft?

When he licked her collarbone, Angelet actually moaned. His need sharpened about a hundredfold.

"How's the moonrise?" he asked, forcing a light tone. God, he wanted to see her naked in the moonlight.

"It's very…inspiring."

"Mmm. Are you even looking at it?"

"Yes!" she said. But she spoke just as he ran his tongue along her neck up to her ear, and it certainly sounded like she was saying yes to him.

"What are you doing?" she asked breathlessly.

"You know exactly what I'm doing."

She opened her mouth when he kissed her again, and curled her hands around his neck and slid her tongue along his. Lord, this woman was going to destroy him.

She sighed when he dipped his head and kissed her neck again. He took his time, teasing her with his lips, exploring her body with his hand, going slowly so he didn't alarm her. Widow or not, it was clear that she'd been without a man for a long time. Too long.

He gathered up the fabric of her skirts to expose her legs, and then touched her. "Angelet? Is this what you want?"

She had closed her eyes. "It feels good," she murmured, and she inadvertently let out another little moan.

In response, Rafe tightened his grip, his fingers digging into her flesh a little more as he explored her body by touch. His hands were roughened by years of physical work, fighting, and riding, but she didn't object, and then, thrillingly, even laid her own hand to guide him upward along her thigh.

"What do you want, Angelet?" he murmured, ready to perform any feat she requested. "Tell me what to do."

She left out a breath, and he felt it across his skin. He wanted to feel her breath on so much more of his skin, unhampered by clothing. He wanted to know exactly how she'd feel under his hands…

Angelet took a ragged breath. Her eyes were wide in the moonlight, and she looked as if she might be a moon goddess herself.

Then she gasped out, "Let me go."

Damn. He released her instantly and stepped away, his eyes still locked on her. "There you are, free."

"I'm sorry. I'm so sorry. This isn't something I can do. It's not right…"

He stifled the disappointment—and the lust—raging through him. "What did I tell you, Angelet? Whatever you want from me, all you have to do is ask. Even if what you want is nothing."

She turned her face away. "It's not about what I want, Rafe." Angelet straightened her skirts nervously. "I should not have… This was a mistake. We should go back."

"As you wish." He pointed to the trail. "Can you see it in the dark? You can go ahead. I'll be right after you." That way he could keep an eye out for danger over her head while ensuring that no one could grab her from behind.

She nodded, then repeated, "I'm sorry."

He shook his head. *She* was sorry? He was the one who was chasing her for the basest of reasons. "Never apologize to me, Angelet. Never."

They returned on the same trail, or what he thought was the same trail. He couldn't get lost anyway. All they had to do was keep following the downward slope toward the smell of a campfire below.

Rafe watched Angelet walk along ahead of him, noting the unsteadiness of her steps. She would be thinking about him all night, which was fair, since his thoughts were increasingly dominated by her. God, he wanted her.

Every time he looked at her or got close to her, his need increased. Something about her tantalized him, and he couldn't name what it was. All he knew was that if he didn't get to touch her again, and soon, he'd lose his mind.

She was obviously interested in his offer, yet she still put an end to their encounter. Not surprising, he told himself. Angelet wasn't the sort of woman to give herself to a virtual stranger out in the woods in the middle of nowhere. She had too much dignity for something like that. And then there was that lock of hair she carried with her, a sign that she still clung to some memory too strong to put aside for a short diversion like Rafe.

At the very edge of the camp, he told her to walk ahead and go directly to her tent. "Don't tarry, don't speak to anyone, and if anyone asks where you were, tell them not to worry, and you didn't have a fit."

He waited a few moments, then moved around in an arc so he would appear to be approaching the camp from the east rather than the north.

A few men saw him come into the circle of firelight.

"Where were you?" Simon asked, looking up from the food he'd been eating.

"Scouting around," Rafe lied easily. "Just making sure no one else was about."

"Did you see anything?"

Rafe shook his head.

Laurence, who just happened to be sitting on a log next to Bethany, now chimed in. "I never like the forest. I feel like I'm being watched."

"Watched?" Rafe asked, remembering his sense of being watched along the road, the feeling that kept recurring even though he never saw any hard proof to confirm it. "Have you seen someone?"

"No," Laurence said. "It's just a feeling in my gut."

"Collywobbles," Tad said knowingly. "The fairy folk do it to keep Christians away from their homes."

A few of the others made noises of agreement. Rafe chuckled and sat down to eat, while the others lay back, joked, and generally relaxed. Bethany excused herself to attend to Angelet, and Rafe took a long breath, realizing how tense he was, for all sorts of reasons.

The incident with Dobson disturbed him far more than he let on. Rafe felt personally responsible for failing to see what the man had planned, though in all honesty, he couldn't have known. Dobson cleverly waited, using the first few days to let the group settle into a routine, a routine he then exploited. Rafe hadn't thought Dobson was that smart, actually. He shifted, willing himself to forget about the vicious fight that resulted in Dobson's death. He needed to relax.

Perhaps a need to relax was driving some of the men's jollity that night.

Simon set up a makeshift target range, and in the flickering light of the fire, he and the other men took turns flinging knives into the soft trunks of the pine trees. Bets were placed, naturally, and the men shouted and joked and laughed as wagers were won or lost.

Rafe took note as Simon won more bets. The young man had a talent—his aim was steady and he struck the center of his target nearly every time.

"I think Simon ought to stand ten paces back from the others," Rafe called out from his comfortable spot by the fire. "Let's make this fair."

Simon grinned. "I could do that. Or someone could fetch me more wine!" He nodded toward the empty wineskin on the ground.

"I'll find another," Rafe said. "Least I can do."

He walked to the supply wagon, where a few spare wineskins were stored along with some food.

There he found Bethany, who was rooting among the boxes.

"Grab a wineskin, will you?" he asked. If she was already inside, no need for him to clamber up.

But she jumped in surprise and looked back at him with an expression that could only be described as guilty.

"Did…did you say wine, sir?" she asked, her voice higher than usual.

"Yes, wine," he repeated. "What are you doing? What are you looking for?"

"Oh, my lady wanted something after her supper. Dried fruit or nuts. I couldn't find them in the dark…" She made a sound of discovery. "Here, sir. A wineskin."

"And the nuts?"

"I just found them. Or dried apples, anyway. Here's the sack."

"Give them to me. I'll take them to the lady. It's on my way." It wasn't, but Rafe seized on any excuse to speak to Angelet.

Rafe ducked his head in through the low door. She was sitting on her bed roll, reading a little breviary by the light of a stubby candle. "My lady?"

She looked up from the book, giving Rafe a slightly nervous smile. "Yes?"

"Bethany said you asked for something to eat."

She took the bag of fruit he offered, though with a puzzled expression. "Did she? I haven't spoken to Bethany since she brought me my supper."

Rafe frowned. So the maid had been lying about why

she was in the supply wagon, claiming an errand for her mistress when she was actually searching on her own. Well, even if she could get to the chest, it was still chained and locked. Any attempt to open it would be heard by the others.

"A mistake," he said, so as not to alarm her. "I must have misunderstood."

"I doubt that," Angelet said. "You always know what's going on."

"That is not true. I wish it were."

She took a piece of dried apple, bit it thoughtfully, then asked, "What are you worried about? Dobson? That it happened?"

"Yes. I expected something, but not that. Not an attack from the inside."

She nodded slowly. "He's the last person I'd have thought would double-cross Otto like that. But then, he probably never saw that much wealth before. Do you think that's it?"

Rafe knew all too well what could happen when a man saw the opportunity to get rich like that. "It must be."

"I'm glad he's dead. Is that shameful?"

"No," he said firmly. "The man would have killed you. You don't owe him anything."

"We're supposed to forgive those who have hurt us."

"Easier said than done, my lady. Get some rest if you can. I expect sleeping outside is a novelty for you."

"It is. But I'll sleep better knowing you're around."

Rafe walked back to the group of knife-throwing men, whose laughter and shouting could probably be heard a mile away. He smiled to himself as he walked, thinking that it was actually fun to be with these people…most of them, anyway. He'd spent too long on his own. Rafe wasn't a loner by nature.

A flicker of movement broke his reverie. There was something off to the side of the clearing. Rafe slowed his pace, then stopped.

He laid the wineskin on the ground and put his hand to the hilt of his sword, prepared to draw at any moment.

His eyes searched the scene in front of him, a tangle of underbrush and thicker tree trunks. The light from the campfire made all the shadows jump about and dance madly. It was impossible to tell solid things from shadows. Still, Rafe didn't take his eyes from the forest. He had relied on his instinct for years, and his instinct now told him something was wrong.

He breathed slowly, in and out, waiting for whatever it was to betray itself. The shadows continued to twist and flicker. Just when Rafe decided he must have been mistaken, he caught something again. A shadow moving the wrong way, against all the others.

Was it an animal perhaps? A deer or feral creature? But what animal waited patiently behind the cover of trees instead of bolting into the deeper woods?

"I see you," Rafe announced, pulling the sword a few inches out from its scabbard. "You can't hide in there forever. Come out."

He wasn't particularly worried about sounding foolish if the interloper was just, say, a rabbit. If it was a rabbit, it wasn't going to understand him anyway. A person, however, would hear him and have cause to doubt how well they were concealed.

The cheerful shouts of the men grew louder all of a sudden, and the moment was broken. There was a rustle in the woods, and then the feeling of being observed left him. He scooped up the wineskin and returned to the group.

He tucked away the issue of his tracker to deal with later. He said nothing of what he saw, or thought he saw. True, he could have explained, and then ordered the others to fan out and flush out the culprit. But to what end? If it was someone after Rafe, he'd have to explain the part of his life he'd rather bury. And perhaps it was only an animal after all.

But when the time came to retire, he ordered two men on each shortened watch. "And keep in sight of each other," he told them. "Take no chances."

"Is something wrong, Sir Rafe?" Simon asked.

"Just being careful. That's what we're being paid to do."

Chapter 12

FOLLOWING A HASTY, COLD BREAKFAST, the men all struck the camp, again following Rafe's instructions for how to do so.

"Next time," he said, "you'll only get half as much time to do it. In an army, you'd all fail."

"Everyone starts somewhere," Simon retorted cheerfully. "At least we're getting experience. Though I hope we don't have to camp again soon. I think I slept on a rock."

"Trust me, that's not the worst thing that will happen to you," Rafe said.

As he spoke, he caught sight of Angelet a little ways away. She gave him a subtle smile, and he had to stop himself from grinning like an idiot. Lord, that woman grew more alluring every time he saw her.

"Nun," he reminded himself.

He directed the packing up of the cortège, finally understanding how a sergeant felt. The other men were learning, and by the end of the journey, they would be considerably more seasoned at this sort of thing.

They continued north along the road, the men still in a good mood. They laughed and exchanged jokes about the betting of the previous night. Laurence was down several coins, and demanded a rematch at the next opportunity.

Rafe listened to the banter, but didn't join in. The sensation of being watched was still with him, an almost palpable creep along his spine. He looked behind him, seeing nothing unusual.

An hour passed with no hint of danger greater than a fox dashing across the road. Rafe rode up to Angelet's carriage. "Need a break, my lady?" he asked. "It's about time."

"That would be appreciated," she replied, with a look toward Bethany, who agreed heartily.

Rafe signaled the men that the cortège would stop briefly. "Stretch out. But stay close. We'll be moving soon!"

After it slowed to a halt, he opened the door of Angelet's carriage. He helped Bethany step down, then offered a hand to Angelet.

At that moment, Simon gave a shout of warning. Rafe looked to see a number of men rushing toward them from the direction they'd come.

"Damn it," he swore. There was nothing friendly in the mood of the approaching group. Fifteen men? Twenty? This was going to be bad.

"What is it?" Angelet asked.

"Get back. And stay down!" Rafe pushed Angelet back into the carriage, and wheeled about. Hell, he knew something wasn't right all day, yet he disregarded all the warnings.

The approaching group split into two, some mounted, some on foot. One second later, all turned to chaos. Simon and Marcus rushed toward the largest group of attackers with swords drawn. Angelet had, thank God, withdrawn into the interior of her carriage. The maid Bethany, however, was still outside of it, shrieking and pointing seemingly at random.

"Bethany!" he shouted.

She paid no heed.

Rafe rushed up and grabbed her by the shoulder. She squealed in surprise and whipped a knife upward.

He blocked it by instinct, striking her arm. The knife fell to the ground.

"Oh, God!" Her eyes widened. "I thought you were one of…never mind."

"Pick up the knife. Get into the carriage with Lady Angelet. It will be safer. Go."

He turned away, hoping she'd follow his instructions.

Rafe couldn't spare the women another glance for the moment, because a big man with a missing eye was charging directly at him, wielding a short, wide sword. The man used it like a scythe, making huge swings to clear his path. Anyone who could rush away did.

By contrast, Rafe stood his ground, despite the natural fear that always flooded through him before a battle. He'd been in this position many times, probably more than any other man in the fray. He flexed his sword arm, taking a deep breath.

When Rafe fought, he felt a sense of calm come over him, despite the madness and the desperation in so much of what happened. He was himself when he was on a battlefield. He understood exactly what was required of him, and he knew just how to move. He knew what to look for when it came to exploiting his opponents' weaknesses. He spun, struck, and parried almost on instinct, relying on his reflexes and his intense training to protect him.

This fight was no different.

Rafe stepped forward to engage the man just at the right moment to put the other off his timing. Rafe blocked several wild swings with small, precise shifts of his position. No need to waste energy. He kept his gaze locked on his opponent, already seeing patterns, guessing the man's next moves.

His opportunity came a second later. His opponent hacked with his blade and overbalanced. Rafe grabbed the other's arm, and swung his own sword upward in a deadly, controlled movement.

The tip of the sword hit just above the man's breastplate, sinking into the exposed flesh. Rafe was in no mood to be merciful, so he twisted the blade, hard.

The man's eyes widened and he gurgled something as his body jerked violently on the end of the sword. Rafe pulled his sword free, and the man crumpled to the ground.

Rafe whirled around, looking for the next fight.

The next fight was easy to find, since the whole scene was now swarming with assailants. Rafe jumped at the nearest one, dispatching him after only a few moments. It was not a fair fight. Rafe was just too skilled at hand-to-hand combat.

Rafe knocked the man's dagger out of his hand, then kicked it away. "If you want to live, lie flat on your belly." What Rafe desperately needed was information.

Instead of obeying, the man sprang like a cat toward Rafe, as if he intended to take him down. But Rafe was ready and slashed the man's chest with his sword, going for a killing stroke.

The man fell in mid leap, crumpling into a pile of

loose limbs and dirty clothing. Rafe leaned down to yank the man's shoulder, turning him over slightly.

A blank-faced stare greeted him, with no hint of who or what this man was. A quick perusal of the corpse showed that he was dressed much like any common man in the area—sturdy but heavily patched hose, and a tunic in a faded green color, along with a newer capuchin with a darker green dye. The dagger was plain but well cared-for, the edge viciously sharp. Rafe leaned over to pick it up.

He glanced up again, taking in the skirmish. Simon and Laurence were fighting back to back as they confronted a group of assailants. They appeared to be doing well, in the sense that they were still alive, but Rafe didn't wait any longer.

He charged toward the group, smashing into the ring of attackers and breaking their formation with a few well-chosen swings of his sword. One man clutched his bleeding arm, falling to his knees. Another fell dead.

"Everyone halt!" a new voice yelled. "Or I'll spill this one's blood all over the road."

Rafe looked to the sound. A huge man held Bethany up. The petite woman was actually dangling in the air.

She whimpered, but was otherwise still.

"There's treasure in one of these carts," the big man went on. "And I want it. Show me where it is, or I'll slit her throat."

No one spoke for a moment. The attackers were waiting to hear where the chest was. The defenders were all staring at Rafe, waiting for him to make the fateful decision of whether to save Bethany's life and give up the gold, or refuse the offer.

Why was this his choice? Rafe groaned inwardly. This

was exactly why he avoided command. Fighting was one thing, but giving orders always led to a situation like this, where lives lay in his extremely fallible hands.

Rafe had a duty to protect both the money and Angelet. But allowing Bethany to die would be unconscionable.

He took a breath, prepared to order his men to stand down.

Then a clear voice broke the silence. "Let her go. I'll show you where the chest is."

Angelet stepped from the carriage, astonishing in her gown and the moonstone necklace and her silvery-blonde hair falling loose around her shoulders. How had she managed it? In that moment, she could have claimed fey ancestry and Rafe would have believed it.

The big man seemed to forget everything when he saw her, and unceremoniously dropped Bethany to the ground, where she lay groaning in pain.

"You're the lady," the big man said, as if he'd never seen a lady before.

"I'm Angelet d'Hiver, and I will give you the chest. But you must not harm anyone else."

The big man glanced around the clearing, obviously judging his odds. Then he nodded. "Where's the chest?"

Angelet pointed to the food wagon. "That cart. It's hidden under the straw at the front. You'll need two or three men to carry it."

The big man grinned and ordered a few of his underlings to uncover the chest. He stayed near Angelet, his axe at the ready.

Rafe narrowed his eyes, sensing exactly what was going on in the other's thoughts. The man wasn't going to let Angelet go free. He would use her as a hostage as soon as he had the chest. Rafe started to shift his position, to be ready to rush over to Angelet. If only she'd stayed hidden!

Meanwhile, two of the attackers had uncovered the chest, and with shouts of triumph, they began to wrestle it out of the cart.

Several of the attackers began to grin, pleased with the imminent payday.

Rafe shook his head. So much for making a fresh start. No one would hire them for another job like this. Apparently, Simon had come to the same conclusion, watching in chagrin as the chest was hauled up to be taken away.

"Oh, no you don't," Simon muttered. Without warning, the younger man whipped a small dagger through the air at one of the men carrying the chest. Simon's aim was true, and the blade sank into the man's hamstring.

He howled with pain, and his whole body jerked. He didn't just lose his grip on the chest. He flung his arm upward, driven by a sudden rush of energy in reaction to the pain. The chest half flew out of his hands.

The other handler lost control as the weight all shifted to him. He cried out, jumping away before the heavy chest could fall and crush his feet.

A fraction of a second later, the chest was loose, spinning oddly. It hovered in the air for a breathless moment.

Everyone watched, mesmerized.

Then the chest fell, hit the rocky ground, and cracked open with a sound of splintering wood. Time seemed to slow as they all waited for the inevitable scattering of gold and silver on the earth. Then it would be chaos as all the men looked out for themselves and scrambled to take what they could.

The chest rotated once more, one corner hitting the ground. The lid separated from the chest, and the contents spilled out. Rafe heard the shout of one of the soldiers.

But there was no glint of metal. Only strange dull pebbles flew through the air. Then Rafe gasped, realizing that was exactly what they were. Ordinary pebbles, stones scooped up from the dirt.

They had been guarding worthless rocks. There wasn't an ounce of gold in the chest.

Chapter 13

ANGELET STARED AT THE MESS on the ground, utterly confounded.

Then everyone around her started to mutter.

"What in hell," someone said.

"This is wrong," came another voice, stunned by what he saw…or rather didn't see. "Where is it? Where's the gold gone?"

"Men! Get ready." Rafe's voice came clear to her ears. She saw him about thirty or forty feet away. He tightened his grip on his sword, ready for what was to come.

The big man near her suddenly let out a roar, his voice ringing out over the whole company. "Where the *fuck* is our gold?"

Someone else growled, "This was a set-up! A trick."

Angelet felt the mood shift. The attackers had been fierce but confident before. They'd had a goal. Now rage ruled them, and they might do anything. And she had foolishly put herself in the middle of them.

Just as the big man lunged for her, she heard someone howl, "Sir Rafe! Look to the lady!"

She dimly recognized Simon's voice as her attacker

grabbed her and dragged her a few feet away from the carriage. His meaty arm curled around her neck, and she clawed at his forearm with both hands, trying to free herself.

She stilled when the big man angled his blade into her neck.

Then Rafe was there, his sword out and ready to strike a killing blow.

"Hurt her, and you'll lose the ransom she's worth." Rafe faced the man. "You've already lost the money." He took two steps toward the attacker.

"We don't want her for ransom," he hissed. Then he yelled as Angelet raised one hand to his face, raking her nails across his skin. The move was desperate, but it worked. The man loosened his chokehold just long enough for her to drop to the ground and scramble a few feet away, against the carriage.

The man made a grab to retrieve her, but Rafe was already moving. He rushed the man, and just as the other swung back, his blade raised, Rafe shifted his attack slightly, compensating for his opponent's moves.

Rafe straightened his sword arm, aiming for the heart.

"Angelet, stay back," he yelled.

Angelet did, but she gasped when something thunked right by her head. She looked to the carriage wall behind her, where a crossbow bolt was now jutting out only inches away from her head.

Rafe reached out, grabbed Angelet by the hand, and pulled her next to him, using his body to block her from the general direction the bolt must have been fired.

"We have to go," he ordered.

Angelet nodded, but lunged to the open carriage, where she grabbed the sack lying on the seat. "We can go!"

She glanced around, but saw no one holding such a weapon as a crossbow. Not that it meant anything. The thick underbrush and densely wooded area could hide any number of bowmen.

Rafe started to move toward where his horse Philon stood, unperturbed by all the noise and shouting, just as a well-adapted war horse should. He muttered to Angelet, "We're walking to Philon. Quick!"

She matched his pace and a moment later they reached the massive creature. "Stay here. Right here. Keep your head low."

"Where are you going?"

"Just wait here!"

Rafe moved away, and Angelet waited for an agonizing time.

She watched the ongoing fight through slitted eyes. How were there so many attackers? What would happen?

Then Rafe reappeared, holding the lead to a white horse. "Let's go," he ordered, as he mounted Philon.

"We can't leave! Look!" She'd just seen Simon get struck by a black-clad man. Simon howled in pain and slid to his knees, still parrying the other's blows. "Rafe, you must help him!"

Rafe looked about to object, but then Simon himself saw them.

"Go, Rafe!" Simon shouted from where he was locked in a grim battle with his attacker. "Get her out of here! Just go!"

Rafe leaned over and scooped Angelet up in one arm. He swung her up into the saddle in front of him, then rode hard back the way the cortège had come. The white horse galloped behind, the lead still gripped in Rafe's hand.

"Where are we going?" Angelet gasped, clinging to him. She was shaking with fear, and the heat of his body made sweat break out on her skin.

"Away," he said, sounding out of breath.

"But Simon and the others. We have to help…"

"We have to get you to safety," he said. "That's what matters. Simon knew that…knows that. The others will defend themselves. But the thieves weren't just after the gold. They were after *you*."

He glanced behind, searching for signs of pursuit. Angelet did too, and thought she could see a horse and rider in the distance. Rafe urged Philon to go faster. The riderless white horse kept pace.

When the road presented a fork leading west, he took it. The smaller trail suggested a local path, perhaps to a nearby village. If they were lucky, the pursuers would continue along the main road, assuming Rafe would retreat to the last large town, or just be too rushed to look for alternate routes.

The road branched again several moments later, and Rafe once again took the westward-leading fork. Only when a huge felled tree blocked the path in front of them did he slow the blistering pace.

Both horses came to a halt yards before the tree trunk. Angelet glanced behind them again, relieved to see nothing that hinted of pursuit.

Rafe stilled the horses and listened.

Angelet remained quiet, so quiet she could feel the thudding of her heart in her chest. The sounds of the forest around them were ordinary, and even though she strained her ears, she couldn't identify any hoofbeats.

"I think we can rest for a moment," Rafe said at last. He circled his horse around to stand parallel to the massive trunk. "Angelet. Hold my hand, and you can slide down. There you go."

A moment later, she stood on the trunk, well above the ground itself.

Rafe dismounted and took both horses by their leads.

Angelet, still on the tree, pointed to the left. "There's a little opening that way to get around the trunk. The path is clear on the other side."

"Keep watch," Rafe said.

Angelet dutifully stood looking at the way they'd come. The landscape remained silent and empty.

Once Rafe and the horses cleared the trunk, she slid down to the ground on her own.

"We should go back," she declared, knowing it was a lost cause.

Rafe shook his head once. He looked tired, dirty, and sweaty. "No. They're either waiting there, or on the path between here and there. There were still twelve or fifteen of them when we rode away. That's too many. I couldn't fight fifteen men on my own."

"Especially since a few of them had crossbows." She shuddered. "One shot at me!"

Rafe frowned. "I saw that. Are you sure? I mean, are you sure you just weren't in the line of someone else?"

"No. Remember, I was by the door of my carriage, trying to keep well out of the way," Angelet reminded him. "The bolt hit the side of the carriage wall about a half a foot away from my head. I was the target. Not you or that big man. I got splinters from the impact."

His frowned deepened. "Why would they be so reckless? You're worth nothing to them dead."

Rafe took her by the hand and led her to the white horse. "Come, mount up. We need to keep moving. You can ride bareback?" The white horse hadn't been saddled.

She nodded. Rafe lifted her up so she could scramble onto the white horse's back.

Then Rafe remounted and started down the path. "Let's go. Just because we haven't seen them yet doesn't mean they're not still on our trail."

"What about the others?"

He shook his head. "I don't know. Either way, we can do nothing. By this point, they're either alive or dead. I'm not trying to be cruel, Angelet. But no skirmish lasts long —and this one is over, one way or another. Simon and the others would understand why we fled. Hell, Simon was yelling at me to take you out of there."

"I hope he's all right. All of them. I hope Bethany got to safety."

"She was hardly a devoted maid."

"But to be a woman alone in the wilderness, or to be captured among a band of thieves…I wouldn't wish that on any woman."

Rafe looked at her. "Ever the noble." Then he flicked the reins of his horse. "Come. We need to ride."

"Rafe?" she asked. "Where are we going?"

He looked over his shoulder, then directly at her. "I've got no idea. But we can't go back there."

Chapter 14

ANGELET WAS VERY WILLING TO let Rafe make all the decisions as to where to go and what speed to take and when to rest. She was numb from the events of the morning. Several times she almost convinced herself that it was a dream, and that she wasn't alone in the woods with only a single knight for company. She'd wake up to find the whole group alive and well.

But then she'd feel the twinges of pain in her body from the splinters that struck her after the crossbow bolt hit the carriage. She grew conscious of the growing ache in her muscles from riding the white horse. She wasn't used to riding for hours.

Rafe was used to it, of course, but he seemed distant, rarely speaking, and frequently circling back to look behind them. He did that again, apparently saw nothing, but didn't seem relieved in the slightest. "Damn," he muttered.

"What's wrong?" she asked.

"Nothing."

"You look as if you want to kill."

"I've been thinking." He sighed. "Back there…I was careless. I should have been paying attention to the road, and I wasn't."

"A man can't be on alert all the time," she said.

"I can," said Rafe, his tone much angrier than usual. "I'm not some boy who's never been out in the world before. I'm a soldier. My task was to get the whole cortège safely from Dryton to Basingwerke, but I was too distracted to keep my mind on my work. And now people are dead because of it."

"Rafe, there were more than twenty of them! Even if you had eyes in the back of your head and never slept, you couldn't have fought them all off. Anyway, all the men-at-arms were supposed to be watchful too. Everyone was surprised. Whatever happened was no one's fault but those who came at us."

"Still, I should have…"

"If anything, this is *my* fault," Angelet interjected.

"Don't," he said. "It was the fault of the thieves on our trail. They were willing to kill for what they thought we had."

"Rafe," she asked then, "the chest was truly empty?"

He took a breath. Clearly, that had been on his mind too. "Not empty, but there were stones where there should have been coin. The weight was meant to reassure us, make us think nothing was amiss."

"But when could that have happened? The chest contained gold when we left Dryton. Otto showed us all! It was locked and chained and guarded every moment since. What happened?"

"I don't know, Angelet. Believe me, I've been thinking of it. I don't know how or when it was done. Or why, come to that."

"The why is simple enough. A thief, but one who worked by stealth instead of force."

"Perhaps," he agreed. "A clever thief, too, to get into the chest to replace the coin with stones, and get away without any alarm. It defies imagination."

"Could it have been two people? Or more? What if Dobson wasn't working alone?"

"I wish I knew." He swiped his hand across his face.

Angelet knew he was tired, but he'd never admit it to her. Men never liked women to know that they were mortal. Even when her husband had been in the last stage of his illness, when he couldn't rise from his bed, he insisted he needed no help.

"We could pause for a while," she suggested tentatively.

"Why?" he asked, suddenly fixing her with a sharp, searching look. "Are you not feeling well?"

"I'm quite all right," she said. "But I'm not the one who was in a fight this morning."

Rafe shook his head. "That was barely a fight. It's been too long since I've fought for real. Those show fights at the tourneys aren't the same."

"But participants die in those."

"Sometimes. But trust me, the experience is entirely different in an actual battle. I'm just a little out of sorts. I'm perfectly capable of defending you along the road."

"I wasn't implying otherwise."

"Good. Because I want it known that I am still the best knight in the whole country."

Despite everything that had happened, she laughed. "Did you mean to say the most arrogant?"

"That too. I excel in many fields."

"Well, I hope one of them includes orienteering. I've no idea how long it is to the next town, or if we'll have to sleep in the forest again. This time without tents or any comforts."

"I'll keep you comfortable if it comes to that," he said. "But with luck, we'll reach some sort of lodging by nightfall. The longer we ride, the better chance we'll be able to pass a whole night before anyone catches up."

Just after dark, they reached a village called Wynlow. The inn was easy to find, being the largest and loudest place along the road. Rafe told her to keep her hood up and to wait outside near the horses while he arranged everything with the innkeeper.

A short while later, Angelet walked into the private room they rented, and was very aware when Rafe followed her in. He closed the door behind him, but didn't step toward her.

She made her way to the brazier, soaking up the heat from the embers while Rafe stalked around the whole room, staring suspiciously at everything.

Finally, he joined her, kneeling down to look directly into the flames.

"You're not going to prod the chimney with your sword?" she asked. "I doubt there's an assassin lurking there, but it's possible."

He shook his head, evidently too tired for jokes now. "The room is safe enough. No one can get in that window without making a lot of noise, and there's no other door but the one to the corridor."

"It doesn't have a lock," she pointed out, feeling a bit nervous.

"I'm the lock," Rafe said simply.

"What do you mean? You can't stand watch all night."

"No, I can't. But I can sleep in front of the door. No one can open it without waking me."

"Oh." Angelet looked everywhere but him. "You intend to sleep in here?"

"It's the best way to keep you safe," he said.

"From everyone but you."

"Angelet, if I come to your bed, it will be because you ask me to and for no other reason." Rafe stood up then, and she mirrored his movement. "Do you believe me?"

"I…do. And I'm *not* asking," she added hastily.

"Just as well that I'm needed as a bulwark then," he said with a wry smile. "You'll have to make do with dreaming about me."

"I do not dream about you!" she said, a statement that was not entirely true. She had daydreamed about him, and specifically what it would be like to spend a night, or two, with him. She missed being touched, being held. Before Rafe came into her life, she'd been able to more or less deny the urge. But ever since he first smiled at her, she recalled just how lonely she'd been over the past several years.

"What a shame. You should try…it would be an improvement over your usual visions of heaven."

"You're insufferable," Angelet said, and turned back toward the bed. She pulled off a pillow and a woolen blanket, pushing them into Rafe's arms. "Here, these are for you. How can you sleep on a hard floor?"

"Wouldn't be the first time. I'll manage." He looked her over. "Now, my lady, you should go to bed yourself. You've had a long day, and you need rest."

Angelet washed her face in the basin provided, and carefully removed her overskirt, feeling as shy as if she were taking all her clothing off, even though she still wore a shift. But Rafe didn't seem to be paying attention, for he was at the brazier once again, adding fuel to keep the room warm through the night.

She lay down and pulled the remaining blanket up. A wave of fatigue rolled over her, and she heaved a sigh she didn't know she was holding in.

Rafe let out a low laugh. "So you are tired."

"Exhausted," she admitted. She curled up on her side. "I'll never learn how to live like this, traveling for miles day after day."

"You shouldn't have to deal with it for very long, my lady. I'll get you to a safe location…once we decide where the danger is coming from."

She lay awake for a while, the darkness only broken by the dull glow from the embers. Rafe was little more than a dark shape by the door.

"Rafe?"

"Yes?" He didn't sound nearly as tired as she was, but he must be yearning for sleep.

"I just thought of something. We could shove the whole bed in front of the door. Then no one could open it."

"True. But then you would also have no escape if there was a fire…or if I turned out to be an untrustworthy rogue and murderer. You need to have a path of retreat."

She asked, "Do you always think of things in that way, as if it's a war?"

"When people are trying to kill me, yes."

"And here I'd have trapped us both."

"It's not your duty to think of those things, Angelet. That's why I'm around. I'll plan the attacks and the escapes and the marches."

"What do I do?" she asked.

"You stay alive."

She murmured some reply, feeling sleepier by the moment. Rafe's words circled through her mind. *You stay alive*. Good advice in the circumstances, she supposed. But it wasn't enough. A person needed something beyond simply staying alive. She needed a hope, or something to dream about. She was just about to ask Rafe what he hoped for, but then sleep took her and she drifted off, the question stuck on her lips.

When morning came, she sat up in bed, feeling infinitely better and more charitable toward the world. She saw Rafe lying across the bottom of the doorway, dozing in the pale dawn light. He was stretched on his side, looking quite peaceful. His unsheathed sword lay a foot or so away from him, the length of it paralleling his own body. For all his joking, he was serious about guarding her from threats. Angelet felt reassured, though she hoped they never again encountered the thieves from the day before.

She slipped out of bed and padded to him. She bent over and reached out to shake his shoulder. "Rafe?"

As she did so, her hair tumbled down, the loose braid falling till the ends hit his cheek.

Rafe caught the braid in one hand, looping the end around his palm once, twice. His eyes were still closed, but he was smiling. He brought his hand to his mouth and kissed the braid around his hand before letting it go. "Definitely a good way to be roused in the morning."

"You're still dreaming," she retorted, straightening up again.

He chuckled, and sat up on his blanket. "A whole night alone with me, and you're not even a bit ravished," he said cheerfully. "Disappointed?"

A tiny part of her was, actually, but she just sniffed, pretending to be annoyed. "Certainly not!"

He wasn't fooled, to judge by how he laughed at her tone.

"Well, I am," Rafe said. Then his demeanor became serious. "We'd best get moving. Who knows if someone chose to keep pursuing you, but the further away we get from the path we were on, the better off you'll be."

"Would they assume we'd continue on to the abbey?"

"That's the logical guess, based on what everyone has heard. Certainly, no one would expect us to be here. Chance brought us to this place."

She nodded. "Then let's move on. Let chance help us stay hidden, for now."

They had so few supplies that packing up was easy. They made their way out of the room and toward the ground floor.

Just at the top of the stairs, the hem of her dress got caught under her shoe and she stumbled. She flung one arm out to the wall to get her balance, but that same moment, Rafe's arm circled her waist and held her firmly on her feet.

"Are you all right?" he asked, his eyes scanning her anxiously.

"Yes. I just tripped. My dress got snagged by something."

They both looked down and there indeed were a few long threads of her gown, caught by a splinter in the floorboard. Rafe relaxed, loosening his hold a little.

"I worried you might be having another fit."

She shook her head. "No. The symptoms of that are entirely different. You've seen them."

"By the time I found you, you were already unconscious," he pointed out. "So I don't know how it looks when it begins."

"Well, I'm not suffering from another fit," she said, hoping to reassure him. "Just a rough floor."

Angelet became conscious of just how close they were, and remembered the way he'd kissed her the evening they'd been out during the moonrise. Just how terrible a person would she be if she wanted a little more of that closeness? "Rafe…"

"Yes?" The way he was looking at her suggested he might be thinking along the same lines.

I accept your offer. Angelet took a breath. No, she couldn't say that. "You can…you can let me go now."

He released her. "You'll tell me if you ever start feeling unwell."

"Of course."

Rafe stepped around her and offered his hand.

"I can walk down a flight of stairs myself," she said. "I've done it for years."

"I believe you." Still he didn't budge.

Finally Angelet put her hand in his. "If you insist."

"I do insist, my lady."

She allowed Rafe to escort her all the way from the second floor, rather enjoying the attention. She'd been so used to being ignored at Dryton, where she was expected to fend for herself.

The innkeeper's wife gave them bread and cheese, and even some sausage. Angelet smiled when she smelled the loaf, still steaming from where it had been resting in a warming oven.

"We should eat now," she told Rafe. "It's a shame to let this get cold."

He glanced at the door, obviously tense. "No more than a quarter hour," he said. His nose twitched a little. Even he was susceptible to the aroma.

It took less than ten minutes to devour all they had in front of them. Rafe paid for another two loaves before they left. Angelet also saw him mutter a few words to the innkeeper's wife as he offered her a coin. The woman nodded vehemently.

"What did you tell her?" Angelet asked, once they stepped outside.

"I suggested that she forget what we looked like, should anyone come asking."

"Will that work? She'd probably make just as much profit again to remember."

He shrugged. "Hard to say. Some people only need a little aid for their sympathy. Either way, I can afford it."

"Can you? How much money have you got? We hardly got anything away from the cortège."

"I always keep my money on me," he said. "And I have some supplies in Philon's saddlebags. A lesson learned long ago. And as for how much I've got, Lord Otto paid well to see you safely to your destination."

"Speaking of which, what is our destination now? I don't even know where we are!"

"Nor do I, exactly. Somewhere south of Glossopdale, evidently. But the innkeeper's wife said we're already on the best road in this part of the shire. I think we can follow it till we reach a town of decent size. Then we'll decide."

He helped her onto the white horse. Not for the first time, Angelet considered the puzzle of Rafe's personality. He was such an odd combination, deferential yet arrogant. He claimed he was only out for himself, yet he noticed the instant she showed any sign of distress and was ready to help her.

They followed the road, which ran roughly southwest, though with many twists and turns due to the increasingly hilly landscape. They rode in silence, each intent on their own thoughts. For her part, Angelet couldn't stop thinking of how someone had spirited away a lifetime's worth of precious coin with no one the wiser.

"Here's an idea," Angelet said suddenly. "Someone drilled into the chest from the bottom, and got the gold out that way. You didn't notice a hole in the chest because it all happened in the middle of a fight, but it's possible."

He shook his head. "Even if someone had the tools for that—an awl? A saw?—he would have made too much noise. One of us would have seen or heard something. There was a man to guard it at all hours." From how quickly Rafe responded, she realized his mind had been on exactly the same subject.

"But what…" she started to say.

"What?"

"What if one of the other guards was an accomplice? Or was promised payment to keep his mouth shut?"

"If it was a guard," he asked, "who? Who would you suspect?"

"Not Simon!" she said instantly. "Nor Laurence or Marcus."

"So quick to absolve."

"I just know you and your friends wouldn't have done this."

He smiled at her confidence. "Thank you. But that puts the blame on Otto's very own men. Does that make sense?"

"Gold makes men strange," Angelet said. "Still, I don't know which of them might have been the culprit, or how they might have done it."

"I was trying to remember all the shifts the men took. On the second night, Dobson and Tad also shared a watch. Perhaps they did steal it then, and hid the gold somewhere nearby."

"But why keep traveling with us?"

"To allay suspicion, or to simply get further from the gold, so that no one else could chase after it. Perhaps they were wary of news getting back to Dryton too soon. I'm not sure."

"If they did steal the gold on the second night, why try to kill me a few nights later?"

Rafe shook his head. "Again, I have no answers. Maybe Tad had enough stomach for theft but not for murder. So then Dobson tried to murder you on his own and when it went wrong, Tad lied about his involvement to save himself."

"If Dobson had killed me without raising an alarm, then he and Tad might have taken the chest out of the inn, but then emptied it and abandoned it. Everyone would still think the gold was just stolen. But they would have been able to run away much faster—because they were actually unburdened. Then they'd go back to where they'd hidden the gold once the search for them died down."

"That's plausible. But there's no proof."

"Does proof matter at this point?"

"I'd like to know the truth," said Rafe, "or at least enough of it to explain my own innocence."

She frowned. "Why should anyone blame you?"

"Why not? Otto will seek to blame *someone* once he gets word of the loss. And I rode away from the skirmish after the empty chest was discovered…taking along his daughter-in-law."

"I see your point," Angelet said, "but I am also your defense. I will explain that I kept the key the whole time, and that everything you did was to protect the chest, and me."

Rafe gave her a skeptical look. "Women aren't considered suitable witnesses in a court. Particularly not beautiful, rich, unmarried women who travel in the company of the accused man for days on end."

"Oh." He was right. "Then we'll just have to ensure that doesn't happen. We'll both find somewhere safe."

"And where in all England would that be, my lady?"

Angelet sighed. "I know not. But there must be a place, and we will find it."

Chapter 15

THEY RODE ONWARD THROUGH THE woods. Rafe had been quiet, occasionally checking over his shoulder as they rode. But he seemed pensive rather than worried.

At last he spoke. "Perhaps we're going about this wrong. I'll return you to Dryton, and…"

Alarm welled up in her. "No, please don't! I beg you not to do that."

Rafe looked surprised at her vehemence. "I know it wasn't the happiest place for you, but you'll be safe there."

"I'm not certain of that."

"Why?"

She shook her head. "It's difficult to explain. But I have this sense that it would go badly should I return, if only because I'd have to explain a journey alone with you. Otto would lock me up in the closest nunnery to hand. And you'd likely not get a chance to explain anything. Otto isn't the most temperate of men."

"Then what? We can't just wander."

Angelet had been thinking of precisely that issue all morning. What she wanted was to get to her son. More than anything. If she had Henry safe by her side, she could face down Otto, no matter what. But she wasn't sure she could tell Rafe that. Judging by how he'd spoken of his own parents, he wouldn't understand the depth of her own need to find her son. She had to think of another plausible destination. Then one came to her.

"Would you escort me to my true home? That is, my family's home in Anjou?"

"You want me to take you across the channel?" he asked in surprise.

"My family has the means to pay you for your trouble," she promised recklessly. "And in any case, you've already told me that you have no plans."

Rafe frowned, considering her request. "Even if I agree, there are obstacles, not least of which is who you are…of who your family supports. Any port city held by the king may not allow you to leave, even if you could afford to pay passage."

"Then we'll go to a port city held by the empress," she said. "Like Wareham!" Wareham was in Dorset, near where Henry was being fostered. Once they got closer, Angelet could reveal her true plans to Rafe.

He shook his head once. "Wareham? That's a long way, Angelet."

She felt his resolve slipping, and pressed on. "I'll pay whatever price you set for your services. From where we are, the fastest way to Wareham is through Shropshire, is it not?"

"Yes," he said, looking displeased. "I don't wish to travel that way."

"Why not? Is it dangerous?"

Rafe didn't answer directly. "I have to think on this. I'm not agreeing to do it yet. For now, let's just find somewhere safe for the night."

Angelet held her tongue after that. She wasn't sure what else she could do to persuade Rafe to agree to her new plan, and from what she knew of him, he liked to come to his own decisions. But if only she could get to Henry! Without Rafe to guide her, she had no hope of doing so.

She had to persuade him somehow. She bit her lip. She knew of one thing that often made men more agreeable. If she accepted Rafe's offer, he'd be more inclined to indulge her, wouldn't he? And she had wanted to say yes long before, anyway. She'd just been too nervous to take the step. But with this added incentive, perhaps accepting his offer would benefit them both. She closed her eyes. *Oh, be honest*, she told herself. *You're dying of curiosity.*

The day was quiet, with no hint of pursuit. A little after nightfall they reached another village, this one tucked into the bend of a river, running high from the previous early rains.

Rafe arranged for a room and food, and care for the horses, all while Angelet stood about feeling useless. She attracted puzzled looks from the patrons of the main room, and no wonder. She wore the same gown as she'd been wearing when they escaped the robbery, and now it was quite dirty from days of riding and negotiating forest paths. Her cloak fared no better, now sporting patches of mud and several rents she would have to mend when she had a moment's peace. The quality of her clothing and shoes told the world she was a lady, but the state of them suggested she was little more than a beggar. She pulled the hood of her cloak a little tighter over her head. Before they entered the village, Rafe suggested she hide her hair, since the silvery-blond was so noticeable.

As if Rafe himself could escape notice! He stood there dressed in all black, commanding attention with his stance and his looks. His thick, black hair fell across his face, making her itch to push it back behind his ear, partly to reveal those deep blue eyes. From the way the barmaid kept staring open-mouthed, Angelet knew virtually all the women in sight felt the same way. And why not? He was by far the most handsome man around. And he could be hers, if she asked.

Her gaze drifted to his shoulders and arms, the outline of the muscles evident even under the thick knit fabric of his clothing. She remembered when he'd helped her down from the horse with those arms, and blushed to think how much she wanted to linger in that embrace. To be so close to him that she could simply wrap herself around him and forget everything that happened.

"My lady?" Rafe asked quietly.

She jumped, not realizing that he'd rejoined her, and now stood in front of her, those lovely eyes searching her face. "What? Excuse me, my mind wandered…" How it had wandered.

"You're tired," he said, putting a hand to her elbow to steady her. "The good news is that we've got a private room upstairs."

"What's the bad news?" she asked anxiously.

"The bad news is that the bath is in the innkeeper's home at the back of the property, so you'll have to walk a bit."

"The bath?"

He smiled. "The innkeeper is named Sarah. She mentioned she had a bath and that you might want it. So I paid the fee for you."

"Oh, that would be a *marvel*," she said.

He chuckled at the feeling in her words. "I thought you would enjoy that. Let's find the room first, though. Follow me."

Upstairs, the room was one of the best they'd seen thus far. Sarah kept a very tidy inn. Angelet put her small bag down while Rafe walked around the perimeter of the room, in a ritual she now recognized as his usual security.

Then Rafe turned to her. "I can risk letting you go to the bath on your own, yes?" he asked. "There's been no pursuit, and the village seems calm. Everyone I've seen appears ordinary enough, and no hint of unsavory types… other than me, of course."

She smiled at that. "You're not the rogue you claim to be."

"I'm twice the rogue I claim to be," Rafe said jovially. "But I've been acting honorably for you. Well, as honorably as a man like me can, anyway."

"Rafe," she said quietly. "About that. I have been thinking." Oh, she'd been thinking.

"Yes?"

"Your offer to me," she said, her voice trembling despite her efforts to sound cool and calm about it. "The one you made before all this happened. I would like…I might…we could discuss it further." Lord, this was embarrassing.

Rafe was evidently enjoying her discomfort. His smile was slight, but unmistakable. "You mean my offer to be your lover, on your terms?"

"I'm not agreeing to anything yet," she said hastily, heat coursing through her and no doubt making her cheeks cherry red. "I only meant I was…am interested."

"Well, if you're interested, my lady, then we can discuss it further. Tonight."

"Yes. Tonight."

"As you command." His tone was mild, no more sensual than before. But she still nearly fainted at the promise in the phrase. *As you command.*

"I'm going to find that bath now," she announced, as if the matter were closed. Too late she realized that talk of her bathing was hardly likely to distract him from the previous topic.

"Enjoy yourself," Rafe said. "Sarah will meet you downstairs and show you where to go. And don't take *all* night," he added. "I'm looking forward to our discussion."

She forced herself to walk slowly out of the room, instead of running away from that knowing smile.

Downstairs, Sarah led her though an inner courtyard busy with activity from the visitors and workers. There was a tremendous din, partly because a couple of dogs had been cornered by a large orange cat.

"Hark! Stop playing, you beast!" Sarah yelled toward the cat. "You've mice to be killing!" She turned to Angelet. "He's normally quite good at keeping the mice down. But any tom will get diverted from time to time. You've been on the road a while."

"It feels as though we've been traveling forever," Angelet confessed. "But in truth, it's only been a sennight. Or so. We ran into bad luck, and lost most of our things to thieves."

"May the Devil pinch all thieves and brigands!" Sarah said. "At least you have your lives. I expect your husband made them run. I know a soldier when I see one!"

"Ah, yes," Angelet said nervously. Was it a sin to allow someone to think that she and Rafe were a married couple? "He's always defended me."

"Would that I could have said that about my man, may he rest in peace. But all he defended was his wine and ale. Left me the inn, though, and I thank him for that." By that time, Sarah had ushered Angelet into what must have been her own bedroom. A wooden tub sat near the fireplace and a maid was already filling it with steaming water. "We like to bathe on Saturday, before we all go to Sunday mass," Sarah explained. "The town's women can pay a penny for a bath. But this water's fresh boiled, and Grisa here makes a good oat soap."

The maid gave a pleased nod.

Sarah made to leave, but Angelet said, "One more request, if I may."

Angelet needed a new dress, yet brand-new dresses weren't laying about, waiting to be purchased. She had to either find a woman with a spare dress to sell, or purchase fabric to sew her own. Both options required time, which was not in abundance. Angelet had asked the innkeeper's wife last night, but got a mere shake of the head. However, she was in luck this time.

"I've a gown that would fit your frame," Sarah said. "It's a plain one, to be sure."

"I do not require ornament," Angelet said. "Just a good, clean, sturdy outfit. For I've got more travel ahead. If you can give it to me to wear after my bath, I'll get the money for it from my…husband."

"You wash up and I'll find it. Grisa, attend this lady, and don't be saucy, for she's a fine lady, anyone can tell. A lady is still a lady in rags, while gold cloth won't make a churl into a king."

Chapter 16

BACK IN THE PRIVATE ROOM in the inn, Angelet stood alone, her mind leaping like a deer as she considered her options: be bold or be modest, risk all or retreat.

She heard a soft knock at the door. "My lady?" Rafe asked from the other side. "May I?"

"Come in," she responded, turning to face him.

She had taken great care with her appearance. She had bathed, reveling in the hot water and soap. She had washed her hair and brushed it so it gleamed as it fell down her back. She wore the secondhand gown, but had added one accessory. Around her neck hung the moonstone necklace.

Rafe took it all in silently, his eyes roaming over her, up and down.

"I wanted to look…better," she explained, feeling rather embarrassed.

"You look gorgeous," he said. The admiration in his voice was direct, unhidden, and as arousing as a kiss. "Is this when we discuss my offer?"

She nodded, but said, "I haven't made a decision."

He took a step toward her. "Then tell me what you need to know. What would you have me do?" he asked.

"Everything I tell you, no matter what." She tried to keep her voice from shaking. She was not used to giving orders or ultimatums. "The *moment* you disobey, we are done. Can you agree to that?"

"Yes," he said. "So order me, Angelet. I'm yours to command."

"I need to hear you promise."

"I promise." He watched her carefully. "You look unconvinced."

She took an unsteady breath. "Words and promises are worthless," she said, finally addressing the central obstacle. "You're stronger than I am, you're bigger, you're…"

He took another step toward her. "Angelet. Think about it. I've had every opportunity to take you, had I wanted to. These last few nights, or on the ridge, by the pond, even the first night at Dryton." He stepped closer still, his eyes locked on hers. "Yes, you've got grounds for suspicion. I did steal you, after all. I warn you that I'm selfish and—"

"Hush," she said.

He stopped talking the instant she put a finger to his lips.

Angelet smiled a little. "So you do know how to take an order from a woman."

"The right woman." He caught her wrist in his hand and kissed her fingers. She nearly fainted when his tongue grazed her skin of her palm. "I wanted you the very first moment I saw you leaning out of the window, high above everything, just watching your world like a queen."

"Hardly a queen," she said. "I was a prisoner, with no say over my life or my destiny."

"Then be a queen tonight. You'll have all the say. I promise."

She inhaled, dreaming of it. Queen Angelet, with a single subject.

"Let me go," she whispered. He did.

She took a step back, partly to get a moment to build up her courage, and to take another look at him. "You're always telling me you're the handsomest man I'll ever meet. Why not prove it once and for all?"

"Don't I do that just by standing here?"

She crossed her arms, wondering if he was perhaps a little nervous as well, and just better at concealing it. Well, no more. "Your clothes. Take them off."

Rafe laughed. "You don't waste time. Very well, do you want to help?"

"No, I want to watch." Queens weren't maids, after all.

So Rafe stripped himself of his simple clothing, starting with his tunic, since he'd removed his armor earlier. When he was nearly naked, he hesitated, obviously not used to being on display. But the hose came off. And he stood in front of her, fully naked…and fully aroused.

Angelet experienced a thrill as she surveyed him. He *wanted* her. He wanted her enough to literally strip bare and stand in front of her awaiting her command. Angelet never knew what it was to have any power. If it felt at all like this, she suddenly understood the appeal.

"Well?" he asked, not at all ashamed. "Am I the finest man you've ever seen, or not?"

Angelet laughed in delight. "You are *so* arrogant."

"But also correct…correct?"

She bit her lip against a laugh. "Yes! I admit it. You're the very finest man I've ever seen naked, which is not saying much."

"Of course it is. First place is first place. What now?" he asked, obviously eager to continue.

"Now you must stand there *patiently* while I undress."

"I can't undress you?" He sounded disappointed.

"No! I don't wish it." She had almost agreed, due to the ingrained habit of acquiescing to whatever anyone asked of her. But she was afraid that she'd lose her tenuous control of the situation if she indulged Rafe's very first request. She wanted one night where she ruled.

She turned away from him, shyness making her clumsy. She lifted the gown above her head, and let it fall to the floor next to her feet. She then gathered up the shift, slowly, from the hem, exposing her legs inch by inch. She could have pulled everything off at once, but she wanted to draw out the tension…and perhaps to hide under clothing a moment longer.

When the thin shift also lay discarded on the floor, she turned to face him again, and was rewarded with an intake of breath.

All that was left was the necklace. She started to remove it.

"Leave the moonstones on," he said. He hadn't taken his eyes from her, and the expression on his face was enough to make her flush. She wasn't used to being admired like this.

She paused, her hands raised behind her head, her fingers at the clasp of the chain. "Why should I?"

"They suit you."

"Even naked?"

"Especially naked. I won't beg for anything else tonight. I swear it."

She considered his words, unaware that the pose she

was holding, with her arms raised and her breasts thrust outward, with the precious stones accenting her body, was challenging Rafe's ability to hold still. She unconsciously let her fingers trace the chain downward and then petted the largest jewel in the center of the necklace, feeling the smooth, cool moonstone under the tips of her fingers. "I'll keep them on. Your *only* request," she reminded him.

"I'll remember." He half-clenched his hands, and in a moment of intuition, she knew he ached to touch her, and only the lack of permission kept him from doing so already. So Angelet touched herself, cupping her breasts lightly with her hands, lifting them up a little.

The strangled gasp he gave told her that her guess was right. She looked at him from under her eyelashes, watching his reaction to her moves.

His gaze was riveted to her, and every time she shifted or moved her hands, his eyes followed.

Finally, he said, "You are planning on inviting me to join you at some point, yes?"

"Perhaps," she said, loving the rush of power she felt.

"Then for God's sake, tell me what to do."

She paused. Here was the issue. Despite her long-ago marriage, Angelet lacked the experience to know exactly what to ask for. Her memories of nights with her husband had grown hazy. She remembered that he had tried to please her, but not how he'd done so.

Rafe must have sensed her indecision, because he said in a low voice, "I want to taste you. Please. However you like."

She looked Rafe over, all six feet of him. "Kneel down," she instructed.

He was on his knees instantly, and Angelet stepped up to him, now understanding exactly why some nobles always insisted on being seated higher than those they interacted with. She looked down at him and smiled. "This is better. You look a little less arrogant this way."

"A little," he agreed. His head came to just below her breasts. He moved his arms up, preparing to embrace her.

"No," she told him shortly. "Hold still."

He stopped, and looked up at her expectantly. Angelet put her hands on his shoulders, then moved her hands to the back of his head, tipping it so he had to look directly at her belly. "You may not use your hands."

He froze. "Then how would you have me touch you?"

"You said you wanted to taste me. Use your mouth."

He leaned in to obey her.

At the touch of his tongue on her skin, Angelet felt a fire start inside her body.

Rafe kissed and licked his way across her flesh, and it seemed he really intended to cover every inch of her that he could reach in his position. He knelt so far as to kiss the tops of her feet, then worked his way up her legs, easing her knees apart, and then going until he reached her inner thigh. He continued, without any hesitation, his tongue invading places on her body she would never dream of ordering a man to touch.

But he touched her there without even asking, and before she could get over the shock of what he was doing, her body reacted, revealing just how effective his touch was.

Her knees buckled, and just as she wobbled on her feet, his hands clasped her hips, steadying her. She gasped out loud, and he froze.

"You might have fallen," he said quickly. He released her, probably wondering if she would declare an end to the whole endeavor.

She put her hands on his shoulders, restoring her balance. "How did you know I would like that?"

He glanced up at her, his lips curving into an easy smile. "You're a woman. I know women."

"Stand up," she murmured.

He did instantly, so he once again towered over her.

Angelet laid the flat of her hand on his chest and pushed him back. "Go to the bed."

"At last. Come with me." He held out a hand and gave her a look that struck her as a little too triumphant.

She crossed her arms. "That sounded like an order."

"Not meant to be," Rafe said quickly. "More of an invitation. But you're in charge."

"How lovely," she said. "Go to the bed and lie down. On your back."

"Yes, my lady." He didn't exactly mock her as he made his way to the bed, but Angelet sensed his confidence. He thought she'd slide right next to him and put herself in his hands. He was wrong.

She padded across the floor to the bed, climbing onto the mattress next to Rafe. He watched her with intense interest, but knew enough to not reach out to her without permission.

Every time she'd lain with her husband, Angelet had been beneath him, pressed into the bed, watching as he took her and then lost himself in desire. She'd rarely felt the same ecstasy at the end, and decided that perhaps being above was what mattered. Strange how the old thoughts, long forgotten, suddenly returned.

Now with a seemingly obedient Rafe in her bed, Angelet wanted to know how it felt to be the one on top. She positioned herself over him, sliding one leg over his body so that she was straddled across his hips, his erection just between her legs.

Rafe's eyes lit up. "Tell me what you need."

Angelet surveyed the man under her. She put her hands on him, sliding over his stomach. "It's probably shameful to admit," she said, "but when you fought Dobson that one night, I couldn't stop looking at you. Even in the midst of all that chaos, the sight of you half-naked was nearly all I can remember."

"Well, if it distracted you from being terrorized by the fact that someone was trying to kill you, that's something."

"You're always so flippant," she criticized.

"Not always. Please notice how very sincerely I'm following your orders, my lady."

She slid her hands along his arms from his shoulders to his wrists, drawing them up above his head. Rafe knew exactly what she was doing, of course, but he didn't object.

"You can't touch me," she instructed.

"Your loss," he returned easily, even as he stretched out his arms to keep his hands well out of danger.

"My choice," she corrected him.

She kissed him then, over and over, her mouth tasting him freely as she explored his body. He was a pleasure to touch, and even to tease, such as when she ran her hand over his erection and heard his breath change in response. She ached to know exactly how he'd feel inside her.

But though she knew what she should do next, she hesitated. Flashes of remembered awkwardness and pain came to her. What if she was no longer made for a man?

"Angelet, let me show you what to do."

She turned her head aside, hating that Rafe had seen the weakness in her, the lack of decision.

"Just for a moment?" he pleaded. "To serve you."

At her nod, he took hold of her hips and eased himself into her body. She gasped in surprise at first, almost regretting her agreement to spend the night with him. What had she been thinking? He was large and she hadn't been with any man for so long. She moaned as he entered her, and heard the sound echoed by Rafe, who closed his eyes and looked almost as if he'd been struck.

"Damn, you're so…"

"I'm what?" she asked fearfully.

"Perfect."

"Oh."

"Take your time, love," he said. "Sit up if you like. Shift till you feel me the way you want to."

She took his advice. She kept her eyes closed and began to rock her hips slowly against his.

"You're no novice to this. Did you do it this way before?" he asked.

"I don't remember," she lied. "And get your hands back by your head."

He obeyed, laughing. But his laughter soon died as Angelet leaned back and rocked her hips, reveling in the sheer virility of the man she'd claimed as her own, if only for tonight.

She loved being above him, feeling him inside her while she could control the pace and intensity of their lovemaking. Every movement made her shiver with delight, as little waves of pleasure swept through her, building slowly into something much more momentous.

Beneath her, Rafe was alternately enjoying what she did to him, and growing frustrated with the restrictions she'd set. His arms remained above his head, but it was a chore to keep them there, to judge by how tight his muscles were as he strained to hold still.

"Please let me touch you," he begged. "Angelet, you've got no idea how it hurts to look at you and not be able to touch you."

She paused. "I know exactly how it feels to see something and know I'll never attain it."

"Not like this," he said, his breath ragged. "You're so close, and so gorgeous."

"Rafe," she reminded him, "you're *inside* of me."

"But I want to touch you with my hands too."

She tapped the moonstone necklace. "Remember what you begged for already. Isn't it enough? Don't you like looking at me?"

He nodded, his eyes raking over her in a way that made her shy all over again.

"You can touch me with your hands next time," Angelet said, "if you continue to obey me this time. Understood?"

"Perfectly."

"Good." She lifted her body up once more, drawing out the exquisite sensation of his flesh sliding along hers.

After a few moments of that, Rafe asked in a strangled tone, "Jesu, just *end* this, Angelet! You're going to destroy me with all your teasing. Why are you doing this?"

"Because it feels good," she breathed, her eyes still closed. "If you want to end it, just disobey me," she whispered.

"No." His voice became softer. "If you like it, then that's all that matters."

"You're stronger than I thought," Angelet confessed.

"Not stronger. Just more desperate."

"Why desperate?" she asked.

Just as she uttered the word, all the pleasure building

within her suddenly burst out, and she gave a little cry of surprise and relief. Her hands flattened out on Rafe's chest as she leaned over him. She whimpered a little, lost in the deep thrumming pulse rippling through her limbs. She didn't know how she ended up pressed against Rafe's body, but she knew he was just as lost as she was. He'd stiffened as he came, then murmured her name, his lips at her ears. She couldn't move and didn't want to. She felt so warm and pleased, and she only wanted to be cradled close as she slid into oblivion.

Rafe's breathing slowed along with hers. His fingers swept her hair aside as he fumbled at the back of her neck. The weight of the moonstones suddenly disappeared. Rafe put the necklace away somewhere—she couldn't care less where. Then his hands were at her hips, drawing her off him.

She gasped as he did that, feeling a last, unexpected shock of pleasure as he slipped out of her. Then she was lying next to him, her head on his shoulder, burying her face in the crook of his neck. She inhaled, smelling sweat and salt, the raw scent of her single subject.

"Rafe, I order you to..." She closed her eyes before she could complete the thought...*hold me.* She dreamed the words she was too far gone to speak.

Chapter 17

RAFE SAW ANGELET'S EYES CLOSE as she nestled into place alongside him. She wore a beatific smile, and he felt a jolt of satisfaction, thinking he'd been the one to put that smile on her face.

Well, partly. In fact, Angelet had done quite a lot of the work all on her own, taking control of him in such an unexpected way that he honestly didn't know what to think. He'd *never* had an encounter like that before. And he never would have suspected that the outwardly mild Angelet would be the sort of woman who could dominate a bedroom. Or him. But she did, with her tantalizing rules and restrictions. Right at the end, he lost it and broke the rule about not touching her. He couldn't stop himself—he had to hold her while she was coming undone above him, triggering his own climax. Rafe wasn't even sure she had noticed his hands on her body, on her hips as he spilled inside her.

Christ, he hadn't intended to do that. As if he needed another complication in his already complicated life. Angelet had completely derailed his better intentions, and now there was a chance she'd have to pay for his failure.

Just one more person you hurt.

The thought soured his soul, displacing all the good feelings Angelet had just given him. Damn. Every time he thought he'd changed, he discovered he was the same heartless bastard he'd always been.

He'd have to get her somewhere safe as soon as possible, then get the hell away from her for her own good. And despite her seductive promise that next time he could touch her, Rafe knew that he'd already gone too far. He'd treated her as a woman, but Angelet was a lady. And despite what just happened between them, she was not *his* lady.

After a moment, he said, "I'll take you to Wareham, and across to France, if we can find passage."

Angelet's eyes flew open. "What?"

"I said I'll take you to Wareham."

She gasped and tried to pull away. "I didn't do this just to get you to agree to take me home!" But the way she looked made him suspicious.

"Wait. Did you agree to this because you thought I'd not take you home otherwise?" Rafe didn't like the idea that she thought he could be tricked like that.

"No! Not quite."

"Not quite?"

"It crossed my mind," Angelet whispered. "And you didn't say you'd take me before…this."

"I didn't say anything before because *before* all I could think about was you."

"And now I'm off your mind?" She moved to get up.

"Stay, lovely." He reached out to her, stopping her from scrambling off the bed. "You know that's not true. And it's not why I'm agreeing to take you."

"It isn't?" she asked, with narrowed eyes. But she remained on the bed, now sitting up to face him, her long hair drawn over one shoulder to partially cover her chest. She seemed remarkably comfortable in her nakedness.

"No." Rafe struggled to explain what he assumed she would be overjoyed to hear. "The truth is that I've tried to think of any other safe place for you…and I can't. You have a family, so you should be with them. I don't care about the war, and I don't care if it helps one side or hurts another. I've got no side. Not anymore."

"But you once had a side," she said, still not fully convinced. Lord, what was her objection? She was the one who offered to pay him to take her home!

"I served a lord who swore for King Stephen," Rafe admitted. "So naturally I fought on Stephen's side in the battles."

"What changed?"

"I left that lord's service." He kept his voice cool. That was not a subject he wanted to discuss. "Since then, I've only fought for myself. And I only take orders when it suits me."

"It suited you tonight?" Angelet asked, in a different voice.

He smiled at her. "Oh, yes. Even though it was not what I was expecting."

"Was I too demanding?"

"You were perfect. And I think you enjoyed giving your demands."

She looked thoughtful, then said, slowly, "Yes…but I wouldn't want it to always be like that. Being in command is rather nerve-wracking."

"Oh, that's what was wracking your nerves?" He leaned forward and kissed her.

She kissed him back, her good humor evidently restored. "You know what I mean."

"I do," he agreed. "Honestly, I never did well with command. Even a few troops in a battle, scarcely enough for a squad…it was too much responsibility for me. My life now is much easier. No one expects anything from a free lance, bastard knight. I can do what I like. Feeding, fighting, and fucking."

"You've never spoken so crudely before," she said, though she didn't sound offended. What an unusual lady.

"You're seeing my true nature," Rafe said, imagining how fast she'd turn from him if she ever learned the whole truth about his unpleasant nature.

"Am I?" Angelet asked, unaware of his darker thoughts. "Or are you trying to convince me of that? That all you care about is feeding, fighting, and fucking?" The last word sounded strange in her soft voice.

"It is all I care about," he insisted, remembering his mistake from earlier. "Though as for the fucking, I usually avoid the part where I make another bastard of my own. I suppose I can tell the child it was done on your orders, not that it absolves me in the least."

She went still. "The child?"

"You do realize there's a possibility you'll bear our child."

"No. You've no need to worry on that count. Not with me." She sounded so certain, so clear that it snapped Rafe from his own turmoil.

"Why not? After all…"

"I cannot have another child." She said it very quietly, without much emotion.

"Another?" Rafe heard the pain beneath her voice. "You had a child?"

"Yes. I was fourteen, less than a year married, and less than a month till I was to be a widow. The delivery was difficult." She shook her head. Though she still sat up, her back straight, she now trembled a little. "I say difficult…it was devastating. I don't remember much, praise Mary. But I am told that my son and I both nearly died. It was a hard labor, and my body not the right size for bearing. I bled and bled, even after the midwife got the baby free of me. He was blue, they said. Almost too long without air to breathe. Thank God he lived. My only child, and the only reason I was worth anything to Lord Otto. So long as I nursed the babe, Otto knew I was necessary. My baby would not take milk from any other woman, no matter how they tried to find one."

"But who said you could never have another child?" Rafe asked.

"The midwife. She said I was lucky to have survived, and that never again would I ever even get with child, let alone bear it to term."

"How could she know that?"

"The herbs she used to quell the bleeding. She said she's used them before, and barrenness is the price. I lived to nurse Henry, but I would never be a mother again." Angelet choked out the last words, her unnatural calm finally collapsing as she shared something he knew she'd kept secret for a very long time.

He reached for her, and she all but jumped into his arms. A little while ago, she'd been a confident, sensual woman, and now she was in tears, shaking with emotion and as fragile as he first assumed her to be.

He wasn't good with crying women. He had no idea what to say or do. But it seemed natural to hold her until she'd cried herself out. The way she clung to him suggested that she needed support from someone, and he was the only available option. Poor Angelet.

"I'm sorry," she whispered then. "I don't mean to sob all over you. You'd think I'd be reconciled to it by now, but…"

A fresh bout of tears cut her words off, and Rafe just held her closer. "It's nothing," he said. Inane, but what could he say? That he didn't mind her crying?

"I don't mind," he said out loud, realizing it was true. "No one is happy all the time."

He stroked her head, marveling again at the light, almost silvery strands. He wondered if her son had her hair.

"Where is your son now?" he asked.

"He's being fostered with another family that holds an alliance with Otto." Angelet raised her head, and she looked a little more present than she had a moment ago. "Otto sent Henry there when he was only eight, and he did it partly to keep me biddable. He dangled a visit like bait. Whenever something happened that made me think I could change my life at all, there it was: Do you want to return home, or see your child again? Do you want to meet a new suitor, or keep your only boy?" Her tone turned harsh as she mimicked Otto's questions. "He knew me. He knew I'd always bow down, because he had the one thing I loved most in the world."

Rafe didn't know what to say to that. He'd never loved anyone that much, or been loved that much.

"All I have of my boy is a lock of his hair," Angelet whispered. "I look at it every day, instead of his face. How is that just? I told Otto whatever I had to tell him, just for the chance to get to see my Henry again."

Rafe went utterly still. Her son didn't have her hair—because it was her *son's* lock of brown hair in that little box. Not her husband's. He sighed, relief coursing through him. All this time, he had thought he was pushing Angelet to betray the memory of her first love. But it was her child she thought of, not her late husband.

"What is it?" Angelet was looking at him, having sensed his shift in mood.

"Nothing," he said. "Just…hearing you speak of a child makes things clearer now."

"Otto warned me not to tell you the truth before. If I told anyone that the nunnery wasn't my choice, or if I revealed the true reason why I agreed to take vows, then he'd punish me by withholding access to Henry for the rest of my life. I couldn't take that chance. Until chance threw everything aside with that attack that separated us from the rest."

Rafe held her close, kissing her forehead. "I can see why you thought that way."

"That's not all," she said, sounding nervous.

"Go on."

"The family he's living with is in Dorset." Angelet looked nervous, and he understood why.

Rafe shook his head. "We're not going to France, are we? You want to get your son back."

She nodded.

"Do you have a plan for that, my lady? The family won't just let you walk out the gate with him."

"I hadn't thought that far ahead."

"Why did you lie about heading to Anjou? Why not just tell me?"

"Because I didn't think you'd agree! And because I don't have the means to pay you for anything. Well, there's the moonstones. The necklace is worth something."

"I don't want your necklace."

"You need to be paid. That's why I mentioned my family. I'm certain they have the means to pay you…I just couldn't be sure I'd ever actually reach Anjou if I tried to get Henry first. But I knew you'd tell me it was hopeless, or you wouldn't take me anywhere at all—"

Rafe sighed. "Angelet. From now on, you need to tell me the truth. If you want to get your child back, we definitely need to devise some plan to do it safely. If we're lucky, we can come up with something before we reach Dorset. And afterward…actually, we may have to cross the Channel. If you can reach your family, then both you and your son will be safe."

Her eyes widened as he spoke. "You think that's possible? We could all reach Anjou together?"

"It's possible. But it will take some work."

"You're not angry that I lied to you?"

"I've no standing to take offense at anything you've done, Angelet." He kissed her again. "Remember, I'm only here to serve you."

"Oh, hush." She gave a little laugh, tinged with sadness. "You make it sound as though I own you."

"You do tonight."

Rafe made her lie down again, and stretched out beside her on the bed.

She took a deep breath then let it out in a whoosh. "Oh, I don't know what to *do*."

"Then do nothing," he said, laying a hand on her skin, feeling how perfectly smooth she was. "At least until tomorrow. We have some time to plan this out."

He couldn't seem to stop touching her, though at the moment, he was satisfied by running his fingers up and down the side of her body, from her shoulder down to her waist, over her hip, and down her thighs. Then he'd reverse course, and repeat.

"You're so lovely," he said quietly.

"I'd say you're rather handsome yourself," Angelet returned, "but I wouldn't dare feed your pride."

"Too late," he said. "As we both know, I'm already as arrogant as they come."

"It's earned." She tipped her head back, offering an invitation for another kiss. He took it, enjoying the sweetness of the gesture.

Then he found the place at her throat where her pulse beat and licked her skin. Her sigh was gold.

"Rafe," she murmured. "Go on. With your tongue. Just like that."

"As you command."

Several moments later, she melted against him in an entirely new way, moaning his name, and he loved every moment.

In the morning, Rafe woke up to find Angelet curled up against him, her breathing slow and soft. For all the times he took a woman to bed, it was rare for him to wake up with one. And waking up to Angelet felt far better than waking up alone.

He almost kissed her, then drew himself up short. She wasn't seeking affection from him, and the last thing he needed was to complicate a very simple arrangement with any suggestion that he wanted more from her than what she'd already offered.

Rafe was content with enjoying her in bed, and only in bed, and only for the short time they'd be together. Angelet was an intelligent woman, and though she wasn't sure of her future, she obviously knew that permanently attaching herself to a bastard knight would do nothing for her own security. No, what she needed was to retrieve Henry, and then get safely to Anjou. After that, Rafe had no role in her life.

And he didn't want any role. Rafe could go anywhere once he was on the continent. He could offer his professional services to any lord or king who could pay. Or hell, he could journey to all the great cities of the known world. In a few weeks, he'd deliver Angelet to her home, and he'd be free forever.

Beside him, Angelet stirred and stretched, then opened her eyes. When she smiled at him, Rafe momentarily lost his highly rational line of thought.

"Good morning," she said.

"Morning, my lady." As he spoke, he brushed some hair from her face. She would age well. Angelet would be as lovely in thirty years as she was now, with a head of silvery hair and those same clear green eyes. Too bad he wouldn't be around to see it.

"What are you thinking?" she asked, looking at him curiously.

"Nothing," he said, with an easy smile. "Nothing important. We should get moving. The faster we're away from here, the safer you'll be."

She nodded, and her playful, sunny expression faded. "Do you think someone is still following us?"

"If someone is, let's make their task more difficult."

Chapter 18

LEAVING THE VILLAGE, RAFE AND Angelet took the south road. They now had a destination, and Rafe said he wanted to make as much progress toward Dorset as they could. The weather favored them at first. It was a fine spring day, the air soft and warm, and the sky clear. Angelet delighted in the scene passing by. Even in the worst situations, it was difficult to be downcast on a spring day.

Rafe wasn't quite as at ease. He kept looking over his shoulder, though he tried to conceal his concern from her for most of the morning.

"Perhaps they've given up altogether," Angelet suggested at last. "You've seen no signs of pursuit."

"No," Rafe said, but he sounded uncertain.

"*Have* you seen any signs?" she asked. "You don't have to shield me, you know. I won't faint…not from hearing bad news, anyway." Was Rafe keeping information from her in some sort of attempt to keep her affliction from recurring?

"I haven't," he said, more firmly. "Nothing definite. But there's a feeling I can't shake, and when you've been followed as much as I have, it's wise to heed that feeling."

"Excuse me, but who's been following you?" she asked.

"Never mind."

Angelet nudged her horse with an ankle to bring her closer to where he rode. "Rafe, what aren't you telling me? Why would someone be following *you*?"

He weighed his next words. "I've annoyed a number of people in the past few years."

"*Annoyed?* You annoyed them enough to warrant being physically pursued? What did you do? Does this involve a woman?" Lord, maybe Rafe made a practice of seducing all the ladies he escorted from place to place. Though he did once mention that he usually didn't do this sort of work. Still, he could have seduced some lady, and now her family was chasing him down to seek retribution.

"There's no woman," Rafe said. "This is entirely different."

"Does it have to do with your competing in all those tourneys? Did you kill the wrong opponent?"

"No."

"Is it a mistake of some kind? A misunderstanding or…"

"No, they understood perfectly what I did," Rafe said, with a bitter laugh. "And so did I. But I did it anyway. Which is why I started competing in tourneys in the first place. It pays me and it gives me a reason to keep moving."

"Moving away from Shropshire?" she guessed. "That's why you didn't want to go this way. You're worried you'll meet someone you wish to avoid. Who?"

"It doesn't matter who," he said. "And I won't be interrogated by you. Just because you've seen more of me than most people, it doesn't grant you any special rights to my past." He nudged his horse to advance a few lengths ahead of hers.

Angelet didn't try to catch up. The last thing she wanted was to anger the one person she was traveling with. If Rafe decided she wasn't worth the effort, he could leave her right on the road. Who would ever know?

And in a way, he was right. Angelet and Rafe's new intimacy didn't come with any promises—just the opposite. The reason she accepted his offer was that it came with no hitches. The less she learned about him, the better. For both of them.

After a little while, Rafe looked over his shoulder, in that same gesture he'd done all morning, scanning the road behind them. But this time, he wheeled his horse around, and rode back. Angelet turned too, thinking he'd seen something. But there was no hint of anyone.

"What is it?" she asked.

Rafe looped around and came up to match her pace. "Nothing. But it was stupid of me to ride ahead of you when the danger is behind us." He was once again the soldier, speaking of tactics, keeping all emotion out of his voice. "I won't do it again."

"I won't ask you more about your past," she said, hoping to soothe him. "It's not as if I could alter it, so there's no benefit in my knowing."

Still, she was curious. What could Rafe possibly have done that angered someone enough to chase down and presumably drag him back to…wherever? Granted, Rafe showed a blatant disregard for the state of his soul when it came to certain sins, namely lust. But he also displayed an incredible amount of bravery and intelligence, and he never once hesitated when he needed to protect Angelet or anyone else in their party. And even his sinful side was actually rather chivalrous—he made his offer and then left it to her to accept it. He flirted and teased, but never took advantage of her. To Angelet, he seemed like a perfect knight.

"May I ask just one thing?" she said hesitantly.

"What?"

"The people who might be following you…do you think they'd hurt me?"

Rafe's brow furrowed. Then, "No. I'd expect that they'd only want to get me. And not to kill. They'd take me back to—" He broke off, but his point was made. "You would be safe from them."

"That's good news, yes?"

"Yes." Rafe fell silent for a few minutes. Then he said, "I'm sorry. I should have told you about…that complication."

"You should have," she agreed. "Though I suppose you knew it would have cost you the job. Otto never would have hired you and the others if he knew."

"I was confident that whoever was after me would be deterred by the greater numbers of the escort. Overconfident," he amended.

"Rafe, remember that those men who attacked us did mention taking me. And someone shot at me. So our first guess is still more likely."

He nodded, but didn't add anything.

"I truly didn't mean to anger you," she said. "Please don't leave me."

"Leave you?"

"You could. At the next town, or even here. I know that you'd prefer to be on your own, and now I understand a little better why that is."

Rafe stared at her. "You think I'd *leave* you somewhere? As if you were a sack of onions?"

"Well, you could. It's possible."

"It's impossible. You asked me to take you to your son, and then Anjou. I'll do that unless one of us dies on the way."

"Truly?"

"Yes, Angelet."

"Why?"

"Because that's what I'm supposed to do! That's what a knight *is*."

"Oh." She smiled tremulously. "Then I'm glad I hired you to be my knight."

He stared at her for a moment more, then laughed. "I hope so."

They rode on, having restored their alliance.

But their luck with the weather did not hold. A cold wind from the west started to blow in the early afternoon, bringing heavy, blue-grey clouds along. Rafe kept a wary eye on the western horizon, and judged their few periods of rest very carefully. He was too well-trained a soldier to ride their horses to exhaustion, but they also needed to reach some shelter before the rain came.

However, the road was taking them through a particularly desolate patch of countryside. They saw no farms or homes, and the nearest village could be around the next curve in the road…or hours away.

Angelet kept quiet for the most part. Rafe was obviously on edge, and she could offer nothing to help them on the journey. The clouds grew darker and seemed to undulate, as if a huge wind stirred them from above.

When a few fat drops of rain spattered on the ground, Rafe cursed under his breath. Angelet winced when the rain hit her face, pulling her cloak more tightly around her.

"Rafe? What should we do?" she asked.

He looked at the horses, patting the neck of Philon. "We're going to hurry," he announced. "Match my pace. If we find a town before the horses tire, then good. If not, it won't matter what shape the horses are in."

Within moments, they were moving at a steady gallop. Angelet kept pace with Rafe. The horses began to kick up mud as the road grew wetter. They raced past trees and meadows and more trees, the rain always chasing them.

But the horses, however fast, could not outrun a storm, and soon the rain pelted down more fiercely.

After they'd covered perhaps two miles, Rafe called out for her to bring her horse to a halt. He did the same. The beasts slowed to a walk, panting heavily.

Angelet sighed. There was still no sign of civilization. And the rain still came down.

"What now?" she asked.

Rafe shook his head in frustration. "I don't know. I'm afraid to press the horses when—" He stopped talking, and tilted his head up. The rain fell onto his face and his closed eyes. But then he smiled.

"What is it?" she asked.

"Can you smell that?"

She smelled only rain and wet earth.

"Smoke," he said. "There's some shelter along this road and it can't be that far. Come on. I think we'll be out of the rain soon."

The time couldn't come soon enough for Angelet. The rain never let up. By the time they reached the source of the smoke, which turned out to be a little town, Angelet was sopping wet and miserable. Rafe took one look at her and abruptly told her he'd take care of everything.

Indeed, within a quarter hour, she found herself in a small, warm, dry room with—praise Mary—a crackling fire. Rafe lost no time in stripping her of her wet clothes, then wrapping her up in a thick wool blanket from the bed. He sat her directly in front of the fire.

"Better?" he asked.

"Lord, yes. This is heaven."

"The place looks a little humble for heaven," Rafe said, bending over to kiss her. She was already warming up from the heat of the flames, and Rafe's mouth was cool. His stubble scratched her.

"You need to shave," she noted.

"Is that an order?"

"It wasn't meant to be."

Rafe stood up. "Listen, I've got to take care of a few things, but I'll be back shortly. Stay there and warm up."

He left the room, and only after the door closed did Angelet realize that he was still in his dripping wet clothes. He must be freezing.

She leaned closer to the fire, letting the warmth soak into her bones. How bizarre that she was here, in a town whose name she didn't even know. She should be at Basingwerke by now, handing off a chest of gold and an embroidered cloth in order to beg the abbey's physicians to heal her.

Angelet hadn't thought of her affliction much over the past several days, even though it was the whole reason she started on the journey. True, she'd been rather distracted, and she had so much more to think of. At Dryton, she'd spend most of her days confined in a room, worrying about when the next vision would come and how much the aftermath would hurt. Now she thought about the road, and the weather, and who was trying to catch her, and who was trying to catch Rafe, and why Rafe wouldn't tell her about his past, and why she wanted to know about his past in the first place.

But before she could fall too deeply into her thoughts, the door opened again. A maid entered, with a big clay pitcher of water. She was about twelve years old and wore her long dark hair in plaits. She put it carefully on the floor, then curtseyed awkwardly and gave a beaming smile to Angelet. "Welcome, m'lady. You can call for me if you need anything. I'm Martha."

"I thank you, Martha," Angelet said gravely, aware that she didn't look a thing like a lady, huddling under a blanket while she sat on the floor.

But Martha acted as if she saw nothing odd about it. The maid gave a quick, very practiced look around the room, assessing the supply of firewood, the blankets, and the cleanliness of the room. Nodding in satisfaction, she turned on her heel and scooted out of the room.

A moment later, Rafe came in, carrying his sword and daggers, all in their sheaths.

"What did you have to do?" she asked.

"Rain isn't good for armor or weapons. I had to dry them all off and re-oil the metal. One of the stable boys is getting an extra coin tonight. He sleeps in the loft above the stalls, and he'll see that no one steals the armor from where he's keeping it." The weapons were clearly another matter. Rafe wouldn't part with them for anything. He put the weapons down near one side of the bed, then moved to the wash bowl.

"What are you doing?" she asked, watching avidly as he stripped off his shirt.

Rafe held up a razor. "Shaving."

Angelet stood up, wearing the blanket like a cloak. "You're doing that for me?"

"Self interest," he said. "I'll get more kisses if my skin doesn't scratch like sand."

"Isn't it curious how your self-interest always benefits me as well?" she asked, walking over to the bed, choosing the side opposite all the weapons. She didn't want to trip over those things in the night. She sat and watched him as he shaved.

After he'd taken care of that, he peeled off the rest of his clothing and hung everything up to dry. Then he crawled into the bed, reaching for her with a smile. "What's your first order, my lady?"

Angelet looked away, feeling shy. "That's not a game we have to play. You were kind to indulge me once, but I never expected you to remain…subservient."

He took one of her hands and kissed the palm. "I liked it."

She sighed at the kiss, and he caught her shoulder in his other hand, lowering her back onto the bed.

"Why does it appeal to you?" she asked.

"Normally, it wouldn't," Rafe said. "Not at all. I offered myself that way because I didn't think you'd accept any other way."

"I wouldn't have," she said.

"Lucky for me, then. But the truth, Angelet, is that I'll want you any way you care to have me. I'll order, I'll obey. I'll be gentle, I'll be rough. Whatever you like…just tell me."

"Rafe, I hardly know what I like."

"Then use me to find out."

"For the time we're together? Then what do I do with my newfound knowledge?" She didn't mean to get contemplative, and Rafe must have heard the unwanted sadness in her voice.

"The only thing I know, Angelet, is that the future is hidden. There's no point at all in worrying about what will happen. Just live for now. Tonight."

She reacted by clutching at him with both hands, pulling him down to her.

"You're right," she whispered, her voice now husky with need. "Tonight we're together. So my first order is for you to kiss my breasts. Show no favoritism. Lavish both with attention."

He looked pleased with her request. "Yes, my lady."

* * * *

The next morning dawned grey and misty. Rafe took one look outside and declared that the horses needed another day of rest. "And so do you," he added, with a wink.

"As you think best," she replied, imitating the tone of her mother-in-law, Lady Katherine. She'd heard the woman say that so many times to Otto, and all it meant was that Katherine knew Otto would do whatever he wanted, whether it was best or not.

Rafe, though, gave her a skeptical look. "Don't start trusting me, my lady."

They spent the day quietly, using the morning to discuss a more detailed plan to get Henry safely back with Angelet from where he was living in his foster family's home. After that, Rafe checked on his armor and horses. He talked with the innkeeper and a few guests in the common room, inquiring about the roads to the south and west, and any news from London.

Angelet spent a large part of the day in their room,

partly because Rafe worried her distinctive appearance would be noticeable in the day, unlike the night before, when the driving rain had observers scarce.

They spent the evening together again, and Angelet discovered a few more things she liked, especially when Rafe was the one to teach her about them. He confessed that his past contained more scandalous incidents than the one he wouldn't talk about.

"And some of those encounters taught me a lot," he explained with mock seriousness. "And now I can pass that knowledge on to you, my lady. Or a sliver of it, anyway. I know too much to teach you everything in the short time we've got."

She laughed. "Rafe. I order you to shut up."

He obeyed, but as it turned out, he could still do many things without talking.

* * * *

The next morning dawned soft and warm, leaving no opportunity to linger. They rode at a slower pace that day, a choice that turned out to be fateful. But all through the morning, Angelet's spirits were high, and she looked out on the world with a renewed sense of hope.

After the cold and wind and rain, this was another true spring day, with a sky the color of a robin's egg, marked only by streaks of thin, high clouds. Birds darted madly through the air, twittering and singing as if they'd only just discovered how to do it. They argued fiercely over branches and trees, all of which were now bursting into leaf, looking like a veil of green cast over the whole forest.

She smiled at Rafe whenever their eyes met, which

was often. The path was clear and relatively straight, so he could relax, riding easily in his saddle.

Angelet watched him as they rode, noting things about him she'd missed at first. There was something essentially sad about Rafe. Even when he was acting at his most carefree, there was a tightness around his eyes, as if he could not forget something unhappy. She was certain the mysterious event in his past was to blame, but she was also certain he'd never speak of it to her, not ever, and so there was nothing she could do to relieve his sorrow.

They stopped to rest beside a stream running near the road, about fifty paces from the track itself. Angelet retrieved bread and cheese from the packs. She grabbed the wineskin for Rafe, but as it turned out, both of them preferred the water from the stream. Angelet dipped her hand into the cold, clear water over and over. "The rain must have filled all the streams with fresh water. This tastes better than anything I've drunk for years," she commented.

Rafe murmured agreement, but he seemed distracted. He looked around, his bearing casual. But Angelet knew him well enough now to see that he was wary.

"What is it?" she asked quietly, not moving from her place at the side of the stream.

He didn't answer for a moment, but then visibly relaxed, looking over at her. "Nothing. I thought I heard something out of place. I must be imagining it."

"What did you hear?"

"Hooves."

She stood slowly, hoping to catch a hint of the sound Rafe mentioned. She heard only birdsong and the breeze.

"It's nothing," he said again. "I tend to always be searching for signs…even when they're not there."

She accepted his answer, but started to grow uneasy.

They rode on, but an hour later, just after they rounded a bend in the road, he took hold of her horse's reins and drew her aside, off the path.

"What is it?" she whispered after he helped her dismount.

"Hush." Rafe's expression was stone. He was alert, watchful.

Angelet kept as quiet as she could.

He waited, listening for something she couldn't hear.

Finally, he put one finger to her mouth.

"Stay here," he breathed, his lips at her ear. "Don't move. Don't say a word. I have to move, but I'll come back. I won't let anything happen to you."

Angelet was taut with fear, but she nodded once. She would keep silent and still while he flushed out their pursuer.

He stepped away and seemed to somehow vanish into the trees. How could a man like Rafe, who commanded attention, suddenly become invisible?

She remained where she was, her breathing shallow and unsteady. She tried to be calm, but how could she? Someone was stalking them, and Rafe was God knows where in the woods, and she was standing there like a simpleton, unarmed and unable to fight back.

I won't let anything happen to you.

She repeated those words in her head, as true a prayer as anything she said in church. But what if something happened to Rafe? What would she do then?

Chapter 19

RAFE LEFT ANGELET, SILENTLY SWEARING that if anything happened to her, he'd shred her assailant to pieces.

He knew someone was following them. He'd suspected it all day. Losing a full day of travel had been stupid. They could have pressed on through the mist, but he chose to stay in the warmth of the inn, lured by the desire to have Angelet to himself for another night, especially when he wasn't drawn out from a full day of travel.

Well, he'd got his night. And now he was paying for it.

Rafe continued to circle around to the road, listening intently for the slight sound of a horse's hooves. He caught a shuffling, and loosed his dagger from its sheath. The close cover of the trees made his sword less appealing just now. But his dagger never failed him.

The shuffling came again, along with a low mutter. The pursuer, whoever he was, realized Rafe and Angelet had stopped. Fortunately, he didn't seem to know that he'd been detected. Or that Rafe was so close.

Twenty paces, ten paces. Rafe could move silently

when he wanted to, a talent that often surprised people who only saw his swagger.

It would definitely surprise the short, hooded man who was now five paces away, facing the other direction. He gripped a dagger in his right hand.

Rafe lunged, knocked the dagger from the man's grasp with a well-aimed strike, and then used his left hand to seize the shorter man by the shoulder and swing him around.

"At last I got you," Rafe spat.

"Got me?" a voice squeaked.

Rafe's eyes widened. "What the hell?"

The person following him was hardly more than a boy.

The kid took a huge breath, then without warning, flung himself at Rafe, attacking with wild blows.

To fight him at his full strength would be murder, so Rafe simply parried the boy's untutored attacks until he saw an opening. Then he used one leg to sweep under the boy's feet, upsetting his balance, and then delivered a quick punch to the left temple.

The force of the blow—restrained compared to Rafe's usual strength—sent the boy staggering backward a few steps. Then he fell heavily on his bottom. He groaned, clutching his head, capped with what could best be described as an explosion of orange curls.

Rafe sheathed his dagger. "Why are you following us?"

The boy maintained a sullen silence.

Rafe knelt and grabbed the back of the boy's mantle, scruffing him like a kitten. "Speak. Are you a scout? Were you bringing back information on me, or the lady I'm traveling with?" he demanded.

"No!" the boy burst out, horror coming over his features. "I don't know a thing about a lady."

"Then why follow her?"

"I was following *you*!" the boy cried.

Rafe let him go, and leaned back on his heels, keeping level with the boy, who was still sitting in the dirt. "Tell me. Did Alric of Hawksmere send you?"

The boy looked confused. "Who?"

"Or perhaps he now calls himself Alric of Cleobury," Rafe went on, though for the life of him, he couldn't imagine Alric using a child as an agent.

"I don't know any man of that name," the boy swore. "I'm on my own business."

"Business? What business could you have with me?" Rafe asked.

"A fight!"

He laughed out loud. "A fight?"

"Don't you mock me! I want to fight you!" the boy said. "That's what you do, isn't it?"

"If you saw me fight, boy, what possessed you to attack me just now? You didn't honestly think you'd win?"

The boy sounded miserable as he spoke. "I thought that you'd be vulnerable if I could sneak up and strike from behind…"

"Thieves strike from behind, boy. Are you a thief?"

"No!" The boy looked up, his glare suddenly hot with emotion. "But you are!"

Rafe was truly confused now. "I'm no thief, boy."

"You stole my brother's life."

Brutal as the accusation was, Rafe relaxed, thinking he now knew what ate at the boy. He said, more calmly, "Child, I've killed many men on the battlefield, true. But they were soldiers, just as I am."

"Don't call me a child. He wasn't a soldier. You didn't

kill him face to face."

"Explain yourself."

"There was a tournament in Ashthorpe. You won. My brother was watching, and he begged you for a coin. Everyone heard that the Knight of the Raven is generous," the boy explained, sounding distinctly unimpressed.

"So I gave him a coin and you're accusing me of his death? How?"

"You gave him a few silver coins—so bright, almost white. He showed them to me, and I never saw anything so fine. But I wasn't the only person he showed. Some others who came to watch the tournament had more in mind. They enticed him to play at dice with them. My brother was so dazzled by the silver that he wanted to add more to his stock. He followed them to where they said they were gambling. But as soon as the group was out of sight of anyone in town, the others turned on him. They attacked him and stole the coins."

Rafe still wasn't sure how that made him responsible for anything. "Then what?"

"One had a knife, and used it," the boy explained. "My brother was stabbed in the belly for the sake of his new fortune. He managed to crawl to a street, and someone recognized him. I was sent for, and I ran to him. There was no hope. He told me what happened as he lay dying. He begged God for mercy, and none came. He died in front of a tavern, with only me to hear his last words."

"Sorry I am for your loss, but I was not his killer," Rafe said.

"No? *You* gave him the coins. He thought the angels had smiled on him at last. But you're no angel. If you hadn't given him charity, he'd still be alive. I swore I'd find you and take vengeance."

"You're young for vengeance, boy. How will your death help your brother now?"

"At least I'll join him. We'll be in a world where a few silver coins mean nothing. Kill me."

"No," Rafe said.

"Kill me! Or give me coins in charity, so I might die the same way my brother did! I've followed you this far. You owe me that."

"I owe you nothing." Though if the boy followed him all the way from Ashthorpe, he deserved something for his trouble. That required dedication and sheer grit.

"You took my only living family from me with your showy charity. Others might be fooled, but I'm not. You're a fraud. A murderer who pretends to be a pious saint."

Those words hit Rafe hard, in a way the previous accusations did not. "I'm not a murderer."

"But you're no saint, either. You curse everything you touch. A gift turns into a death sentence. I'll tell the world about the Knight of the Raven!"

"Tell the world," Rafe said, shaking his head. "I care not."

"You do! Why else do you act as you do, offering all your winnings to the church and to the poor?"

"Because I do not need them."

"Then why fight for such prizes in the first place?"

"Fighting is what I do."

"Then fight me! Damn you, fight me!" the boy hissed, once again pushing at Rafe.

"Stop it! There will be no fighting!"

Rafe looked up to see that Angelet had found them. He'd been so intent on the boy's story that he hadn't even noticed her approach.

"You should have waited for me to tell you it was safe, my lady," Rafe said gruffly. He wondered just how much of the conversation she had overheard.

"I decided it was safe enough." She stepped up to them both and put her hands out. The boy stared at her in wonder.

"What's your name?" she asked the boy as she helped him up. It occurred to Rafe that he hadn't thought to ask the same simple question.

"Goswin, my lady," he said, offering a clumsy bow as soon as he was on his feet.

"Goswin, you must not fight Sir Rafe. You wouldn't win, and to go in hoping for death is no better than suicide. Would your brother have wanted for you to die like this?"

"I've got nothing left, my lady," Goswin protested. "Nothing."

"You have your life, do you not? Come with us, at least as far as the next town."

"*With* us?" Rafe said. "How do we know he won't stab me in my sleep?"

"Because Goswin will not break a promise to me," Angelet said.

"He's made no promise."

She asked the boy, "Goswin, will you promise me that you will not hurt or kill Sir Rafe?"

"Or Lady Angelet," Rafe added.

The boy looked between them, torn, then looked back at Angelet and whispered, "Yes, my lady."

"Excellent." She smiled at Goswin. "And I promise to protect you while we travel together. You know, you're not much older than my son."

Goswin was startled, casting looks between Rafe and

Angelet. "You've got children?" he asked.

Rafe was about to correct the boy's misapprehension that Rafe and Angelet were married. But then he caught Angelet's quick shake of the head. She put a hand out to touch Goswin's arm, and captured the boy's attention again.

"Henry is just ten years old now, and we're going to fetch him from his foster family. I wish you could meet him. But you can't do that if you die in some foolish duel of honor. Understand?"

The boy nodded, his big eyes locked on Angelet's face. Rafe guessed that he'd agree to practically anything she asked by this point.

She looked about. "Surely you didn't run after us?"

"I hid my pony in the woods," he said, pointing to the left side of the road.

"Then retrieve him and let's get moving again. We have a long way to go."

"Where are you going?"

"We'll discuss that on the way," Rafe said, still not trusting the boy.

While Goswin left to fetch his hidden horse, Angelet said to Rafe, "It's all right if we keep him close, isn't it? Better to know where he is."

That was true. Rafe said, "He can come along for a while. I certainly don't want him wandering around, telling anyone who asks that he's seen us."

Angelet smiled, pleased at his agreement.

They continued on, now with the addition of Goswin. Angelet, fortunately, seemed to have a knack for handling the boy. She suggested he ride ahead a little in order to scout out any potential dangers. "Would you do that for me?" she asked.

Of course the boy would. He was already urging his horse faster before Angelet got the whole request out.

"Stay in sight!" she called out after him.

"Why did you do that?" Rafe asked.

"Children like to be given responsibility…and that boy needs to feel useful, considering his bold quest for vengeance just got thwarted."

"You've gained yourself a disciple," Rafe said. "Goswin looks at you as if you're the sun."

She smiled sadly. "He's lonely. He lost the family he had left, and now he clings to the first kindness someone offers. He'll heal in time. Children are very hardy. They can endure so much more than we think."

Rafe wondered if she was speaking of her own childhood, so abruptly ended with an early marriage and motherhood.

"You let him think we're married," he said next.

"It seemed simpler," she replied. "He has enough on his mind. If ever we need to explain the true situation to him, we can. But why complicate things further?"

Why indeed, especially because the current misunderstanding meant that Goswin wouldn't raise any questions about Rafe staying with Angelet every night. Which he definitely intended to do.

Assuming that she still wanted Rafe near her. Depending on how much she overheard, she might want to keep him at arm's length.

"About what he said…" Rafe began.

"Don't let it concern you," said Angelet. "He was devastated by the loss of his brother, and he looked for someone to blame."

"I was to blame." Rafe had given the young man some money, and the young man was promptly killed for those same coins. Even when Rafe tried to do good, it ended badly.

"You were not! It's just like the attack on the cortège. The only ones to blame were those who snuck up on unsuspecting people with the intent to murder them. It's not as if you've ever tried to kill a man for the purpose of taking what was his!"

Rafe winced. Angelet's blithe reassurance did nothing for him, because it hovered too close to the truth. If she ever found out what he did, all her confidence in him would evaporate.

"It doesn't matter. Goswin will think what he likes," Rafe muttered.

"He'll come around once he gets to know you," she said. "You'll be a good example for him."

"What a terrible idea." Rafe was a good example for no one.

"Oh, I just had another idea. Goswin should be your page."

"What?"

"You need one," she insisted. "You do the work of a page in addition to your own, and there's no reason for it. Why else do you have to pay stable boys to watch over your armor and such? Teach Goswin what he needs to know."

Rafe sighed. "This is an order, isn't it?"

"It's a gentle recommendation," said Angelet, with the pleased smile of a person who has just won an argument.

"All right, I'll teach him what a page does, though he's only going to be around until I can find a safe place to drop him off. But no more arranging people's lives, my lady. We've got enough to worry about."

She nodded, satisfied. Rafe almost laughed out loud in

spite of himself. For someone who was never in a position of power, Angelet showed a natural aptitude for it. She had a dignity and grace that attracted attention, and she knew just how to wield her influence.

If only he was the sort of man Angelet thought he was. Rafe would disappoint her in the end, and he wasn't looking forward to that. In fact, he wasn't looking forward to the day he'd have to leave her. But it would come soon enough, and if he was lucky, it would happen before she knew the facts of his true nature.

As they traveled onward, Rafe realized he had another, more practical problem. Somehow, though he'd been aiming to go directly south, they'd been forced somewhat to the southwest, and now they weren't just skirting the edge of Shropshire…they were well inside the northern borders of the shire. Exactly what he didn't want. It was as if his inner demons drew him along all the roads he meant to avoid.

Still, if they traveled quickly and kept to themselves, it was a manageable problem. Perhaps Goswin could even be useful here.

They came to another village in the late afternoon, called Dunfield. Rafe knew the name, though it was far enough from Cleobury that he had never come this way, and no one would know him by sight. He hoped.

Once they rode into the courtyard of the large inn, Rafe quickly made arrangements for a night's room and board. Then he returned to where Angelet and Goswin waited. The two were deep in conversation, and a casual observer would mistake them for mother and son.

"Goswin," he called. "Come here."

"What do you want?" The boy sounded sullen, but he walked over.

"Listen, after you get your supper, you're to sleep in the stables. There's a loft for the inn's stable boys, with extra pallets for the pages of guests. I've paid for it already—don't let any of the boys try to make more coin off you."

"Aye."

"You're to feed and water the horses, and keep watch. Get the horses ready early. I want to leave here at first light."

"Anything else?"

Rafe rubbed at his jaw. "If you see anyone near our horses, or asking after us, or if anyone just gives you a bad feeling, come find me."

"I'm not the only one who was following you?"

"Evidently not. And at least one person has shot at Lady Angelet, so I'd rather not run into them again."

Goswin's eyes narrowed. "I'll watch," he vowed.

They ate, then Angelet went upstairs to the guest room while Rafe went out to the stables to see that Goswin knew what he was doing. When Rafe returned to the room, he stopped short in the doorway.

Laid carefully across the bed was a length of cloth, so dense with color and pattern that it was like looking through a window at a real scene. Except this scene was not anything he'd ever seen before.

"What is this?" he asked, approaching it.

Angelet, who'd been folding some clothing in the corner, said, "It's the altar cloth I embroidered for Basingwerke Abbey. I had it packed in my own bag, and just remembered it. Do you think I could sell it for passage for a few people across the channel, and your horse as well?"

"You could sell it for a small ship of your own," Rafe said. He'd been in many churches over his life, but he couldn't recall seeing something as detailed and as rich as this art. He knew nothing about needlework, but he did know that this was unique in design.

A city in ivory and gold stood at the center, surrounded by fields of spectacularly intricate flowers and green plants. The whole thing seemed to invite him to walk directly into it, to walk up to the gates of this magnificent city.

"Where is this place?"

"Nowhere. Not in the world, that is. I saw this in one of my visions. It was so clear that for months afterward, I could close my eyes and remember the exact scene. I tried to imitate it as closely as I could, but it's still not what I saw."

"This is amazing."

She gave a little shrug of her shoulder. "It's cloth and thread. Nothing more."

"It's your vision."

"I'd happily forgo all future visions if it meant I wouldn't suffer the aftermath. You saw what it did to me at Dryton. And that one wasn't nearly as powerful as some previous experiences. I fear I'm not made to be a vessel for divine revelation. It will break me at some point."

Rafe looked over at her, concerned. "Is it getting worse?"

"I don't know," she said, though the possibility obviously scared her. "Both the visions and the pain afterward varies. And I never know when one will strike. The promise was that at Basingwerke, I might be healed."

Rafe looked back to the cloth. If he ran an institution like an abbey, he'd promise nearly anything to gain such a skilled artist, especially one who couldn't leave.

He ran his hand along the edge of the cloth. "How long did it take you to do this?"

"Mmmm, a few months, all told. I had a lot of time on my hands at Dryton. Just imagine what I had to look forward to if I'd made it to Basingwerke." She shook her head. "What a legacy. *Here lies Sister Angelet. She could embroider with rare skill.* How inane."

Rafe got a sudden inspiration. "If you desired a new skill, I could teach you to fight."

She laughed. "Impossible."

"Why? What's a dagger or sword but a piece of thin metal with a point at the end? If you know how to wield a needle, you could learn to wield a sword." He smiled, thinking of the image.

"I don't attack the cloth as if it were my enemy."

Rafe grew serious. "No, but you do have some enemies. Even today, when I had to leave you alone for a few minutes, wouldn't you have felt better if you knew how to defend yourself, at least?"

"It would take far too long to teach me." Angelet's expression had grown speculative, though. She was interested in the idea.

"To master any skill takes a long time," Rafe agreed. "But there are a few tricks that anyone can learn. With knowledge and a bit of practice, you could surprise someone."

Her eyes narrowed. "Are we still discussing swordplay?"

Now he laughed. "It wasn't meant to be an innuendo. Though now that you mention it…" He leaned over to taste her lips. "You have surprised me."

She kissed him back, but then said, "Could you teach me to defend myself? I have a dagger, but I've never used it for anything but slicing meat."

"I'll teach you, starting tonight. Now."

Chapter 20

HEARING RAFE'S WORDS, ANGELET GOT a little nervous. "Right now? In this room?"

"Why not? When Dobson tried to attack you, it was in a room this size. There's more than enough space to learn how to use a dagger."

She quickly folded the altar cloth back up, then retrieved her dagger from her pack. She'd used it at supper, though it was also her only weapon.

Rafe took one look and told her to put it back. "Your little knife will serve you perfectly well at table, but for this, think seriously."

The dagger he handed to her was longer than her own, about a foot in length, but not much wider. It rested in a scabbard of boiled black leather, shiny with wear.

"But this is yours," she said.

"It's a purely supplemental weapon for me. You need it more than I do at the moment."

She withdrew the blade, and it gleamed silvery in the dull light of the room. The hilt was also metal, but wrapped in soft leather so it was easy to grip. The crosspiece was minimal, barely extending past her curved fingers. It was a beautiful weapon, and the point was deadly sharp.

Rafe said, "It's intended to pierce through your opponent, whether that means clothes or flesh. So you need to point it at them and thrust forward, not swing and slash sideways. Understand?"

She held the dagger out and made an experimental lunge toward the closed door, pretending someone stood there. "Yes, I think so."

"You *can* use the side of the dagger blade to block a blade coming at you," he said, "but that takes practice, and perhaps more arm strength than you have. So let's concentrate on the dagger's use as an attack."

Rafe moved next to her and squared her shoulders with his hands. Despite how close he was, Angelet sensed that he was now totally focused on teaching her to fight.

"You can draw it and hide the blade in the folds of your skirt, like this." He put his hand on hers and pulled it down to her thigh, where she held the blade, tip pointing at the floor. He stepped around to the other side and squinted. "Good. I can barely see it. So if you're nervous, you can draw a bit early and hold it there."

"But eventually I'll need to use it."

"Very true." He held his dagger out now. "Let's say someone threatens you like this." He approached quickly, swinging the blade up to hover in front of her chin.

Angelet instinctively took several steps back, and promptly ran into the wall behind her. "Oh, bother."

"It's natural to want to run," he said, dropping his blade and extending a hand to help steady her. "God knows, if running is an option, you should take it. But let's say you are backed against a wall, as you are now. When someone comes at you like so"—he resumed his previous stance—"you need to go on the attack immediately, or it's over. He'll slam you against the wall and you'll have nowhere to go."

That sounded horrible. "So how do I attack?" she asked.

"Like this." He shifted again, moving to stand beside her, showing her how to stand. "See where my feet are, staggered? Do that."

She did her best to imitate his moves.

"Good," said Rafe. "Now, move forward with your shoulder leading…good…and lunge with your arm out… straighten your elbow! You're not offering someone a drink, you're defending your life. Very good."

After performing the same series of steps he'd done, Angelet gripped the hilt of her dagger tightly. "It's not very good if I'm only fighting an imaginary foe."

"You're going to fight me." Rafe moved once again, blocking her path to the door. He raised his dagger. "Try to get past me."

"Are you sure of this?" she asked. "What if I make a mistake and hurt you?"

"If you hurt me, darling, it's proof I never should have been knighted in the first place. But I'll risk it. Now stop dallying and try to get past me."

She took a deep breath, then lunged at him, just as he first instructed.

A second later, her dagger clattered to the floor and she was caught in his arms, her back pressed against his chest. She gasped. She couldn't even wriggle out of his embrace.

"Do you understand what happened?" he asked.

"No! What did you do? What did I do wrong?"

"You hesitated," Rafe explained. "I suspect that you didn't want to perforate my liver, which is extremely flattering, but not helpful. You need to think of me as an enemy." He released her and stooped to pick up the dagger, handing it to her. "Now, step back and we'll try it again. As soon as I say, you need to move fast. Don't think about me at all, don't worry about my health. Just go."

"All right." Angelet closed her eyes, trying to picture an enemy in front of her, instead of Rafe himself. She envisioned Dobson. "I'm ready," she said, opening her eyes.

"Go."

This time she kept the image of Dobson in her mind, and tried to go faster. She lunged forward with her arm held straight. A second later, Rafe grabbed her arm in a defensive move, keeping her from attacking again.

"Well done," he said.

"But I didn't do..." She then saw that she *had* done something. Her dagger pierced his cloth tunic, leaving a ragged hole.

"Oh, sweet mercy," she gasped, putting her free hand to her mouth.

Rafe grinned at her. "That was perfect."

"I nearly stabbed you!"

"Yes. That was your objective."

"But...your clothing! I'll mend it," she added. "I can, you know."

"I have every confidence in you," Rafe said. "But don't try to change the subject. We're not done yet."

"Surely you don't want me to come at you again?"

"You did it once, very well. But you need to practice. You need to be confident and know how to move without stopping to think about it. Now try again."

She did. Time after time she lunged toward Rafe, and time after time she got a little better at the move. Granted, Rafe was far, far more experienced than she was, so his reflexes and training meant he was in no actual danger, despite the fact that she had assaulted his tunic once. He admitted he didn't expect her to be so accurate so quickly, and thus had been a little slack. She never managed to strike him again.

On the most recent attempt, Rafe stopped her in mid-stride to show her that she was instinctively shying away from a direct attack.

"Keep your shoulder up, and don't veer away. That leaves you less able to defend yourself. Remember how your body moves. Remember this pose. That's what you need to be able to do almost without thinking. Try again."

She did.

He caught her arm and swung her close to his body, effectively entrapping her. "Very good, but never lose your balance. You leaned too far forward and I was able to take advantage of that. Understand?"

"You keep saying very good," she said, "but you keep winning."

"Darling, I've made this my profession for years. You started tonight. What else do you expect?"

"I hoped I'd be a better student."

"You're an excellent student," he said. "Never doubt it."

At that moment, there was a knock at the door. Angelet dropped her hand, concealing the dagger in the folds of her skirt, just as Rafe instructed.

Meanwhile, Rafe stepped around her to answer the door, his dagger now sheathed but close to hand.

He found the innkeeper standing there.

"What's going on?" the alarmed innkeeper asked. "I heard stomping around as if there was some sort of fight!"

"Oh, please forgive the noise," Angelet said quickly. "He was just teaching me a lesson."

The innkeeper's eyes flicked over to Rafe, and he gave a single, curt nod. "I see. Well, it's wise to keep a woman in line. Just don't be all night about it. It might keep the other guests awake."

"Apologies," Rafe said, offering a small coin, which undoubtedly helped soothe the innkeeper's nerves.

After the innkeeper left, Angelet wrinkled her nose. "Wise to keep a woman in line? Ugh. Just as well I didn't try to explain what was really going on."

"He wouldn't have believed you if you did," said Rafe.

"Nor cared if you *were* hurting me." She sighed and put the dagger she'd been gripping onto the little table. "I suppose that concludes the lesson."

"For now. I'll teach you more when there's opportunity."

"You don't mind?"

He shrugged. "It's a dangerous world. Why shouldn't you have a chance to even the field? After all, I won't be around to protect you much longer."

"What can you really teach me in a few weeks?" she asked, not looking at him.

She gasped when she was suddenly swept off her feet and pushed against the wall, exactly where her lesson had begun.

Rafe stood directly in front of her, keeping her in place. "I could teach you not to turn your back on an armed man."

"That's not fair, Rafe! We weren't fighting anymore!"

"You should always be ready, Angelet. And alert."

She looked up into his eyes. "If I'm ever in this position again, with a stranger, I will be alert. I promise. But this time didn't count!"

"Why the hell not?"

"Because I trust you!"

"You shouldn't." Rafe looked her over, in a way that made her breath catch. "I could do whatever I wanted with you right now."

"What would that look like?" she asked, heat building in her core.

He held her to the wall with just one hand laid against her shoulder, emphasizing exactly how much stronger he was than Angelet. "I'll show you," he said, his voice low and deliciously promising—and a little frightening.

"What if I don't care to be shown?" she whispered.

Rafe laid a kiss on her neck, one that left her wanting another and another. "Angelet, the choice is yours. If you want to give the orders, I'll obey. Always."

"But you want something else."

"I think you need something else tonight. And I can show you what."

She inhaled. Looked him in the eye.

"Show me."

He bent down to kiss her full on the mouth, seeking her tongue. It was a rough, demanding, possessive kiss, and she didn't want it to end.

But he did end it, with a ragged breath. Then he grabbed her skirts and gathered them up around her waist, revealing her bare legs.

His hands lifted her higher against the wall, then using his own body to hold her in place, one leg between her own. She gasped when he pressed that leg against her, rubbing exactly where she'd feel it most.

"Rafe," she gasped. "What are you doing?"

"What I want. And you want it too."

He slid one finger inside her, then said, "Damn me, you're wet already."

She gasped again as he stroked her.

"Say yes if you like it," he hissed.

"Yes," she echoed faintly.

"And again. Every time. Every touch. I need to know you want it."

His voice urged her on, in time with his devastating touch.

"Yes," she moaned. "Yes. Yes. Yes."

Then it happened, a flash of lightning she couldn't see, only feel as it lit up inside her. She pressed herself against him, grinding her body against his hand. She gasped as she felt a wave of heat roll through her. "Oh, yes, please."

He held her fast for a long moment, and she pulsed against his hand, desiring him even more than before. He teased her with a few more slow strokes, each of which made her whimper his name.

She clung to him, her arms wrapped around his shoulders. She felt so…smooth, as if all the sharp edges of her existence had been pushed away, replaced with silk.

Angelet laid her head on his shoulder, sighing contentedly.

Then Rafe swung her into his arms and carried her over to the bed. He pulled her gown and shift over her head in a quick movement, leaving her naked. He lowered her back on the covers, her legs hanging over the edge of the bed.

He remained standing, watching her. Then he stripped

off his own clothes and stepped to the edge of the bed, pushing her legs apart so he stood between them.

She reached for his erection, and circled her fingers around it. Rafe's intake of breath was all the motivation she needed. She pulled him closer, but he resisted, even pulling her hand away, though he'd obviously liked her touch. He was far, far stronger than she was, and there was nothing she could do to force him to obey. Except beg.

"Please," she whispered. "I still need you. You were right before. I need something different. Whatever you want to do."

"Whatever I want," he echoed.

With no restrictions, Rafe's hands roamed freely, cupping her breasts, grazing her hips, stroking her legs. Angelet loved every touch, and loved that he wanted to touch her like this. Perhaps it wasn't always a loss to let a man do what he liked. It just depended on the man.

"Rafe, please," she said again, aware of how desperate she sounded.

His eyes raked over her and he smiled. His hands found her hips, dragged her to exactly where he wanted her, and then he pushed his hips roughly against her, parting her legs further. He slid into her without a word, pushing, pushing, pushing until she was moaning his name, her back arching upward. She was still resonating from the climax he'd brought her to with his touch. She could hardly stand the sensation of his body penetrating hers like this. It was too full, too big, too heavy, and far too wonderful.

She didn't know she was clutching at him, her nails digging into his sides. She closed her eyes and simply felt him slide into her, and out, and in again. She wrapped her legs around his waist without being conscious that she did it, and only dimly heard him gasp with pleasure.

She moaned low in her throat. "You feel so good," she said. "I love how it feels to have you inside me."

"That's it, angel. Let yourself go."

Another climax broke over her just as she felt him go rigid. He clasped her hips to him as he found his own release. He now covered her body with his, leaving just enough space to avoid crushing her. She slid her hands up his body, feeling the sweat-slicked flesh. Then she tangled her fingers in his hair, and his face hovered over hers. His eyes reminded her of blue pools, easy to dive into, easier to drown in.

"Angelet," he murmured, sounding very different than his usual self. "Tell me I gave you what you wanted."

"I thought you were showing me what *you* wanted."

"It's the same thing."

"Oh."

"So?" he asked. "Was this what you wanted?"

"For now," she said with a smile.

"Oh, God." He looked astonished, then hungry, and then his old smile returned. "I think I've met my match."

She reached up to kiss him.

"Release me, darling," he said in a low voice. He reached to run one hand along her right leg, still locked around his body, keeping him tight against her.

She untwined her legs from him, and sighed as he withdrew from her. She held her hand out, a wordless entreaty for him to lay beside her. He did, stretching out on his back, closing his eyes. He kept her hand in his for a moment, then let it go.

She watched him for a moment, shamelessly appreciating his body. He was gorgeous, and she didn't want to forget a single detail. If only her visions could be of him.

Angelet giggled inwardly. She would have made a disappointing nun.

She flipped onto her stomach, looking across the floor. The dagger lay within her reach. Idly, she picked it up once more and slid it out of the sheath. She tilted it toward the candlelight, bemused at the play of fire along the blade.

"Are you having any vengeful impulses I should know about?" Rafe asked from where he lay on the bed, watching her. He hadn't fallen asleep as she thought.

She looked back over her shoulder, smiling. "You're safe from me."

"Thank God."

"But I thank you for teaching me." She brandished the dagger, a little too showily, but she was feeling exuberant. "Now I feel as though I'm not quite so helpless on my own."

"Like you were before we met?" he asked, his eyes narrowing.

"Well, yes. I suppose."

"Was it only Ernald? Or were there others?"

She looked away, re-sheathing the dagger. "Very few men around Dryton would have dared assault me, even if they'd found opportunity. I am of noble blood."

"So it was only Ernald you had to fear."

"Why does it matter? Will you challenge him to combat?"

"Say the word and I will. I *am* good at it."

"But you have no grounds. He never actually carried out the threat, not once."

"Making the threat is enough!" Rafe said. "I should just challenge him anyway. I'll doubtless be avenging some woman, if not you specifically."

"You're God's instrument of justice?"

"Entirely possible," he said. "I meet an inordinate number of people who are in need of divine retribution."

"You move in circles filled with the worst sort of people then."

"I'm a fighter by trade. So yes. On the other hand," he added, "I've met good people too. Like you."

"You say that while lying in a bed after we have sinned together."

"We are offering ourselves freely. Not all marriages have that," he added darkly. "I refuse to accept that sharing a night with you is a sin." He kissed her again, slowly.

Desire reawakened in her, and she kissed him back, savoring him in a decidedly sinful way. "We're sharing more than one night," she pointed out, between kisses.

"Mmm. Well, I'm not the person to ask when it comes to questions of proper moral behavior. If you want to know about immorality, though, I'm your man."

She smiled. "Tell me more."

Chapter 21

THEY PRESSED ON THE NEXT day, taking the road heading south, now with a boy in tow. Angelet was delighted to have Goswin with them, even if the circumstances of their meeting had been a little less than ideal. She recognized the boy's frustration with the world, since she'd felt the same thing herself. Even if he only traveled with them for a while, perhaps she could help temper that anger into something more healthy. And it would be good for Goswin to understand that Rafe was a person, not a monster out to destroy his happiness. Goswin was speaking to him, at least. That was a hopeful sign.

Goswin's pony needed to rest more frequently than the other mounts, so Rafe sometimes declared that he and the boy would walk, holding the leads of their horses, while Angelet continued to ride at a leisurely pace. Her own weight hardly inconvenienced the big white horse.

During one of those periods, in the late morning, Angelet overheard Goswin and Rafe talking up ahead.

"She's so beautiful," Goswin was saying. "She looks like one of the fair folk."

"Her family hails from Anjou, not fairyland," Rafe

said, putting a quick end to Goswin's speculations. She understood why—the last thing they needed was for someone to draw a connection between Angelet's affliction and some fairy curse. She also hoped that they'd find a safe place for Goswin long before he might see her have a seizure, which would only frighten him.

In fact, if she regained Henry and reached Anjou, both Rafe and Goswin would leave her life soon after. *It's for the best*, she told herself. Rafe had made it very clear that he intended to be gone the moment his obligation to Angelet was over. If only she could persuade him to stay. She'd already seen that he had the experience to lead others, however much he declared that he didn't feel comfortable as a commander.

Her inner voice slyly pointed out that perhaps her real reason for wanting to keep Rafe near her was not his military skill, but rather the way he occupied her nights. Angelet fought off a rising sense of embarrassment as she recalled their last encounter. Rafe had wakened a part of her that even her late husband couldn't. Maybe if Hubert had lived, their marriage would have grown, and they would have shared the sort of intimacies that she'd experienced with Rafe. But Hubert had been young, and preoccupied, and singularly focused on getting a child—for both his sake and hers.

Lost in her musings, Angelet let out a sigh. Both Rafe and Goswin looked back at her.

"Is something the matter, my lady?" Goswin asked immediately.

Rafe didn't say anything, but gave her a searching look.

"Don't concern yourselves," she said. "I was just thinking."

"About what?" asked Goswin, absently pushing his curly hair off his forehead.

"Nothing important. Merely pondering the future."

The boy looked more interested. "Are you going to seek vengeance?"

"What is your obsession with vengeance?" Rafe said. "Why would she want vengeance?"

"Or retribution," Goswin said. "For what happened to your party before, on the road. I'd want vengeance if I had all my goods stolen and my retinue attacked."

"You know about that?" Angelet asked.

"Course. It's how I was able to find *him*," Goswin explained, glaring at Rafe as though just remembering that he was a mortal enemy. "I was following about an hour or so behind the carriage, when I came across four men on horseback. Evil-looking men, too. They asked if I'd seen a man and a lady riding along the road, he on a black horse, she on a white one. They were looking for you, too."

"So what did you say?"

"I told them yes! I said the couple rode right past me at a breakneck speed, aiming south along the road. The men spurred their mounts and sprang away. Didn't even thank me."

"Well, you did lie to them," Rafe pointed out.

Goswin made a face. "But they didn't know I lied. Anyway, I knew you hadn't actually backtracked, so you must have taken a different turn. I keep traveling, going faster, and came across the broken carriage and cart, and a few dead bodies."

She winced at the picture, remembering how young he still was. "Oh, how horrible for you to have seen that!"

"Not the first death I've seen, my lady," Goswin said

simply. "And it won't be the last. Peaceful or violent, death is everyone's lot."

"What did you do next?" Rafe asked.

"I couldn't do anything for the ones already dead, so I retraced my steps, looking for a path that turned off before the point where I met the four men. When I saw one with fresh tracks, I took it. Kept going, but my pony needed rest, so I moved much slower. I had to sleep in the woods two nights in a row. Then it rained the next day, and I thought I'd lose you for certain."

"Why didn't you give up?" Angelet asked, astounded at the boy's tenacity.

Goswin looked sidelong at Rafe again. "Because I've got nothing to go back to. No one waiting for me. I kept on the roads, kept asking after a man and a woman riding black and white horses. When I met someone who had seen you, I just kept on."

"Goswin, you may have saved my life," Angelet said. "You misdirected those men, who surely would have tried to kill Sir Rafe and hurt or kill me too. We didn't know how we eluded them."

Goswin stood up straighter. "I saved your life?"

"Quite likely. I am so grateful to both of you," she said, pointedly to Rafe.

"Yes," he agreed, with only a slight roll of his eyes. "Goswin seems to have helped…inadvertently."

"I'm more help than *you*," the boy said. "Look! There's a crossroads ahead. I'm going to see." He sprang up onto his pony's back and rode ahead, to where his sharp eyes must have detected a crossing.

After Goswin charged off, Angelet smiled sweetly at Rafe. "Just think. If we hadn't been detained for an extra day by the poor weather, the lad might have lost our trail entirely."

"We should have ridden through the fog," Rafe said. "What was I thinking?"

"I hope you were thinking that we'd have got lost if we rode in that mist," she countered. "For myself, I am glad we stayed at the inn another day and night." She emphasized the last word just a little, and saw Rafe's lips quirk in a half-smile.

"Well, if it pleased you," he said quietly, "then it was worth it."

Rafe mounted up, and they quickened their pace to meet up with Goswin, who was waiting impatiently at the intersection of their road with another.

"Come on," he said. "Which way do we go? East or west?"

Angelet saw what he meant. Though technically a crossroads, it was really a T, since the path to the south quickly petered out from a true road to a mere narrow footpath. A few miles ahead, due south, she saw a dark hill rising from the forest.

She turned to Rafe, expecting him to simply point left or right.

Instead, Rafe was staring at the hill with narrowed eyes. "God damn me."

"Don't swear in front of the boy," Angelet said. "What's the matter? Are we lost?"

"No. I know exactly where we are," he said, exhaling heavily. "That's the problem."

"Why should that be a problem?"

"Because where we are is exactly where I don't want to be." Rafe's voice grew louder as he spoke. He looked around the peaceful scene, as if expecting something terrible to be revealed.

"What's around here?" she asked.

"Nothing," he snapped. "No other roads, no towns, no easy way around those hills unless we go east and then we'll spend days getting back to a proper road south. Damn."

"What's to the west?" Goswin asked. "The path looks well-traveled."

"That's a royal forest, then a few towns, and then Wales. We're not going that way. How did we get here?" he added, to himself. "We came too far west."

"Rafe?" Angelet asked, concerned.

"Just give me a moment," he said in a distracted tone. "I need to think. There may be another road that leads away…"

He turned Philon around in a circle, scanning the forest. "Stay here." Rafe rode for a few hundred yards along the path leading east.

Goswin edged closer to Angelet. "What's he so angry about?"

"I don't know," she said. "He doesn't like this part of the country." She kept her gaze on Rafe, who'd turned about and was riding back to them, with a stormy expression.

Thus, she didn't know why Goswin suddenly shouted in alarm, or why someone hit her hard in the chest, almost knocking her off her horse. She clutched at the reins to keep her place.

"What was that?" she gasped out.

No one answered.

Goswin was screaming, "Over there, over there!" as Rafe rushed past her and rode on to something beyond her.

Angelet turned to look, but didn't see anything more

than the hazy wash of green leaves comprising the edge of the woods by the road. She blinked, trying to clear her eyes. What was the matter with them? Her vision wavered as if she was crying, and why would she be crying?

She took a deep breath, and felt a strange heat all over the front of her body. Then she looked down and saw why. The back half of a crossbow bolt stuck out of her chest. The warmth she'd felt was fresh blood, now soaking through the wool of her gown. "Oh."

She put her hand to the protruding bolt, more in wonder than in fear. *How very, very strange*, she thought, her mind still rather hazy. *This is something Rafe would have an opinion on.*

"Rafe?" she called out. Only a rush of breathy air made it out, and the name was only a whisper.

She tried again. "Rafe?" A little louder that time. What was he up to?

Hoofbeats pounded in her ears. Someone rushed up to her, reining in at the last moment.

"Got him," Rafe said, gripping his sword in his right hand, the blade looking red in the light. "I don't know how the hell he got this close to us, but he's never…"

Rafe stopped talking when he inched forward and got a look at her. His face went white. "You were hit."

She tried to nod, but her head suddenly felt very heavy, and she slumped forward, lost her balance, and fell.

Chapter 22

AS SOON AS RAFE HEARD Goswin yell, he cursed in frustration. The moment he turned his back, something bad happened. He knew it.

The boy was waving his arms frantically, urging Rafe to hurry. Angelet had ridden a few paces to the south, and now faced away from Rafe. She was seemingly unconcerned by Goswin's behavior. That was a little odd in itself. From the moment she saw Goswin, she took to him as if she had been charged with his care. Rafe had chalked it up to her missing her own child and wanting to help another in his place. But now she didn't even look over at Goswin.

Rafe spurred his horse and covered the distance in no time.

"What is it?" he asked Goswin.

"Over there, over there!" he shrieked, pointing to a spot in the woods. "Someone shot at us! I saw the bolt fly right past my nose!"

Following the line of Goswin's outstretched finger, he

peered into the trees.

"I'll find them!" Goswin shouted. His pony was already in motion, riding down the road parallel to the trees.

"Goswin!" Rafe shouted. "Don't! Stay back here with Angelet!"

The boy ignored his order.

Cursing again, Rafe rode directly into the trees along the line the boy had indicated.

Branches whipped out at him as he plunged into the newly-green woods. Seconds later, Rafe spotted a big man who was fully armed and ready to fight, based on the fact that he held a sword in one hand and a long dagger in the other. Several feet behind him, a crossbow lay on the ground.

That was all Rafe needed to know.

He howled a challenge even as he drew his own sword. It was not fair that Rafe was mounted while his opponent was on foot, but then again, it wasn't fair that the man shot at an unarmed woman. Thus, Rafe felt absolutely no compunction about holding the advantage. He intended to give the other man no quarter at all.

The other man didn't ask for any. He braced himself against the wide trunk of a tree and yelled a few insults about the unsavory sexual habits of Rafe's mother. As it happened, those insults had no effect on Rafe, because he had no idea what sort of person his mother was.

So his mind was clear and cold when he charged the man's position. The man seemed as though he was going to stand his ground, but Rafe had long since learned to read body language, and he was unsurprised when his opponent skittered over to the other side of the tree, hoping to block Rafe's right-handed attack.

At a distance of twenty paces, he subtly angled his

horse's path slightly away from the tree, he swapped his sword into his left hand, and swept it in a wide flat circle just about level with the man's chest.

The mercenary raised his own sword to block the stroke, and a tremendously loud clang rang out when the two blades connected.

The man grunted, and Rafe knew why. His arm would be numb with pain right now, having taken much more of the impact of the blow than Rafe had. Rafe pulled hard on the reins to circle around the tree. He then switched the sword back to his right arm, which was perfectly sound.

The other man sensed Rafe coming, and turned to face him again. But Rafe now not only had the advantage of height, he also had a strong sword arm and more experience.

"One chance to live," Rafe said. "Throw your weapons down and tell me who hired you, and why."

The man only tightened his grip on his blades.

Rafe gave the man a more careful appraisal. Everything about him said he was a professional, and that he wasn't going to go as far as attempting to kill someone only to give himself up now. This man was never going to talk. He wouldn't reveal his employer or tell Rafe how he'd tracked him. He'd rather die.

Rafe could accommodate that.

He dismounted, springing down to the ground several paces from the other man, who was so surprised that Rafe gave up his advantage that he hesitated for a moment, which was a moment too long.

Rafe executed a series of moves so familiar to him that he could do them asleep. His opponent was a competent fighter, and parried well for the first few thrusts. However, Rafe didn't just follow a learned sequence—he always adapted to his opponents' response. He had a knack for seeing a fighter's move an instant before it actually occurred. Some people thought it uncanny, and it was the primary reason why Rafe kept winning battles—few things surprised him.

This time was no different. The man's actions seemed clumsy to Rafe, as though he was moving through mud while Rafe moved through air. The conclusion was inevitable, and when Rafe saw an opening, he took it without thinking twice.

His sword pierced through the other man's lower torso, just below the edge of his breastplate. Rafe retracted it instantly, confident in the result.

Sure enough, his opponent dropped his own weapons to clutch at the wound, desperate to keep his guts inside his body.

"You bastard," he hissed out.

"Yes, I know," said Rafe. "I've just killed you, but you have a while before you die. Hours. Maybe a day. Did you have anything to declare? Please skip the confessions. I'm not qualified to forgive."

"Go to hell." The other man sank to his knees, his face paling as blood began to seep through his fingers.

Rafe shrugged. "That's all you have to say? Goodbye then." He turned to fetch Philon, who'd only gone a little ways away, being very used to noise and violence.

"You can't leave me to die!" the other man said.

"I can. I will. Unless you tell me something useful."

"And you'll take me to a village?"

"No," Rafe explained. "I'll finish you off quickly. Choice is yours."

The other man grimaced as some great pain rolled over him. He seemed to be having some realization of his change in fortune. Rafe always wondered at the sort of soldier this man was. They thought they were invincible right up to the moment death took them. Rafe always knew how close death was. Though he put on a show of nonchalance, he respected the deadliness of a sword.

The man opened his mouth, about to say something, when he suddenly hunched over in pain and coughed up blood all over the ground.

Rafe sighed, seeing the signs of a brutal ending. "Very well," he said, more to himself than to the man. "Though he doesn't deserve it."

To the man, Rafe said, "Straighten up. Now!"

He followed the order, though it obviously hurt to do so. He faced Rafe on his knees.

"What's your name?" Rafe asked.

"Morton."

"Close your eyes, Morton."

The man did. Rafe took a step forward and swung the sword in an arc. A red line colored Morton's neck, and then he slid to the ground, dead.

Rafe quickly checked the body for any indication of where he might have come from or who he might know, but found nothing. Just as he expected.

He glanced at the crossbow, then stomped down hard on it, breaking the mechanism. He turned back to the corpse, intending to snap the remaining crossbow bolts in two, but he didn't see any. Had that bolt been the only one the man had? Strange.

Rafe seized Philon's reins, mounted up, and returned to the crossroads. In all, the fight lasted less than a minute.

Angelet was still there, alone. She sat on her horse, staring at the hill to the south. It was not an interesting hill, and Rafe didn't like her silence.

"Got him," Rafe told her, still gripping his sword. "I don't know how the hell he got this close to us, but he's never…"

Rafe trailed off, seeing that Angelet held her hand to her chest in an unnatural way, and that the front of her gown was deep red.

He felt his heart go cold. "You were hit."

She began to slide off the horse. Rafe dismounted and rushed to catch her before she hit the ground. He pulled her into his arms and put her gently down onto the road, keeping her upper body cradled against him.

"Rafe," she said softly. "What do I do?"

"Just stay calm," he told her. "I'll take care of you. I need cloth. Where the hell is that boy? Goswin!"

He thought he heard the hooves of Goswin's pony but couldn't be bothered to wait. He kept his attention on Angelet. "How's the pain?"

"Not very much," she said.

"That's common. The pain comes after, but it's nothing you can't endure."

"There's so much blood."

"I know." God, he knew that. Far too much blood. "But don't worry. The bleeding is already slowing and soon you'll be bandaged up." Lies, lies, lies.

She closed her eyes.

"No, no. Stay awake, love. I'll deal with this." He kept his voice low, to keep her calm and to stop the shaking he felt when he saw the location of the bolt, jutting out of her rib cage at a disturbing angle. If the shaft punctured her lungs or her heart, he'd lose her in moments.

"Just breathe," he told her. If she couldn't breathe without coughing, or if there was blood on her mouth, it was over. And Rafe could not accept that.

The clatter of hooves stopped abruptly and then Goswin was there in the dirt with them, his expression horrified. "She was struck!"

"Goswin!" Rafe yelled, furious at the world and needing to take it out on someone. "You rode ahead when I ordered you to stop. Do you know how stupid that was? Don't *ever* do that again."

The boy looked a little chastened by Rafe's vehemence. "I'm sorry."

"Sorry won't stop you from getting killed. There could have been more than one person!"

"There was! I saw someone running away!" Goswin reported breathlessly. "I couldn't catch them though. The underbrush was too thick. But they definitely came from where that shot was fired."

"Damn," Rafe muttered. That was another bad sign. It meant that the person who escaped could easily inform their partners what happened and where to go. "We can't stay here."

"You want to move her?" Goswin said.

"Yes! Now go look in our gear for something to stop this bleeding. Cloth or something. Christ." The boy scrambled up and disappeared.

Rafe lowered her so she lay on the ground.

Angelet reached up with one hand, grazing his face with the tips of her fingers. "You're so angry."

"Of course I'm angry!"

"It's bad for me, isn't it?" she asked. It was the most lucid statement she'd made so far.

"No, love. The blood makes it look worse," he told her. In truth, it did look bad, but telling Angelet that wouldn't help at all. "Trust me, it just needs a bandage and some time. It will heal."

"If it does not..."

"It will."

Goswin was back then, thrusting a few wads of fabric at him. "Here! Use these!"

Rafe took one and almost pressed it to Angelet's chest when he realized it was her altar cloth. "Jesu," he muttered, snatching it back. He gave it to Goswin. "Keep that one clean!"

He took the other wad, which turned out to be his only spare shirt. He ripped one sleeve off, then hesitated. He needed to take the bolt out and then block the wound with the cloth. That would hurt her.

"Angelet," he said. "I'm going to do something now. It will hurt, but it's necessary."

"I trust you," she breathed.

Rafe told Goswin, "Tear the rest of that shirt into strips. Use your dagger. And don't look if you'll get sick!"

Goswin nodded, his eyes wide.

Rafe laid one hand on Angelet's chest, the protruding bolt between his thumb and forefinger. He took hold of the bolt with his other hand, and prayed. Then he yanked the bolt out.

Angelet's choked off gasp of pain was the worst sound he'd ever heard.

"It's done, love," he said, pressing the dry cloth to her chest. "I'm so sorry. But the worst is done."

"It's not," she murmured, her eyes suddenly dark, the pupils widening.

"Listen, you'll recover. I promise," he added recklessly.

"Rafe, no," she said. "It's not the wound."

"What is it?"

"I feel so strange. I think I'm about to..." she trailed off.

"Angelet? Angelet. Stay awake." Rafe said urgently. But she couldn't answer. Her face took on a slack appearance. Her eyes remained open, but he doubted she could see anything. It was very similar to how she looked when he first found her in the church at Dryton. Angelet told him that the seizures rarely occurred close together, but the violence of her injury must have triggered one.

She stiffened in his arms, her body falling prey to the seizure in her mind. Rafe never felt more helpless, watching Angelet be attacked by something he couldn't even see.

"Angelet! Say something if you can. Anything. Please!"

She said nothing, and her body twisted further.

Rafe took the new shreds of cloth Goswin gave him, and began to bind the cloth to her body by wrapping the longest strips about her.

"What's wrong with her?" Goswin asked urgently.

"She took a crossbow bolt in her chest, for God's sake!"

"That doesn't explain why she's staring at nothing and can't talk. What *else* is wrong with her?"

"Goswin, shut up."

"What if they smeared poison on the tip of the bolt? That happens."

Oh, Lord. Rafe didn't need something else to worry about. "Goswin, *shut up*."

Goswin did for a moment, but then said, "The lady needs help. We must find a physician, or a wise woman, at least."

"We can't stop anywhere. You saw someone get away,

and we have to assume they'll be back with more friends. All they need is for us to stop moving. They'll attack as soon as they catch up."

"You can defeat them!"

"I don't know how many there are," Rafe explained wearily. "One man against many rarely ends well for the one man."

"But she told me you're the finest fighter in Britain!"

Rage only shook his head. "Won't help against an archer. Or if one of them slips past and kills Angelet while I fight the others."

"There must be a safe place around here. A place that would protect a lady. Someplace the others can't get in."

Rafe took a breath. As Goswin spoke, the image of the right place came to him. And the road to get there was the one he'd just refused to travel down.

"Jesu," he muttered. What a trick of fate. The only place Angelet would be safe was the one place he couldn't dare go.

"Sir Rafe?" the boy asked. "What is it?"

Rafe wanted to strike out in frustration, but there was no enemy about...only his own past folly. "God hates me," he said. "It's the only explanation."

"Sir?"

"All right, Goswin. There's a place we can go. It will be a vicious hard ride to get there, but both you and she will be safe once we arrive."

"What about you, Sir Rafe?"

"No time to explain."

So they rode. Rafe knew every turn and every stretch of road. Even though he avoided the whole shire for years, it was where he grew up, and the landmarks remained anchored in his soul. The hunched back of Waterstone Clee to the east, the twist of the river that would join the Severn miles downstream, the massive trunk of a lightning-stuck oak tree at the crossroads north of Bournham, the little village closest to the manor of Cleobury. They were all there, and guided Rafe as he rushed toward the one place he didn't want to see.

But he had no choice. Rafe held Angelet on the saddle in front of him. The rough binding over her wound was already splotched with red. More disturbing than the physical injury, though, was her unresponsive state. Her eyes often opened, but she seemed to see nothing, hear nothing.

Before Rafe was ready to confront it, they reached the shadow of Cleobury. Rafe pulled his too-tired horse to a stop, then pulled his hood over his head.

"Goswin," he said. "This is Cleobury. You're going to have to speak for Angelet."

"Me? Why not you?" the boy asked, taking in the scene. The manor looked to be in an excellent state, with freshly ploughed fields surrounding the walls, and quite a few people moving about. Any one of them could recognize Rafe.

"I won't be welcome here, boy," he muttered. "I can't explain now. When we reach the main gate there, just ask for Lady Cecily. Tell the guards that Angelet needs her care."

Taking a deep breath, Rafe kicked his horse back into movement. Goswin followed on his pony. When they neared the gate, Rafe slowed again, this time out of caution. Cleobury was a fortified manor, after all, and the men on watch were trained to be wary of strangers.

One guard shouted down for them to state their business.

"Hallo! Hallooo?" Goswin shouted up toward the tower. "Help! Please let us in. We've a lady with us who needs care!"

A moment later, the wicket gate opened, and two guards came out.

Rafe kept his head lowered. "Keep chattering, Goswin. And no matter what happens, *don't* say my name."

"Friends!" Goswin said. "We seek a Lady Cecily! This woman was hurt on the road, and needs aid!"

Rafe still held Angelet in his arms, and when a guard approached, he slowly lowered her prone body down to the other man, though he hated the idea of giving her up to any man. Luckily, the guard's attention was riveted on her face, pale and unconscious. Rafe's plain cloak and hood made him almost invisible, at least for the moment.

"Dear Lord," the guard said. "Is she breathing?"

"She's alive, but she was struck by a bolt!" Goswin said, leaping down from his pony. The concern in his voice was very real. "Please get her inside!" He rushed to help the guard who was now holding Angelet.

"Send for Lady Cecily," the guard told his companion. He glanced back at Rafe, but didn't seem to recognize him, or even look at him very hard. "You can take the horses to the stable," he instructed, already dismissing Rafe from his mind.

The guard and Goswin went ahead of Rafe, who deliberately hung back, using the horses as a shield from unfriendly eyes. However, all the focus was on Angelet as they passed through the gatehouse and into the courtyard.

"What has happened?" a voice called out.

Rafe looked over to see a woman striding out of the great manor house, and was hit with an overpowering sense of regret. Yes, it was Cecily, that same person he first met as a child, and one of the people he'd betrayed.

At the moment, she looked as though she might have been roused out of sleep. She took in the spectacle of Angelet and instinctively pushed back the sleeves of her gown, already preparing to do whatever needed to be done. "Who is this woman?"

"Her name is Lady Angelet," Goswin supplied. "She needs help! We were traveling, and—"

"Enough! Tell me more later. She must be brought inside," Cecily said.

As she spoke, the whole party moved toward the manor house—all except Rafe, who walked backwards until he was in the shadows of an outbuilding. He knew Cleobury very well, and he could get inside these walls again if he had to…at least, if Goswin did not betray him. If he did, Alric would tear the place apart stone by stone, and the surrounding area tree by tree, until Rafe had nowhere to hide.

Until that moment came, he *could* hide. He knew that Angelet would be cared for. Cecily was a healer by nature and training. She would do everything she could to make Angelet comfortable.

But all Rafe could do now was wait.

Chapter 23

ANGELET AWOKE IN AN UNFAMILIAR place. She blinked, looking around in confusion. Soft spring sunlight filtered in through the open window. The room seemed too large to be meant for one person, and certainly too lavish for her. This was someone's home, not any religious house or infirmary run by a holy order.

She felt the bed linens under her fingertips...marvelously smooth and soft fabric, finer than anything she'd slept on during her years at Dryton. The tight weave of the linen was closer to that of the altar cloths Angelet embroidered. As she turned her head, she reveled in the feather pillow. The scent of lavender—dry, warm, and summer-sweet—surrounded her. Something had gone wrong, and she'd been mistaken for a princess.

Then she remembered something had gone *very* wrong. She'd been hit with a crossbow bolt. Angelet put her hand cautiously to her chest. But the wound was now padded and bandaged. There was still pain, but it was only a dull pulse.

Someone had cared for her in an expert manner. Who?

Before Angelet could sit up or call out, she heard a voice from the other side of the door. Then a woman walked into the room and went directly to the open window, all the while humming quietly to herself. She had golden hair looped and braided around her head, a style suited to a highborn wife. The lady's left hand rested on her belly, which was rounding with an obvious pregnancy, and she tapped her fingers in time with her little song.

She's singing to her coming child, Angelet realized with a pang.

"Hello?" she asked out loud.

The woman broke off singing and turned from the window. She smiled at Angelet with a warmth beyond mere politeness. Had they met before? Angelet felt as if she knew the other woman, though she couldn't think where or when they ever would have met.

"Good day, my lady Angelet," the woman said. "You are doubtless confused, but I assure you that you're safe here."

"Where is here?"

"This is the manor of Cleobury, in Shropshire. Do you not know the name?"

Angelet shook her head, and promptly groaned at the wave of dizziness that assailed her.

"Oh dear, lay back. You need more rest." The woman was at her bedside in seconds, pushing Angelet back against the pillows and smoothing her forehead with a cool hand. "I am Lady Cecily. My husband is Sir Alric Hawksmere, and my father is Rainald de Vere. Do these names sound at all familiar? Your boy asked for me specifically."

"My boy?" Angelet felt so confused. Had she somehow come to the place where her son was being fostered?

"Goswin."

The image of wild, red-haired Goswin floated into her memory. "Goswin. Oh, yes. I'm sorry, but I remember nothing of what happened. I suffer an affliction, you see…"

Cecily gave a crisp nod. "One that strikes your brain first and then your body, leaving you unconscious and unable to move. It appears that the wound you received must have caused you to suffer a fit. No surprise—when the body suffers, the soul feels its pain. All healers worth their salt know this, whether a midwife or the most learned doctor."

Something in Cecily's tone—the lack of fear—made Angelet say, "*You* tended me? You're a healer? I thought you the lady of the manor."

"I am both of those things," Cecily said. "I have worked for years to help my people with whatever ailments come their way, from winter coughs to more serious illnesses. The plants from my garden are very useful in many cases."

"You spoke as if my symptoms were familiar. Have you seen anyone like me before?"

Cecily's eyebrow arched. "No. But I will do what I can for you. Have no fear."

"You don't even know me." Why was this stranger offering such assistance? What did she want from Angelet? Money? A favor of some sort? Did she think that Angelet was more important than she actually was?

"But I *do* know you," Cecily was saying. "You're Angelet, and I am Cecily. Women in this world are all sisters, in a way. That is enough, is it not?"

"My family ties are much more knotted than that," Angelet said miserably.

"Well, tell me when you're recovered. I think we shall be friends by the time you leave here."

"Leave?"

"Not till you wish to," Cecily said, patting her hand. "You've been through too much to hurry outside of the gates again so soon!"

"How do you know what I've been through?"

"Goswin said that you were being chased by someone. Was it brigands? This part of the shire is generally clear of such bands, but they are always a risk for travelers. Where did it happen?"

"I cannot say," Angelet answered, honestly enough. "All I remember was a crossroads, and a hill…but yes, someone was after us, and meant us great harm."

"Us…meaning you and the boy Goswin? Was there no other?" Cecily's voice held a newer, sharper curiosity. And no wonder. It would be very odd for Angelet to travel all alone, without any protection like Rafe's.

Angelet frowned. Cecil had not yet mentioned Rafe. Was he not here? Had something happened to him? Her gut went cold at the thought. "There was another! I must speak to Goswin. Now. Please, it's important!"

"Hush, dear, hush." Cecily restrained her from getting out of bed. "I'll send for him immediately."

To her credit, Cecily did just that, and soon Goswin entered the room on tip-toe, looking about as if he were entering a shrine.

"You asked for me, my lady?" He spoke in a near whisper.

"Goswin," Angelet said, gesturing to a stool set by the bed. "Sit. You must tell me what happened."

The boy's eyes slid toward Cecily, in a clear warning that what he wanted to say had to be kept private. Oh, what had she missed while in her seizure?

Cecily, however, seemed oblivious to any strain. She got up from the edge of the bed. "I'll leave you two to chat. Just call out if you need anything." She glided out of the room and pulled the door mostly shut.

Goswin stared hard at the door for a long while, his head tipped carefully, listening for footsteps.

Then he sighed. "I think she's gone." He leaned toward Angelet. "This place is like a town, my lady. There's a wall around, and men-at-arms on guard at all times."

"You're saying we're prisoners here?" she asked.

"No! Nothing like that. Everyone's rather kind, actually," he added, with heavy suspicion. "I can pass through the gate whenever I like."

She held out her hand to Goswin. "Where's Rafe? Why did Lady Cecily think we came here alone?"

Goswin looked over his shoulder and leaned even closer. "He's around, but he's hiding."

Relief warred with confusion. Thank God Rafe was all right, but why on earth would he hide from their rescuers? "I don't understand. What's going on?"

"He wouldn't say," Goswin told her. "He knew all about Cleobury though, and insisted it was the only safe place to bring you. But I gather it's not safe for *him*. He said he must not be seen by any of the inhabitants."

"That makes no sense. Surely people who would care for a stranger would welcome the knight who brought her!"

"I don't know, my lady. He won't talk about it."

"So you've seen him since you brought me here?"

"Yes. He meets me outside the gates just after sundown. He always asks about you. I'll tell him you're awake again."

Just then, the door squeaked open and Cecily stepped in. "That's long enough, boy! Lady Angelet must not be agitated."

"Be careful," Angelet told Goswin in a low voice. "And tell him to be careful too. I can't lose either of you."

"Yes, my lady!" Goswin sprang up from where he was sitting and dashed away before Cecily could ask him anything or detain him.

"My goodness," Cecily said, looking after him. "That's an energetic youth."

"Boys are like that," Angelet said, thinking of how Henry used to run for hours, seemingly without tiring.

"I hope my little one will be more calm," Cecily said, putting her hand to her belly again. "Or mayhap I don't! What's more delightful than watching a child be a child?"

"Your first?" Angelet asked.

Cecily nodded, bliss covering her features. "I cannot wait to meet him. Or her! I shall find out in June."

"I wish you all happiness now," Angelet said, "for I will be gone by then."

"Where will you go? Where are you from?" Cecily asked, turning her attention to Angelet. "Your boy Goswin was a little vague on that point. And his own memory concerning the event seemed quite hazy. Very few people earn such loyalty as that boy has for you."

"I've not earned it," she said. "Goswin is naturally cautious, that's all."

"So what did happen? Surely you didn't ride though the forest with only a page."

"No. I was part of a much larger entourage. I had intended to go all the way to Basingwerke Abbey, near Sheffield. I was to be a postulant. But then our whole group was attacked on the road, and I fled…and now I am here."

"This is a long way from the Nottinghamshire road."

"I'm afraid my plan was not well thought out. Goswin probably was trying to protect me. If he told the story as it happened, I'd sound as if I wasn't in my right mind."

"Your wound was fresh, though. You were attacked again, closer to here?"

"Yes. Or at least, I don't think it was far. I'm afraid I am useless," Angelet confessed. "I wish I could give you a better answer."

"It's understandable, considering what you've been through. All travel carries greater risk now. War is rupturing this country. We are lucky that the king has kept order here in Shropshire, more or less. But there is always the threat of violence. And then with the Welsh so close..." She looked at Angelet and gave her a sunny smile. "Not to fear though! My husband Alric is a knight by training, and he has made Cleobury the safest manor in England."

"That is reassuring. I will have to repay you for your hospitality."

"You may begin by recovering from your wound," Cecily said. "I've prepared a tisane that will help you sleep."

Behind Cecily, a maid approached, bearing a tray on which sat a little pot. From the top, fragrant steam wafted upwards in a languid curl. The smells of mint and apple and honey teased Angelet's nose. Cecily poured a cup and served Angelet herself, behaving much more like a healer than a great lady. "Drink this. It will help you sleep. Don't mind the bitterness."

Angelet did detect a sharp note under the honey. "What is it?"

"Willow bark. Most pungent, but good for many ailments. Perhaps even your other affliction will be eased. Who knows?"

After she finished the drink, Angelet lay back down. Cecily pulled the shutters on the window closed, dimming the room. "Call out if you need anything. There's always someone close by."

Cecily left. In the ensuing silence, Angelet pondered the changes in her circumstances. She been sent away from one manor, attacked on the road, and barely escaped with her life thanks to Rafe. They then traveled for days in an attempt to retrieve her son and return to her childhood home, all the while growing dangerously close to one another. Angelet was even having second thoughts about her determination to go home. But before she could gauge Rafe's feelings, that second attack came out of nowhere. And once again, Rafe had managed to save her from the worst fate, leading her to this new place that seemed as welcoming as Dryton had been cold. So why was Rafe unable to share the welcome? She wouldn't know until she could speak to him. Maddening.

She lay against the pillow and closed her eyes, wishing he could be with her now.

Where *was* he?

* * * *

Rafe was tantalizingly close to Cleobury, able to see through the gate, but not willing to walk through it. Spring was advancing in this part of the country, and the leaves were bursting out on all the trees now. The undergrowth was even further along, which was fortunate, because the green wall created by the shrubs and vines gave Rafe somewhere to hide while he watched the walls. The manor bustled with activity from before dawn to after dusk. Merchants from the village came and went on errands, and the many residents of the manor were constantly passing through the gates as they went about their tasks. Workers marched out to the farm fields and gardens outside. Women washed clothing and gathered water from the nearby stream. Some people even had work to do in the forest, and Rafe was careful to avoid them in particular.

Only Goswin knew where he was. For the past three days, the boy had come out to the woods to tell Rafe how Angelet fared. Rafe couldn't rest till the time Goswin told him that Angelet seemed to be recovering. According to the boy, she was now awake and seemed in good spirits. Hearing the news secondhand wasn't good enough for Rafe.

"Where is she? You say you were in her chamber. Where precisely in the manor house is it located?"

Goswin looked alarmed. "You can't go in there! You said so yourself."

"I need to see she's well with my own eyes."

"You'll get lost. I can't describe it well enough."

"I know the place well. Just tell me."

Goswin told him the location of the room, but he looked unconvinced about the wisdom of Rafe's decision. "If it was unwise for you to go there in the first place, what's changed now?"

Now Angelet is there, he thought. Rafe only shook his head. "Don't worry about me, boy. You go back in, and follow the routine you've started. Tonight, go to sleep in the dormitory with the other boys."

"How do you know about the dormitory?"

"I used to sleep in it myself, when I was a boy," Rafe

said.

Goswin looked a little surprised, perhaps at the idea that Rafe had ever been a boy. "If you get caught…"

"You'll be out of the way," Rafe told him. "Now go."

Goswin ran back to the manor. Rafe waited until darkness fell, then used his knowledge of the manor's defenses to slip in a small back gate that was rarely used, and never guarded in times of peace. At least not when he used to live there.

Rafe found that not much had changed. The little back gate remained unguarded, and he could move easily around the compound of the manor, avoiding the people who were still out and about—not many, since work was hard to do once the light faded from the sky. He heard voices in the stable as the boys tended to the animals before they headed off to bed. A few men-at-arms crossed the courtyard toward the main gate for night watch, but they didn't even look around, so Rafe was safe in the shadows.

When it was quiet, he slipped into the manor house itself. Here, more people came and went, but he knew the way and how to avoid being seen.

When he stood in front of the door Goswin claimed was Angelet's, he paused. What if the boy was wrong? Or what if she was moved? There was no sound at all.

He eased the door open just enough to get through. "Angelet?"

"Who is it?" Angelet asked from the bed, past the curtains that would enclose the bed during cold nights.

"Lower your voice," Rafe said quietly as he closed the door.

"Rafe?" Her eyes widened, taking him in. "What are you doing here?" She flung off the covers, preparing to slide out of the bed. Then a look of pain crossed her features. "Oh, no."

"Don't dare get up." He had her in his arms a moment later.

She clung to him, and he heaved a breath of relief. Until she actually touched him, Rafe hadn't quite believed she was going to be well.

"Rafe, I thought you couldn't be here!" Angelet pulled herself out of the embrace and put her hands on his shoulders, gazing at him in wonder. "How did you get in?"

"Goswin told me where you were." He looked her over, keeping his touch light when he passed over her bandaged chest. The memory of seeing her wounded cut through him once again, triggering a visceral response, as if he needed to go into battle. He deliberately took a long breath to relax. He said, "How are you? Recovering?"

"Lady Cecily is a very good healer," Angelet responded, still surveying him in the dim light of the candle by her bed.

"That's why I brought you here."

"How do you know these people? Why all this secrecy?"

"It's a long story, Angelet, and you've got enough on your mind."

"Rafe, you're on my mind. I didn't know where you were, and I worried that something happened to you. You're sleeping outside," she added, running her fingers through his hair.

"I'm used to that."

"While I'm cared for like royalty. It's not fair."

"You deserve the care. I don't."

Angelet's brow wrinkled. "Why do you say that? Tell me what's—" She broke off at a sound in the corridor.

"Someone is coming, Rafe. You have to go. Or stay out of sight."

He could hide. The room was large, and nearly all in shadow. But suddenly Rafe was sick of hiding. And the idea of walking away from Angelet a moment after he'd just rejoined her made him furious.

"No." He remained exactly where he was, and kept her hand in his. "I'm done sneaking off into the night."

"But you said…"

"Never mind what I said. I'm not leaving you." Rafe leaned over and kissed her to make his point.

"Isn't it dangerous for you?" she asked.

"I kill men for pay, Angelet. I'll decide what's dangerous."

The sound of footsteps came closer. Both Rafe and Angelet faced the door, and both saw when Cecily entered.

Her warm smile for her patient froze, then faded. She stared at Rafe in pure shock. "Oh, my God," Cecily whispered.

Angelet said quickly, "Don't be alarmed. Sir Rafe is the knight who brought me here. I owe him my life."

Cecily took one step forward, then stopped, as if uncertain what was happening. "Rafe," she said.

Seeing her up close after two years, looking so different and yet still the young woman he remembered, Rafe actually smiled. "Hello, my lady. I suppose you'll run for your husband in a moment. You should—Alric's been looking for me long enough."

Chapter 24

IT DIDN'T TAKE LONG TO summon Alric. The man had once been a simple knight like Rafe, but he was now married to Cecily de Vere, an heiress and the daughter of a proud family. The changes in his appearance were subtle, but evident to Rafe, who once knew him very well. His clothing was finer quality, and that belt and the leather shoes cost more than Alric ever would have spent when he was a knight. Still, he was Alric. The brown hair held a little grey now, and he probably slacked off his military training since becoming lord-in-waiting here at Cleobury. But he was just as tall, and just as insufferably straight-laced in outlook.

When Alric entered the room, he immediately crossed the floor to join Cecily, putting one arm around her shoulders in a gesture that said louder than words that he'd protect her against any threat…and that the presence of Rafe implied considerable threat.

The couple spoke to each other, just a few low-voiced words Rafe couldn't hear. Next to him, Angelet gripped his hand.

"Do you know him?" she murmured.

"Like a brother," Rafe said wryly.

Then Alric faced Rafe. He'd been forewarned, of course, but even so his expression was admirably steady. "I knew I'd see you again someday, but I didn't picture it like this."

Rafe actually laughed. "You mean where I come to you on my own two feet, unbound and unshackled? You have sent people after me to drag me back. Admit it."

Alric and Cecily exchanged glances, and she said, "I think you should tell him."

"Tell me what?" Rafe asked.

"Come with me," Alric said. It wasn't a request.

Rafe gave Angelet a careless smile. "Back in a moment."

"Make me no promises," she said, looking doubtful.

Rafe had his own doubts, but he followed Alric until they reached another room on the same floor, this one much smaller than the room Angelet was using.

Alric closed the door, then looked Rafe over for a long time. At the end of the inspection, he just shook his head. "I will admit, I did *not* foresee this." His tone was resigned, amused…and deeply, painfully familiar. Rafe never felt more homesick than right at that moment. But Cleobury was not his home anymore.

"Believe me," he said, "it wasn't by design. I tried to avoid this whole shire. But you guessed that, since your people tracked me elsewhere."

"No. Not my people," Alric said instantly. "True, I wasn't happy that you ran away. But your life is your own."

"Don't play me for a fool. There have been men following me for years. I noticed the first signs only a few months after I left."

"I didn't say that you weren't being followed," Alric said, "just that it wasn't me who sent them."

"Who, then?"

"Lord Rainald is keen to speak to you."

Rafe closed his eyes. Even if Alric forgave Rafe for his transgressions, it sounded as though Rainald de Vere had not. "What's his plan for me? Why haven't you dragged me to his feet already?"

"Because he's not here," Alric said. "He's gone to a meeting the Lord Halbeck called. Many of the lords in this part of the country went to discuss the progress of the war. It might be many weeks before he returns."

"Good. We'll be gone by then."

Alric snorted. "You'll go when I let you go. And it won't be for a while."

"You don't understand. It's the lady who needs to hurry."

"Ah, yes. Tell me, who is the lady?"

"Exactly who she says she is. Angelet d'Hiver. Yarborough. She's the widow of one Hubert Yarborough. He was the son of a Lord Otto, who holds Dryton Manor. Stephen's man."

"I don't know the name, but that means little, since I'm so bound here. What happened?"

"She must have told the story, more or less."

"I'd like the more. The version she related to Cecily was rather light on detail."

"I was hired to escort her on a journey," Rafe said, "along with several other men-at-arms—some locals, and some who served Lord Otto. We were attacked on the road, taken by surprise. I had the opportunity to get her out of the fray and I took it. If we'd stayed, we all would have been slaughtered."

"Surely she'd be ransomed," Alric objected.

"I doubt it," Rafe said. "They meant to kill her that day, and that was confirmed when someone attacked her again several days later. Same weapon, same method. But they hit the second time, and forced me to bring her here."

Alric was following the story, watching Rafe with narrowed eyes. "Where were you going?"

Rafe paused. He wasn't sure if Angelet had explained she had a child, and intended to retrieve him. He'd better stick to the more obvious story. "We'd been heading south. She wants me to take her to Wareham, in hopes of getting passage to the Continent. Her own family hails from Anjou."

"So all this was just professional pride on your part?"

"What else would it be?"

"You rode halfway through the shire to get her to a healer you trusted."

"Well, I didn't want her to die." Rafe swallowed, suddenly very uncomfortable with how Alric was prodding at his motivations. "I'd get a bad reputation if a client died before she got to her destination."

"*That*'s the part of your reputation you think will suffer?"

"What's your point?"

"My point is that you are not treating this woman as an obligation."

"I am. I was paid to take her to Anjou, and that's what I'm going to do. She's offered more money when she gets home. So you can understand my haste to resume the journey."

"Don't be too eager. The lady seems to have cheated death this time, but her recovery will take a while, according to Cecily. And then there's Lord Rainald."

"What's he intend to do with me?"

Alric shrugged. "He's been very secretive about his reasons, and it's not for me to question him. But he's not been at all secretive about his eagerness to find you."

"He blames me for working for Theobald," Rafe said, referring to one of his many past mistakes. "Serves me right for getting involved in a family matter. Rainald will punish me for that."

"That's up to him," Alric said. "My duty is to keep you here until he returns."

"So *you* don't intend to punish me in the meantime?" Rafe asked.

"No. You showed remorse for what you did in the end, and I don't think you knew the extent of Theobald's plans."

"That's all too true," Rafe muttered. No one knew just how far Theobald de Vere had gone to take power from his brother, or just how far he was willing to go to keep that power. However, Theobald's plans didn't go as he intended, and now Rainald was once again the head of the de Vere family.

Unfortunately, Rafe had been a willing pawn in Theobald's game for too long, and the price of losing was steep. Steeper than he'd anticipated. Rafe hadn't considered how valuable his friendships were until he destroyed them.

"Any word from Luc?" he asked, remembering their other close friend from the early training days.

"He's well," Alric said, his expression changing to one of genuine happiness. "I saw him just before Christmastide, in fact."

"I expect he's at court. He was always eager to play

politics."

"Less eager than he used to be. His interests are now more domestic."

"Domestic? Luc? What happened?"

"He married, and is now a father."

Rafe blinked. "I'd have heard! If Luc of Braecon married, it would have been into one of the great families—the news of that alliance would have been talked of everywhere. Who'd the king pick for him?" Rafe couldn't believe he missed that news. He made a point of checking for such tidbits whenever he could.

"It's a long story, in fact. His wife isn't from one of the families you would guess, but he's well content. And not too far away, since his new lands are only a few days ride south of Cleobury."

"Don't tell him I'm here," Rafe said. It was bad enough to face Alric. He couldn't face Luc too.

"No promises."

Rafe accepted that. Alric didn't owe him anything.

"You can sleep in the southeast room," Alric went on. "No more lurking in the woods outside."

"Well, at least it will be a comfortable imprisonment. Do you want me to surrender my weapons?"

"No," Alric said. "You're too intelligent to do something stupid when your *client* is forced to remain here at Cleobury for her own health."

"Speaking of which, are we done? I'd like to talk with her." Rafe began to walk to the door.

Alric stepped into his path. "I don't think that's necessary. After all, she doesn't mean anything to you. And now that she is at Cleobury, we're all responsible for protecting her, not just physically, but her reputation as well. Wouldn't want anyone to get the wrong idea, would we?"

Rafe rolled his eyes. He'd be damned before he admitted the truth of what happened between him and Angelet. Let Alric guess if he wanted to. Rafe didn't have to make it easy for him. He said, "I don't need to see her. It doesn't matter to me one way or the other." The words came out easily enough, but for some reason Alric just looked more annoyed than before.

"Maybe you haven't changed at all," he said.

"Don't tell me about myself," Rafe warned. "You don't know me."

"Of course I do," Alric retorted. "We grew up together, we fought together, and we fought against each other. And when you had the whole country to choose from, you came here for shelter. Goodnight, Rafe. Welcome back to Cleobury."

* * * *

Rafe spent his night dead asleep. He expected to be restless, disturbed by the return to his old home and anxious for the health of Angelet. But after days of sleeping outside and the whole time running from whoever was after him and Angelet on the road, Rafe couldn't resist the appeal of a clean mattress and the soft linens of a real house. Everything about the manor spoke of comfort, and Rafe woke up feeling amazingly refreshed and even somewhat optimistic.

The good feelings didn't last long, of course. Everywhere he went, he felt the eyes of the residents on him, and knew they were talking about him. Exchanging old gossip and new guesses about his plans. He could sense their interest, much as he could sense when someone on a battlefield was getting ready to go for him in particular.

His reaction, predictably, was to tense up, to prepare to fight, even though there was no actual attack coming. Still, it reminded him of what he should be doing.

As he left the manor house with his weapons and gear, he encountered Alric.

"Not running away, I hope," Alric said by way of a greeting.

Rafe said, "I'm going to the practice fields."

"Why?"

"Because I need to practice." Not everyone married the heiress of a manor. Alric might be able to forget about his training, but Rafe still had to make a living.

"Want company?" Alric asked.

Rafe stared at him, incredulous. How the hell did Alric expect him to respond to that? Finally, he said, "I don't think that would be a good idea."

Alric gave a shrug. "Another time, then. Good luck."

So Rafe practiced. Alone. Goswin did show up later in the morning, and Rafe was able to show the boy some of the rudiments of what a page or a squire did before and after a fight. Perhaps Rafe could persuade Alric to keep the boy at Cleobury. Goswin showed no inclination to return to Ashthorpe, despite Rafe's prodding.

"Why should I?" Goswin had said. "One town is the same as another. By the time I got back there, everyone will have forgot who I am."

"You need a trade," Rafe told him. "Something to keep you fed."

"Then I'll be a soldier, like you. When did you start your training?"

"Eleven or twelve, I think. But it took years. The war will be over when you're old enough to join an army."

"The war will never be over," Goswin grumbled. "The

king and empress will fight until they've got no soldiers left. Is that why you left your lord's service?" he asked.

"No. I had other reasons, none of which matter to you." He then changed the subject, keeping Goswin busy answering detailed questions about the care of arms and armor.

Afterward, he tried to visit Angelet. At the door of her chamber, he saw a woman he knew.

"Agnes!" Rafe gave the older woman a smile. She'd been Lady Cecily's nurse for years. "Did you miss me?"

"Not a whit," the woman replied, though she still accepted a peck on the cheek. "I've got my hands full with all the young people running about this place. No sense, some of these maids. What's the world coming to?"

"You'll keep order as you always have," Rafe assured her. "May I see Angelet?"

"She's sleeping. My lady has given very strict orders that she's not to be disturbed. By anyone," she added before Rafe could wheedle an exception from her.

"Just a peek? To see that she's well."

"No. The woman needs rest, not to be leered at."

"I don't leer," he objected.

"Ha! As if I'd forget the sort of rogue you are. Get on your way, sir knight, or face my wrath." The old nurse crossed her arms.

"I'm going, I'm going," he promised. "You will tell her I tried, won't you?"

Agnes chortled. "No promises. I'm not your messenger. Now get on with you." He left, wondering if Cecily gave orders regarding him specifically. Very probably. How irritating, to be so close to Angelet and still not be able to even speak to her.

The next few days passed in the same way. Angelet

slept—he was told—and he could do nothing but wait. He practiced every day, always alone, though often some of the servants would come to watch him for a while. Perhaps Alric told them to, because Rafe had the sense he was never unobserved. Alric took his role seriously, and Rafe sneaking away would be difficult, though certainly not impossible…if he went alone. He'd never be able to spirit Angelet away, which meant he had to either brazen this whole situation out, or cut and run as he did before.

Before he made any decision, Alric summoned him one day. He wore what Rafe thought of as his "serious" expression.

"What's the matter?" Rafe asked.

"I spoke to someone this morning, and heard an interesting tale. I want to believe what you told me, Rafe…"

"But you don't," Rafe interrupted, "because of who I am."

Alric frowned. "Regarding your earlier, ah, error in judgment—"

A kind way to describe attempted murder, Rafe thought.

"—I have forgiven that. Truly," he added, on seeing Rafe's skepticism.

"So?" Rafe asked. "What is my new crime?"

"You told me your account of what happened when Lady Angelet's cortège was attacked."

"Yes," Rafe said impatiently.

"But you didn't tell me that there was a large quantity of gold in a chest. And now I've heard that there is speculation that you were the very person who stole it."

That annoyed Rafe. "What?"

"There are rumors among travelers. You stole the gold, allowed the others to be killed, and made off with the woman as a hostage."

"Does she look like a hostage?" Rafe sputtered. "I did everything I could to save her life. I even came back here! A mistake, I now know."

"So you deny the theft?"

"Yes, I deny it! I'll march into the chapel over there and deny it again, if that would help."

"It wouldn't," Alric said flatly.

"Then what would convince you?"

"The whole truth?"

Rafe sighed, then proceeded to tell Alric the few details he'd withheld from the original account. At the end, Alric shook his head.

"Why keep this a secret?"

"Perhaps because of the accusation you just leveled at me? I know I'm not the trustworthy, upstanding knight you are. But I'm no thief, and I didn't have anything to do with the disappearance of that gold. Angelet will confirm it. I couldn't have brought along so much treasure, even if I did steal it. Which I didn't."

"You might have hid it somewhere."

"There were nearly a dozen other people with the cortège. Someone was always awake—because *I* set watches. There's no way I could have spirited the chest away, snuck the key from Angelet to unlock it, unchained the whole mess, removed the money, refilled it with rocks, rebound it, relocked, and hauled it back alone, without someone seeing. And who in the world would be dumb enough to hide a cache of treasure in a countryside he barely knows? I'd be better off tossing it into the sea."

"All right, I believe you."

"You do?"

"You're not the type of man to leave something that

valuable behind."

Rafe sighed. Even when he was exonerated of something, his worst traits got brought up. "Ask the lady. She'll tell the same story."

"Cecily insists that we don't distress her while she recovers, so I haven't brought it up."

"Speaking of her recovery, can I see her at some point? She always seems to be asleep when I try."

"Well, a crossbow bolt to the chest is no small matter. It's amazing the bolt didn't pierce a lung, or her heart. She'd be long buried by now. So don't begrudge her a nap."

"I don't begrudge her anything. I just want to see for myself."

"Speak to Cecily," Alric said. "One thing I've learned is that it's unwise to ignore my wife when she's made her wishes clear."

As it happened, Cecily found him first. Rafe had gone to the top of the outer wall, the one facing the eastern woods. He was enjoying a moment of peace, simply looking out over the greening woods, when the lady of the manor joined him.

"Did you miss Cleobury?" she asked, surveying him rather than the scene.

"Occasionally." Every day, but he wouldn't tell Cecily that. "Thank you for letting me stay. And for caring for Angelet."

"Did you think I'd turn the poor woman away?"

"I knew you couldn't. That's why I risked the ride here."

"You did risk quite a lot for the lady Angelet," Cecily noted. "I want to discuss that."

"You do?"

"You've seduced her, haven't you?"

Rafe glanced at her. "You've grown blunt."

"I'm not the innocent girl I once was. I know much more of the world, and I know what you're like…what you've always been like when it comes to women. You see one you enjoy and then charm her to you, with no thought of what comes after. So you've done to Angelet."

"No," he snapped. Then, before he could stop himself, he hedged, "Not exactly."

"How do you not exactly seduce a woman?"

"It was…are we really going to talk about this, you and me?"

"You're in my home, Rafe. You once served my father. You once betrayed my husband and my family. And now you quail at a little crude talk? What did you do to her?"

"Nothing she didn't ask for."

"That's no defense, if you persuaded her to ask."

"It wasn't like that," he said. "Not at all."

"Then what was it? If you played with her heart simply to tumble her into a bed once or twice, it proves you've not changed and you'll never change. You'll be the same selfish knave you showed yourself to be years—"

"I'd die for her," he said, louder than he intended.

Cecily's eyes widened as the words fell between them.

"I'd die for her," Rafe repeated, more calmly. "In fact, I was attacked multiple times on her account. If things had gone a bit differently, it might have been me with a wound in my chest. Sorry to disappoint. Again."

"You love her?" Cecily asked softly.

"I've never been in love," he said, shrugging off the suggestion. "I protected her because that's what I was hired to do. That's all I meant. Anything more would complicate things, and they're complicated enough as it is."

"You've slept with her, though," Cecily guessed.

"Dear God, what's it to you if we have? She's a widow. She was no innocent for me to ruin. We both wanted something. If there was a seduction, it was entirely mutual."

"So it might have been, but the consequences are not equal! What if she bears your child?"

"No."

"That's your defense? A simple denial? That's—"

"She had one son, and that is all she will ever have. She told me she can no longer bear children."

Cecily suddenly put a hand to her mouth, her cheeks reddening. It wasn't hard to guess why. Cecily's rounding belly made her current state obvious. She must have chattered away of her hopes to Angelet, who naturally would have said nothing to destroy the happy mood.

"Whatever is between Angelet and me is our problem," Rafe said.

"But now you're both here," Cecily countered. "And I insist that until you both leave, you treat her as a lady, not one of your conquests. Your reputation at Cleobury is damaged enough. Don't make it worse."

"Thank you for reminding me," he muttered.

"Was there a chance you'd forget?"

No, not till he died. One more reason to get out of Cleobury as soon as humanly possible.

Chapter 25

ANGELET SEEMED TO SPEND A long time adrift, half asleep, half awake. She remembered fragments of conversations with Cecily and a few other women, but no details. The room was sometimes light and sometimes dark. Breathing occupied much of her attention, since every time she inhaled, an ache pulsed through her whole chest. She was very lucky to be alive, and she sent several prayers to Mary in thanks. The mother of God must have extended a hand to deflect the shot, protecting another mother out of compassion.

Her dreams sometimes included scenes of the visions she had in the past, from the golden city in the clouds to the black figure she thought of as an angel. But she never lost control of her body as she did when the seizures came upon her, and for that she prayed thanks to her nameless angelic protector.

Even after she awoke from her deeper dreams, Angelet still felt adrift and lost. But at least she could enjoy a new gown. When Angelet was well enough to get out of bed and walk around the chamber, Cecily offered her one that she had recently put away due to her pregnancy. It was a lovely soft blue wool. Along with a new shift in a crisp white, Angelet felt like a different person. Perhaps she was, considering how much had changed for her in a few short weeks.

While walking, she stumbled, and Cecily reached out to steady her. "Careful! You don't want to turn an ankle and be stuck abed longer!"

"I don't know what I want anymore," Angelet said miserably, as she shuffled to the bed. She felt winded after only a few steps.

"Then you should stay here while you decide," Cecily replied.

"You've done so much already, my lady. I cannot impose."

"Nonsense. Guests are rare enough. Don't deny me a lady's company for a while. I'll send word to your family at Dryton—"

"No, you must not do that!" Angelet said.

"Why ever not? They will worry once they hear you've not arrived at Basingwerke. They're likely already worried, if news of your broken carriage and the bodies of the slain are reported to them."

That had undoubtedly already happened. But Angelet still shook her head. "Please don't send word, at least not until you've spoken to Sir Rafe about it. Heed him—he'll know what to do. There were men following us and I'm not sure it's wise to alert anyone to where we are. Not yet."

"You set great trust in Rafe," Cecily observed.

"He earned it! He defended me, and brought me here. Without him, I would be dead."

Cecily said, "Rafe does seem to have cared for your well being. But if I may be so bold as to counsel you, don't blind yourself with gratitude."

Angelet blushed. Did the other woman somehow guess that she and Rafe had shared a bed? "I don't think Rafe is like most men."

"No, he's not at all, and that's what worries me. You think you know Rafe, but I'll wager there's much in his past he's told you nothing of."

"What?" She knew there was something, but Rafe had never confided in her.

Cecily sighed. "I'll leave him to tell it, if he dares. I would not tell the story properly. We're all too close to it."

It was a cryptic line, but Angelet didn't want to press the other woman since the topic obviously distressed her. But when she next saw Rafe, she would try to steer the conversation to learn more.

In the great hall, she slowly ate some hot broth with warm, crusty bread speckled with green bits of wild onion. Rafe joined her at the table, his eyes filled with questions he couldn't ask out loud. Beneath the innocuous talk they exchanged, she sensed his concern. She also recognized how fiercely she'd missed him during their time apart. Cecily's warning seemed to evaporate when she looked at the face of the man across from her. Still, she wanted to know more about him.

Angelet asked him, "How did you come to be in training here? Under de Vere specifically, I mean. Isn't that usually reserved for sons of relations, or friends, or those in alliance? That's why my Henry was fostered where he is now."

"I don't know," Rafe said. "I asked him directly, only once. He said he did it out of Christian charity, and could tell me nothing more. Perhaps he owed a favor to someone, and taking me on was sufficient to repay it."

"Or someone owed him a favor," she countered. "After all, having you as knight must have benefited him. He had one more to send when the king asked, and one more to defend his own walls. Although no one could have predicted your skill, not if you were only…eleven, did you say, when you came here?"

"Eleven or close to it. Too young to know if I had a gift for fighting."

"Well, no one can now dispute that you have." She gave a little laugh, then winced, putting a hand to her aching chest.

Rafe leaned forward. "What's wrong? Should I find Lady Cecily?"

"No, I just need to mind how I react. Too deep a breath or too sudden a movement and I can feel it."

"I can walk you up to your chamber. You should rest."

"I'm sick of resting," she said. "I'll go mad if I'm confined to that bedchamber another day."

"You won't, and it's not worth it to push yourself if you only collapse back. Don't you want to get to your son in Dorset? Think of him. I can't escort you there if you can't even walk from one floor to another."

"It feels so far away."

"Yes, but if that's where you want to go, then that's where I'll take you. You didn't hire me to sit around, after all."

Was he annoyed by the diversion in their journey? Well, of course he was. He didn't want to be at Cleobury. "If you wish to leave, Sir Rafe, you can. You can make a better living if you return to fighting tourneys, or hiring out for someone else. I have no claim on you."

He didn't respond for a moment, then said, "Not many tourneys to fight in, once summer comes. That's when the real battles begin again. Who knows what Stephen or Maud have planned for England? I don't want to be in the midst of that."

"So you'll stay?" she asked, trying hard not to sound as if she were begging.

"I suppose," he replied. "But you must rest. The second I hear you're violating Cecily's instructions, I ride out that gate."

She smiled, unreasonably happy with that response. "Thank you."

"Good. Now, I'm taking you to bed."

"Rafe!" she warned.

He gave her a too-innocent smile. "So you can rest. What's the matter, my lady? Did you think I meant something else?"

"Stop that," she said in a low voice, though she had to bite her lip to keep from smiling. "This is hardly an appropriate time."

"But eventually it will be, and we still have an agreement, don't we?"

Was *that* why he agreed to stay on? Angelet doubted it, since Rafe could have any woman he wanted. Still, the idea that he was only interested in her recovery so they could resume their more intimate relations chilled her.

"Angelet?" Rafe took her hand. "You know I'm only teasing you."

"Of course I know that. I'm just tired. I should rest after all."

Rafe walked her back to her room, behaving perfectly the whole time. He'd always been able to do that, she recalled. Proper in public, and very improper once they were alone. She wished he wasn't so good at switching his demeanor. It made it impossible to judge his true feelings, assuming he had any feelings for her deeper than lust.

When she was alone in the bedchamber once more, sleep eluded her. Instead, she thought of Rafe, realizing how little she knew of his past actions or his future intentions.

* * * *

The days passed quietly. In general, Angelet was recovering well, and soon felt much closer to normal in a physical sense. She could move and walk and perform all her usual tasks just as well as she used to. She explored the manor's house and grounds as her strength returned.

Cleobury was about the same size as Dryton, but it felt much busier, with steady traffic coming through the gates from the nearby village and the surrounding countryside. Some folk carried in goods that had been made by the town's craftsmen. Others brought in food—a cart of grain in one case, several braces of rabbits in another, or a basket full of pungent mushrooms harvested from the forest to the west. Everyone seemed to know each other, at least to call out greetings or chat for a few moments. Laughter broke out frequently, and the whole mood was so different from the grim atmosphere of Dryton.

The reason had to lie with those who ruled here. Lady Cecily appeared to have business in every building and field at some point. If she wasn't directing some effort, her lord Alric was. The man was on his feet from sunup to sundown. Angelet had to struggle to remember Otto when he wasn't at ease. Apparently, the real lord of the manor—Cecily's father—was away. But Alric seemed to be well prepared for the part. Cleobury would be in good hands for another generation. Or two, considering Cecily's condition.

Watching the lady absent-mindedly put her hand on her belly made Angelet think of her own child. She had to reach Henry before Otto found her. And she couldn't do that until she got well enough to travel. Everything was in the air till she recovered, so she dutifully swallowed every tisane and followed every command when it came to her health. At Cecily's orders, she did not overexert herself, though she did not enjoy feeling useless.

She didn't have funds to repay Cecily for all her charity, so she instead offered her labor. Luckily, she could mend, and the ladies of Cleobury had plenty of mending to do. There were so many people about, there was always a supply of things to be repaired or improved—clothing, linens, sacks, and more. Angelet joined the group of women as if she had every right to, and soon she was quite happily stitching away.

She sewed several items for Cecily's expected child, and used her skills with embroidery to make those items special. The women who worked as seamstresses in Cleobury all cooed in approval, and several of them asked for advice. Angelet gave it happily. At last her few domestic skills were proving useful in a small way. As she worked, she listened to the ladies gossip around her.

"Have you met Robin yet?" one of the ladies asked one day, gesturing to a new face in the room. "She's a ward of Lord Rainald, and we are attempting to teach her some of the skills of a lady." The woman's tone hinted at how difficult the task was.

Robin stabbed at her work with the needle, muttering every time she made a mistake, which was frequently. She huffed out sighs, and generally acted as though she'd rather be plunged in an icy river than make another stitch.

Angelet smiled. Robin was several years younger than Angelet, with a slim body that was nevertheless fully into womanhood. The way the girl's eyes kept flicking to the window made it clear she wanted to fly out of the room.

"When the weather grows warmer," Angelet said to her, "you can take your work outside. It's pleasant to embroider in the sun, and never a worry about having enough light for the task."

"Aye, but I'd still be sewing, wouldn't I?" Robin sighed.

"What would you rather be doing?"

"Nothing appropriate to a lady," the matron in charge interjected. "Robin must learn calm and comportment. And patience. Sewing teaches all these things."

Robin rolled her eyes.

"And respect!" the matron added darkly. "I despair of you, Robin. You're a hoyden at heart."

Angelet sought to rescue the girl. She stood, wobbling a little for effect, and said, "I fear I must lie down again. Could someone walk me to my chamber?"

"Yes, of course!" Robin was already on her feet and stepping toward Angelet before anyone else could reply. Her sewing lay unregarded on the floor.

Angelet let Robin take her by the arm, playing up her unsteadiness. Once they left the room, however, she suggested a detour to the courtyard. "A little bit of fresh air may help me."

Robin nodded, just as eager to get outside. The courtyard of the manor bustled with activity. Workers brought in firewood and supplies. A young boy led a sheep on a rope toward the kitchens. Grooms exercised and brushed down horses by the stables.

"That white one is yours, is it not?" Robin asked, pointing toward one of the horses.

Angelet walked toward the paddock. "She is the one I rode before, though she's not mine. Beautiful animal."

"I love horses," Robin said. "Being able to ride is the one good thing about being a lady."

"You speak as though you haven't always been one."

"Of course I wasn't!"

"You mean you were a child."

"I mean I was free," Robin said hotly. "No long heavy skirts to trip me up. No sewing. No sitting for hours and hours inside the manor because that's what ladies do."

"But as a lady, you'll be protected and cared for. Is that so very bad?"

A look of remorse filled Robin's face. "I shouldn't say anything. Lord Rainald has done everything for me and I owe him my life. I don't mean to be ungrateful, but no one asks what I want to do!"

"No," Angelet agreed. "No one ever asked that of me either." Well, Rafe asked. Asked and asked and asked until she revealed her very deepest desires, and then he did his very best to fulfill them. She grew hot under her clothing, and tried to get her mind back to the actual topic. "They mean well, our families. At least most of the time."

"Is it true you're going to take the veil?" Robin asked, looking at her sidelong. "I heard that you were on your way to a nunnery when…things went wrong."

"That part is true enough. As for whether I will take the veil now, I cannot say."

"What's changed?"

"The nunnery wasn't my choice," Angelet said. "It was a compromise."

"A compromise? Lord, what was the alternative worse than a lifetime of being trapped behind walls?"

"It doesn't matter." Just then, a flurry of movement at the other end of the courtyard made her look over. There he was. Rafe, dressed in black as usual, walked along with several other men, who all seemed to be guards or men-at-arms. They were headed for the practice fields and didn't see the two women.

"Look at that. He's got a retinue now. Surprised anyone would spar with him," Robin muttered. "After what he did."

"Who did?"

"Sir Rafe." Robin's eyes narrowed. "Do you not know?"

"Know what?" Was this the same thing Cecily hinted at? She knew that Rafe had some falling out with Alric, and that he had been very reluctant to return to Cleobury until Angelet's dire state demanded it. "Tell me what happened. Please."

"Sir Rafe tried to murder Sir Alric."

Chapter 26

"EXCUSE ME?" ANGELET MUST HAVE misheard. Or the girl suddenly spoke in Welsh. Or Angelet was having another seizure. "Did you say *murder*?"

"I wasn't here when it happened," Robin hedged, "but I heard the story. Many times. Sir Rafe was sparring with Sir Alric on the practice field, but he had more in mind than…are you well?"

"No!" Angelet felt genuinely sick. Something must be wrong with her, because Robin's words made no sense and yet she *said* them. Why would she lie?

Robin put a surprisingly strong arm around Angelet's waist. "Come with me. You need to sit down. Your face is white."

As the two walked over to a nearby bench, which was just a plank of wood set over two stumps, Angelet whispered, "I need to speak with Rafe."

"You mean Lady Cecily," Robin said. "Because you're ill."

No. She meant Rafe, but it was no good telling Robin that. "Both of them, please. Could you fetch them? I'll wait here."

"Don't collapse," Robin warned. "I'll get in trouble if you collapse."

"Just hurry. And find Sir Rafe *first*, if you please."

Robin picked up her skirts and ran toward the practice fields, moving as if she did that sort of thing all the time. Angelet didn't remember the last time she ran anywhere. Ladies did not run.

She waited, sitting in the sunny spot, undoubtedly looking much calmer than she felt. The word *murder* kept crackling in her mind, interrupting all other thoughts. She tried to explain Robin's brief, startling statement to herself. It was obviously false. Rafe would never murder someone in cold blood. He was a knight, and she saw him fight. She even saw him kill Dobson, but that was purely to defend her.

But then she remembered Goswin's accusation of murder, and how Rafe had reacted to that, with a split second of horror before recovering. Granted, it turned out that Goswin exaggerated the situation in his anger, but the fact remained that he thought Rafe a murderer too. What did Robin and Goswin see in Rafe that Angelet missed? Was she so starved for affection that a little flirtation from Rafe was enough to blind her to his true nature?

No. She'd seen his true nature. It was impossible for him to be a murderer because she couldn't fall in love with a murderer.

"Oh, no," she whispered, putting her head in her hands. She loved him. Not just cared for him, or felt a passion for him, but *loved* him. How careless of her. How incredibly foolish.

"Angelet?"

She lifted her head.

Rafe stood in front of her, his face the picture of concern. "Robin just said you asked for me. What happened?"

"What happened?" she echoed. "What happened is that Robin mentioned something no one else here thought to bring up! She said you tried to murder Sir Alric."

Rafe's expression changed from concerned to chagrined. "Oh."

"Oh," she mimicked, taking refuge in ridicule. "Is this the awkward matter that kept you outside the walls at first? Is this the reason Cecily and Alric keep talking around your return here?"

"Yes."

His simple admission hurt to hear. "So it's true?"

"In short, yes, it is. Look, I never claimed I was a saint. In fact, I warned you that I was anything but."

"I never expected you to be perfect. However, attempted murder is completely beyond anything you hinted at! And I refuse to believe the matter is simple."

"Why?"

"Because if it were simple, and it was just a case of you hating Sir Alric enough to try to murder him, you wouldn't be allowed back here. But you were—"

Rafe interjected, "Solely because de Vere himself has been seeking me for some special retribution of his own. Alric wants me here so I can't avoid my fate."

She hadn't known that was what was keeping him here, but she should have suspected it wasn't because of her. "I see," she murmured. "Why did you try to kill him?"

"The usual reason," Rafe said. "Money. Same reason I agreed to escort you to Basingwerke. I'm a very simple man, Angelet. And not a good one. So when someone presented me with what looked like a profitable opportunity, I took it."

"Are you referring to the attempted murder or guarding me on the journey?"

He gave a short laugh. "The murder, but it applies to both. I'm out for myself, darling. Growing up with no wealth and no family connections meant that I always had to look out for myself."

"You were fostered here," Cecily interrupted. She'd just walked up, with Alric beside her. "You may not have had a noble name or lands to inherit, but you did have a family."

"Perhaps I did," Rafe conceded. "Until I betrayed that family when Theobald came to me with his plan."

"Who's Theobald?" Angelet asked.

"My uncle," said Cecily. "A snake of a man. We're well rid of him. But we're doing this piecemeal. Rafe, tell her the whole story."

"Please," Angelet added.

He looked away. "Let Cecily and Alric tell it. No one wants to hear my version."

"Everyone wants to hear your version," Cecily said. "And you owe Angelet the truth, since you were the one who brought her here."

"Do I have a choice?" Rafe asked.

"No." That came from Alric, who didn't look ready to compromise.

The whole group moved back into the manor house, since Cecily was worried about Angelet's condition. In the quiet solar, Angelet was offered the best seat, and Rafe was left standing to give his account, with both Cecily and Alric in attendance, to ensure he told the truth.

Rafe began with his arrival at Rainald de Vere's manor

so many years ago. "I had no idea what to expect. I was just a boy, and all I knew was that this…lord decided I was to join these other boys for training. I met Alric, and Luc…as well as the lord's daughter." He glanced toward Cecily. "I had nothing to complain about. The training was hard, and the days were long. But I was fed, and had a place to sleep."

"And you had friends," Alric added.

Rafe gave a short nod.

"Those three were inseparable," Cecily told Angelet. "They trained together, played together, ate together…everything. Together, they teased me horribly, too." But she smiled a little, suggesting that her memories of those days were fond ones.

"Then the attack happened," Rafe said. "And Lord Rainald de Vere died, or so we thought."

All smiles in the room disappeared.

"We didn't know it then—we were children—but the attack on the manor had been orchestrated by Theobald de Vere, who wanted the title and lands for himself. He forced his older brother to flee into exile, then pretended he had died so he could take over." Rafe's voice was quiet. "We all spent most of the next decade under his rule. It didn't matter much to me. I kept on training, and then we all went off to fight when the new king called for soldiers. I fought with Alric and Luc for the next few years, battle after battle. It's amazing we all survived."

Alric said, "We did it because we stayed together. That was what the oath meant."

"Ah, yes. The oath." Rafe chuckled. He looked directly at Angelet. "I swore an oath, you know. With Alric and Luc. Just the two of them. The oath was simple enough. That we have each other's back and be as brothers, not just in battle, but in life."

He sounded so distant. Angelet wanted nothing more than to pull him close and embrace him, but of course she couldn't. "What happened to change your heart?"

"We came home. Here, to Cleobury. The war was in a lull, and we'd finally got enough time to rest for a while. But Cleobury wasn't a place of refuge for anyone, not with Theobald in charge. He wanted even more power. So he arranged to marry his niece Cecily off to some lord. Theobald knew Alric worshipped her, though, so he offered me a deal. If I arranged for an accident during training, and Alric died, then I would be rewarded for my loyalty. More money than I'd ever imagined I could have at once. With that fortune, I could go anywhere, start a life in any place I chose. And all I had to do was murder my childhood friend."

"But you didn't actually do it," Angelet said.

"Not for lack of trying. We were sparring one day. Did I mention I'm a better fighter than Alric?"

"Sad but true," Alric admitted.

"He can't defend against me," Rafe went on. "I saw opening after opening, and finally I took one. I struck him. Drew blood."

Angelet put a hand to her mouth. "How did he survive?"

Rafe shrugged. "I stopped the fight and called his squire—after all, it was supposed to be an accident. But Alric took fever from the wound I gave him. I wished I hadn't struck him," Rafe said suddenly. "The instant I pierced the skin, I knew I'd made a mistake. No, not made a mistake. Committed a sin."

"Sins can be forgiven," Alric said. "And obviously, I did survive."

"You stayed at Cleobury?" Angelet asked. "Even after…"

"At that point, Alric didn't know I meant to kill. He has a better heart than I do. Everyone does."

Just then, a servant hurried in. "Pardon! My lady Cecily, your father returns. Octavian de Levant rides with him. An advance rider has just come. The main party will be here well before dark."

"Ah, how wonderful!" Cecily said, with a huge smile. Then she turned toward Rafe. "A little early, though. Your story isn't done."

"It doesn't get better," he said. "I did a host of despicable things after that. I even fought Alric again."

"Your heart wasn't in it that last time," Alric said. "And you knew it."

"The rest of the tale shall have to wait." Cecily looked at Angelet apologetically. "Come with me and we'll make ourselves presentable. I can't wait for you to meet my father."

"I'll stay with Rafe until Lord Rainald arrives," said Alric. "Just to make sure he doesn't slip away."

Angelet's gaze caught Rafe's, and she read the defeat in his face. Rafe looked as if slipping away was exactly what he had in mind.

Chapter 27

RAFE STEELED HIMSELF FOR THE arrival of the lord who'd been hunting him for years. Whatever his plans to slip out of Cleobury and evade the reckoning, now he had no choice. Part of him actually welcomed what was to come. Running was exhausting. The unknown was exhausting. At least now the worst would come out.

At Cecily's instruction, everyone gathered in the courtyard to greet the party so Rainald would have a proper welcome…and also to make Rafe's appearance known as quickly as possible.

When the party entered the courtyard, Rainald rode alongside someone else Rafe knew well. The young, dark-skinned knight scanned the group, and when he saw Rafe, his eyebrows lifted in surprise. He leaned over to say something to Lord Rainald, who nodded slowly. Then the knight leapt down from his horse and went directly to where Rafe stood near Angelet.

Cecily stepped forward. "Octavian! What a pleasant surprise."

"Surprise is a good word for it," the knight replied,

with a glance at Rafe.

"Angelet," Cecily said, taking her by the elbow. "This knight is our friend, Octavian de Levant. He has fought beside my Alric—as well as Rafe—during battle. I think he has saved all our lives once or twice."

Angelet, not yet fully healed, gave a wobbly curtsey. "Then I am most pleased to meet you, Sir Octavian. For Lady Cecily saved my life. She could not have done that if you hadn't saved hers earlier! I am Angelet d'Hiver."

The knight bowed. Rafe had forgot how intensely formal Octavian could be. "Lady Angelet."

Cecily said, "And you noticed that Rafe has returned."

"Indeed." Octavian looked Rafe directly in the eyes, and Rafe saw the suspicion there. Octavian was younger than him and Alric, and they hadn't met him until about five years ago. Of all of them, Octavian had the least reason to trust Rafe, since he'd only seen Rafe at his worst.

Still, he took his tone from his hosts, and Cecily obviously allowed Rafe to be there. "We'll have to talk soon," the knight said. "I'm curious as to where you've been."

"First," Alric said, "we all need to hear what happened at the meeting. It took long enough!"

Now Octavian smiled. "Our visit was useful, I think. The lull in fighting has meant an increase in discussions."

"Will Stephen and Maud finally agree to a peace?" Angelet asked. Rafe knew why. If they did, it would make it easier for her to reunite with her family.

"That I don't know, my lady. There are still many obstacles, not least of which is that both cousins still desire the crown."

Cecily frowned. "There won't be anything left to rule, the way they keep bickering. This country will revert to wilderness."

Octavian had been looking around the courtyard. "Speaking of the wild, where's your ward? Any luck housebreaking Lady Robin yet?"

Cecily sighed. "We're making progress…of a sort."

Octavian gave a knowing laugh. "Sounds like a *no* to me. You're better off opening the cage door and releasing her back into the forest."

"She'll make a fine lady," Cecily insisted. "She just needs time."

"And a miracle or two."

"Then pray for her." Cecily took Angelet by the arm, saying, "Now, dear, you must meet my father."

They all turned as Lord Rainald de Vere walked up to them. He accepted Cecily's exuberant embrace, then bowed to Angelet, who was introduced as a guest—again, Cecily kept the association between Rafe and Angelet quiet.

Then de Vere stood in front of Rafe. The older man's expression was one of wonder, not anger. "Rafe, you have come back."

"By chance, my lord," Rafe said. Despite everything that had happened, it still felt natural to defer to Lord Rainald de Vere. "Circumstances brought me to Cleobury for a short time."

"You have not come to stay?"

Rafe glanced at Alric as he said, "I do not wish to trouble the household further, my lord. I plan to leave as soon as…" He trailed off. What was holding him here? Angelet was already being cared for by Cecily, and she could not be in better hands. Rafe had no claim on her, and no reason to linger. Yes, he'd promised earlier to help her get her son back. But that was before all this happened. Alric and Cecily would be better allies even for that task. "I'll leave when you're done with me, my lord."

"Then you'll stay for a little while more. For I have much to say to you." Rainald spoke kindly, but there was no mistaking the order.

"As you wish, my lord."

Cecily said, "You must want to wash off the road, Father."

"So I do! And I hope supper will be prepared, for we're all famished."

As evening fell, everyone gathered in the great hall. The return of the manor's lord meant that the kitchen went to extra effort, and it was rather like a holiday, there was so much food and drink.

However, toward the end of the meal, Rainald gestured to Rafe, in a wordless order to join him. Rafe did.

"Now that I've finally got you here," the lord said, "it's time we speak. Follow me."

Alric, who was seated next to Rainald, asked if he ought to join them.

Rainald shook his head. "Rafe and I will speak alone."

"You're sure?"

"Sure as I am the lord of Cleobury."

That ended any more argument from Alric, though he watched Rafe as the two men left the hall.

"Alric worries overmuch, don't you think?" Rainald noted, as if they had conversations like this every day.

Rafe said, "Were I in his position, I wouldn't trust me."

"Alric knows only part of the story." Rainald opened the door to his private study and Rafe followed him in, sitting as instructed. The older man went on, "And indeed, you know only part of the story."

"Part of what story?"

"The story of your past. My dear boy," de Vere said with a heavy sigh, "I must beg your forgiveness."

"Ah…what?" As far as Rafe knew, he was the one who briefly allied himself with Rainald's traitorous brother Theobald. Rafe was the one who nearly murdered Rainald's future son-in-law, and it was Rafe who treated Cecily shamefully when she should have been able to rely on him. "You owe me nothing, my lord."

"Oh, I do. I've thought of you so often since I returned to Cleobury. How I wish I could have done things differently. Through my carelessness, I have stolen from you."

"My lord Rainald," Rafe said. "You are mistaken. I have nothing to my name. How could you have stolen anything from me?"

The older man smiled. "If only it were so. The truth is that I failed you, Rafe. There was so much I should have told you before. But you were a young boy, and I didn't want to burden you. Then I was forced to flee Cleobury when my brother moved to usurp me, and all seemed lost."

"You returned. Thanks to Alric and Octavian."

De Vere nodded sadly. "But then you left so quickly, and things were so turbulent here. By the time I realized I had to speak to you, no one could find you."

"Alric said you hired men to go after me."

"I did, but you're a hard man to find. I think providence has led you back here, so I could share what I should have shared so long ago."

"I don't understand. What is so important? What do you know that you didn't tell me?"

"Listen," de Vere said. "I must tell you a story. It may seem overlong, but it is necessary."

Rafe sat back, not at all sure what to expect.

"Once," Rainald began, "during the reign of King Henry, a rebellion rose up, as happens to all kings in all times. This one took place among some of the Marcher lords and their dubious Welsh allies. Naturally the king could not allow the rebellion to grow, so he sent men to quell the uprising.

"One of those men was a knight by the name of Sir Michael, who commanded a company so loyal that they were once rumored to have all swam across an icy river at night at his order, just to be in place at the battlefield by dawn. Now, during this rebellion, his task was to besiege the castle of one of the rebel lords. Dhustune was a most formidable prize—built high upon a rocky cliff-face, with stout walls and a natural defense of boggy land at the base of the cliff to one side. A siege would be long and difficult, but Sir Michael was a patient soldier.

"He first worked to cut off supply lines and seal up the castle from any outside assistance. Everyone settled in for a long siege. However, the rebel lord was a subtle and tricky man. He took advantage of a dreadful rainy night, when even the most dedicated sentries were less willing and able to keep a sharp eye out. He took his immediate family and a few retainers, and snuck out of the castle in the black of night. They managed to reach the edge of the bog when a sentry finally sighted them. An alarm was sounded and Sir Michael's men gave chase.

"The lord and nearly all of his people escaped into the woods—they knew the pathways better than the attackers. However, by chance, one person was captured. Lady Clare, the daughter of the lord, was brought to Sir Michael.

"Now this was like discovering a key to a lock. Sir Michael had a fine hostage in the lady Clare. He ordered the soldiers guarding Castle Dhustune to open the gates, lest Lady Clare be killed. What else could they do, given such a choice?

"They opened the gates and surrendered to spare their lady's life. This shifted everything in Sir Michael's favor. After only a few weeks of siege-work, the knight captured the castle with scarcely any losses, and now he had a noble hostage of the rebel side, rendering the rebel lord's escape almost moot. He took over Castle Dhustune in the name of the king, and sent word that he had Lady Clare, to be ransomed once terms could be reached. The king and the rebel lords would negotiate for her worth, and in the meantime, it was Michael's responsibility to keep the noble hostage safe.

"He took this responsibly very seriously, but Lady Clare was treated with all the courtesy due to her class and station. She was a sort of guest in her own home. Now, ransoms can take a long time to raise, and the negotiations would likely take months. This left plenty of time for Sir Michael and Lady Clare to get to know each other.

"This they did, for they were close in age and station. Over the weeks and months, their feelings grew from wariness to mutual regard to respect, and then of course to that most dangerous feeling…love. Sir Michael knew that Lady Clare was utterly unavailable to him, for so many reasons. Yet he had grown to love her most desperately. He might have been able to hide his feelings, but then Lady Clare herself forced his hand.

"She used a secret means to flee the castle one night. Sir Michael learned of her departure and gave chase. He found her quickly enough, in the woods past the castle. He asked her why she ran. Did she receive some secret signal from her father? Did she fear for her life? Had

Michael harmed her or insulted her in any way? He'd done all he could to make her life comfortable and safe. As a hostage, she was in no physical danger.

"The lady confessed that she ran not because she feared Michael, but herself. For weeks, she fought her own heart, for she had grown to love Sir Michael for his strength and great kindness and courtly manners. She fled the castle, knowing that she could no longer hide her feelings and her own desperate desire for a man she was supposed to hate.

"Naturally, once they both understood each other's hearts, the next step was inevitable. Michael took Clare back to Castle Dhustune, concealed her attempted escape, and promised to love her and serve her in any way he could without breaking his oath to the king. They began a secret affair, too much in love to wait any longer. A few months later, the lady Clare discovered she was with child."

De Vere fell silent for a long moment, taking a drink after the long speech.

Having listened in perplexed silence so far, Rafe said, "So that's my past? I'm that child. Bastard of a hostage and the soldier sent to watch her."

"My boy, you must learn patience," de Vere told him. "I'm not done with my story. Your parents' love for each other was great, and so was their honor. Your father would never allow the woman he loved to be shamed, or for his child to be born as a bastard."

"What are you saying?"

"Your parents married."

"Married?" Rafe took a long breath.

"Yes. In secret, in the Castle Dhustune, by a priest they knew and trusted, for he'd been priest to Lady Clare for years. He married them, and swore to keep the ceremony secret until Sir Michael could properly explain what had occurred to his own family, and to Lady Clare's, and to the king. It was a delicate balance, you see. Sir Michael did not want to give an enemy an advantage due to the unsanctioned marriage. Nor did he want to risk King Henry's wrath with the news that he'd married the daughter of a rebel! He wanted to speak to the king directly first, hoping to soften the blow."

"Obviously, something went wrong."

"Yes. I'll tell you how it happened, but first I must confess that I erred greatly. You see, I knew part of the story for a very long time. You came to Cleobury as a boy, and that was because your mother had long before asked me to watch over you."

"You knew who my mother was from the first?" Rafe tried to keep his feelings in check, but it was hard. Even he never knew that! He'd been raised by a family of tenant farmers that treated him well enough, but admitted he wasn't their son.

"I knew that you were Lady Clare's child," de Vere said. "Back then, I didn't know the name of your father, or that you were born legitimate. A trusted servingwoman to Lady Clare brought you to Cleobury, and from her I was given the name of the priest and told to seek him out. But before I could contact him, my own life was upended."

"I remember." Rafe would never forget the night they all thought Rainald de Vere had died, though in reality he'd been forced to flee his home and family.

"As you can imagine," Rainald said, "survival was my first goal in those years, and I had no means to pursue the matter of your birth. But I did not forget. When I was restored as the lord of Cleobury, I set about rectifying the many injustices brought about by my brother Theobald's actions.

"Though you'd left soon after my restoration, I knew I still owed you the truth. I did find the priest, and heard his story. I had him dictate his testimony, which was witnessed and signed. There will be no dispute as to the legitimacy of the marriage or your birth. I wish that I could also tell you that you are due to inherit lands or some chattel, but alas, I have only your history to give you."

"That's enough." Rafe was stunned by the revelation that his parents were married. He'd lived his whole life under the assumption that he was a bastard, completely unwanted and unneeded. That belief shaped his entire existence. It was why he fought for everything he wanted, because he knew no one would give him anything, he had to take it. "Wait. No, it's not! What happened to my parents?"

"Ah, I forgot to say. Sir Michael left Castle Dhustune, precisely for the purpose of joining the king and reporting all that happened. But on the way, he and his companions—he rode with only a few men, for speed's sake—were killed in a skirmish. It was not certain if the attackers were masterless men, or a group sent by the rebel lords. But the result was the same.

"Lady Clare was devastated when she heard, and fled the castle herself, for she no longer trusted her own family to treat her well once they learned she married a knight from the opposing side and was carrying his child. She went to live with a tenant family she trusted, who lived far from the castle."

"The Fowler family." That was who raised him.

"Exactly. She went there because she had known the

family since she was a young girl. At their home, she hid. She bore you, and named you Raphael, an angelic name like your father's. She had sent word to my wife of the news—they had known each other, and Lady Clare trusted her. My Matilidis told her to come to us with the baby, that we would protect you both as needed. Clare was too wary though. She said she felt safer hiding with the humble tenant family. I think she would have been persuaded in time. But she died when you were only about two years old. I expect you never had any memories of her."

"None." Rafe always tried to forget his early childhood. Now he regretted doing so.

"You have her coloring, that same dark hair. But the eyes are your father's gift, I am told. Even as an infant, you charmed everyone who saw you. A harbinger of things to come. When you were old enough, I sent for you. I hoped that by training you as a knight, I might give you the same legacy your own father would have."

"So you wanted me here."

"Of course! Who would leave a child among strangers if they could prevent it? I blame myself for withholding the partial news from you while you were a child, but I wanted to discover the whole story, in order to pass it on to you. Then my own brother usurped me here, and I thought I'd lost everything, all my connections to my blood and my friendships. In truth, I forgot about your difficulties in the midst of my own. And then you fled from Cleobury after my return. By the time I remembered how vital it was to speak with you, you were gone."

Rafe closed his eyes, thinking of how impetuous he'd been. "I should have stayed."

"Don't berate yourself for what you might have done differently. It's a fool's game, and unwinnable."

"I wasted years of my life, when I could have known the truth. I kept running. I assumed Alric sent men after me to drag me back to face justice for my crimes."

"No, it was my doing. I asked him to help me find you…though he hoped to find you anyway, for his own reasons."

"I thought you meant to punish me."

"No, dear boy. I only wanted to give you what you should have already had. A name. Two names."

"Michael and Clare," Rafe said slowly, testing the sound of them.

"Wait, did I not say? His family name was Corviser, and he always used the device of the raven. A play on the Latin word for raven: *corvus*."

Rafe laughed out loud. Had some remnant of his father managed to influence Rafe's choice of the raven for his own symbol? He chose it all on his own, back when he was training with Luc and Alric. *Rafe* and *raven* sounded similar enough that when his name was shouted across a practice field, or a battlefield, it often sounded like raven. But perhaps there was something more to it. Had his mother told him of his history when he was so young that he had no conscious memory of it, yet it settled into the recesses of his mind, ready to be called up?

"So I'm my father's son," he said quietly.

"Perhaps an angel took an interest in you, Rafe, though you always behaved like a young devil. You survived how many battles? Formidable fighter you may be, it's not all skill that saved you. It was grace."

"Grace, and having Alric and Luc to watch my back." Rafe grew somber once again. "Where was the angel when I decided to betray my friends?"

"Closer than you think. You stayed your hand when

the moment came, didn't you? You could have killed, and you chose not to. You never truly lost your moral center. You just...muffled its voice for a while."

"I need to think about this," Rafe said, standing up. He felt light-headed, even dizzy. Was this how Angelet felt when one of her visions came upon her? Surely this story counted as a revelation?

At the thought of Angelet, Rafe suddenly found it hard to breathe. He had a *name* now. He didn't have to be just the soldier paid to escort Angelet across the channel. Now he could be more, if she would let him.

"I need to go," he said to de Vere. "I need to find someone."

"I know the feeling," the older man said, with a smile. "Good night, Sir Raphael."

Chapter 28

AFTER RAFE HAD GONE AWAY with de Vere, Angelet lost all ability to focus on the simplest conversations at supper. She wanted to be in the room with Rafe. She wanted to hear what de Vere thought so important that he chased Rafe for months on end to tell him. She could only imagine that it was connected, in some way, to the fateful action he'd taken against Alric. But she couldn't puzzle out what it might be.

As she often did when her mind was in a tumult, she sought the dim, silent peace of the chapel. The one at Cleobury was deserted when she entered that evening, since the priest had just celebrated the office of Compline, and would not return until the late night office of Lauds, following the endless, reassuring cycle of holy hours.

Out of long practice, Angelet lit one of the candles at the base of the altarpiece and said a prayer to Mary, asking for protection for her son, Henry. "I cannot watch over him, so I appeal to you, Mother of God. Though I am unworthy, I beg you for aid. I love him so, and all I want is to know he's safe and well."

Then, she sank to her knees in front of the altar. The candles cast steady, gold beams of light into the space. She bent her head and closed her eyes, praying silently. The rote Latin took only a moment, leaving her mind to wander. Angelet often spoke to Mary, using French or even English as the words came to her. For years, these one-sided conversations were her only safe way to pour out her sorrow and her worry. She always asked Mary and her army of saints to watch over young Henry, who Otto had so deftly snatched away from Angelet. She prayed for her distant family, wondering where they were and how they fared, and why no word from them ever reached her. Most of all, she prayed for an end to the royal squabble that affected her life along with so many others.

This night, however, her words had a different subject. She prayed for Rafe, who seemed so tangled up and unhappy with everything. She hoped he could at last reconcile with the friends who he obviously missed, though he pretended not to. Alric insisted more than once that he had forgiven Rafe. But Rafe had yet to forgive himself. Angelet wished she could help—her fingers threaded together as she tried to think of any way to do it. But she was a near stranger, and she barely knew these people or the events that had occurred years ago. What could she possibly do to help? She wasn't sure if her help would even be wanted.

And now he was talking with Rainald de Vere himself. Was he learning something that would make his life even more difficult?

"Just…take away a little of his pain," she whispered. "Give it to me, if someone must bear it. I don't mind." Whether Mary would hear her words, Angelet didn't know. Father Mark once warned her of the futility in demanding a response from prayer. Silence was an answer in itself.

As she knelt there, her head bowed, she sensed someone else enter the church behind her. She turned, and saw Rafe standing just inside the doorway, dressed in dark clothing, as always. And he was still so arrestingly handsome. She should stop being dazzled by this point, but she realized that would never happen. She delighted in looking at him, for looking at something beautiful ought to delight.

And he was smiling, making him even more attractive. She rose to her feet as he closed the distance between them.

"Angelet, I have to tell someone," he said, his voice holding a barely restrained excitement. He slid his arms around her waist and his body met hers, like a shield against the world.

"Rafe," she whispered. Having him so close, after so long apart, affected her more than she could have guessed.

He looked her over, his expression growing tentative. "Can I…can I tell you? You might not care to hear anything I have to say, considering what I kept from you—"

"No! I want to hear. Please. You've had good news. It's in your face. Tell me."

Rafe looked a little stunned, but he smiled again. "May I introduce myself?"

"What?"

"Angelet, I have a name." He took a breath, clearly bursting with joy. "I'm Raphael Corviser. My father was Sir Michael Corviser, and my mother was Lady Clare of Beaumont. And they *were* married."

She put her hands on his chest, and felt the beat of his heart underneath all the layers. She repeated, "Sir Raphael

Corviser. The name fits you well."

Rafe rambled out the whole story to her, probably just as de Vere told it to him.

At the end, she was smiling just as widely as he was. "Oh. Oh, Rafe. I'm so happy for you, to have finally learned your past."

"I would have learned it earlier, if I hadn't run."

"Don't blame yourself, Rafe. You did what made sense at the time. Your friends have forgiven you, and you have your life back. What more could you want?"

"You." He kissed her.

Angelet's lips parted as she responded to him. She'd been aching for this, to taste him again, ever since he'd touched her last.

"You missed this, too," he said, pleased.

"Yes." Her hands were all over him then, as if she'd forgotten what he felt like. She hadn't forgotten at all, but she didn't mind relearning the shape of his body.

He bent to kiss her neck, and she stretched to allow him the best access.

"I've gone far too long without you," he murmured. "I need you, sweetheart."

"We can't."

He kissed her again, drawing out a gasp and the truth that she was just as aroused as he was. "We can. Come with me."

"Now? Where?"

His lips were at her ear and his laugh sounded wicked. "Here."

"This is a church!" she gasped.

"I'm aware of that."

"Rafe, you can't even joke about that." And yet she was so tempted to say yes.

"I'm not joking. I want you. We have the place all to ourselves. Why shouldn't we enjoy the privacy?"

"It is not private. Anyone could walk in."

"They won't."

"The priest will return…"

"We have half the night till the next office. And I happen to know that the priest here is a sound sleeper."

"Rafe—" Angelet's next protest was cut short when he slid his hands over her breasts. He knew her too well, and knew exactly what she liked.

"Sin with me, love," he begged.

Angelet's eyes slid closed. "I want to. But I'm not strong enough. I'm still healing…"

"I'll be careful," he promised. "Trust me this time. No orders, no games. Just let me be with you."

"Yes," she breathed, still clinging to him. "But Rafe…"

"No one will see anything," he said. He kissed her again. "Come with me."

He took her hand and led her to the side of the church, where the design of the apse created the alcove for the lady chapel, not much more than a little room with an altar specifically set up for the veneration of Mary. Behind the stone altar there was a shadowed space, just large enough for two people to lay together.

She was flushed and distracted, but she still realized just how…knowledgeable he was about this hidden place. "You've taken other women back here, haven't you?"

Rafe looked wounded. "Never."

"Truly?"

"I swear." He gave her a quick grin. "But I have thought about it. Plenty. They forced me to attend mass, but mass is boring. And I was young and easily distracted by pretty girls in the next row."

"Now that sounds like truth."

He cupped her face in his hands. "You're so beautiful," he said suddenly.

"So are you." Her voice was raw. "Rafe…I…" Angelet's stomach was in knots. Rafe's touch destroyed her calm, made her think only of him and how much she wanted to be with him.

"Are you still nervous about being found out? No one will bother us here." Rafe took her in his arms. "Do you mind the dark?"

"No."

"I do," he said, his voice low and provocative. "I wish it was full daylight and I could see you." He found her mouth and kissed her, making her knees weak by the time he had her lower lip in his teeth.

She reached for him, pulling him to her and twining her fingers in his hair. "I dreamed about you," she confessed. "I woke up sweating, so certain you were with me in bed."

"Believe me, I had the same dream, love," Rafe said. "I'd wake up, reach for you and feel nothing there. Tonight will be different."

He used their cloaks to arrange a makeshift bed, then he pulled off his shirt and bundled it into a pillow, apologizing for the crudity of the materials.

"I don't mind," she told him. "As long as we're together."

"You're the perfect lover, Angelet. Discreet yet daring. And very accommodating." He started to loosen the lacing at the sides of her over-gown.

She smiled, but his words needled at her, though she knew he meant nothing cruel. She had been a perfect lover for Rafe. Discreet enough to hide their relationship. Daring enough to accept his proposition. And accommodating of his every suggestion. And safe, since she'd never bear him a bastard child, something Rafe feared, living so long as a bastard himself.

But now he had a name. And a legacy. He'd want to build on that legacy, reclaim his family line. That meant marriage…to a woman who could bear his children.

Angelet blinked back tears. The very thing that gave Rafe hope was the thing that meant she'd lose him.

She gasped, and Rafe took it for physical pain. He paused just as he was about to remove her gown.

"What's wrong? Did I hurt you?"

"No. It's nothing," she said, putting the thought aside.

"You need to lie down, love," he told her.

A moment later, she was lying down, completely nude, with Rafe kneeling between her legs. He'd stripped off the rest of his clothes, and she eyed him greedily, wanting as much of him as she could take while she could, before she had to give him up.

Rafe took his time, evidently being quite serious about treating her with care. He first looked over her wound. By this time, she didn't even need it covered with a bandage. The tissue was growing back in a way that promised a scar, and there was bruising that discolored her skin.

Anger flitted over his face when he saw it all.

"It's healing," she told him. "It looks worse than it is."

"You shouldn't have got hurt at all," he said. "I wish I could have…" he trailed off. "Angelet, you'll always be beautiful. You know that."

"You've always made me feel beautiful," she confessed, feeling unexpectedly shy.

"I will again," he promised, looking more like himself. "But don't worry. I'll treat you carefully. I can do that, you know. Being a civilized man and not a mere bastard soldier."

She reached out to pull him closer. "Enough chatter. You brought me here to sin with me."

And Rafe knew all about sin. He knew just how to touch her and when to wait, and always he treated her like glass about to shatter. He ran his hands over every part of her body, but kept his touch light. When he kissed her, his mouth was gentle, not the greedy, demanding kisses from their earlier encounters. Angelet reveled in his attention, her arousal building bit by bit.

At first, she tried to listen with half an ear for footsteps beyond, or any hint that someone else was in the church. But soon enough she was so utterly seduced by what Rafe was doing to her that she forgot what to listen for, and even forgot why she should care.

All that mattered was that she was with him, the man who made her feel as if she was special all on her own. She watched him in the near darkness, and fell in love with him again, even though she knew it was foolish of her. But he was so gorgeous on the surface and so intriguing underneath. And how could she not love someone who made her feel so lovely?

He took his time, alert to her breathing and any hint that she might be past pleasure and into pain, even though he did nothing more than touch her with his hands and mouth. She was certain he'd grow impatient, and give in to his own obvious desire. But he never did. Instead he devoted himself solely to pleasing her, each stroke and touch building on the last until she forgot everything but him.

When she came undone, it started so gently that it

took her a moment to realize it was happening, and then she was barely more than one long sigh as she clung to him, enjoying his warmth as she felt the sense of completion ripple through her.

After a moment, he moved above her at last, ready to enter her. There was a pause, and she understood he was waiting for her permission, still not quite sure that she was healed enough to tolerate actual coupling.

She gave that permission with a few whispered words, and he sighed in relief as he slid into her. Still, he kept his word to treat her gently, and he showed incredible restraint as he took his own pleasure from her body, and all she wanted was to make him happy with her, to have a little time when they could be content with each other and need nothing else.

He let out a low moan and then kissed her to muffle any further sound when he finished inside her. Angelet wrapped her arms around him, keeping him as close as she could.

"Oh, I missed you," he said finally, his voice no louder than breath.

He withdrew, shifted to lie down on his back, and then pulled her to him.

She sidled up till she could tuck her head under his chin. He held her tightly, one strong arm around her shoulders, cradling her to him. She sighed. She never felt more safe and happy than when he held her like this.

Neither of them spoke for several moments. Rafe kept running one hand over her back and her side, then slid his fingers to hover over her chest. "You're all right?" he asked, his voice a little shaky. He was scared he'd hurt her after all, despite all the care he'd taken.

"I'm marvelous," she assured him.

"Good." His arm tightened around her. "There are only so many hours until dawn, and I don't know how long it will be until the next time."

Angelet felt cold intrude on her lassitude. There could never be a next time, and the sooner Rafe understood how their lives no longer had any intersection, the less painful it would be. She reached up and pushed his black hair away from his face. "Rafe, we can't keep meeting like this."

"We can after I find sufficient bedding." He smiled and then kissed her nose.

"I meant…we can't continue this dalliance."

"You're afraid of being caught?"

"Well, that and…it's not right. Not here, among these people. They're your friends and they've taken me in. I can't abuse their protection by sneaking off like this." She gestured to the dark surroundings. "And if we should be discovered, then what? What's the outcome for you or me? I'll wager you hate to have your hand forced. No matter what happens, you'll resent any choice that isn't your own."

He looked at her, his brow slightly furrowed. "What's your alternative then?"

"That should be obvious! We need to behave. Not continue this…"

"Dalliance."

"Yes."

"However," he added, "Since we're already here…" He leaned forward to capture her mouth with his, and she immediately felt the heat spiral through her.

"Oh," she sighed.

"That's what I thought," Rafe murmured. She could hear the smile in his voice, the satisfaction he got from knowing how much she needed him.

"Please," she whispered.

"Please what?"

"Please don't waste a moment."

He wasted nothing.

Chapter 29

ANGELET HAD SLIPPED back into her bedchamber in the manor house before dawn, and Rafe had gone to his own bed after seeing she was safe. Her absence had been noticed the previous night, but when she said she'd gone to the church to pray for a while and then had fallen asleep —which was not precisely a lie—the answer was accepted instantly, not only by the various servants who tended the house, but by Lady Cecily as well.

"You must be careful," Cecily reprimanded her. "Even praiseworthy tasks such as prayer can be overdone. And you are still weak. I hope you did not suffer from cold, or exert yourself too much."

"I assure you that was not the case," Angelet replied, her eyes on the floor. *Not at all.*

"And today? What do you have in mind?"

"I have some items to work on," she said, "and with the day being so warm, I thought I would embroider in the gardens."

"Very good. I'll send one of the maids out to check on you around the midday meal."

The day was indeed finer than any before it that spring. The air was marvelously soft, the breezes gentle and the sun warm. Puffs of clouds raced in the sky above.

Below, a pack of boys raced around at about the same speed as the clouds, dashing more erratically, and shouting the whole time. Angelet spied the bright orange head of Goswin among them, and was glad he could enjoy some simple pleasures. After a time, the whole rowdy pack ran through the wide open gate to play in the fields and woods outside. Spring days seemed to be specially made for children.

Angelet settled down beneath a spreading apple tree to work. She wanted to complete the embroidery she'd started on the gown for Cecily's coming infant. It was an inadequate repayment, but she had to start somewhere.

She lost track of time, but when a shadow eclipsed her work, she looked up.

The man towering over her was a stranger, but since he was dressed in the same manner as all the men-at-arms she'd seen at Cleobury, he must have been one of them.

"My lady," he said. His tone was in marked contrast to his size—diffident and very soft. "I'm sorry to tell you that your boy Goswin is hurt. He wants to see you."

Angelet's sewing dropped into her lap, and her breath caught in fear. "Hurt? How?"

"The boys were climbing trees, and he fell."

"Oh, no! Where is he?"

"Still there. The boys feared to move him. Will you come? He asked for you specifically."

As she started to scramble to her feet, she said, "Yes, of course, but shouldn't we also bring Lady Cecily? She's the healer."

He offered a giant hand to help her up. "Someone's already gone to find her, my lady. Please, we ought to hurry."

"How far?"

"Not very. Just in the woods past the western fields." He started to walk, assuming that she'd follow in his wake. She cast about briefly, confused about whether she ought to take anything, and if so what. She ended up bundling several things in a sewing basket, but she was far too distracted to know if she was bringing the right things. She didn't even know how Goswin got hurt.

Angelet hurried to catch up to the big man. "What happened? Did he break a bone? Is he bleeding? It's not his head, is it?" she asked fearfully.

"Not sure," the man said. It was hard to hear him, since he spoke so quietly and also because he was facing the woods, not her. "He asked for you."

That didn't clarify much, but at least it meant Goswin was conscious. She kept up the pace set by the big man, though it meant that she was nearly breathless by the time they crossed the fields to the fringe of the woods.

"Wait. A moment," she gasped, putting her hand against a tree trunk. "I need to rest."

The man stopped abruptly, looking back at her, then at Cleobury. "Yes, a moment. But we can't waste time, my lady."

"No," she agreed. "It's just that I was hurt too, not long ago. I'm not supposed to…" She stopped talking, gasping again.

"Just breathe," the man said, looking alarmed. "They didn't say you were so weak."

"Who said?"

He gave a shrug. "Everyone, my lady. People talk. No offense meant."

She closed her eyes, trying to get her breathing back to normal. "I'm better now…what's your name?"

"Ulmar," he said.

"Very well, Ulmar. We can go on."

The man-at-arms looked rather uncertain, but he nodded and turned to keep walking. "Follow me. It's not far."

They went a bit slower through the woods, but Angelet thought they'd reach Goswin soon, and instead Ulmar just kept walking. She also expected to hear voices—boys shouting, perhaps. Or running to see when help would come.

"Where is he?" she asked.

"Not far. Almost there." Ulmar slowed his pace to let her catch up, then took her by the elbow. "Just a little further."

Something made her hesitate, and she stopped in her tracks. "This is too far."

Ulmar's grip tightened. "Sorry, my lady."

She tried to pull away, but there wasn't much she could do against a guard twice her size. "Let me go," she said. Her heart sped up, and she could feel the pricks of pain in her chest from the exertion.

"Can't do that, my lady." Ulmar's voice was still soft. "Orders."

"Whose orders? Where's Goswin?"

"He's got him," Ulmar said. "Lord Ernald. So you see, my lady, the boy does need you. Ernald will hurt him if you don't arrive soon."

Angelet swallowed, tasting a metallic bitterness in her mouth as her limbs shook in fear. She took a deeper breath, then tried to run. She had to get back to Cleobury.

She made it about twenty paces. And only that far because Ulmar stumbled on a tree root for a moment. But he gained on her immediately, and she screamed when he grabbed her by the arm.

Ulmar jerked her toward him, swinging her body to his and muffling her mouth with a big hand. "Don't scream, my lady. Won't do a bit of good. You're too far from the manor and no one will hear."

She struggled for a moment, but already her lungs protested. She slumped in defeat.

The big man removed his hand, and she gasped several times.

"Scream again and I'll have to do something about it," he warned her.

"Let me go."

"Can't. And there's still the matter of the boy. You don't want him to suffer."

"Where is he?"

"Close." Ulmar took her by the elbow once more, this time making it clear that she'd be stupid to try to get free. Angelet stumbled along beside him, furious with herself for getting into this mess. She should have known something was wrong! She should have told someone, or insisted on more people joining them. But she had been so worried about Goswin.

A moment later, they entered a clearing, where several horses were tethered at one side, and people gathered on the other.

One of them turned at their arrival. "Oh, there she is. The elusive Angelet!"

Angelet took in the sight of Ernald, who appeared incredibly satisfied with himself. Next to him stood none other than Bethany, who clearly survived the attack to the cortège—and was probably never even in danger. The way she hovered possessively close to Ernald suggested that she was his lover. So that was the reason Bethany volunteered to join Angelet on the journey. Ernald must have told her to.

She noticed another man dressed as a soldier, who held a bound and gagged Goswin. Angelet saw the fear in the boy's eyes, and understood exactly how he felt.

Ernald circled Angelet like a wolf around a sheep.

"You're looking well, sister," he said. "Despite all that's befallen you since your departure from Dryton. And I know about everything you've done because I've been tracking you for weeks now."

Considering Bethany had obviously been passing on information to him during the first part of the journey, that news was not surprising. Still, she knew Ernald wanted to be dramatic, so she indulged him. He'd tell her more that way, since Ernald adored the sound of his own voice.

"How did you find me here?" she asked.

"Silly girl, it was simple. One of my hired men saw you flee from the site of the original attack. Your champion, dressed in black armor, riding a black horse. You in your fine gown and jewels, with your lovely blonde tresses, riding a white horse. That's a remarkable looking pair. It was not hard to follow the trail once we found someone who had seen you." Ernald's grin widened. "Where the hell did you plan to go, though? I never could tell."

"We were riding for Wareham," she said, deliberately avoiding mention of Henry.

"Ah, yes. You'd get aboard a ship and sail back to your family!" He laughed.

"Why does that sound so funny to you?" she asked. "It's not as if I ever could call the Yarboroughs family. After Hubert died, I was forgotten."

"Hardly forgotten, Angelet." Ernald put a finger on her throat. "I thought about you quite often."

"All the more reason for me to return to my own family," she said, jerking away.

He chuckled again. "Ah, yes. One small hurdle for that course, Angelet. You have no family in Anjou."

"What do you mean?"

"I mean the d'Hivers are no more. Both your parents are dead now, your brother is who the hell knows where. A rival has taken your lands by force… You have no allies, and no home to go back to."

Her heart quailed, but she kept a brave face. "I don't believe you. These are lies to hurt me."

He shrugged. "You may think that if you like. But did you never wonder why no one came to claim you? Why Otto could keep you in his grip as he did? Why your mother or father never wrote to you? Never asked after you?"

"Otto kept letters from me," she guessed, uncertainly. "Or stopped messengers from speaking with me."

"A few, early on. But then there were no more letters. Because there were no more d'Hivers to write them."

"I don't believe you," she repeated, except this time her voice shook.

"Oh, it's true. Otto was just waiting for the right opportunity to unload you, since you long outserved your purpose as the vessel for the heir. Hence the nunnery."

"That was a compromise," she said. "I would be allowed visits from my son, and that abbey is known for healing. My affliction could be cured there."

He chuckled. "Basingwerke is not known for its healing or its infirmary. It's known for its visionaries. Both men and women touched by God with divine visions that they shout out or mumble or ramble on. You'll embroider yours, I suppose. The abbot doesn't seek to cure anyone's suffering. He collects people like you, and then profits from the spectacle of the visions. Whether they're beautiful or terrible or prophetic…it doesn't matter. People come to watch."

"The abbot permits that?"

"He encourages it! If your sufferings are dramatic enough, you'll be locked up in an anchorite's cell, or chained to the wall, and there people will come and gawk as you go through your ordeal. They call it a pilgrimage, like visiting a shrine of a saint. But they leave…you don't. You remain there on display until you die, or you bring in no more money. See, the gawkers pay the abbey in coin for your care…a donation, which the abbot keeps for himself."

"That cannot be true."

"As if you'd know, woman. Otto told you nothing of the place. He didn't allow you to visit first, or decide for yourself."

Angelet swallowed nervously. "What do you care if I end up in a nunnery or run off alone. I don't know why anyone in your family cares what happens to me!"

Ernald leaned in, his mouth right by her ear. "Because you *are* family, little lamb."

She shivered at the feel of his breath on her skin. "Get away from me. This isn't seemly."

He straightened up, saying, "Neither is riding around half the country with only a nameless bastard of a soldier for company. You're no better than a common slut."

"Then why bother with me? Just let me go."

"Ah, no, I still have some business with you, Angelet. First, after your behavior, you've dishonored the family name, which is intolerable. Second, there's the matter of your missing dowry. Third, I intend to discover exactly how depraved your nighttime activities have been, by testing you myself, starting tonight."

"You will *not*," Angelet retorted. Her words were echoed strangely, and she realized someone else said the same words.

Bethany stood aghast, staring at both Angelet and Ernald. She had also spoken. Now she added, "My lord, you can't. Not her. Not after she's given herself to that man. She doesn't deserve you!"

All at once, many things became clear to Angelet. Bethany's often rude behavior, her cutting remarks. The maid wasn't just a casual lover. She truly *loved* Ernald. No wonder she'd hated Angelet for so long. Angelet felt sick.

But Ernald just said, "Silence, lamb. No woman orders me."

Bethany looked as if she was going to retort, but then clenched her fists and bowed her head. "Yes, my lord."

"Good girl. Don't worry about what transpires between Angelet and me. She'll be dealt with soon enough."

Angelet closed her eyes. That did not sound promising. She had to get away from Ernald. "You tracked me for weeks just to punish me?" she asked.

"No. I tracked you for weeks because what I wanted to retrieve from your cortège wasn't there. What happened to the gold, Angelet?"

She blinked in confusion. "Surely Bethany told you. The thieves—*your* thieves—dropped the chest and we all saw it. There was no gold."

"Yes, everyone saw it. No one liked it." Ernald's eyes narrowed. "Those men almost turned on me afterward. They thought I lied to them, but I managed to convince them you were at fault."

"But I wasn't!"

"Otto gave the key to you. You had half the men-at-arms dancing to your tune. You must have used them to sneak the gold out of the chest. How'd you do it? A little night by night? Or one bold move? Where'd you hide it all?"

"Nowhere! For the last time, I didn't open that chest at all. Whoever stole the gold did it without using my key, and without my knowledge."

He raised a hand, about to strike her across the face. "Don't lie to me, Angelet."

She watched his hand, certain that whatever she said, it would result in pain. But she wasn't going to be made into a thief. "I had nothing to do with the gold going missing," she said, very slowly.

Ernald's arm jerked, but he stayed his hand for the moment. She saw the calculation in his eyes. "Perhaps it wasn't you. That knight could have done it, maybe by stealing the key after he enjoyed you."

"Stop it."

"If it was him," Ernald went on, ignoring her, "then I'll need to chat with him. And keeping you close will make that easier." He looked to Ulmar. "Now that we have her, it's time to ride to meet the others. When we get there, take her to the stone hut and make sure she stays locked up inside. I have to consider my options."

The way Ernald smiled at Angelet made her grow cold.

Chapter 30

RAFE WAS STILL OVERWHELMED BY the news he'd received the day before, and he wanted to tell everyone he'd ever met. In particular, he wanted to hear more of what Angelet had to say. He knew that he couldn't court Angelet, much as he wanted to, until his status was known more generally. Still, he could talk to her. After hearing that she was awake and working in the orchard he decided to find her, but he was intercepted by Alric.

"Well?" the other man asked bluntly. "What was the news? Rainald can be an oyster when he wants—won't let a word slip about his plans."

"He told me about my family," Rafe said.

The surprise on Alric's face was completely authentic. "Your family?"

So Rafe shared the story once more. He'd tell it for the rest of life and not tire of it. Alric sat back in amazement and listened to it all. At the end, he said, "That's a marvel. A tragedy for your parents, but still a marvel. That you should have gone so long without knowing, just because of all the obstacles fate put in the way."

"Better late than never."

"Who else knows?"

"So far, I only told Angelet."

"Ah." Alric crossed his arms, and looked intolerably smug.

"What's the *ah* for?"

"The woman you insisted was just a client was the first person you told. Interesting."

"Well..." Rafe didn't have an answer. "Yes. I did. But it doesn't mean anything."

"No? My mistake. Come, you need to tell Cecily what's happened."

So Rafe was dragged along to tell Cecily. Then Rainald joined them, and talk turned to the more legal ramifications of Rafe's new status. Rafe was jolted when servants brought in some food for a midday meal—he'd got lost amid the swirl of discussion about what he should do next.

Alric thought he should petition the king for the privileges that had been his father's. Cecily suggested he travel to find his mother's people. Rainald also offered a few ideas for Rafe to take advantage of his legacy. Rafe nodded and listened to them all, but the only thing he could think of was the fact that he was now elevated to a station just high enough so he could ask Angelet to marry him without being rejected out of hand. Granted, she'd still want to speak to her family and he'd need to prove himself worthy of them. And they still needed to get her son back to her. Would Angelet's being married again actually help with that? Possibly.

He just wished he could feel more certain about Angelet's response. She'd seemed a little strange the previous night, especially with the suggestion that—how had she put it?—he'd resent any choice that wasn't his own. Why had she said that? She'd meant that if their relationship became common knowledge, marriage would be the quickest path to restoring reputations. But why would Angelet think he'd resent *her* for it? Even with his parentage known, Rafe would still be the one ascending in rank by wedding her, a truly well-born woman. Perhaps she just hadn't been thinking clearly when she spoke. After all, Rafe had done his best to keep her mind occupied elsewhere.

"Rafe?"

"What?" He looked up to see the others watching him. It was Cecily who'd asked him a question. "Yes?"

"Did you want to send word to Luc? To help you craft a petition for the king. You know Luc has the most experience at court—he'll know just what to say."

"I need to speak to Angelet," he said, not quite following.

Cecily glanced at Alric, then they both smiled knowingly. Cecily said, "Perhaps that's best. I'll ask for her to come here."

She called for a servant, then gave the order. They sat waiting. Rafe tried to ignore Alric and Cecily's smug expressions, which was difficult, since they sat directly across from him. Rainald, in the large, padded seat close to the fire, hummed to himself, then said, "That was the song they played at my wedding feast! Never forgot it."

Rafe rolled his eyes. So he was beset on all sides. "You did tell the servants to bring her here, didn't you?"

Cecily nodded, but then looked to the door. "I do wonder what's keeping her. It's been long enough."

But Angelet did not come. Another quarter hour passed. Rafe stood up. "Something's wrong."

"Don't be silly." Cecily rose to her feet. "She's probably just freshening up. I'll go to her room and see."

Cecily left, but Rafe didn't sit back down. Alric watched him pace. "Aren't you overreacting? What could possibly happen inside the walls?"

"She could have had another seizure, like the one she was suffering from when she came here."

"Then we'd have heard about it," Alric said. "Someone would have come to Cecily immediately."

Rafe was just about to admit he was right when he heard footsteps. He turned to the door, grateful Angelet wouldn't hear his worrying.

But it was only Cecily who came in, her brows drawn. "No one's seen Angelet," she said. "Not since this morning."

"She was in the orchard," Rafe said.

"I've just sent someone to look. Perhaps she walked to a different place, to sit under shade or…"

A maid hurried in. "My lady, she's not in the orchard, but her sewing was under an apple tree. She wouldn't have simply left it there. She was very careful of her work."

Rafe's fists balled up. "Something's wrong," he repeated, more vehemently.

Alric put a hand up. "Let's not jump at shadows. She must have seen something, or been needed."

"Find Goswin," Rafe instructed the maid. "He might know what happened."

The maid nodded and hurried out.

By then, Rafe wasn't going to sit back down until he knew what was going on. He told Cecily to summon him with any news, then he left the room, followed by Alric. They encountered Octavian almost immediately.

The younger knight didn't look unduly worried when Rafe explained the situation, but he said, "First things first. She's likely somewhere within the walls, but I'll go ask the gatehouse if she's left. Then we can focus the search inside." He turned and walked briskly toward the gatehouse.

"So it's a search now," Rafe muttered.

"Just a term," Alric said. "She'll be under a tree somewhere, and she'll laugh at all the fuss over nothing."

But the fuss was not over nothing. Another servant said that Goswin couldn't be located either. Rafe grimaced. "Jesu, I never thought I'd miss seeing that boy's face."

Then Octavian returned with one of the gatehouse guards.

"Listen to this man's report," the knight said, then gestured to the guard to speak.

"My lords," the guard began nervously. "The lady who's a guest here…she walked outside of the walls this morning."

"When?" Rafe demanded.

"Um. About mid-morning. She was with one of the men-at-arms."

"Who?" Alric asked. "I'll have him summoned."

"I don't know, my lord. Peter? No, Peter's not so tall. Gunter, maybe…" The guard looked confused.

"Did the man come back to the gate?" Rafe asked.

"No. No, they walked west toward the woods, and then…no one saw anything."

"Angelet wouldn't have just walked off," Rafe muttered to Alric. "And certainly not with someone who was a stranger to her."

"Unless he told her something to get her to go with

him. A threat."

"She was in the manor walls. She would have screamed."

"Then he tricked her?"

"How?" Rafe burst out.

"Her boy went missing too, you said." Octavian turned to the guard. "How about the boy? Did he leave the manor this morning?"

"Oh, a whole pack left. But they're like wild animals, running about and chasing each other. I couldn't say if he was among them."

Rafe shook his head. "Goswin and Angelet both left the manor, possibly with a stranger, and now no one has seen them for hours. That's no coincidence. I have to find them."

"You're not going alone," Alric said.

"You don't trust me?"

"Of course I trust you, but two swords are better than one."

"Excuse me, but by that logic, three are better still," said Octavian.

Rafe regarded the other two knights. "You're under no obligation. I brought all this here. I'll deal with it."

"Don't be an idiot." Alric put a hand to Rafe's shoulder. "We want to help."

"Yes," Octavian agreed. "At least, I do. Sir Alric *is* obligated, because of that oath you three took. I'm just joining you out of Christian duty, and a desire to find a man who seems to have something against the lady Angelet. Who, from what I can tell, nobody could possibly hate."

"Well, someone does," Rafe said.

Alric said, "Then let's go."

Soon the three rode out of Cleobury, fully armed and wearing chain mail. They had only a vague idea of where to search, and no proof that anything evil had befallen either Angelet or Goswin. But Rafe knew something was horribly wrong.

* * * *

Angelet had been confined for hours in a tiny hut, with the guard Ulmar posted just outside. Somehow, Ernald had found a deserted farmstead not far from Cleobury, and he'd spent the last few days watching the manor to see when and how he could send someone to steal Angelet away.

If only she'd spoken to someone before leaving! Even a maid. Then they'd know. As it was there was no way Rafe would have any idea where she was, or that she was captured. "Sweet Mary, please help me," she whispered. Then she sighed. Why would she merit help? She had just spent a night sinning in a *church*. If anything, this was a direct punishment for her actions.

She bent her head. "I'm sorry. Forgive me, *please*."

"Why should anyone forgive you?"

Angelet's head snapped up, and she saw Bethany in the doorway. The former maid thrust half a loaf of bread toward her. "Eat."

She took the bread, ravenous since she'd missed the midday meal.

"Bethany, I don't want to be here any more than you want me here," Angelet said, trying to reason with the maid.

"God knows I'd rather he never found you," Bethany agreed with a snort.

"Then help me get away."

"Help you? Ernald would kill me."

"Only if he knew you had anything to do with it. Please." She put a hand on Bethany's arm, but the maid jerked her arm away.

"Don't touch me, you freak!"

"You're afraid of me?" Angelet asked, surprised. Bethany's eyes, shifting between Angelet's hand and her own sleeve, told her the truth. "You think you'll get the same affliction, just by being near me? You've been my maid for years!"

"And I hoped to never see you again!" Bethany hissed. "Why does he want you so?"

"I don't know. I've never encouraged him."

"You draw him on with your aloofness then. Men always want what they are denied."

Angelet closed her eyes. "So it's my fault if I encourage a man and it's my fault if I discourage a man! I can't win!"

The maid sighed with vexation, but then said, "That's truth, I grant you. Any woman knows that."

"Then as a woman, please help me out of this mess. I'll slip away. Ernald will never find me again."

Bethany leaned closer. "All right. A deal. I'll let you escape…if you tell me where the money is."

Frustration gnawed at Angelet. "I don't know! I never did anything to the chest, and I was just as surprised as anyone when it broke open and there was no gold in it."

"You had the key. You must have done something."

"I swear I know nothing of it. I'd tell you if I did…all I want is to get away from here. I don't care about any money."

"That's what people who've always had money say,"

Bethany said. "Still, I believe you. I bet it was the knight who took it."

"Maybe. I don't know. Please, Bethany. It's not that long until dark." Until the time that Ernald threatened to force her to bed with him. Angelet shuddered.

Bethany glanced behind her, then beckoned Angelet closer. In a low voice, she said, "I'll draw Ulmar away from the door for a moment. Watch and sneak out. Go to the left and hug the side of the hut to hide behind it. Then you're on your own. Head to the woods for cover. But if you're caught again, it will be worse than before."

"Thank you," Angelet breathed.

"Just go quickly."

Bethany stepped outside, leaving the door cracked. She chatted with Ulmar, in that flirtatious way she had. The guard laughed at something she said, then the sounds of their conversation drifted away.

Angelet, peeking through the opening, saw her moment. She slipped out and hurried to the back of the hut. She took a moment to get her breath and survey the land. No other buildings were in sight from this side, and the forest lay not far beyond. She could run.

But that left Goswin alone. How could she abandon him? No, she'd have to bring him along somehow. She had a little time. The late afternoon light was still bright, and it was at least an hour until sunset, possibly more. Ulmar would assume she was safely in the hut, so he had no reason to sound the alarm.

Angelet peeked around the other corner of the hut, toward the main farmhouse. Was that where Goswin was?

She then looked toward the stables and saw a familiar figure. Not content with merely kidnapping him, they had put Goswin to work feeding and watering the horses. He was lugging a wooden bucket filled so full that water sloshed over the brim with every step. Then he disappeared into the darkness of the stable building itself.

She waited until she saw another guard walk out the door, heading to the main farmhouse. Seeing nobody else, she picked up her skirts and ran around the perimeter of the open area until she reached the back of the stable building.

There she leaned against the stone wall, trying to catch her breath. She heard no shouts, and it seemed that she had succeeded. She waited several moments more, but the quiet endured. The only sounds were the wind stirring the highest branches, and the twitterings of hidden birds. Angelet moved to where the stone wall of the building gave way to wood. In one spot, a plank was missing.

"Goswin!" she called in a low voice.

"My lady?" Goswin's voice was excited. "Where were you? They wouldn't say!"

"In a hut, but I got free. Listen, we can wait until dark, then—"

At that moment, a huge hand clamped down on her shoulder. She turned to see Ulmar standing over her.

"Did you think it would be so easy?" he asked. "One of the men by the house saw you running."

He dragged her around to the front of the building, and she faltered when she saw Ernald approaching with several others, including Bethany, who regarded her with cold eyes.

"I heard," Ernald said, "that you were attempting to escape."

"Should I have just sat there and accepted my fate?"

Ernald just looked at her in confusion, and she realized that was exactly what he expected her to do.

"You were stupid to go to the stable," he said at last. "The woods would have hidden you."

"Goswin was in the stable."

"And you wanted to save him? Silly. You'd have got away if you hadn't bothered with the boy."

"I wouldn't have left without him."

"Well, now you won't leave at all." He grabbed Goswin, thrusting him toward Ulmar. "Tie the boy to the post and take his shirt off."

"What are you doing?" Angelet said.

"You disobey, but he's the one who will take the punishment. I'm whipping him ten times." He retrieved a whip from inside the stable.

"No!" Angelet tried to grab Ernald's arm. "You can't do that."

"Well, I can't hurt *your* pretty flesh, Angelet. I have other uses for it. And you don't want to be stripped bare to the waist in front of everyone, do you?"

She followed him. "Ernald, please. I beg you. Don't do this. I'll never run away again. I promise."

He paused, flicking the whip against the ground, where the end of it twisted like a snake. "Promise? You give me your word?"

"Yes. I swear it. Leave Goswin alone. He did nothing."

"What if you're lying, Angelet? You planned to run away, didn't you?"

"I give you my word I won't ever again. Please."

"You're sweet when you beg, Angelet. Very well."

She sighed in relief.

Then, without warning, Ernald swung the whip in an arc, directly toward Goswin's unprotected back.

Goswin screamed once, a high piercing shriek that

split the air. A bright red welt appeared on his back.

"No!" Angelet shouted. "Why did you do that? I promised!"

"A little reminder that if you break your promise, others will suffer."

She broke past two guards in the way and rushed to Goswin. She fumbled at the rope until it came untied. "I'm so sorry, Goswin. Oh, Lord, you're bleeding."

"It's nothing, my lady," Goswin said, fighting back tears.

"I'll get the wound tended."

"Don't make pronouncements you can't keep, Angelet." Ernald stood above them. "You're not in charge."

"Then you can tell someone to tend his wound!" she said.

Ernald sighed. "You're almost more trouble than you're worth."

"How much is that?"

He laughed. "That depends. Though even if I don't recover the money, I'll still get you to that nunnery, and soon. After your behavior with that knight, you ought to be locked away, to restore the tarnish you'll bring to our family. Then I'm going to Northampton, where the king will hold his Easter court. That will be my opportunity to make an impression. My father has been holding me back long enough. I'm sick of it."

"So you'll tell the king that you fixed Otto's mistake, and that's why you deserve to run Dryton?"

"Possibly. Or the king might offer me another position. Or a wife."

"Kings don't just hand out rewards," she said in disgust. "You need to earn them. Prove your loyalty."

"Don't lecture me on loyalty, woman."

Just then, one of the soldiers in Ernald's retinue gave a shout. "Someone's approaching!"

"Send them away!" Ernald growled.

"Armed!"

That got everyone's attention. They all looked to the track leading west, the access point of the isolated farm to the main road.

"My lady," Goswin said. But Angelet had already seen the same thing.

On the road, on a small rise so the sunlight shone behind him and turned him into a silhouette, was a black-clad knight on an equally black horse.

"Rafe," she murmured. The image was so similar to the one she saw in her visions that she wondered if a seizure was imminent.

Then the horse reared once, and Rafe began to ride directly toward her.

Chapter 31

EARLIER THAT DAY, THE KNIGHTS had made one discovery very quickly—a group of boys ran toward Alric, shouting that one of their number couldn't be found.

"We've been looking for ages!" one shouted.

Rafe asked, "Was it Goswin?"

"The new boy, yes!"

"Where did you see him last? Were there any others in the woods today?"

The boys conferred, and reported that a big man asked one of the boys the way to Cleobury, and if they were at hide and seek—which prompted the boy to start exactly that game. The man had been armed, and he was described as a giant.

"A stranger," Alric said under his breath. "And a giant, if he's bigger than Peter, as the guard described. He must have watched the boys playing and took Goswin when he was hiding during the game."

"But where?"

The boys directed the knights to the area of the woods where the game had been played. There, they found evidence of several people walking. That led to a clearing, where they found signs that a whole group of people had been there, with horses and all.

"Too many riders," Octavian said. "Too many to be hiding out in the woods, that is."

"They were afraid to use the road this close to Cleobury," Alric agreed. "We'll have to track this backwards. They might have gone through Bournham without resorting to stealth. We'll ask if a party of this size rode through today, and which direction."

In the nearby village of Bournham, where Alric was very well known, several residents told him that a party of at least ten men came through in the morning, and then again later in the day.

"There were women too," added Margaret Dyer, whose giant tubs of fabric dye sat in the yard of her business. She always saw who passed by, since her work kept her outside much of the day. "One or two, I think. Odd, for the men looked to be soldiers. They rode out the north way."

Alric thanked her, and they rode on.

"North could be anywhere," Octavian said. "They could be hours away by now."

"We'll keep looking till we find a reason to stop," Rafe said. He hated to think that Angelet was getting further from him by the moment. Why had he wasted a whole morning talking to everyone but her?

"There's a place I've got in mind," Alric said suddenly. "If they've been following you, Rafe, they might have come across it. You wouldn't have noticed on your ride here—you had other concerns."

At Alric's instruction, the three men rode toward the abandoned farm he told them about, one that had yet to gain another owner after two years of neglect. "They might be using it, if they needed to stay close for a few days."

The knights rode on. Though anxious to reach their destination, Rafe still had the impression that someone was following them. He looked back often, but saw no one. He decided that he'd been trailed for so long he no longer had any ability to forget the feeling—he would simply have to get used to the creeping sensation of being followed for the rest of his life.

The bright sun crawled across the sky, then began to drop toward the horizon. Rafe felt that everything was taking too long. It took too long to discover Angelet's absence. Too long to hear about Goswin. Too long to prepare to ride out.

Then, Alric pulled his horse to a stop where the road climbed a small rise, obscuring the other side. The others followed suit.

"The farm is up ahead, just beyond this hill. It's possible they took Lady Angelet there."

Octavian nodded, saying, "We should plan how to approach the place."

"Here's the plan," Rafe interjected, already nudging his horse to the front. "I'm riding directly there. If I see anyone I don't like, I'm killing them. You two can follow me." He kicked once and was off.

"You used to make better plans!" Alric called after him.

Rafe didn't care. Hitting the top of the rise, he reined Philon in so he could judge the scene before him. The startled horse reared once.

"Stop that," Rafe muttered. He saw a farm below, where people moved about. He nudged Philon once, and the horse sped down the slope toward the ramshackle clutch of buildings. A small group of people stood near what looked to be the stables, and a few more were emerging from the house. Several horses cropped grass in a paddock.

One of the figures wore a pale blue gown. Angelet. She was being held in place by a huge hulk of a guard. But her eyes were on Rafe.

He picked out the other figures, identifying the irritating Ernald, as well as the maid Bethany, and Goswin. The other men looked like hired soldiers.

Rafe jumped down from his horse, drawing his sword.

"Ernald!" he yelled. "This is your doing?"

The lordling lifted his chin into the air. "You shouldn't have come after us. You shouldn't have taken Angelet away in the first place. Made my life quite inconvenient these past few weeks."

"I offered to fight you before, at Dryton," Rafe said to Ernald. "I won't wait any longer."

"Don't be absurd," Ernald retorted. "You're alone, and I've got ten men with me. In fact," he added, raising his voice, "the first person to kill you will get an extra reward!"

"No," Angelet protested. But her cry was drowned out by the shouting of others. Some came from the soldiers who stepped forward to fight Rafe. Another was a cry of dismay, howling that two more riders were coming.

Rafe turned to see Alric and Octavian galloping toward them.

"Ah. Reinforcements," he told Ernald.

"Not enough. Anyway, you can't do anything while I've got Angelet under my command. One word from me and she dies at Ulmar's hand." He nodded toward the big man, who stood by Angelet, his blade drawn.

Then Ernald's expression changed. He was looking at Angelet with puzzlement. "What in hell are you smiling about, woman?"

Angelet was indeed smiling. Though she faced Ernald, her eyes didn't seem quite focused on him, but rather on a distant point. She lifted one hand and pointed toward Ernald. "I see you," she said, speaking slowly.

"I'm standing in front of—"

"Surrounded by gold," she went on, oblivious to his outburst. "Gold as bright as the sun. Like the ocean at dawn."

Rafe got a twinge in his gut. He'd seen that vacant look before. Angelet must have been under tremendous strain all day, and now another seizure was imminent.

Before he could say anything, Angelet took a step toward Ernald, then another. Ulmar remained rooted to his spot, unnerved by what was happening.

"I see you above this gold," she continued. "No other but you."

"And?" Ernald demanded, interested in spite of himself. "What else?"

Her voice was dreamy, disconnected. "Now you're falling. You're drowning. You'll die."

"Shut up with your rambling!" Ernald snapped. "Get back!"

Angelet didn't react to his command. Her gaze was locked on Ernald, who appeared truly shaken by her words. Then she swayed on her feet, and crumpled to the ground. Goswin yelped and bent down to check on her, leaning in to see if she was breathing.

Rafe's first instinct was to get to her as fast as possible, but there were too many other people in the way.

"Damn, she's having another fit," Ernald said. "Of all the times to suffer a vision."

"What's your order?" the massive guard named Ulmar asked.

"Leave her. She's not going anywhere for hours. I've seen it. Everyone, get these men!"

Ulmar dutifully walked forward, though he clearly didn't want to engage an armed, angry knight. And now Alric and Octavian had joined the fight, wreaking havoc.

Before Rafe could do anything—whether fight or try to get to Angelet—Goswin rushed toward him at full speed.

"Distract them!" he hissed. "She's fine. She's only playacting now!" Then he started to run in a circle around the group, drawing several pairs of eyes due to the way he was waving his hands and yelling.

Rafe glanced at the still form of Angelet on the ground. She certainly didn't seem to be pretending. But he had to trust that she was. He rushed Ulmar, keeping the gigantic guard's attention on him.

Fighting always made Rafe's muscles tense and his whole body heat up as though a fever was coming on him. He always felt like he could hear everything, smell everything. No matter how many times he fought, each time felt like the first, the primal fear of death reaching out to him. But having faced that fear so many times, Rafe also knew how to get through it, using his heightened senses to focus within the inevitable chaos that all fights created.

Ulmar swung his blade like a woodcutter swung an ax. Rafe could tell the other man relied on pure mass and intimidation to win his fights. However, Ulmar had probably never fought a trained knight before, and not one as well-trained as Rafe. The big man showed not a trace of the fear Rafe always felt, but he knew it was there.

Despite his earlier hasty words, Rafe didn't want to kill him, so he kept parrying, waiting for an opening to deliver a blow that would just incapacitate the man. But the situation grew dicier when another guard rushed up to attack Rafe from behind. He dodged the first blow, and ducked out of the way.

Ulmar howled as his next swing hit not Rafe, but his other ally. Rafe took advantage of Ulmar's second of surprise to hit him hard in the side of the head with the flat of his blade. Then he kicked at Ulmar's knee, causing it to buckle. The giant slid down, clutching at his head, moaning.

Rafe moved away, and saw that Alric and Octavian were both fighting just as he was. The two knights had started fighting as a pair, but got drawn away from each other, exposing their backs.

Yet another fighter went for Alric, wielding his own sword with much more skill than Ulmar did. Rafe yelled out a warning.

Alric turned just in time to avoid being struck. He shifted to avoid being trapped, and regrouped with Octavian.

Rafe turned, intent on getting to Angelet. All of a sudden, a crossbow bolt rushed past him and buried itself in the ground a few feet beyond, not far from Angelet's prone form.

"Hell," he muttered, tracing the path back to see where it had come from.

The path led directly to Bethany, who stood yards away from the farmhouse, holding the weapon. She cursed at missing and set about reloading.

"Bethany." Suddenly, Rafe knew she'd been the one

who was responsible for the previous attacks, that she regarded Angelet as more of a threat than any of the knights.

"Bethany, get over here!" Ernald had avoided the fight, instead moving to one of the saddled horses in the paddock. "This is not the time for revenge."

"Everyone's always fighting over her," Bethany said. "Why? She's a freak, and she should have run while she had the chance!" Now Bethany held the weapon at the ready, sighting the unprotected form of Angelet, ready to shoot once again.

"Don't you dare," Ernald yelled, furious that Bethany wasn't listening. "She still has a use."

"I will!" Bethany shouted back at her lover, her composure gone. "I won't miss this time!"

But she didn't fire. There was a whistling sound, and Bethany dropped the crossbow, transfixed by the shaft of an arrow protruding from her neck.

Everyone was silent for an endless moment, as Bethany collapsed, dead.

"They have archers!" Ernald shouted. "Mount up! Ride!" He went for the nearest horse, got up and rode off, without waiting to see if any of his men were with him, and without any more thought for his slain lover.

"He's getting away!" Rafe yelled to his fellow knights.

"Let him go."

Rafe looked down, where Angelet lay, her eyes now open and alert. "Let him go," she repeated quietly. "Don't leave me."

"I won't," he said, helping her up.

Once on her feet, Angelet embraced him, heedless of how it would look. He held her tightly for a moment, absurdly happy to know she was safe. Then he released her. "Enough of that," he muttered. "Tell me exactly what happened."

Angelet sighed. "What happened was simple. Ernald followed us all this way, and then took Goswin in order to get me out of Cleobury." She explained everything, concluding that she had been foolish to trust Ulmar. By then Octavian and Alric joined them, and Goswin also hovered near.

"I should have known something was wrong," Angelet said at last.

"It wasn't your fault," Rafe said. "You thought it was an emergency, and you couldn't have known Cleobury's guards all by sight."

"You were really worried I was hurt?" Goswin asked.

"I was," she said. "And you were hurt in the end!" She looked angry.

At last Rafe noticed that the boy's shirt was stained red on the back. "You were whipped?"

"Once," Goswin said. "It doesn't hurt."

The boy was obviously lying, wanting to appear strong in front of Angelet. Rafe gave him a nod. "If you say so."

"We should return to Cleobury," Alric said, looking worriedly at the darkening sky.

Octavian said he'd retrieve the horses, who had wandered away somewhat. But the moment he spoke, another rider appeared.

Rafe squinted, since the rider was backlit by the setting sun. "Is that…"

"Robin," Octavian said, sounding unsurprised, and also unhappy. "Our hidden archer."

"What the hell is she doing here?" Alric asked.

By that time, Robin reached them, holding her bow. "I followed you," she said bluntly. "And a good thing too. Three against twelve? Plus a crossbow? Not good odds."

"A battle is no place for a lady," Alric said.

"I attended as an archer," Robin said defensively, plucking at the leather bracer she still wore on her forearm. "And some thanks would be pleasant."

"Thank you for saving my life," Angelet said. "But Sir Alric is correct, it's time to go."

They rode back to Cleobury in the deepening twilight. The lack of extra horses meant Angelet rode with Rafe, while Goswin rode behind Alric. As they rode, Octavian and Robin dropped back, immersed in a heated argument about Robin's "whim," as Octavian put it. The word seemed to infuriate the young woman, whose cheeks had gone beet red.

"I will say that having that first arrow appear was convenient," Rafe said quietly to Alric.

"But she's barely more than a girl," Angelet said worriedly.

"A girl who can shoot," Alric said. "I know all too well. I met her at arrowpoint, an experience I don't want to repeat."

Suddenly, Robin's voice grew louder. "Because I was *bored!* And I wasn't in danger at all. Not with three knights in earshot!"

Octavian said, in a more measured tone, "It was irresponsible." The rest of his argument was too low to hear.

Rafe didn't think the knight had much chance to influence Robin. "And Octavian's argument will…do what?"

"Chasten her, perhaps," Alric said. "At least she listens to him sometimes. She never listens to me."

Angelet said, "I'm glad she followed. Ernald might

have succeeded if she didn't. He was going to force me to go to Basingwerke. Which sounds like a horrible place." She told what Ernald shared about the abbey's practices.

Rafe's arm was around her waist, holding her so she wouldn't fall. Now he tightened his grip. "He's probably telling the truth. Lord Otto acted strangely about it when he first hired us. We were told not to bring you back. He ordered me to ignore any pleas you might make. I was to see that you passed through the gate, and then leave when the gate locked behind you."

"And you agreed to that?" she asked, aghast.

"I made no complaint," he corrected. "I let Otto believe what he would—my reputation is that of a man out for himself. But I didn't like his words, and I never let another decide my course. If I didn't like what I saw, or if you'd asked…Otto's orders meant nothing to me."

He laid a kiss on her head, enjoying the silky feel of her hair. By that point, the sky had changed to a purple-blue, the last shade of twilight. Rafe used the darkness to hold Angelet closer to him than he otherwise could. He almost didn't want to see the gates again.

Back at Cleobury, the party rode in to find an audience, despite the late hour. Many of the residents knew of the crisis and found reasons to be in the courtyard when they returned. At the sight of Angelet, many shouted in relief. She smiled happily. "I don't ever remember being cheered upon my arrival anywhere."

Cecily made much of Goswin, and took him away to tend the wound across his back. Alric asked if Angelet felt up to talking briefly. "Rainald ought to be told what's happened."

She nodded, but leaned against Rafe as they walked.

"Are you well?" he asked in a low voice.

"Well enough, if you are here to help me."

The warmth of the statement kept Rafe going during the discussion that followed. Angelet related all that Ernald told her, including the fact that he intended to go before the king after Easter.

"He'll do everything he can to advance his own cause and hurt any other. He hoped to have me behind walls, and also to recover the stolen gold. But he'll settle for destroying reputations. He'll destroy mine to ensure that I'll never get to see Henry again. And he'll destroy Rafe's because Rafe thwarted his plans, more than once."

"Then we should go there too," Rafe said.

"Go there?" Angelet said. "Away would be a better choice!"

"Ernald just threatened to blacken my name with the king. He might be able to do it, especially if he gives his story before I can tell mine. I'm not going to let that miserable excuse for a man ruin the name I just regained."

"Your name is important to you," Angelet said softly.

"Of course it is. It's all I have. Without it, I'm nothing."

She smiled, but her face looked even paler than usual. "Then we should go. To Northampton. You can put your case to the king, and he'll see the right of it."

Chapter 32

EASTER CAME IN MID-APRIL that year, leaving less than a fortnight for Rafe to gather any witnesses he could find to support his case, travel to Northampton, and prepare a defense before an audience with the king himself. He was not optimistic.

Fortunately, however, he was no longer alone. Alric and Octavian both helped him. In addition, Luc was sent for. Luc's family was close with the king, and Luc could advise Rafe on what to say—and not say.

Luc did even more than that. He arranged for some of the group to stay with his own family in Northampton, and assured them that he'd help in any way he could. Rafe could hardly believe it.

"Why are you doing this for me? After what I did?"

"What are friends for?" Luc replied. Then he grinned. "Besides, it wasn't me you impaled during a practice session."

"Be serious."

"I am serious, Rafe. We practically grew up together, and I know the truth of what happened—Alric told me the whole story. So stop dwelling in the past. You've got a problem in the present, and that's the only time we can affect our fates. So let's get to work on mounting a defense against whatever accusations the Yarboroughs will make."

"They will accuse me of theft and kidnapping, and possibly murder. I should have taken care of Ernald back at that farm." Rafe walked from one end of the room to the other and back again, full of energy he couldn't get rid of.

"You can't solve this with a sword, Rafe," said Alric. "How will you being executed for murder help Angelet?"

"She'll be safe once Ernald is dead."

Luc put a hand to his head. "Rafe. For God's sake, stop pacing. We'll find a way through this. And blood will not be involved."

"Otto must have already spoken to the king," Rafe said worriedly. "He'll have lawyers, local friends, and witnesses. I may as well give up now."

"You have the truth on your side," Luc said. "That counts for something. Usually."

A group left Cleobury for the town of Northampton, arriving a few days before Easter. Both Robin and Goswin had to stay behind at Cleobury, and both complained bitterly about it. Yet they were children, and Cleobury was the safest place for them.

Angelet rode most of the way in a carriage with Lady Cecily, which must have been more comfortable for both of them than a horse would have been. But it separated her from Rafe, which annoyed him. He liked to see Angelet as often as he could.

When they arrived, the group went directly to the home of Luc's family. The house they came to was impressive, but not cold. Indeed, the whole family—father, mother, and daughters—welcomed them as if they were all old friends. They fussed over Cecily's expectant condition and chatted with Angelet as if she'd always been part of their circle. Rafe had always been somewhat in awe of Luc and his noble upbringing. He had access to the sort of life most people never even dreamed of. Yet Rafe was welcomed, and that was before his true parentage was even revealed.

"Luc has told us something of what's happening, Sir Rafe, but I'd like to hear more," the Lord of Braecon said.

So Rafe told the story as best he could. It was not the final retelling either. As it happened, wheels were already turning, and an agent of the king was conducting something like an investigation before the king held an audience with them all. He was interviewing all parties, trying to discover what really happened.

The day after they arrived in town, Luc took Rafe to meet the man at an inn close to the center of town. "Be careful what you say," Luc told him before they entered. "I've met Lord Drogo before. You don't want to antagonize him."

"Sounds charming," Rafe muttered.

The man waiting for them was anything but charming. He was an ascetic-looking man somewhere near fifty. He had a thin face and deep-set eyes that seemed to miss nothing. His clothes were very fine in quality, but in dull, drab colors. He'd fade away in most rooms filled with people. Rafe suspected he liked it that way.

"Sir Rafe," Luc said, "may I present Lord Drogo. He has been tasked with investigating this whole matter, as an impartial servant of the king."

Drogo invited them both to sit. "I've spoken to several other people involved in this matter. Lord Otto and his son Ernald have leveled very serious accusations. And their description of Sir Rafe was not flattering."

"My description of them won't flatter, either," Rafe said, before Luc put a warning hand on his arm.

"Let's stick to facts. Drogo, what do you need to know from Rafe?"

"Everything. Let us begin with who you are."

That Rafe could now answer with pride. "My name is Sir Raphael Corviser. I have served the de Vere family, who swore allegiance to King Stephen very early in his reign."

"Corviser…"

"My father was Sir Michael Corviser. He died in service of the old king."

"Yes, Corviser. Good king's man," Drogo muttered approvingly. "Sterling fighter, was Sir Michael. Never knew he married."

"It was only a few months before his death," Rafe explained, skipping over the details. "To Lady Clare of Beaumont, who has also now passed away."

"What brought you to the manor of Dryton?"

Rafe told him the whole story from beginning to end, leaving out only the parts that would compromise Angelet's reputation.

At the end of the tale, Drogo regarded him with those glittering eyes. "Much of the early part of your story rings true—up to the time of the initial attack on the cortège. I questioned another witness who confirmed it."

"Who?" Rafe asked, puzzled.

Drogo gestured to Luc. "Go fetch him, please."

Luc grinned at Rafe, then left the back room. He returned moments later, along with none other than Simon Faber.

"Sir Rafe!" Simon almost shouted. He surprised Rafe with an embrace that nearly cracked a rib. "It's a miracle to see you again! I feared that you never got the lady to safety, and you both perished after the attack."

"I thought the same of you," Rafe said, after he got his breath back. "What happened? I assumed the thieves would have slaughtered every possible witness."

"So they would have, but then they fell apart after you stole the lady away. Some wanted to go after you, some wanted to loot the wagons and flee north, and the others wanted to march back to Dryton and demand satisfaction from Ernald, who'd hired them. The few of us who survived the first round regrouped by the supply wagon and held off a second attack for a precious few moments. God be praised, another party came into sight from the north. It was a caravan of wool merchants, and they were well-guarded. The thieves scattered, and the newcomers came to our aid. We were able to take our dead and wounded to the nearest town."

"What happened to everyone? Marcus? And Laurence?"

"Marcus was wounded but survived. He's back in Ashthorpe. Laurence didn't…" Simon took a heavy breath.

"I'm sorry." Rafe knew all too well what it was like to see companions fall in battle. "But how did you come to be here? In this town?"

"That was my doing," said Luc. "I had a few men go to Dryton and Ashthorpe in search of any witnesses who might be able to tell us something of what happened. And Simon was one who answered the call!"

"I'm not usually one for believing in miracles, but this is close to one. I never thought to see you again, Simon."

"Ah, it would have been sooner, but they said I was not to talk to you earlier. Something about getting stories straight."

"Indeed," Drogo said. "I am most interested in where people's stories diverge. That is always where it gets intriguing."

"And you've learned something?" Luc asked.

"Many things. Someone is lying, and I will find out who it is. By the time this matter is brought before the king, I will know exactly what happened, and all that will be left is to decide the punishment."

Rafe didn't like the way Drogo looked at him as he said it.

* * * *

The days of the holy week preceding Easter seemed to drag for Angelet, who attended mass every day, but otherwise stayed close to the house. She usually had company, because with three other noblewomen and a number of female servants, there was always someone about. Angelet knew that everyone was subtly—and not so subtly—working to hide the extent of her relationship to Rafe while they were in Northampton. That was why he was staying in another house, and why they were not permitted to be in the same room alone together when he visited to meet with the family. She recognized the wisdom of it, but she hated it. After this, whether it ended well or not, Rafe and she would travel separate paths. Why did she have to be denied even the pleasure and comfort of being near him for these last few days? Though she tried to mask her feelings with the calm face she learned to use at Dryton, it seemed she wasn't doing well.

"You're melancholy," Cecily told her one day.

"I'm worried about the audience with the king," said Angelet. "I'm terrified I'll say something wrong and hurt Rafe's case. It's the last thing I'll ever be able to do for him. What if I fail?"

"Last thing?" Cecily asked, puzzled.

"I'm just being practical. We've no future."

"You and Rafe, you mean? Why should that be?"

"It just is. He's told me exactly that, again and again. From the very first time we met, Rafe made it clear that our meeting was purest chance, and that soon enough we'd be parted again....though when he first said that, he never could have envisioned how tangled our paths grew. Still, he said it."

"Yes, but was he saying that for your benefit, or his own?"

"What do you mean?"

Cecily said, "Perhaps Rafe mentioned the end so often because he needed to remind himself of it...or else he'd start dreaming of another future. One with you in it."

"No. He's got his future...or he will, once the king hears his side of the story. Rafe will undoubtedly receive some sort of commission, or be granted a role in Stephen's military, perhaps. He's too good a warrior for the king to waste."

"And what path will you take?" Cecily asked.

"I don't know." Angelet felt helpless as she pictured her future. "Otto will keep his grip on Henry more than ever now. I think my chance to be rejoined with him is gone." The unfairness of it stung her. All she wanted was to provide her child with a home, where they could be happy together until he grew up. But she lacked the political power to do that. "I could go to Anjou—perhaps my family isn't entirely lost, though unless we're able to get an army together, there's little chance we'll be able to reclaim anything of our legacy. But I've no means to support myself."

"Your gift of needlecraft might be more useful than you think," Cecily said. "That altar cloth you showed me is an object worthy of princes. But I think you are too concerned with the future. See what happens during the audience with the king. Who knows what will come of it?"

"That's what concerns me most," Angelet said. "It is one thing to know that Fortune's wheel is always turning. It is quite another to feel it crushing you into the mud when you finally think you could rise."

"Have you had a vision as dire as that?"

"No. I never see myself in visions."

"Then don't fear a future you haven't even seen, dear."

The next day, Cecily came to Angelet with an excited expression on her face. "Listen, I had an idea! Your altar cloth…would you consider offering it as a gift to the king?"

Angelet said, "I wouldn't dare presume it was good enough for a king. But it would be an honor."

"I knew you'd think so. And I asked Luc's father to exert some of his influence to beg a favor from the king. If you come with me to Northampton Castle this evening, you can present it to his grace. And if he happens to notice that you're a modest and pious lady who deserves justice, so much the better!"

Angelet wore a gown borrowed from Luc's sister. The undyed linen of the fabric glowed almost white in firelight, and the tunic-like overskirt was a pale grey-blue that appeared more like silver. She wore the moonstones around her neck, since they were the only jewelry she had.

She took care to braid her hair tightly and bind it up on her head so as to show restraint and modesty. If she were a nun, she'd have to cover her hair completely. As she prepared, she idly thought of young Robin. The girl felt caged at Cleobury…Angelet guessed that Robin would literally climb the walls of an actual nunnery.

"I am not so wild," she said aloud, rather regretting her nature. She'd had her moment of wildness, when she accepted Rafe into her life so very briefly. Those few weeks had been filled with passion and excitement and danger, and she should be happy it was now over. There would be no more wildness, not for her. And not for Rafe either, since he would no longer be an itinerant knight. She refused to think of what might happen to him should Otto prevail during the audience. Rafe could be branded a criminal, despite all her efforts to defend him.

"That's what tonight is for," she told herself. "I'll beg the king for mercy if I must."

Cecily and Angelet rode to the castle in a carriage, escorted by a few men-at-arms from the household. It seemed Cecily kept the visit a secret from nearly everyone, except for Luc's father, who arranged it. Angelet wondered if that was because she feared it would be a failure.

Angelet held the folded altar cloth in her lap, feeling more nervous by the second. What if the king refused to see them? What if he accused her of something terrible? What if he despised the gift?

"We should go back," she whispered to Cecily. "This is a mistake."

"It would be a mistake to miss this opportunity to advance your cause," Cecily returned, taking Angelet's hand. "Be bold."

"I am not bold."

"Then be strong. Whenever you fear you'll fail, think of what you love and you'll be able to go on."

Angelet closed her eyes. Immediately she saw whom she loved. Henry, who needed to be removed from Otto's control. Rafe, who needed to clear his reputation. If she could help either of them, she had to try. "I will do it," she whispered.

"Good. Because we have arrived."

The ladies were shown into a small receiving chamber that was grander than anything Angelet had seen in a private home. A massive fireplace dominated the space, and dark wood paneling covered the walls. The floor was covered with a plush carpet woven in a pattern based on some fantastical garden, and the chairs all had carved backs and velvet cushions. A round oak table with elaborately carved legs stood in the middle.

"All this wealth for one room of a castle the king only visits a few times a year," Angelet said in awe.

"Royalty lives differently," Cecily said, looking overwhelmed as well.

Then the door opened. A thin, rather pinched man came though, followed by a much larger, broad-shouldered man dressed like…a king.

Angelet gasped when she realized who stood in front of her. She dropped into a curtsey alongside Cecily. "Your Grace," they both murmured.

"Rise, my ladies," King Stephen said. "Which of you is Lady Angelet?"

"I am Angelet d'Hiver Yarborough, widow of Hubert."

"That makes you Lady Cecily," the king said, looking Cecily over. "Traveling in your condition, my lady? Please sit."

"I thank you, your Grace." Cecily sat down after the king did himself.

Angelet remained standing, still holding the altar cloth.

Stephen smiled at her. "I hear you bring a gift to me." With a gesture, he invited her to put it on the table in front of him.

She unfolded the cloth so the scene it depicted faced the king. "I embroider, your grace, and I hope this work may please you. The scene is of a…dream I had."

"A most beautiful dream," Stephen said. He reached out to the cloth with a large hand more suited to battle than to art. Perhaps he came to the same conclusion, for he didn't actually touch the cloth, though his fingers traced the lines of the gold castle and the twisting vines of the border. "I have been told, though, that your dreams are not just dreams, but visions."

"So others say, your grace."

The other man spoke for the first time. "So says Lord Otto, who reports that you fled away from the nunnery where you were meant to go, on account of your visions." He did not smile. Possibly he never learned how, based on the way his face was lined. He looked hard at Angelet, as if she were a puzzle to figure out.

"This is Lord Drogo," said the king, leaning back in his chair. "One of my most trusted advisors. At my request, he has been collecting the facts of the situation raised by Lord Otto and his son. He's spoken to most of the people involved."

"But not to me," Angelet said, before realizing it

sounded impertinent.

Drogo said, "I'll correct that now. If his grace permits?"

Stephen waved a hand. "That's what we're here for."

"And to that end," Drogo said. "I would like you to explain, in detail, all that occurred from the moment you left Dryton to the moment you entered this room tonight. Leave nothing out, and speak only the truth. Fear not that you will suffer any repercussions from any man you may accuse. You are under royal protection now."

She wasn't sure who Drogo thought she was afraid of, but she suspected it was Rafe.

After looking at Cecily, who gave her an encouraging nod, Angelet related all she could, answering Drogo's many questions. Several were sharply pointed, but she never caught herself in a lie—the only things she kept back were the intimacies she'd shared with Rafe, and the fact that she'd lost her heart to him. She knew well that those facts would be detrimental to her cause.

At times, Drogo or Stephen interrupted. The first was when Angelet was explaining how Otto removed Henry from Angelet's care.

"Seems to me most cruel to tear the mother and her child away from each other, when she had nothing else," Stephen said, watching Angelet closely.

Drogo disagreed. "It's no odd thing to send a boy away for fostering."

"But so young? My lady, did you protest?"

"I begged Otto not to do it. But he is Henry's grandfather, and the head of the family. Such is the order of things."

The king nodded at that, and directed her to go on.

She continued the story.

At a later point, Drogo said, "This maid called Bethany—you say she wielded a crossbow? That is remarkable. And she was driven to try to murder you with it."

Angelet said, "Bethany was Ernald's lover, and she did anything he told her. It was also why she hated me, for Ernald wanted me for reasons of his own. Nevertheless, she was his eyes and ears on the journey—that's why she was so upset when we moved the chest from my carriage to the supply wagon. She had to communicate the change to the thieves, but she couldn't do it in time. That's why the attack was so scattered. And why Sir Rafe was able to get me away from the gang."

"Did he take advantage of you?" the king asked abruptly. "At any point, before or after the attack?"

"Your Grace?" she asked, nervously.

"You can speak freely. I'm not a priest to judge you for any sins. But I want to know the truth."

Angelet bowed her head, thoughts rushing through her. Then she looked up at him and said, "The truth, your grace, is that Sir Rafe always defended me from danger and he treated me well. He made a point of obeying any order I gave, and never did I fear he'd force himself on me. I wish I could say the same of Ernald Yarborough, who more than once threatened me with just that."

Stephen kept his eyes on her. "So you do not accuse Sir Rafe of any…violation?"

"No, your Grace."

"You are quite a champion for him. What has he done to earn such sympathy?"

"Your Grace," she said, "have you ever been shot at with a crossbow?"

"I have, Lady Angelet," he returned with a frown.

"Then you certainly know the terror inspired by one. And your sympathy would be with the one who pulled you to safety!"

"Truly spoken," the king acknowledged. "The chaos of battle does reveal men's natures."

"I never wish to see a true battle," Angelet said, "if what I experienced was even a hundredth of what soldiers face, what you *yourself* have faced, your grace. I have no bravery such as that." She looked down at the floor as she spoke. "But I am grateful to Sir Rafe and everything he has done for me. I know I'm only a woman, and not an important one. But that's the truth I can offer you."

Drogo inhaled. "If that's so, I've nothing further to ask the lady."

The king rose to his feet, then extended a hand to help Cecily rise as well. "Then that is that. Tomorrow is Easter. And the day after we will hold the formal audience to have it all out. Good night, ladies." He bowed, and began to leave.

"If you please, your grace," Angelet burst out. "I do have one request, should it please you to indulge me once this is all over."

The king looked back with a curious expression. "And what request is that, my lady?"

"I know that I'm no prize in marriage. I bring no lands, and I'm too old for most to look at me favorably as a wife. If your judgment is that I should be a nun after all, I only beg that I be placed somewhere close to where my son is. So he may visit me."

"Do you wish to be a nun?" he asked.

Angelet was tongue-tied, unsure how to respond. No, she wanted to scream. It's the last thing I want. But I'm afraid to ask for more.

"All that matters to me is that Henry is safe, among people who truly care for him. The request to be near him is just a mother's selfish desire."

The king watched her for a long moment. Then he said, "I see. I shall consider your request, my lady. But until the audience is concluded, I can promise nothing."

She curtsied as he left, feeling more desperate than before.

Chapter 33

EASTER MASS WAS CELEBRATED IN the Church of the Holy Sepulchre, and everyone who was anyone attended, in order to be in the reflected glory of the king. Angelet and the others went along with the Lord of Braecon and his family. They all sat on one side of the church, while Otto and his family sat on the other. Most of the people pointedly ignored the other side, a task aided by multiple, huge stone columns that held up the roof of the round church.

Angelet prayed fervently—for justice and forgiveness and mercy, things she wasn't sure could be reconciled. Then she went back to the house to worry about the coming audience. Despite the king's graciousness during the private meeting, she had no idea how he'd rule. Otto was a baron, and Rafe merely a knight. The little she knew of politics suggested that power and influence mattered far more than who was right.

For the audience the next day, she dressed in the same white and blue gown. She nearly fainted when she entered the large audience chamber where the king would hear

Otto and Ernald's grievance. If ever a place was designed to make a person feel insignificant, it was this lofty, cold room.

She saw Rafe, who wore his usual black. He sat between Alric and Luc, with Octavian nearby. Whatever animosity had disrupted the men's alliance, it was over now. Angelet was grateful, though she hoped that Rafe wouldn't need their help by the end of the day.

Rafe caught her eye and gave her a tiny wink. He appeared much more confident than she felt. But then, she felt as if she were made entirely of butterflies.

Otto and his entourage came in, filling many seats. Ernald glared at everyone, and sat far from Otto. That was interesting. Had the two quarreled? Lady Katherine sat just behind Otto. She looked down at the floor and never anywhere else, from what Angelet could tell.

Once everyone was assembled, the king entered, along with Lord Drogo, who seemed to be in charge of orchestrating the proceedings.

He began by listing the details of the grievances, and then said to Otto, "You are Lord Otto Yarborough, and you hold the manor of Dryton, as well as other properties in Leicestershire and Lincolnshire."

"Yes."

Drogo turned to Rafe. "You are Sir Raphael Corviser, son of Sir Michael Corviser."

"Yes." Rafe stood proudly. Otto leaned over to mutter something to his aide.

"You hold no properties," Drogo continued. Otto smirked.

"Not yet," Rafe said, though he didn't look downcast by that.

Drogo proceeded to recount the whole sequence of

events, based on the accounts people had given him. Where they conflicted, Drogo questioned the parties involved until he seemed satisfied.

Unfortunately, he was not often satisfied. Too often, there was no hard evidence to fully prove that one person was lying or another person told the truth. Witnesses were accused of showing bias, or being blind. Angelet began to despair. If no one could *prove* Ernald planned to rob the cortège and hurt Angelet—and with his confidante Bethany already dead—he could easily win his case.

While her mind wandered, Drogo had just asked Rafe something, and he was responding vehemently.

"...and my own defense," Rafe was saying. "There has been an accusation of theft and kidnapping. You heard the evidence, and you can see there's no proof for them. I refute both charges."

Drogo glanced to the king, then said to the gathered assembly, "When we questioned the lady Angelet in private, she declared that you are innocent of any charge of kidnapping. Indeed, she says she implored you to take her south, relying on your knightly oath to protect her."

"After the attack, we could not be sure who was responsible for it," Rafe agreed. "So yes, I escorted her south with the hope of finding a safe place for her. As you know, circumstances prevented us getting any further than Shropshire."

"I heard her," Stephen added. "The lady's testimony was not that of a woman frightened. She gave her account very ably, and without contradiction. She seems credible, even though she is a woman."

"Your grace," Otto objected. "That she is a woman is all you need to know to discount her testimony! She has doubtless been seduced by this man, and will now say anything he wants her to."

All eyes turned to Rafe. He took a breath, weighing his response. "Even if I wanted the lady to offer a particular answer to the king's questions, I wasn't there, and I could hardly dictate her responses. Whatever answers she gave were her own."

The king put up a hand to call Drogo to him. He whispered to his advisor for a few moments. Then he nodded. "Truly, she seemed honest and forthright. And as for having her head turned by a handsome face…well, then she would not have asked me to find a place in a different nunnery for her, once this is all over."

Angelet looked at the floor, too embarrassed to meet anyone's gaze, and in particular Rafe's. After all this, she would end up essentially where she started.

Otto looked annoyed by all the talk of Angelet being credible, and stood up to regain control of the situation.

"Your grace!" he said. "Everything I did, I did out of concern for my daughter-in-law. She was a dutiful wife to my son, and bore an heir. Even later, when she suffered visions and disrupted the household, I saw to it that she was cared for. Angelet, tell them it is true."

Angelet regarded her father-in-law, feeling nothing but distaste. "I will not."

Otto's eyes narrowed. "What ingratitude, after all I have done for you."

"You've done nothing for me," she told him. "Don't pour me poison and tell me it's wine."

"What?" he gasped.

"You used me at every turn," said Angelet. "First I was a simple wife to your son to get an heir. Then I was a bargaining chip in your negotiations with other barons during the war. You even used my sewing for your own ends!" She turned to the king. "The altar cloth I gave you, your grace, was intended for the Abbot of Basingwerke. Otto insisted I make it as a gift, probably to soften the abbot's annoyance once he learned he'd get no other payment."

Drogo said, "Perhaps some of this is true, but the last part is an invention of a lady's overwrought mind. We know Lord Otto sent other payment, for everyone saw it at Dryton. He could not have known it would not arrive."

Otto grunted in satisfaction at the point, sitting down in the wooden chair.

Angelet felt ready to cry, so she closed her eyes and recited a prayer, trying to remember counsel the Lady of Braecon offered that morning—a woman who cried was a woman who lost.

Then a thin, wispy voice said, "He knew."

Everyone looked in astonishment at Lady Katherine, Otto's usually silent wife.

"What do you say?" Drogo asked. "Stand and speak up, my lady!"

Lady Katherine stood awkwardly, uncomfortable with all the masculine authority staring at her. "He knew that the gold would not arrive, because there was no gold sent along with the cortège."

"Katherine," Otto began in warning, but he was quickly hushed by the king.

"Everyone has recounted seeing the gold before the cortège left," Stephan said. "Explain what you mean."

"First," she said, very nervously, "I must go back much further, back to the marriage of Angelet to Hubert."

"Well? Do so!"

She cleared her throat. "It is true that the Lady Angelet was married to Hubert Yarborough, and Hubert's death left her a widow in our house. However, according to the terms of the contract, she was *not* to remain with the Yarboroughs."

"How do you know this?" Drogo asked.

"I read the contract drafted by Lord d'Hiver before the marriage took place. It was in Otto's study."

"What were the terms of this contract?"

"Most were what one would expect of a marriage contract. Angelet's dowry was agreed upon, and there was a list of items she would retain possession of in her own right—some household goods and jewelry, a breviary worked in ivory leather, and such.

"But d'Hiver insisted on a special clause. Because Hubert was already known to be in poor health—though we still hoped for his recovery—there was an agreement that Angelet *and* her dowry would be returned to the d'Hiver family if her husband died before Angelet was sixteen, which he did."

Drogo nodded. "Because d'Hiver would have arranged another marriage for a daughter still young enough to breed. But then Angelet was kept at Dryton anyway?"

"At Otto's wish, yes," Katherine explained. "The baby was the excuse at first, and I kept quiet because I did not want to part mother and child. Little Henry would feed from none but his own mama."

"He would be weaned soon enough. What happened?"

"Otto told me to forget what I read in the contract, and not to speak of it to Angelet. She was too young to truly realize the implications of the contract, even if she'd known to ask for it. Otto said the war changed everything, and he had mind to keep Angelet close. I was scared to oppose him. I am his wife; it is my duty to obey him…but

I never liked it. I knew it was wrong to keep the poor child from her family."

"Did Otto seek to marry her again, to his own advantage?"

Katherine shook her head slowly. "At first I thought that was in his mind, but he never seriously looked for other suitors. It is my belief that Otto concealed the contract and held Angelet at Dryton so he could keep her dowry for himself."

Otto looked furious at his wife's betrayal, and sat staring at her in hatred, his face growing red.

"Where is the dowry now?" Drogo asked Katherine.

"It is nowhere. Otto ended up spending it all, or almost all. That was part of the display at the dinner before she was sent to the nunnery. He arranged the chest with mostly false filling, and a thin layer of gold and silver at the top. It looked to everyone as if the whole chest was filled with precious stones and metal. But it was a trick. By the time the chest was chained up and lashed to the wagon, it was already emptied of all value. It was filled with only rocks and gravel for weight."

"This would have been revealed at the end of the journey," said the king.

"Only if the chest reached the end," she said meekly. "You see, Otto planned to accuse the hired men of theft. His own man Dobson was to slip a little gold coin into all their purses, then empty the chest and leave it to be found. Otto's word as lord would be enough to cast doubt on Sir Rafe and the three others. It didn't matter to Otto if they were actually convicted or not—only that everyone believed the treasure was lost. That way, no one could demand any payment from him, whether in the form of the dowry, or the gift to the nunnery, or anything else."

"But I woke up when he tried to get the chest out of the room while everyone else was sleeping," said Angelet.

"And you screamed," said Rafe. "And we all assumed Dobson was trying to steal a chest full of gold for himself. But it sounds like he never intended to kill anyone—it just got out of hand."

"Very well," said Drogo. "But what of the thieves?"

"Ah." Lady Katherine now looked truly pained. "The thieves were Ernald's idea, and Otto is innocent of that. This is what comes of pretending too well. Everyone believed that chest was full of gold…including Ernald."

"You hag!" Ernald burst out. "I never said that!"

"Ernald, you are not nearly as subtle as you think," his mother told him, a new tartness in her voice. "I heard you plotting and planning at Dryton. Why do some men think that women are deaf and blind, just because we do not always speak? But I will no longer stand here and let both of you avoid justice."

"You overheard Ernald's plans, then?" Drogo pressed, now eager to get to the meat of the tale.

Katherine nodded. "I did. He wanted the money for himself, and he was irked at Otto for keeping him subservient for so long, even years after his older brother's death. He plotted with his own cronies and came up with a plan to have the cortège robbed of its treasure."

Drogo said, "This I believe, based on what I've learned. But Ernald was more brutal than his father—he gave instruction that all traveling with the cortège should be killed…except for the few loyal to him."

"Even Angelet was to be killed?" It was Rafe who spoke now, just as caught up by Katherine's revelation as everyone else. "I thought that was Bethany's doing, because Ernald wanted to marry her himself."

"That I could not say for certain," Katherine admitted. "Both Otto and I knew Ernald held a certain passion for his sister-in-law. It troubled me, and I did urge my husband to find a solution—sending Angelet to a nunnery would keep her safe from Ernald. But he chased after her. It's possible he wanted her alive, and the maid Bethany acted out of jealousy. Certainly, my son would be a fool to say otherwise at this point."

Drogo took a deep breath. "So it was Ernald's plan to rob the cortège by force. But Sir Rafe turned out to be a formidable opponent during the initial fight, and his decision to take Angelet and flee meant that the thieves would have had to give chase. They might have done so....except that they had already learned the truth that the chest was empty. No one anticipated that it would have cracked open during the skirmish—it revealed Otto's deception. Ernald didn't know about the worthless chest, but his thieves assumed he set them up. They abandoned the job and returned to Dryton to confront Ernald. Is this what happened, my lady Katherine?"

The woman nodded. "That was how he learned of the disaster before anyone else, and how he came to be looking for Angelet himself."

Then, all at once, Lady Katherine put her hands to her face. "Years I have lived with them, and I tried to love them. I tried to do my duty as a wife and a mother. I kept silence for far too long, over too many things when I should have spoken out. And look what it has come to."

She looked pleadingly at Angelet, who had no idea what to say.

Then King Stephen cleared his throat. "It seems to me that I have the answers I need. Lady Katherine, you are overwrought, and that is no wonder. You are excused."

"Let me help her, your grace!" Angelet rose to help the older woman walk. Taking her arm, she whispered, "It's all right now, my lady. It is over." She glanced at Rafe as she left, and saw how still and shocked he looked.

Together, the two women left the lofty, cold room, where the king would decide the fate of the men left inside.

* * * *

Rafe watched Angelet go, wishing he could go with her. But he had no time to think about that now. King Stephen was not a man to be ignored.

"Well." Stephen looked over the assembled group. "I have heard enough. Indeed, too much, for it exposes the weakness of a family I counted on as allies. The young heir Henry Yarborough is innocent of wrongdoing, for he is a child, and was far away from the whole mess. Yet that means he is too young to take up the mantle. And the other generations of men have proved unworthy."

"Another steward is needed," Drogo said. "A neighboring baron, perhaps, one who can be trusted."

The Lord of Braecon stood up. "Your Grace, some of my lands are not far from Dryton. I would be glad to take on the responsibility of governing the manor until the boy is of age to claim it. Perhaps Lady Katherine would be permitted to continue to live there, and be the chatelaine. There are no reports of mismanagements of the property, at least. In my experience, it is helpful to disrupt a manor's workings as little as possible."

"That is acceptable, for now," King Stephen said, nodding to Braecon.

Rafe marveled at the political shrewdness of Braecon.

So that was one of the reasons he was so interested in the proceeding, and why he welcomed one side into his home.

The king was speaking again. "As for Otto and Ernald, I cannot permit them to…"

"Mercy, your grace!" Ernald burst out. "I was misled by evil women. I never meant things to go so far. Please show mercy—"

"Mercy? Here is my mercy. Your actions were selfish. Short-sighted. Cruel. Greedy. Unworthy of a man of noble blood. In short, the actions of a sinful man. If you wish mercy, there is only one path to it. You will join a monastery of my choosing, where you will live as a lay brother. You will give up all claims to inheritance, and you will pray to God for forgiveness for your sins. You may study to take holy vows, at the abbot's discretion. But you will never leave the monastery once you enter it."

Ernald looked horrified.

The king went on, "Your other option is to die by an executioner's sword."

"The monastery, your grace," Ernald choked out.

"I expected so. As for you, Lord Otto. In my mercy, I offer you the same choice. What is your decision?"

"The same, your grace," Otto said, with a more even tone. His eyes were narrowed, and Rafe suspected the man was already plotting a way out of his new situation.

Stephen gestured to his guards. "Escort these two out. They are to be confined under armed guard until escorted to their respective monasteries."

Otto and Ernald were taken away.

"As for the matter of Henry Yarborough, I will find a more suitable place for him to be fostered, one that will benefit someone other than Otto."

Luc leaned over and whispered something to Alric, who stood next to him. Rafe wondered what it was about, but then the king pointed to Rafe, erasing all other thoughts.

"Yes, your Grace," Rafe said.

"One last item, while everyone is gathered here," the king said. "The Welsh border is still of strategic importance, and it must be defended at all costs. As you already know, it's not a place for the weak-hearted. Life on the marches is precarious, and we've lost many men and strongholds to both the damned Welsh and twice-damned English rebels. I need reliable castellans to guard the castles I do have. Men to hold the land, and to train new fighters for the battles ahead. Sir Michael Corviser did such service for my father. I think it is only right that you, Sir Raphael Corviser, will do the same for me."

"Yes, your grace," Rafe said instantly.

"There is a place called Martenkeep. It is in need of some repair in addition to refortification. You'll be given enough coin to pay for such work. And once you establish yourself there, we'll send young men to be trained in the matters of riding, swordplay, and all other realms of combat."

"How many can be trained there?" Rafe asked, suddenly aware of the potential enormity of what was being asked of him.

"As many as you feel you and your men can responsibly instruct."

Rafe would have to find good people to handle some of the elements of training. At Cleobury, as many as half a dozen men served as teachers for various tasks. "I'll confer with Lord Rainald de Vere for advice."

"Good idea. Work quickly to make the castle properly

fortified and ready to be inhabited. No woman wants to live in a half-built house."

"Woman?"

"Certainly you don't plan on living as a bachelor. Life in the marches can be lonely, and Martenkeep is isolated. When you're ready, a suitable bride will be found."

"Thank you," said Rafe, "but I already have one in mind."

* * * *

Angelet was sitting alone in her chamber of the home provided by Sir Luc's family. She felt restless and ill at ease, and was startled by a knock. "Yes?"

Cecily stood in the doorway. "You have a visitor, Angelet."

"A visitor?"

Rafe stepped in. "Hello."

Cecily closed the door, leaving them alone.

Angelet rose to her feet. "Rafe. I heard you're to be a castellan. That's wonderful."

"I'm not here to talk about that." He crossed the room to meet her. "What's all this about a nunnery? Why are you determined to stay away from me? What more do I need to do to prove myself worthy of you?"

"Nothing! God, Rafe, don't you understand? It's not that you're not good enough for me. It's that I'm not good enough for you. I was born cursed."

"You were not."

"You have your legacy now, Rafe. You have a duty to carry on your family line. Marry a woman who can actually bear a child…"

"That's what's troubling you?" he asked, sounding

amused.

"Don't pretend it doesn't matter."

"It doesn't matter to me."

"It should," she insisted. "I would serve no purpose as a wife to any man. I have no wealth, no lands, no title to confer, and I can never bear a child again. And that is putting aside my affliction! I'm useless. In truth, a nunnery is the best place for me."

"The best place for you is with me," Rafe said. "Hear my argument, love. I don't care that you don't bring wealth or a title or lands. I have what I need of those. I don't care that you cannot bear children."

"But what worth am I to you—"

"Angelet, you're more than a vessel. Any man who thinks that is a woman's sole value doesn't deserve to have a woman anywhere near him."

He cupped her face in his hands when she tried to turn away. "Listen. Children are never guaranteed from any union, and does that make a marriage any less true? No. I need you, Angelet. I need you with me. I need to hear your voice in the morning, and see you smile at me—or yell at me, when I deserve it, and I assure you I will."

"You want a wife who yells at you?" she asked, starting to feel a crack in her misery.

"I want a wife who knows me, not some name picked by the king's council for reasons of their own. You know me better than anyone. You know my past, and how I've failed. You know how far I need to go to be worthy of the name I've just found for myself. You know all my worst traits, and for some reason you still think well of me."

Angelet sighed, tucking her head under Rafe's chin. She gathered the fabric of his tunic and bunched it up in her hands, clinging to him. "How could I think otherwise?

You saved me."

"I barely got you away from that whole mess in time, angel. If I'd been paying attention, those thieves never would have got the drop on us, and—"

"Oh, Rafe, I don't mean the attack, though you've saved me over and over while we were traveling. I mean you saved me from despair. I was heartsick when you met me. I thought I had lost everything in my life, and I was nothing more than a nuisance, in everyone's way. I was lonely and despised and isolated. Then you rode into the courtyard of Dryton, and it was as if the sun broke through the clouds. You spoke to me as if I mattered. You defended me when you barely knew my name. You protected me when there was nothing in it for you."

"Not *nothing*," he said in a low voice. "I had a goal."

"To seduce me. So you did, but I like to think I seduced you too."

"Very true."

"And you never sought to profit from it, when you thought I was wealthy—wrangle me into a quick marriage or blackmail me or sell me off."

"I hadn't thought beyond those few nights," he said. "I knew I'd never get to keep you, so I tried not to dream of the future. Angelet, do you know the first thing I thought when I learned I wasn't some nameless bastard?"

"What?"

"I thought *Thank God, now I can ask her to be mine.* I had some standing, some leverage. After an entire life of owning nothing more than my sword and armor and horse, now I'm somebody."

"You were always Rafe to me."

"I'd like to be more. If you accept me. Please. I want you as my wife, and if it's not you, then it will be no one."

Angelet took a deep breath. "Oh. Well. I don't want you to be alone."

He smiled at last. "So you'll take pity on me?"

"I'll marry you. We can decide who deserves pity later on."

Rafe captured her mouth for a kiss. "No one will say the word pity about our marriage, love."

Rafe was so new in the good graces of the king that they dared not risk his wrath. Rafe put his request to marry Angelet before the king himself.

Stephen frowned. "Dear Lord, how changeable you both are!"

"Not changeable, your grace," Angelet said quickly. "Our hearts have both wanted this, but misunderstandings made it seem impossible. But those misunderstandings are now swept aside. No offense was meant."

His expression softened as he looked at Angelet. "I suppose this whole affair has been less than simple." Then he shifted in his chair. "But by God, I'll make the ending simple. If you both now want marriage, then you will be married…on the morrow. No more delays, no more prevarications, no more wishes for the cloistered life, no more misunderstandings. Do I make myself clear?"

Rafe nodded. "Yes, your grace."

"After morning mass at the Holy Sepulchre. I will have a man in attendance to report that it is done. And henceforth, I expect nothing but simple, quiet, encouraging reports from Martenkeep, Sir Rafe. You will take on your first batch of trainees by the end of summer, and you will send to my armies the finest squires you can."

"That is my goal, your grace."

"Very well. God grant you both joy. I think the Fates wish you to be together—certainly all plans to separate you have been thwarted."

Epilogue

SIR RAPHAEL CORVISER AND THE Lady Angelet d'Hiver were married the next morning, just as promised. Rafe was perfectly content with the speedy and very public ceremony, since he knew all too well what happened when marriages were delayed or kept secret too long. He wanted Angelet to be protected, no matter what might happen in the future.

They had their wedding night, a night marked by joy and laughter and lust. But then Rafe had to prepare to leave for his new assignment as the castellan of Martenkeep. Angelet would travel with him as far as Cleobury, where she would stay as a guest of Cecily and Alric until Rafe sent word for her to join him.

Rafe traveled to Martenkeep with an entourage—mostly workers from Cleobury and the village of Bournham, but also a few other faces. Goswin and Simon Faber had joined Rafe, each for their own reasons.

When the group finally arrived at the castle, the view was less than impressive.

Goswin, acting as Rafe's page, offered his opinion first. "Lord, this is a ruin!"

"We do have our work cut out for us," Rafe said, surveying the property entrusted to him.

The castle called Martenkeep stood on a small rise surrounded on three sides by the curves of a river. Some parts of the main wall were old and nearly in ruins. The stretches of stone wall that remained upright were covered with thick moss, making it look as if the wall had grown up there, instead of being built by human hands.

The keep itself still stood…partly. Green moss and grey lichen covered the walls in great patches. All the wooden structures, including the stables, the outbuildings and all of the roofs, were nothing more than piles of rotting timber.

"It's not as bad as it looks," one of the men said. "The stones can be reset with fresh mortar. And there are plenty of trees to be cut for new wood."

"True." Simon looked around the forest. "Looks as if I'll become a carpenter after all! Plenty of work here, but I think it will go quickly enough."

"You're more optimistic than I," Rafe told him. "When we're sleeping in puddles from the next rainstorm, I'll remind you of your words."

"Yes, sir," he replied. "Now, what is your command?"

Rafe looked about again. Really, it was not that much different from setting up a military camp. And that was a task he knew how to do.

"First things first. Locate the nearest source of water—make sure it's clean. Adam, clear an area for the horses and livestock to be sheltered temporarily. Neale, search the buildings, and find the best place to set up quarters for sleeping and cooking. I'm going to ride around the perimeter and see if there are places in need of guards during the nights. Simon, you'll join me."

Simon nodded, then shouted, "You heard your orders!

To work!"

All the men dispersed to their tasks without any complaint. Rafe was still surprised that people accepted his word as authority, but every time it got a little easier.

He said, "Very well, let's see how badly the defenses have crumbled, and how long we'll need to rebuild. I won't allow the king to send any boys for training until I know the place is secure."

"Secure enough for the new trainees?" Simon asked. "Or secure enough for Lady Angelet?"

Rafe smiled. "That, too."

"Then the repairs *will* go quickly," Simon predicted.

Rafe worked feverishly to restore Martenkeep to a habitable state. First, the massive gate had to be rebuilt, and the walls repaired, and the ditches and dry moats cleared out and sometimes re-dug. And that was just to keep attackers out. Then there was the matter of the keep, which had a heavily damaged roof and needed a thorough cleaning to bring it up to a level the soldiers considered acceptable. It would require even more work before it was suitable for ladies, and ready to become a proper household with servants and workers and livestock.

Still, despite the backbreaking effort and long days, Rafe didn't mind the work at all, because this was his home. That made all the difference. He would hold this castle in the king's name and he would protect this part of the shire to the best of his ability. He had to, because he would never allow Angelet to live in a place he couldn't protect. His lady was his life.

The day she and her entourage arrived, Rafe felt as if his heart was going to burst out of his chest, he was so filled with anticipation. He was proud of what he'd accomplished at the castle so far, and he hoped Angelet would not be disappointed.

By her smile, she was pleased to see *him,* at least. "Greetings, husband," she said, clearly enjoying the word.

"Welcome to Martenkeep, my lady. How was the journey, and what news from Cleobury?"

"The journey is not a difficult one. I'd hoped to bring a certain kind of news along, but Lady Cecily's child has not quite arrived. It is a matter of days now, instead of weeks. Everyone is excited. But I couldn't wait any longer to see you, or our new home."

There is still much work to be done, but I hope you'll find it adequate."

"It's where you are," she said, putting her hand in his. "I need nothing more than that."

"Well, all the same, I made sure you will have a new roof over our bedchamber, and a new bed." He leaned over to kiss her. "It's been here for a fortnight, but I refused to sleep in it 'til you could sleep with me."

Angelet bit her lip, looking down. "Rafe!"

"Still a rogue," he confided. "Some things will never change."

She looked up then, with a conspiratorial look in her eye. "You must show me to our chamber, husband. And I warn you, travel was so fatiguing, I'll doubtless need to retire quite soon." She looked anything but sleepy.

"This way…wife." He liked saying that word, too.

* * * *

Angelet took a deep breath, drawing in the warm, sweetly-scented summer air with pleasure. Was this what true happiness felt like? She looked over the green treetops visible past the mown fields and smiled. She never thought she'd find a place like this, with a partner such as Rafe. She would work hard as chatelaine, and make life here comfortable and safe for all the inhabitants, whether they would be here for life or only a little while, such as the young men come for training as soldiers and knights.

It was almost like having a family, she thought. These young men were really not much more than boys. She could be a mother to them while they were here, and offer a more gentle influence to complement the harsher treatment they would endure from Rafe and the other men who would act as instructors.

Rafe had initially agreed to train four boys, and three were already here. They all seemed bright and eager to learn. There was Torin, a friendly and brash boy whose body had started to outpace his mind, leading to a certain clumsiness, since he was often in motion before he quite knew what he was actually intending to do. His big blue eyes always seemed startled, and nearly every time he spoke, out came an apology for bumping into someone or knocking over a tower of baskets or for simply standing in the wrong place—he had a knack for forgetting how to walk when any of the maids crossed his path.

"If he ever learns to control those limbs," Rafe had said, "he'll be a terror on the battlefield, especially if he keeps growing taller." Angelet had agreed, but privately she thought he'd be more dangerous among ladies. His hapless innocence, combined with his appearance, was already drawing glances from the girls his age.

Then there was Guy, who was dark-haired with an olive complexion, as slight and short as Torin was brawny. He was the son of a very wealthy baron, and he was conscious of his station and eager to excel, but he was a tentative fighter, overly cautious and afraid to fail.

Angelet suspected that his interests lay elsewhere, and he'd prefer a career in the church. She felt that he'd need the most mothering of the boys she'd met so far, lest his lack of confidence turn to sullenness.

The third boy was from the north, the nephew of one of the rebel barons, and thus something of a puzzle. He was too young to have any knowledge of or participation in the rebellion, but the king was now determined to make sure this new generation belonged to him. Thus all the children and younger relatives of the rebels had been taken for fostering with trusted vassals of Stephen. The boy, Acer, had a quick smile and polite manners, but a very changeable nature. He could be sunny one moment and stormy the next. Doubtless he felt insecure at Martenkeep, not quite prisoner and not quite guest. Angelet would have to make him feel welcome and safe.

A faint clatter in the distance made her look to the road. Yes, there it was. A small riding party was approaching, very likely the final trainee. She went down to greet the newcomer.

But when the visitor climbed out of the carriage, Angelet gasped in astonishment. "Henry?"

"Mother!"

"Sweet Mary, it's you," she whispered.

Henry ran to her and she sank to her knees and wrapped her arms around him, embracing him fiercely. She thought her heart might burst. It had been so long since she'd seen him. The last short visit had been over a year ago. It seemed like a lifetime.

"Oh, my boy." Angelet clung to him, patting his hair, then hugging him again, then wiping her eyes, then starting all over. She was crying freely, and she didn't care at all who saw it or what they thought. "Oh, you're back with me. My prayers were heard. You're going to stay. I'll never let you go again." She could barely think clearly now. She felt him shake a little as he threw himself at her.

Henry's arms circled her neck, still thin, but with a strength she didn't remember from their last time together. Her boy was growing up.

"I missed you, Mother," he said over and over.

"We're together again," she said. "That's all that matters."

Finally, he pulled away a little, beaming at her. "I'm here! When they said I'd get to live with you again I didn't believe them at first. But they said I wasn't going back to Dryton because you married again. Is that true? They won't tell me anything."

"It's true. I've married Sir Raphael Corviser. A knight whose father served the old king, just as Sir Rafe serves our king now."

"Is he a good man?"

"Very good. I'm so happy with him."

Henry pulled out from her embrace and studied her with his solemn eyes, so like his late father's. Then he said, "Very well. If he's ever not good to you, Mother, you'll have to tell me so I can fight him."

Angelet let out an astonished laugh and reached out to tuck a loose lock of hair behind his ear. "Oh, my darling. It will never come to that. But I do want you to listen to everything Rafe teaches you, understand? He's one of the finest fighters the king has, and you'll be a knight like no other if you learn from him."

"Am I to call him father?"

"If and when you're ready to, my love. But first I think you ought to meet him."

She pointed to the approaching figure of Rafe, who

was trailed by the three boys. Henry took a deep breath and squared his narrow shoulders, preparing to meet these new faces.

"Damn," Rafe said first. "I wanted to be here for the moment of revelation."

Angelet wiped tears off her cheeks. "You said nothing!"

"I thought it would be a good surprise." Rafe turned to Henry. "Welcome to Martenkeep. I'm Raphael Corviser."

"I am Henry Yarborough," the boy replied with stiff dignity, obviously trying to seem as though he hadn't just been shedding tears of joy. "Though I may change it to Henry d'Hiver, since the Yarborough name isn't dear to me."

"A matter to discuss with your mother," Rafe said.

"Your mother?" Torin asked incredulously. "I thought you were just married."

"Second marriage, you dolt," Guy said.

Angelet smiled. "Henry is my son, and he will begin training with you three tomorrow."

"He'll be spoiled," Acer whispered, though his whisper could be overheard by everyone present.

"None of you will be spoiled," Rafe said sharply. "No matter your birth or your relations, you are all equal during your training. No one will be punished or indulged differently than the others. You must trust and rely on your companions. Let that be the first and most important lesson. On a battlefield, at court, on the road…you must always watch their backs and be confident they have yours. It's the only way to succeed. Distrust, envy, malice…these things will be your downfall. You can be the best swordsman in the world, but if you're friendless, your skills won't save you."

"How do you know?" Acer said.

"I've seen it firsthand, boy," Rafe answered. "And eventually, you'll all hear the tale. Now, take Henry and show him the dormitory. Supper is in one hour."

"By your leave, Mother," Henry said, beaming at her before running off with the others.

"I'll see you soon," she whispered to his retreating back.

Rafe stepped up to her and slid an arm around her waist. "Pleased?"

Pleased? She was ecstatic, overjoyed, giddy, blessed. "When did you know?" she demanded.

"I suggested the possibility when I told the king how many boys I could offer to train at a time. If it was no great matter to change the location, why shouldn't Henry be with his mother instead of a foster family? But the decision was the king's."

"This is the best gift I could receive," she whispered. "Thank you. I only dared ask the king to look after his welfare. You fought to get him back to me."

Rafe kissed her. "For you, I'll do anything, love."

"Why? What have I done to deserve a champion like you?" she asked.

"A few days before I met you, I could see my whole future in front of me. Fight after fight, all of them meaningless."

"Meaningless?"

"I had no one to fight for. I wasn't even fighting for myself. I was just…following a ritual, doing what I had done all my life. But when I saw you, I again had something to fight for."

"And so you did. You defended me so many times."

"But I didn't just want to protect you—I wanted to be

worthy of you. That's why discovering my name meant so much."

"I would have stayed with you no matter what your name was, Rafe."

"Perhaps, but I never would have asked before I knew."

"So it wasn't my poverty? Or my illness?"

He put both arms around her, pulling her close. "Fortunes can be stolen. Health can fail. But nothing can take away your soul. And your soul is the most beautiful one I've ever known. You believed in me when no one else did. You gave me another chance when I'd lost all my chances. You even agreed to live your life with me. Angelet, you are worth fighting for."

"Rafe, you don't have to fight for me. You have already won my heart, all of it. And I trust you to keep it safe. Forever."

"Forever."

ABOUT THE AUTHOR

Elizabeth Cole is a romance writer with a penchant for history. Her stories draw upon her deep affection for the British Isles, action movies, medieval fantasies, and even science fiction. She now lives in a small house in a big city with a cat, a snake, and a rather charming gentleman. When not writing, she is usually curled in a corner reading...or watching costume dramas or things that explode. And yes, she believes in love at first sight.

Printed in the USA
CPSIA information can be obtained
at www.ICGtesting.com
CBHW021450240424
7460CB00011B/654